THE VOID OF
MUIRWOOD

Books by Jeff Wheeler

The Covenant of Muirwood Trilogy
The Banished of Muirwood
The Ciphers of Muirwood
The Void of Muirwood

The Legends of Muirwood Trilogy
The Wretched of Muirwood
The Blight of Muirwood
The Scourge of Muirwood

Whispers from Mirrowen Trilogy
Fireblood
Dryad-Born
Poisonwell

Landmoor Series
Landmoor
Silverkin

THE VOID OF
MUIRWOOD

The Covenant of Muirwood
Book Three

JEFF WHEELER

47NORTH

Published by 47North, Seattle

www.apub.com

Amazon, the Amazon logo, and 47North are trademarks of Amazon.com, Inc., or its affiliates.

ISBN-13: 9781503948723
ISBN-10: 1503948722

Cover design by Ray Lundgren
Illustrated by Magali Villeneuve

Printed in the United States of America

To Madison

NAESS

BAMBURG

PRY-REE

NORRIS-YORK   Billerbeck
KRUCIS   Forshee
TINTERN   SEMPRINGFALL
Bridgestow
COMOROS
MUIRWOOD
HOLYROOD
Winterrowd   CLAREDON
Comoros   AUGUSTIN
Caspur   Doviur
CEASTER

ROSTICK

HAUTLAND

VIEGG

ANTIMO

PAEIZ

RIVAULX

Watzholt Mtns.

Peliyey Mtns.
SUMEELA

CRUIX   FENTON

LISYEUX

DAHOMEY

The Spike

MON

Briec
DOCHTE   Vezins   Roc-Adamour

Peliyey Mtns.

Argus

CASINUM

Cursed Shores   LOST ABBEY

AVINION

AVINION

• Towns
✟ ABBEYS

TABLE OF CONTENTS

I hail from the land of black sky and midnight day. Where there is darkness, there is courage. Where there is ambition, there is power. Where there is will, there is dominion. I thank the Medium for an unconquerable soul.

—Corriveaux Tenir, Victus of Dahomey

CHAPTER ONE

Leerings

Corriveaux Tenir tried to block out the waspy drone of the celebration and focused his gaze on the blackened visage of the Leering. The air was warm and yeasty with the mingled smells of ale and cinders. The heavy clunk of pewter mugs joined with the thudding of stamping boots, making him scowl. Drunkenness was a loathsome thing to Corriveaux. It addled the wits and inflamed the passions. It was excellent for controlling vast numbers of men. What some of them would do for even a swallow of brandy was almost laughable. Men would kill each other with enough drink. He counted on that.

He narrowed in on the eyes of the pockmarked stone face in front of him. This Leering had been harvested from an abbey in Avinion, moved by several oxen teams, and ferried by ship to Naess to be studied and saved. It was a special waymarker.

Corriveaux was fascinated by Leerings, which served as conduits for the Medium's power. There were boundless varieties, and each one was unique and interesting. Some were small, tiny enough to fit in the palm of your hand; others were carved into mammoth boulders or the capstones of arches. Each had a face— whether it bore the likeness of a man, woman, or child; an animal or beast; or personifications of the sun, moon, or stars. And the range of powers they possessed was practically infinite. There were even tiny ones to stop clothes from wearing out or metal tools from rusting. As he had studied in the tomes, Leerings could be channeled to multiple purposes. Together, a fire and a water Leering could create steam. There was power in steam, he was discovering. His mind always whirled with dozens of ideas for how Leerings could be used in war, machinery, and harvesting. But not everyone could use Leerings. That privilege of power was reserved to the Dochte Mandar, who bore kystrels, and the maston Families steeped in the traditions of the Medium.

Some Leerings could not be transported, or they lost their function. Others retained their power wherever they were located. Each of the ships in the armada had a Leering built into the prow, called a figurehead. They invested the ships with various powers, such as speed and protection. A few of the figureheads could even belch fire.

Slowly, almost reverently, he reached out his hand to touch the waymarker. Closing his eyes, he summoned the power of the kystrel around his neck. A giddy, soothing feeling swept through him, making him shiver with delight. Yes, the men around him were satisfied with brandy, wine, and cider, but such simple pleasures did nothing for Corriveaux. He craved the magic of the Medium and how it made him *feel*—the way his very bones seemed to melt in delight. His pleasure showed: the tattoos from his use of the kystrel already wreathed his neck up to the jawline of his trimmed beard. As his hand touched the rough stone, the Leering awoke instantly.

Waymarkers were special Leerings that were connected to other stones in a web. By touching one, you could *know* the others in the web—you could see through their stone eyes and touch the minds of other humans who were connected to one of the Leerings in the web. If your will was strong enough, you could even take control of that person and command him or her to obey you. Corriveaux's will was impressively strong. He was the only Victus to have subdued a hetaera.

By touching the waymarker, he could see through the eyes of another Leering on the other side of the world. Through the ship's figurehead, he saw the vast armada filling a crystal-blue lake fringed with evergreens. He saw the ongoing construction of a series of decks and harbors, which would allow the brunt of the armada to harvest the Leerings of Assinica and ferry them back to Naess.

Corriveaux.

The thought whispered into his mind as he connected with the Dochte Mandar stationed aboard the vessel. The man's name was Pralt, and he was a seasoned member of the order, having been expelled from Comoros years ago, after the king of that land made the unprecedented decision to banish the order.

Greetings, Pralt. What news?

He could not only hear the man's thoughts, he could actually experience his emotions. Most who used kystrels were not strong enough in the Medium to tap into the deeper ways of the magic, but Corriveaux had Family mixed in his blood, and the power came stronger to him than to many others. He could sense feelings of disappointment and fear. Pralt was dreading this communication.

The mastons fled.

What?

He could feel the bile rise up in his throat. Anger began to churn inside Corriveaux's heart. He would not lash out at the man. Kicking down underlings was not a way to foster loyalty.

The kingdom was abandoned. There was no opposition awaiting us. The Aldermaston sent a delegation to us to sue for peace and—

Tell me! Corriveaux thought firmly. *How can a kingdom flee? Where did they go? Did they leave no tracks?*

Of course they left tracks, Corriveaux. There are no walls or fortification around the city, as you know. The hunters went tracking into the woods and found nothing. All the tracks were within the city. They led to the abbey.

Corriveaux tried to restrain his impatience. From Pralt, he was sensing different emotions now—mingled frustration and fury. They had sent legions of soldiers to Assinica after whispering promises to them about plunder, rape, and riches beyond their dreams. Dreams of the glory to come had been enough to motivate the soldiers to risk the wrath of the Medium by slaying thousands of mastons. And now there would be no battle. It was entirely possible the armada would revolt against their Dochte Mandar overseers.

Pralt, we know that many abbeys have tunnels constructed beneath them, secret passageways that enable people to escape. Surely that is where the mastons fled.

Pralt exuded a sense of contempt for Corriveaux, which only inflamed his anger.

We know this, Corriveaux. I am not a simpleton. You cannot move a herd of kine without leaving a trail of dung. You cannot move a herd of people without evidence either. The trail leads into the center of the abbey, not into the dungeon where the learners are

4

instructed and where underground trails are most likely. There is a screen of wood. The Rood Screen. The markings of their feet were evident all the way to the screen. Then they disappeared.

Corriveaux listened in shocked silence. He could almost see the other man's thoughts, could tell that Pralt had personally led the inspection.

They are gone, Corriveaux thought bleakly.

That is what I am trying to tell you. You must tell the Hand. What would he have us do? I am awaiting orders to raze the abbey and burn the city. The fleet is settling in and occupying houses. They left . . . they left cooked meals for us, Corriveaux. Every table was set as if expecting visitors. They left their belongings. All of them. Clothes, cloaks, vases, looms. Everything was abandoned and left behind for us to pillage. It is difficult maintaining order. The men want to go ashore and begin plundering. They left it all for us to take. Why would they do that?

Corriveaux gritted his teeth in fury. A peace offering. He knew that was what it was. We are innocent and harmless. We give you our city. We give you our possessions. Spare our lives, our culture. Do not hunt us.

The Apse Veil is open, Corriveaux thought.

What is that? Pralt demanded.

You have not studied the maston ways sufficiently. Their legends are as deep as time. The Apse Veil links the abbeys together, much like these waymarkers link us. If the Apse Veil had opened in any other kingdom but Comoros, we would have been the first to hear of it. It must mean they have gone to Muirwood. The mastons have returned after all, just as the Hand feared they would.

What would you have us do? Pralt asked.

Be vigilant. They may have left spies behind to study our reaction. Have the abbey guarded night and day, but in secret. The mastons may be peaceful, but they are cunning. Some may try to slip through the abbey again. Be watchful.

I will make it thus. Farewell, Corriveaux.

Farewell, Pralt.

Corriveaux released the waymarker, and the din from the celebration flooded his ears, making him nauseous. He was sweating beneath his velvet tunic, so he took a moment to calm himself, repeating the dirge of the Dochte Mandar in his mind to focus his thoughts.

As soon as he felt centered, he hurried out of the chamber of the waymarker and down the hall—the racket of the revelers increasing with each step. He avoided the doorway leading into the great hall, where hundreds of Leerings illuminated the vaulted beams and provided heat and warmth for the men gathered inside. After they had their fill of the casks of drink that had been provided, the slave women would be brought in to dance, inflaming them all the more. Every day new ships arrived from foreign ports, bringing a new glut to be enjoyed—whether it be wealth, food, fabric, or art. Though it disgusted Corriveaux, it was necessary. Men would only commit the worst murders when they could drown their senses afterward and if they *truly* believed that those killings would improve their standing in their next life. It did not hurt that any last traces of guilt could be purged by the kystrels.

For a moment he felt an unexpected temptation to join in the reveling. But no, the Victus stood above the ranks of mere men. They were the masters of the fates. The spinners of webs. The patient spider awaiting its prey. He could feel the trembling strain on the lines. It was time to act, time to bite, time to feast on blood.

Corriveaux reached the end of the corridor and opened another door that led down into the dungeons. As he passed, Leerings meant for light greeted him. His boots clipped on the rough stone steps as he hurried his way down. At the base of the steps, a door Leering blocked the way. These had also been taken from the abbeys and would only open with the proper password.

Unconquerable.

The door responded to his thought and swung open with a grinding sound that made him squirm. Flames dimly lit the passageway beyond, and the smell of nutmeg hung in the air. Corriveaux entered and walked down the small arched corridor. Rooms were set into each archway along both sides of the main gallery. Within these alcoves were shelves and tables that sagged under the weight of gleaming maston tomes. Buried deep within the ground, it was a place sacred to the Victus. It was the inner sanctum, the only place where the tomes were allowed to be read. The Leerings were triggered so that if anyone attempted to carry one of the aurichalcum tomes away, all of them would be instantly engulfed in fire.

The tomes contained rich secrets, and one of Corriveaux's favorite pleasures was to come here and glean knowledge from the pages.

Another chamber—Corriveaux's destination—rested at the very end of the corridor. The heavy wooden door gaped open.

"Corriveaux," said a raspy, gravelly voice as he reached the threshold.

He could not see the man behind the voice.

"Where are you?" he answered.

"Where you cannot see me," came the reply. "Put your dagger on the plinth."

That was different. A Victus's dagger was his only safeguard against murder. Being asked to put it down was a request for absolute trust and fidelity. The dagger was a symbol. The members of the Victus did not all know one another's identities. Only the

Hand knew. The dagger was a sign to show the carrier's allegiance, a token that enabled him to walk unmolested past any Dochte Mandar and fulfill his assignment, regardless of where he traveled.

Corriveaux did not hesitate to walk up and put his dagger on the stone plinth positioned beneath a light Leering by the entrance to the room. Standing at the edge of it, he could see a shadow move on his left. He did not flinch.

"One of you has betrayed me," the dark voice growled.

Corriveaux felt a spasm of startled surprise. He dared not utter a word, but the hairs on his neck bristled with fear and dread. Could it truly be him?

A heavy step sounded, followed by a dragging noise. Corriveaux knew the Hand had a stump for one leg. His movement was ponderous due to his girth. A gnarled, meaty fist closed on the dagger hilt on the plinth.

Corriveaux wanted to protest his innocence, but he knew it would be foolish. If the Hand believed it was him, he would die regardless of his innocence. He stood calmly, steeling himself, trying to keep a ball of sweat from dripping down his cheek, through sheer force of will.

"What news from Assinica?" the man rasped, bringing the dagger out of the shaft of light. He coughed wetly.

"They have fled," Corriveaux said tautly, keeping his eyes trained on the light. He wanted to flinch and flee, but he knew it would mean instant death.

"Yes," the Hand said in his guttural tone. "I expected this when you let the High Seer slip away."

"I—" Corriveaux checked himself just in time. He blinked, trying to keep his thoughts collected.

A wheezing laugh followed his self-correction. "There are only three men who know enough to betray us," the Hand whispered.

"You. Walraven. And Gastone. All three of you are uncommonly clever and motivated. All three patiently bide your time for my death. I know that. But the traitor must meet his fate, and soon, if we are to succeed."

Corriveaux could almost feel the Hand's hot breath on his neck as the other man came around behind him. The stump-like appendage thudded once more and fell silent.

"It is you I have chosen, Corriveaux. You are young. You are ambitious. You are impatient." A low chuckle sounded. "You know what happens next."

There was a grunt and then a gasp.

Corriveaux whirled, watching in horror as the Hand pulled the bloody dagger out of his own stomach. The hulk of a man shuddered and dropped to one knee, his meaty fist clutching the front of Corriveaux's tunic. He dropped the dagger to the stone floor, and it clattered away.

Corriveaux stared at the Hand in shock as blood began pattering on the floor.

"You will lead us," the Hand hissed, his voice full of pain. "I will counsel you from the dark pools now. Your rivals must . . . be destroyed. Do not trust them. One of them . . . is the traitor."

His puffy face and jowls quivered. His eyes were fierce with determination.

"Bring back the hetaera," he said. "Destroy the world. Or the mastons will defeat us." And then he collapsed.

CHAPTER TWO

The King's Threat

I t was a beautiful spring day outside Pent Tower—sunlit, a little hazy with miry smoke, and trilling with birdsong. Maia sat by the window, watching as the knights marched in cadence below on the greenyard, their uniforms fastidiously clean and dangling with badges and ribbons and frills. From her view at the window, she could see the chancellor's tower and its solitary window, and her memory suddenly bloomed with the sound of skittering mice and rats, a pair of wooden clogs, and Chancellor Walraven's weary smile.

"I spent many hours in that tower," Maia said, gesturing toward it with conflicting emotions. "Never in this one, though."

Her friend Suzenne was pacing the room, her arms wrapped around herself for warmth, for though it was sunny, it was cold. Her face was drawn with anxiety and worry. When she heard Maia's voice, she came over to the window and stood behind her.

"Which tower?" Suzenne asked.

"The one with the pennant fluttering. A bird just landed on it, did you see?"

"Is that the chancellor's tower?"

Maia nodded pensively. "I did not know about the Ciphers then. I thought that I was the only woman in the entire kingdom who had been taught to read, that because I was a princess, I was above the taboos of the Dochte Mandar." She sighed as she thought on all she had learned about kystrels and hetaera. She had been groomed by Walraven and the Victus to become one, to wreak havoc on the mastons and destroy them. Though Walraven had eventually joined the maston cause at great personal risk, he had not halted the Victus's plot. They had hoped to use Maia as the vessel for Ereshkigal, Queen of the Unborn. Had she agreed, they would have made her their empress, the ruler and commander of all the kingdoms. They had promised her jewels and gowns, power unsurpassed since the days of the Earl of Dieyre. And she had somehow managed to deny them and survive. Until now.

Maybe my purpose has been fulfilled, Maia mused. She had left the dark island of Naess with her grandmother, the High Seer of the mastons, and sailed to Muirwood Abbey. There she had studied the tomes, learned about the maston order, and become one herself. Then she had successfully reopened the Apse Veil, joining the worlds together so that the dead could finally rest in Idumea, and the mastons in Assinica could escape slaughter. She wondered if she had completed her purpose and the Medium would now shepherd her on to her next life. Maia was troubled by the thought. She did not feel ready to depart.

And yet why else had the Medium not warned her to stay away from Comoros?

"You are lost in thought," Suzenne said, resting a hand on her shoulder. Not her left shoulder, where the hetaera brand lurked, hidden beneath her dress. "Did you sleep much last night?"

Maia shook her head. "I dare not," she confided. "The Myriad Ones are everywhere. I think they are waiting for me to grow weary before attacking me."

"Do you think they will?" Suzenne looked even more nervous.

Maia nodded. "I wrestled against them all night," she said, her voice sounding hollow even to her own ears. "I am protected by wearing the chaen, but they intrude into my thoughts most insidiously. I can hardly think without some remembrance of their power over me. Did you not feel them this morning at the execution?"

Suzenne blanched. "That was terrible. You came here to prevent Lady Deorwynn's execution, and instead we became the chief witnesses of her death."

Maia stared sympathetically at her friend. "Are you afraid to die, Suzenne?"

The other girl's anguish deepened. "Yes," she whispered in a small voice.

Maia turned and took Suzenne's hands in hers, squeezing them. "I am struggling with that fear as well, I admit. Chancellor Walraven taught me not to fear death. That lesson is in the maston tomes as well, and yet the urge to cling to this second life is so strong. Let us remember the maston ceremony. This is not our final destiny. Knowing that makes it easier to bear the truth of what may happen." She swallowed hard. "I am so sorry that you and Dodd came with me to Comoros. I hope my father does not kill you because of me. That would be too much for me to endure."

Suzenne tugged one of her hands free and wiped the tears that had fallen from her lashes. She dropped down to her knees in front of Maia. "I do not regret coming with you, Maia. Dodd and I are bound by irrevocare sigil. They may have separated us in this dungeon, but they cannot separate us forever." She blinked quickly, suppressing further tears. "I know you and the King of Dahomey—"

Maia smiled sadly. "I hardly think of him as that. He is Collier to me."

Suzenne's voice was pained. "Your husband is not a maston. If you die, you will not be with him. Does that not make you grieve?"

Maia gave her a sad smile before looking back out the window and nodding. If all had gone according to Collier's plan, he'd ridden through the night from Muirwood to reach his spy, Simon Fox, this very morning. How surprised Simon would be to learn that Maia was in the city! She had not made it very far from the gates of Claredon Abbey before being abducted by the chancellor's men. There had been no opportunity to visit Simon as she'd promised Collier she would do.

"I do not know what the Medium has in store for me," Maia said, shuddering, "but I love him, Suzenne. I am surprised that it hurts so much to say it. Our entire relationship has been fraught with disappointments. We were trothed as infants and then my father reneged on the contract. Collier kidnapped me in Dahomey and forced me to marry him, or he would have killed my companions. Not a wonderful beginning to a marriage." She gave Suzenne a crooked smile. "But he has changed. Muirwood has transformed him just as it did me. I am the same girl who left these shores on a ship to fulfill my father's will. And yet I am so much stronger than I was then. I will stand up to the king, no matter what he threatens." She felt the smile slip from her face. "Even if he kills me."

Suzenne trembled in sympathy. "Do you think that he will?"

Maia shook her head. "No. He will try to break me first. He will let us linger in this dungeon, tortured by the freedom that is

within our sight, but not within our reach, for a while. He thinks
to frighten me into surrendering, but he does not know that I have
already been through the crucible. I know my own strength, and
I do not fear him." She squeezed Suzenne's hand again and then
rose, stretching her tired limbs. She was sorry she could not save
Lady Deorwynn from her fate. Listening to Jolecia's shrieks and
sobs after the execution was painful to endure. All of the lady's
children had been imprisoned. She knew how it smarted to be
deprived of the benefits of rank after years of enjoying them. She
pitied them.

"I wish they had let Dodd stay with us," Suzenne said. "I keep
thinking about what they did to his father and brothers, and I
cannot stop fretting about him."

Maia continued to walk the room, wishing there were books
to read, but of course such a simple pleasure would not have been
provided to two girls who were expected to be ignorant of the skill.

The sound of heavy boots marching down the hallway filtered
into the room, but this was not uncommon in Pent Tower. She
did not give it much thought until the sound grew louder and the
steps started up the stairwell leading to their cell. Suzenne's face
pinched with concern, and she rushed across the room to stand
by Maia's side.

Moments later, the lock on the door rattled and the door
opened. Two knights dressed in her father's colors entered the
room and stood guard on either side of the door. Between them
entered Chancellor Crabwell, followed by the Earl of Forshee and
the Earl of Caspur. To a man, their expressions were stern.

"I wondered how long before we would meet again, Chancellor,"
Maia said with feigned indifference.

"When we last met, the Medium delivered us into your hands.
Now it has delivered you into ours. Or should I say, it was your

cunning that entrapped us at Muirwood." He chuckled to himself and scratched the corner of his mouth. He was dressed in a sable-lined cape, felt hat, and the ceremonious golden stole of his office. His hair was going gray, and despite his bold words, he looked nervous. It did not harm the effect that he was shorter than her and had to look up to meet her eyes.

"Is that how you've managed to convince yourself?" Maia asked him pointedly. "You think we tricked you at Muirwood?"

"Of course it was trickery!" Crabwell snapped. "We had the sheriff's men posted around the grounds all winter. But they were not mastons, and the *only* place they could not search was the abbey itself. We know about the tunnels beneath the grounds, my dear. The High Seer—your grandmother—is a wise and cunning woman. I must applaud her ability with stagecraft, Maia, truly I must. She won the day, and your father was almost convinced. But Kranmir is a persuasive man. He helped him see the truth."

"And the light coming from the abbey?" Maia said in a scoffing tone. "The mists that were sent away?"

"Leerings *all* have peculiar properties, child. They are useful in propagating superstitions from the old days. You cannot imagine what the Naestors believe about us, the simplicity of some men!" Crabwell coughed, then resumed a more formal tone. "Lady Maia, I am here at your father's behest to give you one last chance to join him. If you refuse, you will be executed for treason. It will not be difficult to persuade the people that you were duped by your clever grandmother if you accede to the king's demands and—"

"No!" Maia interrupted angrily.

Crabwell's eyes blazed with fury. ". . . *and* if you sign the Act of Submission with two earls of the realm as witnesses. I have a copy of it here," he said, waggling a leather cylinder at her. "Once you do this, you will be escorted forthwith from Pent Tower and receive all the dues you are—"

"No!" Maia said more forcefully.

Crabwell nearly choked on his impatience. "Let me finish. If you will . . . my *lady*. I did promise your father that I would give you this opportunity." He swallowed, his face suddenly blotchy and red. "Ahem . . . and receive all the dues to which you are entitled as his *bastard* daughter. He will forgive your treason at Muirwood if you cooperate, but you will not be a member of the Privy Council. An oath made under duress is no oath at all and contrary to the laws of the realm. Lady Jayn Sexton and the king will be married this evening. She will become his rightful queen, and her issue will be his rightful heirs." He stuffed the leather cylinder back into his belt. "There, I have completed my task. Is your answer still the same? I charge you, on your very life, not to trifle with us. The king has empowered the three of us to oversee your fate."

"I wish to see my father," Maia demanded firmly.

Forshee snorted, and she finally looked at him. His face was contorted with fury, and his eyes were like twin flames. An imposing man, he looked to be in his forties and very strong and hale.

"Your father will only see you," the Earl of Caspur interjected in a forbidding tone, "if you sign the Act of Submission right now. This is your last chance, girl. Do not be a fool. The king has already promised more mercy than you deserve."

Maia regarded the Earl of Caspur and his grizzled beard. She saw he looked more nervous than angry, his eyes almost pleading with her to acquiesce. Judging by his silver beard and the fringe of hair beneath his velvet cap, he was the oldest of the three lords.

She looked him in the eyes. "You were there, my lord," she said softly, trying to reach him. "What you witnessed was not a deception. I opened the Apse Veil and reached through time itself and drew Lia Demont into our realm. The Covenant of Muirwood had to be fulfilled. We have so many enemies, so many who seek to humble our kingdom and bring us to desolation. I have seen the Naestors' fleet, my lords. They will not succeed in destroying our kinsmen in Assinica, but they will come here next to hunt for them. They are on their way even now, yet here we are, fighting amongst ourselves." She looked back at Crabwell with clear, resolute eyes. "I care nothing for lands or titles. I do not care who is queen or who is heir. Our people are suffering, Chancellor. They are suffering in squalor. They are suffering in ignorance. They are suffering because they have forgotten what the Medium even feels like. *You* have forgotten, sir."

Crabwell looked at her blackly, his eyes smoldering. "I *never* felt it," he said disdainfully. "Oh, it is real. I know that. They say the Medium grants our secret wishes, yes? I am an ambitious man. We all are," he said, gesturing to the other two men. "And look how it has yielded us a ripe kingdom . . . which *you* seek to topple."

Maia shook her head in denial. "I have no ambition, Chancellor. I only seek the welfare of my people."

"That is *treason*," he accused. "They are your father's subjects, not yours."

"They are mine because I love them," Maia pleaded. "My husband is the King of Dahomey. If you put me to death, he will not stay his hand at revenge." She could hear Suzenne's ragged breathing behind her, and though she wished more than anything for her friend to be safe, she was grateful that she did not need to face these men alone.

Forshee almost spluttered with rage. "You know nothing of politics, lass," he said. "Your husband is a penniless, gutless fool who brought his kingdom to ruination by letting himself be captured by the Naestors. Even if he wished to retaliate, he could not."

Maia stared at him coldly. "You are misinformed, my lord Earl. About many things." She turned her gaze on the others, giving them each the same piercing look. "I see, gentlemen, that you act out of fear and hatred. Remember what the Medium does. You are not quite correct, Chancellor, but you are close. It brings our *thoughts* to bear on us. You fear losing power, and so you *will* lose power. The foundation you stand on is crumbling."

"Enough!" Crabwell said disgustedly. He brushed his gloved hands together. "I told your father you would not relent. This is how you repay his leniency and mercy? With insults and infernal preaching? So be it. If you will not sign the Act of Submission, you will pay the price of a traitor's death."

Maia lifted her chin with false bravado . . . feeling indignation, but not remorse. "Then so be it, Chancellor. I will not sign it. If execution is how my father chooses to unbirth me, then I must accept it. You all feed his self-delusions and madness. But though he tells you the sky is red, he cannot *make* it so. And when he tires of you, do not believe you will be safe from his wrath either. You have your answer, Chancellor. I will not sign under duress. He has broken the pledge he made to me at Muirwood. If I die . . . I die innocent. And the Medium will judge you for my blood."

She saw the Earl of Caspur's eyes were wide and wet with tears. He looked shaken to the core. Crabwell seemed incensed, and only too eager to abandon the room.

The Earl of Forshee, however, looked murderous. His cheeks quivered with violence, his eyes were molten with ire. She felt a quick pulse of fear, for he looked as if he would gladly plunge a sword into her ribs. The power of the Myriad Ones emanated from inside him, telling her he was their creature, their plaything. He took a step toward her, his gloved fingers gnarled as if he wished to choke her to death. "You are so *unnatural*," he said in a quivering voice. "How dare you speak to us thus? If you were *my* daughter," he growled, "I would knock your head so hard against the wall that it would cave in like a baked apple." He swallowed, saliva flicking from his lips, and took another step in her direction. "You are a traitoress and will be punished as such. Prepare for death, insufferable girl. I would volunteer to do it myself, though I fear a blade would be too merciful."

The black void of his thoughts pressed into her, leaving a path of queasiness and disgust. He was so thick with the Myriad Ones, she could see them inside his black eyes. The raw hatred was terrifying. Maia felt her knees tremble and buckle, but she held firm, squeezing her fists to give herself the strength to remain standing. The howling thoughts of the Myriad Ones echoed through the small cell. It was a flood. Just like the rats Walraven had summoned into his office that long-ago day.

"Be gone," Maia stammered, her tongue swelling in her throat. "I rebuke you."

The rage in the man's eyes intensified. He took yet another step toward her, and the other men did naught to stop him. Suzenne was shrinking beside her, holding up her hands as if afraid she too would be murdered. The edges of Maia's vision began to flake with blackness, as if scales were growing on her eyes.

The Myriad Ones surged against her once more. In the past, she would have recoiled and surrendered under the force of their attack. This time she did not, for she was a maston.

Maia raised her hand in the maston sign. "Be gone," she whispered again, her voice choking.

She did not feel the Medium come to rescue her, for there was no place for the Medium in that chamber. It was like clinging to a rope in the midst of a churning river, but she held firm, and the blackness could not claim her. She clung to her faith, rooted against the threat of danger.

The Earl of Caspur fled the room. Crabwell winced as he looked at her, as if the sight of her burned him. He was the next to storm past the guards and out of the cell.

The Earl of Forshee remained behind, his black eyes still raking hers. Will against will. He fought her for domination and control. She saw a flicker of silver in his eyes.

"Now," Maia ordered forcefully.

And he obeyed.

The harvest of Leerings is rich indeed. The craftsmen of Assinica have a simplistic but beautiful style. The parks and lanes are clean and tranquil. The flowerbeds surrounding the abbey were sowed for spring flowers. It is almost a pity to ruin so much magnificence. Almost. When the mastons see the devastation we leave behind us, when they realize we will not be swayed by beauty, delicacy, or innocence, they will fear us. They will see that our will moves the Medium. Not with compassion, but with force. Those who defy our aims, even within our order, will repent their disobedience.

—Corriveaux Tenir, Victus of Dahomey

CHAPTER THREE

Hetaera's Mark

M aia held Suzenne close, soothing her friend as shudders rippled through her body. The encounter with her father's emissaries had shaken them both, but Suzenne appeared to be more affected. Maia had been in dark, threatening places before. A kishion had nicked her ribs with his knife, promising coldly to spill her blood if she used the kystrel against him again. A Myriad One had used her body as its own. She had endured many hardships in her life. For the past several years, Suzenne had lived in the cloisters of Muirwood, protected from the unpleasantness of the diseased kingdom around her.

"I have never been so frightened," Suzenne choked back her tears. "Never have I felt such . . . blackness. How did you have the strength to stand against him? I quailed!"

Maia stroked Suzenne's hair and hugged her. "I have faced worse. They were odious men. Caspur was affected by my words. I could see it in his eyes. But the others are quite hardened."

"Ugh," Suzenne moaned. "I feel sick. The Myriad Ones were here. You could feel them . . . sniffing about us like we were dead flesh to vultures. It was disgusting."

"It is over," Maia said. "They are gone."

Suzenne straightened, brushing some of her hair over her ear. "The difference between this city and Muirwood . . . It is almost too vast to describe, like comparing noon with midnight, but Maia, there is no peace here. Even in the daylight, it seems as if the sun were veiled. What a horrid feeling."

Maia nodded in agreement. "I have often wondered what it would be like to live in Assinica, where they know nothing of war. I cannot imagine it, to be honest. And think of the shocking transition the Assinicans will have to make when they come to our realm, chased by the Dochte Mandar? Suzenne, how will they endure it? Yet perhaps they are our only hope."

Suzenne nodded in agreement. She looked slightly calmer, but her eyes were still anxious. "Will they kill us?" she whispered, gripping Maia's hands.

"I think . . ." Maia paused before continuing, wanting to soften the blow without lying. "If the Medium wills it . . . perhaps. Yes."

Suzenne swallowed and bit her lip. "Do you . . . think it is the Medium's will?"

"I do not know." She stared down at their entwined hands. "When I left Comoros for Dahomey, we reached the shores that are still cursed by the Blight. I kept hearing whispers that said it was the land where death was born. Back then, I thought it was the Medium speaking to me. And it seemed to suggest that I would die there."

"But it was not the Medium," Suzenne said, perplexed. "You wore a kystrel. It must have been the Myriad Ones who spoke to you."

23

"Yes, I think so," Maia answered, but a nagging little doubt remained in her mind. "Whether or not that is true, I have suspected for years that I might die before my time. When I was younger, I learned to read, knowing that if my ability were discovered, I would be put to death. When I went to Dahomey, I feared I would not survive the journey. When I went to Naess, I believed the Dochte Mandar would kill me because of the mark on my shoulder." Maia sighed tiredly. "I suppose I have been dreading it so much, it would not surprise me if it happened. The Medium gives us the results of our thoughts. Perhaps I have served my purpose by restoring the Apse Veil." She frowned deeply, keeping her gaze lowered. "For some of the things I have done, I deserve to die."

Suzenne shook her head violently. "That is not true, Maia! You are not accountable."

"But I still carry the consequences," she replied, and began pacing again and wringing her hands. "I *destroyed* an abbey and killed its Aldermaston. I cannot help but feel awful about it, despite the circumstances. And what of my marriage! My husband is not a maston. I wanted to marry one to preserve the lineage of my Family, as we were taught as children. Yet Collier and I were married by the customs of the Dochte Mandar. I have done everything wrong." She sighed again. "I cannot kiss my husband because of what I am . . . and I cannot even say what I am because the Medium binds my tongue. And Suzenne, even if I were innocent, it might not help. The Medium did not protect my mother from dying. Nor did it protect Dodd's father or his brothers." She came to a stop before Suzenne and glanced up into her eyes. "Yes, I am sorry I brought you with me. I should have come alone."

Her eyes moist with tears, Suzenne reached out and hugged Maia fiercely. "I am afraid, Maia. But I made my vows to the Medium in the abbey. If this is how I can best serve, then so be it. Perhaps Dodd and I will join his siblings in Idumea tomorrow. At least that is possible because of you. And Maia, I would have come with you even if I *knew* that would be our fate." She pulled away enough to look deep into Maia's eyes. "You inspire me, and you have made me a better person by your example. Do not lose hope, Maia. If we die, we die together. Friends, if not sisters." She punctuated her comment with a timid smile.

Before meeting Suzenne, Maia had never had a friend her own age and sex. Staring into Suzenne's eyes, she felt the warmth and compassion that had always been denied her. It was not hollow or false. This was true friendship. "Thank you, Suzenne. I am sorry if that is our fate, but I appreciate you more than you know. Having you here with me gives me the courage to face anything."

Suzenne smiled, then hugged her again.

They sat at the one spare table in the room and spoke for hours after that—about Muirwood and how the Leerings had helped save the abbey. About the men they loved. And even though the cell was cold, they soon forgot the chill. For a while, it felt like they were back at the Aldermaston's manor in Muirwood, talking late into the afternoon.

***

Captain Trefew came for them after sunset.

They had just finished their simple meal, so Maia assumed the footsteps belonged to their jailor, come to remove the dishes. But when the jailor opened the door, he was accompanied by Trefew and five soldiers, each heavily armed. The captain had a leer on his face, a look of delight and savagery that turned Maia's stomach.

"Bring them," he ordered two of the guards near him.

"Where are you taking us?" Maia asked, her stomach churning with panic.

"Not to the gallows, if that is what you fear," he answered smugly, the light in his eyes making her worry all the more. "Soon, though."

"Where?" Maia pressed.

Trefew chuckled and motioned for the guards. Each was a salty man, very rugged in appearance—fair hair and blue eyes indicated origins in Naess. They wore the uniform of the king's guard, but bore the slovenly appearance of dungeon keepers.

One of them grabbed Maia by the arm, his grip painfully hard as he dragged her from the cell. Suzenne received the same treatment from another guard, and they were paraded down the hall in front of the other cells. Because of the sunset, there were torches—no Leerings—to light the way. She smelled spoiled meat and sickness, which not even the heavy pitch smoke could quite conceal. The soldiers marched them down the hall toward a cluster of six more guards who awaited them in front of a closed door.

"Suzenne! Maia!"

She jerked her head toward the sound of the noise and saw Dodd straining at the bars of his cell, his eyes wide with fury and concern. Manacles secured his wrists and ankles, and the metal cuffs jangled and echoed throughout the tower. His shirt was stained and scuffed and his dark hair was sweaty and tousled. He pulled against the solid bars, trying to achieve the impossible and shake them loose.

"Do not fret about your lady friends," Trefew said, pausing at the bars. His expression twisted with malicious glee. "That one is your lass, is she not? A beauty. We will handle her gently for you. Rest assured."

"If you touch her . . ." Dodd warned savagely.

Trefew laughed in his face. "What, Maston? Will you raze the tower walls with your powers? Wilt me like a dried reed?" He spit in Dodd's face suddenly, his smile melting into hate. "We will treat them kindly. The Aldermaston wants them checked for certain *marks*." Maia stiffened, and a sickening feeling wrenched her stomach. "I am sure they will oblige us willingly enough. Now back in your corner, whelp." He reached through the bars and shoved Dodd back with his hand. Dodd did not fall, for he was sturdily built, but his nostrils flared with rage and he clenched his hands into fists.

The group of soldiers continued to pull Maia and Suzenne down the hall.

"Take Deorwynn's two brats into the girls' room," Trefew ordered some of the guards. "We will bring up the two gowns after they have disrobed. They will not be coming back up here tonight."

"Yes, Captain," one of the soldiers said. He marched over to another set of cells near Dodd's, where Murer and Jolecia hung back from the bars. As the girls were pulled out of their prison, Maia caught a glance from Murer, whose face was ashen and whose dress was of a far lesser quality than the last one she had seen her wear. Their eyes met, and Murer looked both humbled and pitiful.

The guards at the end of the hall opened the door, and Dodd let out a groan of impotent rage, the sound of which was silenced as the thick wooden door was thrust shut behind them. Maia felt the mewling of the Myriad Ones all around them in the dark confinement of the corridor. The soldiers were grim faced and silent. Trefew walked ahead of them, his expression turning wary at every intersection. Finally he paused before a door, tapped on it gently, and then waited as the lock was opened from the inside.

Maia glanced at Suzenne, and saw that her friend was white as milk with fear. Her own stomach twisted with dread as she imagined the humiliation they would be forced to endure. The door opened, leading to another hallway in the mazelike keep. Leerings provided the only illumination in the darkened corridor, and Maia was tempted to extinguish them all, but she decided not to risk antagonizing her captors further.

"Here we are," Trefew said with a hint of anticipation in his voice. They had turned a corner, and Maia was hopelessly lost. She did not recognize this part of the grounds at all. The walls were dank, the crevices riddled with scum, and there was a damp, musty smell in the air. The pathway led them on a downward slope, and several more guards awaited them below.

"Cannot be too cautious," Trefew said to Maia conspiratorially. "There are rumors the King of Dahomey has spies at court. You will be moved all night to foil any attempts he might make to rescue you. But mastons like to go without sleep, eh?" He winked at her. "Consider it a vigil, my pious prisoner. This way."

The door was unlocked and opened to a small stone chamber with no windows. It was another cell, much more isolated and stark than the last. There was no cot to sleep on, no table to sit at—not even the smallest of comforts or conveniences. It was wide enough to fit a dozen men, but most of the guards waited outside. Only Trefew and the two who gripped her and Suzenne entered. The door was closed and locked behind them. A Leering, set into the ceiling, was the only source of light.

Trefew walked across the room and then tapped on the stone wall with his dagger hilt. After a moment he whispered something that Maia could not hear. The stone swung inward to reveal a Leering on the other side carved to resemble a man in great pain. The eyes in the gouged, worn face glowed orange, and Maia shuddered.

There was another room beyond, in which Maia immediately recognized Aldermaston Kranmir and his mushroom-shaped black hat. He was standing, for there were no chairs.

"Come in," Kranmir said smoothly, gesturing for them to enter. The room was lit by several lanterns and two Leerings. The thought of being in the same room as him made Maia's skin crawl, and she started with surprise when she realized Lady Shilton was also present. Her cheeks flaming, her eyes puffy with tears, Lady Shilton looked abashed to see Maia. The grieving look aged her. Seeing the woman who had tortured her for so long caused a visceral reaction in Maia—a stab of fear, dread, and indignity.

There was a dark, twisted feeling in the room, and though she could not help but tremble, Maia steeled herself to face what would come.

After their escort released them, Maia entered first, followed by Suzenne.

"You will not be harmed tonight," Kranmir said coolly, "if you cooperate. If not, Captain Trefew and his men will compel you. Lady Shilton witnessed this same . . . procedure when her own granddaughters were questioned. Do not think she will show you any more favor than what they received."

Maia stared at the ground. She knew what was coming. Her heart panged with regret for ever having touched that accursed kystrel.

"Remove your gown, Lady Suzenne. You will be examined first."

Suzenne shot Maia a look of abject terror and quailed.

Kranmir's eyes narrowed. "Captain?"

"With pleasure," Trefew said jubilantly, stepping forward.

"Do not touch her." Maia blocked his path. "I will help her." She gave Kranmir a look of loathing, but he seemed unaffected by it. Suzenne shook with fear as Maia stripped away her girdle, then tugged the lacings of her gown loose and helped her remove it. She wore the chaen beneath, protecting her modesty, but Suzenne's cheeks were beet red with mortification to have disrobed before so many men. Maia gathered up the bundle of clothes and turned to Kranmir.

"Are you providing us something else to wear?" she challenged, before handing over the clothes.

"Of course," Kranmir said. He stepped forward, giving Suzenne a critical look. She trembled with embarrassment, unable to meet anyone's eyes. His voice was smooth and dark. Maia could not see the Myriad Ones prowling throughout the room, but she could sense them, their mewling shadowforms snuffling about, greedy to taste the emotions in the chamber. "A kystrel," he said with exaggerated sanctimoniousness, "leaves a taint on the chest bone. A whorl of tattoos that begins to rise up to the throat. You do not seem guilty, my dear, so that is in your favor. Lower the chaen slightly to be sure."

Suzenne flushed even more and tugged limply at the front of her bodice. There was no stain.

Kranmir nodded and clasped his hands behind his back. "There are records, however, that an ancient Family in Dahomey was not afflicted by the kystrel's taint. The only way to be certain is to see the shoulders as well. If you please, my dear. Or as I said, Captain Trefew will be only too eager to assist you."

Suzenne gave him a black, angry look. She nodded in meek compliance and carefully pulled down the chaen to expose her left shoulder, covering herself as best she could. Maia was furious, but of course this was all a playact for what would come next. She knew it with savage certainty. They were drawing out the charade to make their suffering more acute.

"Thank you," Kranmir said. "But just to be sure. The *other* shoulder too."

Suzenne obeyed and revealed her other shoulder, which was also free of any brand.

Kranmir nodded with satisfaction. "Lady Shilton, you are my witness. So are these soldiers. Lady Suzenne Clarencieux is free of the taint. Now, Lady Maia. If you would submit to the same procedure, we shall examine you next."

His eyes looked into hers, and her suspicion was confirmed. Yes, he knew . . . he had probably known for a while. He nodded to Captain Trefew. Suzenne moved forward to help her, but the captain shoved her away. Maia cringed as she felt the hands touch her, yanking loose the girdle and tearing the sleeve of her gown. She wanted to strike out, to scream, but she endured the humiliation as he nearly ripped the dress from her. It was what he had wanted to do on that long-ago day when she had been taken to Lady Shilton's manor, when her remaining privileges had been stripped away, as well as her clothes.

Maia stood in her chaen, feeling the same awkwardness to be stared at by so many, but she lifted her chin in defiance and refused to cower. Trefew gathered up her gown in a heap under one arm and stared at her with vile emotions burning in his eyes.

"Let me see your hand," he said, gesturing for her right. She opened her palm and showed him the pink scar on it. He nodded, frowned, and then folded his arms.

"Even the chaen does not conceal the kystrel's taint on your breast," he said sternly. "I am shocked that Richard Syon did not have you examined when you came to Muirwood. Did he know what you are? I cannot say the word, you know. Obviously a binding sigil is at work here."

Maia clenched her teeth as she stared at him in anger. She said nothing.

"Your shoulder, please," he said, motioning for her to bare it.

Maia kept her expression as calm as she could. "I bear the mark," she said simply, her voice quavering. "But I am not what it implies."

Kranmir smirked at her in response. "Show me."

Maia sighed, anguished, and slipped the chaen over her shoulder, exposing the hetaera's brand. As soon as she did, a veil of blackness drew over her eyes like a cloud blotting out the moon.

And then she was falling.

CHAPTER FOUR

Gallows

It was a struggle, terrifying and sudden. Blackness shrouded Maia, enveloping her in dark coils of smoke and suffocation. She felt a wrenching sensation in her mind and body, as if her soul was about to be sundered. On instinct, she battled it, refusing to yield to the vapor that threatened to stifle her. She groaned and thrashed, trying to repel the invasion. It was like fighting off an ocean's tide. There was nowhere to anchor her feet, no way to shove against the amorphous waves that wished to bury her alive. She was drowning in the blackness of the Myriad Ones.

A sudden light pierced the darkness, knifing through it like a glowing Leering. That blackness melted away from her, unable to cling, and seeped through the stones and crevices of the rock around her instead. The Leering in the ceiling was blindingly bright, and Maia discovered when she opened her eyes that she was curled up on the ground.

As her eyes adjusted to the brilliance, she watched as Suzenne's hand lowered from the maston sign. Her other hand was pressed flush against Maia's brow. Though her friend was strained and weak, she had a look of defiance mingled with fear as she covered Maia's exposed shoulder with the chaen.

"You did that deliberately," Suzenne said to the men.

Kranmir's eyes were wide as he stared at the two girls on the floor. His nostrils were rimmed with white. A look of fascination mingled with dread transfixed his face, and a single ball of sweat trickled down his cheek.

"So it is true," he whispered hoarsely.

Lady Shilton was fanning herself, her eyes wide with unalloyed horror. She cowered by Aldermaston Kranmir's side, trembling, groping for a chair to sit on, though none was there.

Maia gave Suzenne a grateful look and tried to rise, but her muscles quivered and trembled, her energy completely sapped by the ordeal. Suzenne helped her sit up, hushing her gently.

"What I did," Kranmir continued, shaking his head stubbornly, "is prove beyond a doubt that you are a danger and a threat to the kingdom of Comoros. Who wears your kystrel?" he asked.

Maia's throat felt raw, as if she had screamed for too long. "I do not know."

The Aldermaston looked far from convinced. "Whoever it is, they must be found and destroyed. Did Walraven give the kystrel to you? Hmmm? Absolute treachery. Your father will be displeased."

"My father knew I had it," Maia contradicted, trying again to rise, and failing still.

Kranmir clucked his tongue triumphantly. "Please, child. His memory lapses have always been very convenient. You have given me all that I need to secure your father's throne. The people are rioting to see you, and they *will*. Let no one say we do not give them what they want. Yes, I can see it now. There you will be, up on that platform with your shadowstain and shoulder brand for all to see. I cannot say what you really are for the sigil binds my tongue. But the evidence . . . the evidence will be seen with the people's eyes. Your grandmother knows the truth. There is no need to lie and cover for her."

"She does know," Maia angrily contested. "I never accepted this brand willingly. My father sent me—"

"It does not matter!" Kranmir thundered, his voice hot with rage. "It does not matter why you received the brand. It only matters what you *are*. What you let yourself *become*. The people clamored long for Queen Catrin to rule. She was a true threat to your father's power. But you . . . you were always the greatest threat. That is why he kept you so near him. That is why Lady Shilton watched over you. Did you know, Lady Shilton, that Maia had the mark on her shoulder?"

Lady Shilton cringed away from the Aldermaston, her voice trembling. "I swear I did not!"

"She did not when she lived at your manor?"

"No!"

Kranmir looked vindicated. "She visited Dahomey. And she returned to despoil Comoros, to bring the Scourge back to this land once more." He shook his head, clucking his tongue in mock disappointment again. "And the High Seer of Pry-Ree knew it!" he snarled. "She knew what you were. She hid the truth in a tome and sealed it with a binding sigil. Oh, my dear child, how can I ever thank you! All was lost at Whitsunday, but now all is recovered. The people will cry out in rage for your death when they learn what you really are. Of course, there is no heir, but perhaps Lady Jayn will bear a son. She is young still. One heir is all it will take for people to be satisfied. Thank you, Maia. The Medium has delivered you into my hands. Truly it has ordained that *I* shall be the new High Seer."

His eyes were wild with the fervor of power lust, his lips quivering as he spoke his ambition aloud. He turned to Captain Trefew, who was skulking outside Maia's vision. "Captain. She is under your watch. Move her and the other from room to room until dawn. There can be no mistake. When she dies in the morning, you will become an earl yourself."

"Yes, Aldermaston," Trefew said, his eyes as wide as a child with a bag of sweets. He came and yanked Maia up by her arm.

***

"It is selfish, yet I am glad you are here with me," Maia said as they were forced awake, yet again, and marched to another location in Pent Tower. The corridors were thick with guards and torches. "You saved me."

Suzenne smiled nervously and squeezed her hand with affection. They had been given new gowns to wear, simple servants' attire with no fancy trims or edging. "When I saw your eyes roll back in your head, I truly feared you were overcome," Suzenne said. "You started trembling and thrashing, and the room was . . . dark. The Medium told me what to do, Maia. It is still with us."

Maia nodded and squeezed her hand in return. She was grateful the moment with the Myriad Ones had not lasted long. In the past, Ereshkigal had taken over quickly, and it had taken her hours to regain control of her body. Suzenne had drawn power from the Leering in the ceiling and the maston sign. She would not have been strong enough to cast the evil being out if Maia had been successfully occupied. But she was strong enough to prevent the takeover. If Maia had been alone, she knew she would have lost the struggle.

"I need you near me," Maia said with relief. "Until the end."

Suzenne nodded firmly, her eyes determined. "Until then."

"The *end* is not far distant," Trefew chuckled darkly from nearby. "The cocks will crow ere long, lasses. Somehow word got out yesterday that you were in Comoros, Lady Maia. We are suspecting a full riot this morning. Most of the king's soldiers are still returning from the celebrations. But we have enough to hold the tower. Never fear that."

Maia turned to look at him. "And what earldom were you promised?" she asked disparagingly.

"Any will do," he replied smugly. "But I think the Earldom of Dieyre will be open once your marriage treaty is over. Always fancied that one."

"It will bring you as much joy as it did its earlier ruler. That earldom is cursed."

Trefew smiled slyly. "So much the better." He gave her a look that revealed a mind full of darkness and corruption. She could see the evil of his thoughts plainly on his face, in the Myriad Ones dancing gleefully behind his eyes.

They reached their next destination, and the doors were unlocked. Several guards awaited them within the cramped cell and Trefew waved them out and entered after the last man left. He looked around at the small cot, checked the bars at the window to be sure none were loose, and sniffed the air, which was odorous, before gesturing for them to enter.

Suzenne and Maia did, and he went to the cell door, key in hand. He looked at her again, grazing her up and down with his eyes. "I wonder . . ." he said offhandedly. He paused for dramatic effect. "I wonder if those lips will still kill after your head is struck off." His eyes wrinkled with perverse glee as he slammed the door and locked it.

Suzenne hung her head, sighing deeply. "A truly odious man."

"Indeed," Maia answered. "If I am ever queen, I will only allow true mastons to serve me." She shook her head sadly and smiled. "It will lower the costs of the household, to be sure, given that there are so few left."

"How can you joke," Suzenne asked in amazement, stifling a laugh. "Look at the sky. Is it yet dawn?"

"I think it is," Maia replied. "Can you see outside?"

"The window is too high."

"What if we move the cot over?"

They both grabbed an end and arranged it by the window. The narrowness of the cell indicated it had only been meant for one prisoner. Suzenne ambled onto the cot and pulled on the bars so she could see better.

"It *is* dawn," she said. "I can see the greenyard, but it is a ways distant. There are soldiers milling all around it and some coming to and fro with torches." She eased herself down and then pressed her head against the wall.

"What is it?" Maia asked, seeing her expression change.

"I hope Dodd does not watch us die," she whispered, shivering. "Do you think he will join us on the platform?"

Maia felt a stab of sadness. Would Collier be on the grounds? She could not imagine him standing still while she was executed. He would rush the guards and kill as many of them as he could. She had hoped that Simon Fox would have found a way to rescue them in the night, but as a wine merchant, what could he truly do but report the latest court gossip? Maia was struggling to keep her courage as the end loomed ever nearer.

Something clattered and slammed against the door of their cell, startling them both. Maia pulled Suzenne off the cot, and both waited anxiously as the noise quelled. A few moments later, a key entered the lock and Captain Trefew entered, his face dripping with sweat, his look now more wary than lustful.

"Come on," he ordered gruffly.

"What happened?" Maia asked, startled at the sudden change in his behavior.

"Come on!" he barked.

He grabbed Maia's arm painfully and dragged her out, motioning for another set of soldiers to fetch Suzenne. As Maia left the cell, she was surprised to see Captain Carew kneeling in between a few other guards, his face covered in sweat. He looked at her, his eyes panicked. Blood dribbled from his nose.

"Maia!" he gasped when he saw her. "Your father—!"

One of the soldiers clubbed him on the head with a sword pommel, silencing him. Carew's tunic was spattered and stained, and she saw a huge bandage on his leg where he had been injured in the brawl on Whitsunday. She saw some other guardsmen had also been subdued and one man was obviously dead, his face twisted into a rictus.

She blinked with surprise. Something was horribly amiss, and her mind swirled to piece it together.

"This way," Trefew muttered, yanking her after him. "Best get you to the greenyard now before there are more surprises."

Her father's captain had tried to rescue her, apparently. Her mind whirled with amazement. She scanned the bodies of the other knights, looking frantically for any sign of Collier. Could he be the cause of this sudden turmoil?

"Move!" Trefew barked, digging his fingers into her arm.

"What has happened?" Maia demanded.

"Nothing that need concern you," he replied impatiently. Then, to another soldier awaiting orders, he said, "Keep the guards on every doorway."

A soldier came running at them from down the hall, his eyes wide with panic. "There is a mob at the palace gates," he gasped. "They are chanting to see her."

"Let them," Trefew sneered. "We'll give them her corpse."

"But if the king is—"

"Shut it!" Trefew interrupted, his eyes blazing with fury. "I have my orders from Chancellor Crabwell. Go, man!"

Maia looked at Suzenne in desperation, and saw the same startled expression on her friend's face. Something was wrong. Something had happened. Something to do with her father.

"Tell me, Captain," Maia insisted, stopping and wrenching against his arm.

He glowered at her, his eyes full of spite. "You want to be *dragged* to the gallows, my lady? Very well."

"No!" Maia snapped obstinately. "Tell me what happened to my father."

She saw him flinch at the word. His oily assurance was gone now. He was afraid. Desperate. When men were desperate, they were impulsive.

"He is dying," Trefew growled abruptly. "Poisoned."

Maia stared at him in horror.

"His last order was to have you killed," Trefew whispered, his jaw convulsing. "Carew could not stomach it. Neither could some of the others at court." He pulled her hand hard, bringing her face close to his. "But I *can* stomach it. For an earldom. There will be even more earldoms vacant soon."

The feel of his breath wafting against her face almost made her gag. But she stared into his eyes, pleading with him to see reason. "This is *wrong*, Captain. I am the Princess of Comoros. Release me and I will show you mercy."

His teeth clashed together, his lips twitching. "I do not want your *mercy*, lass. But if you promised me something more . . . interesting? Still, I think you will not."

Suzenne gasped with outrage and lifted her hand to strike him across the face, but the soldier who restrained her yanked her off balance and she nearly fell down.

"To the gallows!" Trefew roared, pulling Maia down the corridor after him. As soon as they left the corridor and entered another, she could hear the tumult of the rest of the castle. Everywhere there was shouting, the stamping of boots, and the murmur of voices.

Other soldiers filed in around them as they marched down the tiled floor that was polished to a shine. They were still in Pent Tower, but they were now on the main floor, heading toward the greenyard. Maia's heart was afire with emotions, tumbling and fighting inside her bosom. Her father had ordered her execution as he lay dying. Even at the brink of death, he would not admit he was wrong . . . he would not protect his only heir. It caused her so much pain, she almost felt like giving in to death.

I will obey the Medium's will, she thought in despair. *Whatever that may be.*

"Clear the doors!" Trefew shouted. "Quickly!"

Another soldier ran up. "The Privy Council is assembling on the lawn, Trefew, but some are refusing. They are summoning their retinues."

"Cowards. They are squeamish," Trefew snapped. "It will be over too soon. They will fall next."

The cavernous doors before them creaked open, and Maia saw the first flush of dawn in the sky. There were soldiers outside on the green. Her heart hammered in her chest as she was dragged toward the gallows, where she had watched Lady Deorwynn meet her fate the day before. Then a strange peace suffused her, as if a calming whisper were sounding in her ears. The Apse Veil was open. She had fulfilled the Covenant. No matter what happened now, she had done her duty to the Medium. Maia glanced back at Suzenne, who winced with pain at the grip the soldiers had on her arms. She tried to give her friend a comforting smile.

Suzenne looked back at her, her eyes blinking back tears, and nodded.

Another soldier ran up with a drawn sword. "The mob is trying to force the gate," he shouted.

"Who is guarding it?" Trefew asked. He glanced around at the soldiers alongside, easily more than a dozen men. The numbers gave him confidence. "If any man tries to help them get through, kill him!"

"We have pikemen ready in case the mob breaks down the gate. They are tradesmen mostly, not soldiers. But they fill the streets. Some are even trying to climb the walls."

Trefew looked bewildered at that, as if he had not expected such effort on Maia's behalf. "They are all mad! Have the pikemen stab through the portcullis. Start killing them now rather than waiting for them to burst through."

"Aye, Captain," the soldier saluted, and rushed off.

The gallows were small, but a growing crowd had assembled before them. Foremost was the Earl of Forshee, who was on horseback and surrounded by men wearing his livery. Of course he was present. Some of the witnesses were female. One man in the crowd was shouting at Forshee angrily. Then she recognized him from the day before. It was the Earl of Caspur.

As they marched, Maia saw another man come running up.

They reached the crowd, and the assembled parted like a curtain, opening a path to the threshold. Maia swallowed, still feeling a strange inner calm despite the hurricane of tumult about her.

The page handed the Earl of Forshee a scroll. He took it, snapped off the caps, and then quickly scanned the content of the message. His face contorted into a frown, but he nodded for the boy to run off.

"What does it say?" Caspur demanded.

They were close enough now to hear what was being said.

"The king is dead," Forshee muttered. "That is all. Crabwell issues his first order. The princess must die."

"No!" Caspur shouted, seeing Maia and her escorts for the first time. His eyes widened with outrage.

"Go back to the castle if you are not man enough to watch," Forshee sneered. Caspur's face was white as chalk, but he backed away from the earl with an anguished look.

Forshee's horse jumped a bit. He turned to Trefew and gave him a curt nod. "No speeches. This must be quick."

Trefew pulled Maia to the wooden stairs, followed closely by the men who were grappling with Suzenne, and the two girls were forced up onto the platform. There was a growing rumble of noise from one side of the castle grounds, but they would arrive too late, Maia was suddenly certain of it. Her hair streamed across her face as the wind suddenly breathed across the greenyard. She tried to smooth it away, but Trefew's grip on her arms barred her from even that small comfort.

Maia was escorted to the block at the center of the platform. Glancing up, she could see the tower cell where she had been imprisoned. She could see people at the windows, but it was too distant to clearly see Murer's and Jolecia's faces. Maia struggled to envision a last image of Collier before crossing the mysterious chasm to Idumea, but there was not time. Her body was thrust forward toward the executioner's block.

Then she turned to look at the executioner, whose hands rested on the pommel of a giant sword so sharp its blade pierced the wood of the platform. He looked solemn and impressive and frightening under the leather hood.

The bottom of his mouth was visible, along with a telltale scar. She looked into his blue eyes, his *deadly* blue eyes. His shape, his size—she knew without a doubt it was the kishion.

He smiled when she recognized him.

There were some mastons who remained hidden in Assinica. Some poor souls who hoped to use persuasion to thwart us. They were meek, to be sure. They feared not torture nor death. Courage is often the balm of the fool. I ordered their remains to be hung by chains from the steeples as a witness.

—Corriveaux Tenir, Victus of Dahomey

CHAPTER FIVE

Kishion

"Kneel," Trefew ordered in Maia's ear, then gave her another shove toward the block. She stumbled but managed to right herself and take another look at Suzenne—maybe her last. Suzenne's cheeks were stained with tears, her fingers knotted together in a mute prayer. She was pale, but she nodded at Maia and did not look away from her. Two guards still restrained her friend; Maia was now free. The wind swept across her face again, sending strands floating before her eyes. She smoothed them away this time, facing the kishion with the greatsword.

A memory struck her at that moment. After their escape from Collier's army, she had entreated him that someday he might be called upon to fulfill his duty to kill her. She had told him that she might ask it of him. She looked into those emotionless blue eyes. But no, they were not void of emotion anymore. He stared at her with obvious feeling, but how could she even describe what she saw in his eyes? Triumph? Glee? His smile made him look uglier, if anything, made her want to recoil. Why was he smiling at her? Was he so evil that killing her brought him joy? And yet, he had saved her life at Muirwood Abbey. If only she knew where his true loyalties lay.

Maia took the final steps to the cold plinth. She cupped her hands against her chest and then knelt on the planks. She shivered uncontrollably, but she did not flinch. Glancing down at the crowd, she saw a mixture of expressions there. Sadness, greed, placid unconcern, misery. All eyes were upon her. And there was Forshee, his expression an interplay of hatred and victory. The government was toppling, the stones just starting to crash down in the heath, and he hoped to come out ahead.

"Do it!" Trefew ordered savagely.

The kishion stepped forward. Her heart was brim with emotions as she heard and felt the distinct thud of his boots. At least the Apse Veil had been opened, she reminded herself again. Her mind wandered to those poor souls from Assinica, who would come to this land for shelter, only to find themselves in an evil kingdom that despised mastons. She thought of her grandmother and of Collier, wishing she had been permitted to say good-bye.

Then Maia lowered her head and swept the dark hair away, exposing the nape of her neck. The kishion's shadow passed over her. She could hear his breathing.

"Do you forgive me of my office?" he asked her gruffly, his voice so familiar. They had wandered through the cursed shores of Dahomey together. Of the protectors who had traveled with her, he alone had survived the journey to the lost abbey. He had protected her from Corriveaux and his Dochte Mandar. He had nearly died at a mountain crossing in a confrontation with the Fear Liath.

"I am content to die," Maia whispered, refusing to meet his gaze. Her head dipped lower.

"I know," he answered softly. There was something in his voice when he said it. A familiarity. Compassion. "But you were born to rule."

She heard the sudden stomp of his boot, so she shut her eyes, not wanting to see the blade as it came down to end her. But the cut did not come—at least not for her. Gasps sounded from the crowd, and a commotion erupted on the platform. There were cries of pain, shouts of outrage, and Maia opened her eyes and whirled around to look.

The kishion was attacking the soldiers on the platform, cutting them down one by one with the greatsword. For a moment, she did not understand what was happening, and then her heart burst with relief at the realization that her protector was protecting her still. The kishion kicked a soldier in the ribs so hard he flew off the platform and into the mass of swarming men who had gathered to watch her die.

Forshee barked orders with uncontainable rage. There was no way the kishion could face so many foes singlehandedly, was there? Maia stood on shaking knees, watching the chaos unwind in the greenyard. The kishion cut down another man, and Maia spied Trefew cringing behind Suzenne, using her as a human shield. How she loathed him for his cowardice. Suzenne's face was pinched with pain, but there was no fear there—only triumph.

The kishion untied something from his belt that looked like two glass cylinders stoppered with cork. He flung the vials off the platform, right by Forshee's stamping horse. There was a flash of white and suddenly a mist began to fill the green with snaky tendrils. The people in the crowd began to scream in pain and terror as it licked against them.

Forshee's mount bucked and threw him, adding to the tumult of the scene. People were fleeing in all directions to escape the choking mist, while soldiers charged from the castle to join the fray. Were they there to fight for Maia's freedom, or her death? She could not tell amidst such confusion. The kishion shoved another man off the platform and then ripped off the leather executioner's hood and dropped it at his feet.

"Follow me to safety," he said, his smile savage. He rushed to the far end of the platform, reached into his belt again, and hurled another pair of glass vials onto the ground, which also erupted in a flash of seething smoke. More shouts and cries rocked the greenyard, and Maia heard her name screamed by Suzenne. She tried to turn, but the kishion grabbed her arm and pulled her toward the back edge of the platform.

"Jump!" he growled. Though she strained for Suzenne, the kishion pulled her with him, giving her no choice.

They landed with a jolt on the cobblestones. The mist was already reaching them, and the kishion grabbed a scarf from his pocket and held it to her mouth.

"Breathe through this," he said, grabbing another one for himself.

She pressed the cloth to her mouth and felt its dampness against her skin. It smelled strongly of some pungent odor. The mist swarmed around them, its milky vapors dancing in the air.

"Find her! Find her!" someone shouted.

Wails of pain and suffering surrounded them, but the mist made it impossible to see. The kishion wrenched open a sack partly concealed beneath the platform and withdrew two cloaks. He hurriedly fit one around her shoulders and raised the cowl to cover her hair.

"Always hide your beauty," he told her, his scars twitching with his smile. He tossed the greatsword down under the platform and then grabbed her hand again and pulled her deeper into the fog.

"Where is she?"

"I cannot see her!"

"It was the headsman. He betrayed us!"

"That was no headsman. It was the kishion!"

The panicked masses were escaping all around them as the kishion led her away from the platform. It pained her to realize that the kishion's aim was to save only her. He was one man, and even a trained killer could not hope to defeat all the guards Crabwell would send after them. Her heart thundered inside her ribs from exertion and lingering fear, but she finally felt the thrill of having survived what had seemed a certain death sentence.

A soldier emerged from the mist in front of them, spluttering. "Hold there," he ordered, reaching out to stop them.

The kishion released her and plunged a dagger into the soldier's ribs and then grabbed him around the neck with his other hand and whipped him around, letting him tumble into a heap on the ground. The ruthless dispatch sickened Maia, but she also felt a certain degree of detachment, having seen so much death and violence in the past months.

Once again, the kishion grabbed her hand and pulled her after him. Her sense of direction was completely impaired by the commotion and the haze. She stumbled over the body of someone who had fallen, and saw the fine tunic and glittering vest of a nobleman she did not recognize. His felt cap had fallen, and his hair was askew. The kishion kicked him in the ribs in passing and pulled Maia back to her feet.

"Bar the gates!" someone was shouting. It was Trefew's voice, full of wrath mixed with fear. What had he done with Suzenne? Was he still using her as a shield?

"The crowd is smashing them down!" someone replied. "The mob is coming! We must flee!"

Maia heard the churning roar of the castle that was indeed under siege. Her father was dead, and all law and order in Comoros had crumbled.

"Are you behind this mayhem?" Maia asked her companion, increasing her speed to match his.

"The wood was already cracked and dry," he answered. "All it needed was a little spark. Wet wood only smokes, not burns. This way."

"Where are you taking me?" she demanded.

"The main gates are being forced by the mayor and the ealdermen. But it is too crowded, and crowds are dangerous and difficult to predict. I have the porter key to get us out. This way."

The haze was beginning to dispel, and she could see that only soldiers had remained around the gallows in the stinging smoke. They were clearly searching for something—for her.

The kishion grunted. "Too much wind. I thought it would last longer. Walk fast, but do not run. It will attract too much attention. Over by that arch. It leads to the porter door."

Maia glanced back again, hoping for a glimpse of Suzenne, some sign that her friend was safe, and the kishion scolded her. "Focus, Maia. We are not to safety yet."

She kept the pace he set, trying to stifle the thrill. "Did you poison my father?" she asked him bluntly, staring at the chin jutting from his cowl.

"Of course," he answered flatly. "He betrayed our agreement. He and Lady Deorwynn were supposed to reinstate you."

"Who will pay you now?"

He laughed coldly. "I do not work for your father any longer."

"Who then?" she pressed. He had saved her today, just as he had saved her from the sheriff's men at the abbey. To whom did he owe his allegiance?

"Stop!" someone shouted from behind. "You two. Stop in the name of the chancellor!"

"Run," the kishion said, pulling her in the right direction as they broke into a sprint. Cries sounded behind them, followed by the percussive pounding of boots. The kishion directed her to the arches and then down a long, narrow alley set between two of the outer walls of the castle. The walls were too high to climb, but a narrow iron door was set into the stone at the far end. The stone was chalky gray and cold, the alley spotted with a brown moss that also marred the door.

The kishion thrust a key into her hand. "Unlock it. I will hold them back."

Maia nearly dropped the key as she frantically searched for the keyhole. She found it just as the soldiers raced into the alley with their swords and pikes. She fit the key into the lock, her hands trembling, and tried to turn it.

It was stuck.

The kishion did not wait. He rushed the soldiers and threw one of his daggers, which caught a man in the neck. There was a clash of arms as the soldiers tried to rush him with their weapons, but the kishion struck and twisted like a serpent, wounding an enemy with each jab. He took another vial out of his vest and threw it against the breastplate of one of his attackers. This time fire erupted from the contents instead of mist. The soldier screamed in pain and flailed his arms, exuding the sickening smell of sizzling meat.

Desperate, Maia used both hands to wrench on the key, and it finally groaned and turned. The bolt slid free. Using her shoulder, she shoved at the door, barely managing to budge it. The kishion attacked ten men at once, ducking and weaving and jabbing his daggers into their vulnerable parts. She gritted her teeth and continued to shove against the door, managing to slowly grind the warped wood against the stone, inch by slow inch. Through the gap, she saw another alley, littered with trash and crowded with pigeons. The birds cooed angrily and flapped away.

The kishion was suddenly next to her, and when he slammed his shoulder against the door, it swung open easily, as if without any effort.

"Almost free," he said exultantly. "The city is crying for you, Maia. They want you to be their queen. They *need* you."

He grabbed her arm and pulled her with him into the alley, glancing back several times to see if they were being pursued. How had he struck down so many so quickly? She realized that he had not. His chemicals or devices were causing fear. The soldiers had run away.

She sensed two Leerings built into the stone walls as she approached the mouth of the alley. They radiated fear, and she could sense their purpose through her Gift of Invocation. They protected these walls and especially the porter door. Men feared to enter the alley, and so it was cluttered by debris that had been blown in by the wind.

"There!" someone shouted behind them. More soldiers spilled through the breached porter door and started pursuing them.

The kishion whirled to face them, his eyes full of anger. He was going to dispatch them as he had the others.

"No," Maia said, grabbing his arm. "I can stop them. This way."

She pulled him toward the edge of the alley and directed her thoughts at the Leerings, commanding them to prevent people from *leaving* the alley instead of approaching it. She felt the Leerings respond to her thoughts, and suddenly waves of terror and dread washed over her. She pulled the kishion into the street, beyond the Leerings' range. The streets here were teeming with people, many of them carrying shovels or spades and chanting. She glanced back at the alley, where the soldiers now cowered in place, overcome by the fear caused by the Leerings. They would neither be able to pursue them nor track their steps.

"Clever," the kishion praised. They walked swiftly, putting distance between themselves and Pent Tower. Maia saw the steeple of Claredon Abbey ahead—*escape*. But Suzenne and Dodd were still back at the castle, and she was unwilling to abandon her friends.

"The mayor is part of this revolt?" she asked him.

The kishion nodded. "He is loyal to you, Maia. Most of the city is loyal to you. Most of the realm is as well. They are teetering on the brink. *You* will steady them. You were meant for this."

She stared at him and began to understand the look in his eyes. The cynical, murderous part of him was sloughing off. The look he gave her was almost . . . tender. He respected her. He admired her.

She was surprised. "You did this . . . for me?" she whispered.

He met her look and nodded curtly. "I do not serve the Victus. I do not serve Deorwynn. I serve you. My lady. My queen."

Maia trembled at what he said. Fear coiled in her heart like a serpent. The look in his eyes. He was staring at her with . . . an eagerness she was unaccustomed to seeing in him. The pressing need to find safety brought her back to the present moment.

"Do you know where Flax Street is?" she asked him. "Can you take me there?"

He nodded. "It is nearby."

It was where Collier had told her she would find the business of Simon Fox, his spy from Dahomey. She knew the man was also a spy of the Victus, but he was betraying the Dochte Mandar to support Maia's grandmother.

They walked, hand in hand, through the crowded street. Maia was appalled at the filth clogging the gutters, the broken windows and lopsided houses and shops. Flies buzzed around the commotion, heedless of the human troubles, seeking their foul nectars to drink. The stench in the air was strong. The city was large and had never been as clean as the streets of Rostick, but it had never been this foul. Her father's misdeeds had drowned his kingdom in sorrow and filth.

As they reached Flax Street, Maia could discern the scent of wine from the other odors. She saw several shops before her eyes fixed on the one with Fox's name. They hurried toward it, each step feeling lighter and more hopeful.

"I must leave you now," the kishion said, releasing her hand. "I know you will be safe here." He stared into her eyes without looking away.

Yes, there it was again—something had changed in this hard man. There was devotion in his gaze . . . ardent devotion. What had she done to deserve it?

She had saved his life from the Fear Liath. She recalled the last words they had spoken when he lay crippled by his wounds. He had asked her to leave him. To escape him. She had denied him vehemently and brought him to a healer at the village below Cruix Abbey.

"Where are you going?" Maia asked fearfully.

He smirked. "You would not approve. The chancellor is the next to fall. When the mayor brings you to the palace, you will find it ready to welcome you. Farewell, Maia. I will be near if you need me."

Without another word, he turned and vanished into the crowded street beyond.

CHAPTER SIX

The King's Daughter

W hen Maia pushed open the door to the trading shop on Flax Street, she was surprised to see so many people bustling about frantically. She spotted Simon Fox quickly. He had seemed solemn and almost detached in Muirwood, but now he looked agitated and unkempt. His velvet cap was gone, his brown hair was mussed, and his eyes were bleary from lack of sleep. He was talking to three men at once, but when he noticed her, his eyes blazed wide and he nearly shoved the men aside.

"Lady Maia!" he said, choking. He rushed to her side, staring at her in utter amazement. "But how? You are here? Truly? Or do my eyes deceive me?" He reached out and touched her arm, as if to assure himself that she was not a phantom.

"I am safe," she answered, searching the room. "But where is my husband?"

"In the front lines of the crowd attempting to force entry into the castle. Tanner and Brent—quickly! Tell him that she is here."

"At once," one of the men replied. Needing no further instruction, both of them rushed out the door.

Simon went to the window, looked out quickly, and then steered her into a comfortable, furnished back room. He gestured for her to take a seat in what had to be his chair—a thick, padded leather chair behind a broad desk. She chose a small couch instead and sat down, trying to calm her trembling hands.

"How are you even here?" he asked in utter astonishment.

"I was rescued," she answered.

"By?"

She stared at him. "The kishion whom my father hired to kill me."

Looking even more bewildered in face of her explanation, he went and sat down on the edge of his desk, tugging at the strands of his forked beard. He was young, only a few years older than she was, but he was wiser than most, and his mind worked quickly.

"It is known to the Victus that the new headsman is a kishion. But he had orders to kill you . . ." He looked at her gravely. "I have tried all night to find a way into the castle to free you. They locked every gate, sealed every porter door. No traffic was allowed in for any reason unless the visitor bore the chancellor's seal. Crabwell is clinging to power by his fingernails. And so the king and I suggested a riot."

Maia nodded. "There was talk of it in the tower during the night." She stifled a yawn. "I have not slept at all. They were moving us around on the hour. My friend Suzenne was also on the platform with me, but I could not save her. Her husband, Dodd, is also imprisoned in Pent Tower. Can you—?"

"I will send someone at once," he said, rising swiftly from the desk and disappearing into the other room.

When he returned, he found her in the midst of another yawn. Before either of them said anything, he quickly went to a side cabinet and withdrew a small blanket. "You are exhausted. Here, lie on the couch awhile and rest. My men are searching for the king and your friends. I am sorry for this ordeal, Lady Maia. That your father would stoop to this . . . well, those are the only words available to me. I am truly sorry."

She gratefully accepted the blanket. "My father is dead," she said. "The kishion is going after Crabwell next."

Simon blanched. "Then the government has been toppled, and the country is at risk of invasion. A new ruler needs to be chosen immediately. It will not take long for Hautland or Paeiz to press a claim."

"Or Dahomey?" Maia asked with an arch look. She wrapped the blanket around her shoulders.

"He would not do that to you," Simon replied, smiling benignly. "You have changed him, my lady. He is a different man since coming to Muirwood. You have humbled his pride. I had not even believed it possible."

Maia smiled and then stretched out on the cushions.

A hand jostled her shoulder what felt like moments later. She must have fallen asleep, though she had no memory of it. Simon was bent over her, and as soon as she processed what was happening, she allowed him to help her sit.

"He is coming," he whispered. "Anxious to be sure. I still await word on your friends."

Maia brushed some hair behind her ear and sat up, feeling at once dizzy and lethargic. She heard the authoritative sound of boots marching down the hall, and suddenly Collier was in the room. She was so relieved to see him, it must have shown on her face. He rushed up to her and hugged her so tight it almost hurt. His hand stroked her hair, and she could feel a slight tremor in his touch.

"By the Blood," he gasped, pulling away slightly to look at her, his hands cupping her face. Through his relief, she could see the marks of a long night spent in dread and agony. His eyes were bloodshot, and there were smudges of stubble across his tense jaw. His body trembled with pent-up energy. "You are safe. I almost could not believe it when they told me. It was too much. It was too good. I *begged* the Medium to save you, for I could not," he said hoarsely.

She smiled, so grateful to be here with him after despairing of ever seeing him again, so warmed by his concern and affection. He brought her back down to the couch and sat beside her, holding her close. "Would that I had an army. Would that I had wings to fly over that wall. I could not get to you, Maia, and it nearly killed me. How did you escape?"

"The kishion freed me," she answered, squeezing him hard. She felt grateful for what her protector had done, but it caused her deep concern that he was acting on his own. What would he do next? Who else would he kill? She suspected he had done it because of his feelings about her, which troubled her even more. Worry could come later, though, and she shoved the thought from her mind so she could savor her reunion with Collier.

She pulled back and grazed his cheek with her fingers. "But I believe the Medium was what truly saved me."

"So do I," he answered. He shook his head in amazement. "Poor Simon, I have not been patient. The castle was completely secured, and they were letting no one enter. The streets are rioting, Maia. People are demanding you. They are shouting for the king's daughter to be their queen. Yes! They are chanting for you. They were going to depose your father, but word has gotten out that he died last night."

Maia could hardly contain the feelings cascading through her—there was a sense of loss for her father, though that was tempered with relief, gratitude for her people's support, and the solace of at last being in Collier's arms. Tears pricked her eyes.

"When you were banished and your titles were stripped away, that was all they were allowed to call you. The king's daughter. The people have watched your suffering, Maia. They have resented your father's treatment of you. The mayor is even now rallying the citizens to rescue you and proclaim you queen throughout the land."

Maia wrinkled her brow. "I do not even know him. Why is he so eager to help me?"

Collier smirked. "Because Simon and I told him that the king had abandoned the city to be destroyed by the armada. And then we told him of what had transpired in Muirwood. Believe me, people here have heard nothing of what happened on Whitsunday. Much of court is corrupt, but not all. They resented the king's treatment of you and were ready to depose him even before they knew the truth."

She shook her head, dazed. "They were truly ready to depose him?"

He nodded and grinned. "I told you before. The people cannot abide him. They resented his treatment of your mother, not to mention his attitude toward you. While there were no tears shed over Deorwynn's execution, once word got out about your impending death, the people went mad with rage."

"I told the king about your father's fate and Crabwell's grab for power," Simon said. "There is chaos in the streets. I have reports that the Earl of Forshee has fled the city. Many of the other earls have left too. The army was divided and sent to different parts of the country to prepare for the invasion, leaving the heart of the kingdom unprotected."

Maia nodded somberly. "What of my friends? I am worried about Suzenne and Dodd. Have they escaped? Were they harmed?"

Simon shrugged apologetically. "The outer wall has been breached, but the inner one is still under siege. We have no word from them or about them, but do not be hasty in your concern. Anyone seeking to win your favor would know to protect them. Do not give up hope."

She was restless to hear news of her friends, but she realized it was inevitable for word to travel slowly amidst such tumult. Gathering Collier's hands in hers, she entwined their fingers and gazed into his eyes. "What would you advise?" She looked at both men. "I confess, part of me longs to return to Muirwood and seek the Aldermaston's counsel."

Collier shook his head firmly. "This is not a moment to flinch, Maia. How can I put this gently? The Medium has delivered this kingdom into your hands. It is yours by right. It is yours by grace. It is *yours*." He squeezed her hands. "And your people *need* you!"

Maia was shaking all over. It felt as if a great door was closing in her life and another even larger one was opening. The path ahead was vast and unpredictable. But her husband spoke true; she had been born for this. She understood the need to create calm immediately, to give her people hope.

How quickly her situation had changed. She had gone out into the greenyard expecting to be executed—she had even knelt before the block and bared her neck. Now, before the day was even done, the people in the streets were hailing her as their queen.

She felt a gentle murmur in her heart and realized that her destiny was just about to unfold.

***

To help protect Simon's identity, Maia and Collier left his shop and met the lord mayor in a private room at a nearby inn.

The mayor of Comoros was a worldly man and a cunning one. He had dark hair with a speckling of gray and a small little stripe of beard just beneath his bottom lip. Neither tall nor short, neither heavy nor slight, he was swathed in costly court attire, jeweled doublets, and a fur-lined cape.

"Your Majesty," he said with studied formality, bowing gracefully. "I have taken the liberty of sending for several gowns. The sheriff of Kellinge was only too quick to supply them, as well as jewels to match. I thought you might like a variety of colors and styles to choose from. If you are to ride through the city, you must look the part."

He bowed once more with a flourish.

Moments later, several servants streamed into the room, carrying the costly gowns for her to see. Each one was sumptuous and clearly befitting someone of her station. Collier frowned at the majority of them and subtly gestured toward a green-and-gold Dahomeyjan style.

Maia shook her head. "No, my Lord Mayor. Justin," she said more informally. "This was not planned or anticipated. I will ride without changing my attire."

"But it is a *servant's* gown," he objected. "They will not even know who you are. My lady, I appreciate the gesture of humility— in fact, I honor you for it—but the people need to see you as their queen."

"Thank you for the trouble you took in bringing these to me," Maia said sincerely. "It was thoughtful of you to try to anticipate my needs. Thank you. But this you must understand." She swallowed, trying to compose herself. In her mind, she could practically hear Corriveaux's voice as he promised her gowns and jewels and courtiers and the envy of all. "I am not my father. I am his daughter. My mother spent her final years as queen living as a wretched in Muirwood. I myself have just passed the maston test at that abbey. Our kingdom is on the brink of civil war, but that is far from the only threat we face. We are also on the brink of an invasion by men who care nothing for the sanctity of lives—men who want only to crush us. This is not a time for pageantry or show. A queen *serves* her people. So it is best if I come in that guise. I have come to serve Comoros, not to rule it."

The mayor stared at her as if she had uttered speech in a foreign language. When he glanced at Collier, she did too, and what she saw there was heartening—could his look be *approving*? Of course, if anyone would understand, her husband would. He knew all too well the benefit of a servant's garb.

"Now, Justin," she continued. "Thank you for providing a horse. I do need that. If I ride next to you, I think the people will understand who I am. You mentioned it would be best if we rode through town so that we could rally more supporters."

"It is dangerous," the mayor said, "but also unexpected. Your enemies will not have time to retaliate. The inner grounds of the castle are still locked down, but we now control the outer gates. As I suggested earlier, once we have ridden through town, we should assemble a host of citizens to follow you to Pent Tower. There you can command the castellan to open the gates to you. If he refuses, we lay siege. There are not enough provisions there to last more than a fortnight. But I know the castellan. If you come, I trust he will do his duty and open the gates. The people believe you are the rightful heir, despite the acts."

"Very well," Maia said. "Prepare the escort. We ride at once. I would like to make sure the castle is ours before sunset, if possible. Two of my dear friends are trapped inside, along with any number of other innocent victims. The chaos and looting must end swiftly. We face too many threats from the outside to be this divided within."

"I cannot agree more," the mayor said, mopping his brow with a silk kerchief from his pocket. He turned and left to make the final arrangements.

Maia turned to Collier. "Are you disappointed?"

He flashed her a small smile. "Whether you wear a servant's gown or one made by a master tailor, you still look beautiful." Collier took her to the corner of the room, where a chair sat in front of a table and mirror. "Your hair needs to be brushed. If I may?"

She glanced over her shoulder at him and nodded, giving him a private smile. Then she sat down in front of the mirror and gazed at her weary reflection. There were soot smudges above her cheeks.

Collier took a comb from the table and began to smooth out her long hair with expert hands, as he had done aboard the ship on their way to Naess. She was more comfortable with him now, but his touch made her shiver with pleasure and anticipation as his hands grazed the back of her neck.

"I wanted you to ride with us as well," Maia said, looking at his deep blue eyes through the mirror's reflection.

He shook his head. "Simon said it would be unwise, and I agree with him."

Maia pursed her lips.

"Shall I explain?" he offered.

She nodded.

"The people love you. There is euphoria in the streets right now. Word is spreading quickly that you miraculously escaped your death at the tower and will ride through the city to claim your father's throne. Simon's people are helping to spread the word. All requests for evidence that your father still lives have been met with silence. Half the nobles, including Kranmir, fled the city, and many were robbed as they departed Ludgate." He snorted to himself. "I will not comment on whether they deserved it. This is your moment, Maia. If the King of Dahomey rides beside you, then it will tarnish that moment. You did this, not I. It would not be wise to let people think that Dahomey manipulated your father's death or put you on the throne."

Maia stared at him. "A queen has never before ruled Comoros," she whispered. "I will be the first."

He nodded, teasing out some more strands of her hair with the comb. "Which is what makes it so interesting. The customs of your realm must change. Your struggles are just beginning. You have renegade earls who fear losing their possessions and estates. Men like Kord Schuyler, the Earl of Forshee. And Kranmir will do his utmost to rally the mastons against you. I imagine you will want to invest your friend's husband with Schuyler's title?"

The idea had never occurred to her—the notion of having that kind of power would take some adjustment, it seemed. "I suppose I can do that," she said in an almost awed whisper.

Collier chuckled. "There are certain privileges that come with power, my dear. You can reward those who are loyal and faithful to you. That will show the people what you value and set the tone for their future behavior. Reward the mastons, and more nobles will choose to join the order."

Maia nodded, smiling. "I will need a new chancellor as well."

Collier tugged through a stubborn clump, easing the tangles out gently, and then continued to make long, smooth strokes. She sat patiently, enjoying this moment with him.

"That role is critical," he said firmly. "It is someone you must absolutely trust. Your chancellor will act on your behalf. They will control who gets to speak with you and when. They will lead meetings in your absence and decide policy on your path. I kept my father's chancellor when I became king. Integrity is paramount. He was a maston, and I knew that he would not use his power to reward himself or his friends. Do you have anyone in mind?"

Maia sighed and nodded. Their gazes met again in the mirror. "Richard Syon."

He seemed startled but pleasantly so. "An Aldermaston?" he chuckled.

"Not just *any* Aldermaston. He has already shown himself to be a wise counselor, not to mention a patient and kind-hearted man." Maia also thought about his wife and her band of Ciphers. She smiled inwardly. She had not shared that secret with Collier yet—and indeed, it was not hers to share. "And he is the Aldermaston of Muirwood, the most ancient abbey of the realm."

Collier nodded, and his eyes gleamed with approval. "I do not know of any precedent for it. He might reject the position. Or the High Seer might oppose your choice." He winked at her.

"I shall have to ask my grandmother then," Maia replied.

Collier finished combing her hair and gently played with some of the strands. He crouched behind her, his chin resting on her shoulder.

"And when shall we announce our marriage to the people?" she asked him, feeling her stomach ripple and thrill as she gazed at him.

"Give me a few months in Dahomey," he whispered in her ear. "You have not yet been crowned Queen of Dahomey. I imagine you should be crowned by your own people first."

She turned. "Without you by my side?"

He gave her a small smile. "Setting up a kingdom takes time, my love. And I have problems of my own."

She raised her eyebrows and waited for him to continue.

"When I arrived in Comoros, Simon told me that Paeiz is preparing to invade Dahomey. They think I am penniless and that my future father-in-law is too tightfisted to help. They seek to enlarge their borders at the expense of mine. I think they will be a little surprised to find us more than capable of defending our borders." He smirked at her, but then his face grew serious. "Thanks to your grandmother," he added softly.

She turned in the chair so she could look him in the eye. "I do not want you to leave me."

"It will not be for long," he promised, running his fingers down her cheek until they landed just below her forbidden lips.

A brisk knock sounded on the door, and then the mayor entered, beaming, noise from the streets outside streaming in from behind him. He looked at them askance, then grinned and winked, and bowed with a flourish.

"Your Majesty," he said graciously. "As you can hear, the city is clamoring to see you."

Collier crept his hand into hers, gave it a firm squeeze, and then let her go. She rose and followed the mayor to the front of the inn, where the cheers and shouts were growing louder and louder.

When she reached the door and shielded her eyes from the sun, she saw people on every cobblestone of the street, in every open window, on every roof. Everywhere there were raised caps and waving hands. A few of the escorts who would accompany her and the mayor were mounted, and she could tell they struggled to keep their horses calm in the sustained cacophony of noise.

When they saw her, it was like a rumble of thunder. The cheer deafened her.

I do not disagree that the maston tomes have gems of great wisdom contained therein. We can learn from anyone, even our enemies. Knowledge can be twisted into any shape. Did not one of the wisest men teach that the least initial deviation from the truth is multiplied later a thousandfold? That is the hallmark of the Victus. By small degrees are women wooed. By tiny corruptions will kings fall. I especially love the tome of Ovidius, who has taught all other men the art of telling lies skillfully.

—Corriveaux Tenir, Victus of Dahomey

CHAPTER SEVEN

Pardon

aia rode a quivering stallion through the streets of Comoros to the deafening tumult of cheers and fanfare. The horse had blinders to keep it moving straight, but she could sense the beast's nervousness, which rivaled her own. The mayor of Comoros rode at her side, waving gallantly to the crowds who had assembled en masse to see her. Everywhere there were men and women with tears streaming down their filthy faces, people shouting for her to go forth and claim the crown long denied to her.

It was a moment she would never forget.

She had been prepared to die for her convictions, but now she realized it might require more courage to live for them. So many lives were in her hands, and she could not fail them. The streets were clogged with mud and debris, but it did little to stop the people who were gathering around the cavalcade, or to cool their ardor. She was the first female heir of Comoros, with no legitimate brothers to rival her for the power of the throne. In the distant past, one female heir had attempted to take the queendom and failed, sparking a civil war that had lasted nearly a generation.

Someone from the crowd rushed up to hand her a flower, but the person was rebuffed by one of her escorts who surrounded them on foot, each of them carrying poleaxes to keep the crowd from engulfing them. The lady was grabbed by the shoulder and shoved away.

Without pausing to consider her actions, Maia tugged on the reins and halted her nervous mount. "Bring me that woman's flower," she said in a firm tone of command. The closest soldier gazed at her in confusion for a moment, as if to gauge her sincerity, but then strained against the crowd to make his way to the older woman. When he returned to Maia, he presented her with the flower. She took it in one hand, still clenching the reins in her other, and nodded her thanks to the woman, who stared at her with dumbstruck gratitude. Another cheer went up from the crowd as those nearby realized what she had done. She tapped the flanks of her horse with her boots and pressed on amidst the noise and confusion.

The people wanted more than to see her wearing a humble servant's gown and riding a cream-colored stallion. They wanted to touch her, speak to her, and know her.

All that would come with time. Maia had no intention of sequestering herself away in the castle once it had been seized. She would first seek out Suzenne and Dodd and ensure they were safe. There was a nervous pit in her stomach that would not be moved until she saw them again.

A man hung precariously from a weathercock on a roof, waving his cap like a flag and screaming her name. When she waved up at him, the crowd cheered her all the louder. There were so many people, it was impossible to focus on anyone for very long.

"Almost there!" the mayor shouted to her, gesturing as Pent Tower loomed ahead of them. The walls were crowded with spectators, citizens who had helped storm the greenyard in a selfless effort to save her life. The outer walls were in the mayor's control now. The keep itself had been bolted and shut, but the mayor's men had also taken control of the river leading to and from the palace. Several nobles had already been caught trying to flee, and the rest were hunkering down within the keep for a siege.

"Have your men be gentle with the crowd," she told the mayor. Then she had to repeat herself, yelling this time, for him to hear.

He looked at her askance. "My lady, we are doing our best to hold them back!" he shouted in reply. Then he beamed with satisfaction. "I have never seen such a mob! Not even on Whitsunday!" He gave her a victorious smile and tapped his stallion's flanks with his spurs, urging the reluctant horse onward.

The garbled shouts from the crowd washed over her. She heard men crying out praise for the king's daughter, as if it were a title of the greatest honor. Others shouted out their support for the reign of the new queen. Each clop of hooves brought them nearer to their destination, and Maia could not help but wonder what would happen when they actually reached the gates. Demanding the castellan to open the gates was a risk. If he refused and challenged her authority, it would be an inauspicious beginning. Yet the mayor was convinced that the castellan would surrender rather than face the wrath of the mob that followed Maia. There were not enough soldiers in the city to tame the restless hive. The city's very vulnerability—months, nay, years, in the making—had prepared it for Maia's claim.

As they reached the outer walls, flower petals started snowing down on them. How it had happened, she did not know, but it felt as if every flower seller in the entire city must have gathered their wares together to be shredded and tossed from the heights. Rose petals mixed with daffodils and daisies to create a fragrant, beautiful rain. A small blue forget-me-not landed on Maia's hand, and she snatched it up before it blew away, smiling at the memories it inspired.

The mayor guffawed at the display, his features glowing with the triumph of the moment. He motioned for Maia to ride under the arch and into the main bailey. The greenyard was off to the left, and to her relief, the scaffold was not still standing. It had been broken down, the plinth knocked onto its side and broken to pieces. The greenyard swelled with people—merchants and tanners and weavers all jumbled together and waving and screaming her name.

The mayor beamed. "I have never seen the like," he shouted. "By the Blood, what a scene!"

Maia's heart beat hard in her chest as their horses continued to approach the huge doors of the keep. There were guards stationed on the walls looking down at them. Their helmets concealed their faces, but they wore her father's uniforms.

The mayor reined in his stallion, and the beast stamped nervously. Maia's own mount still trembled with fear, and she tried to soothe it by stroking its mane.

The mayor held his fist high in the air, and the folk in the bailey fell silent, though the roar from outside the walls did not abate. Tension and dread hung in the air. Maia's mouth went dry as she gripped the reins, squeezing the leather straps hard enough to bite into her skin, and stared up at the walls.

The mayor raised his voice loud enough to boom through the courtyard. "In the name of Marciana Soliven, heir of Comoros, I command you to open the gates! She is the rightful ruler of Comoros, upheld by the people of Comoros! Castellan! Open the gates!"

There was a tremor of anticipation as the crowd awaited his

decision. Maia stared at the huge barred gates and heavy doors. It would not be an easy task to burst them down.

A few moments passed with no action on either side, but then there was a clattering sound, then a groan, and the gate started to rise as the winches began tugging on it.

The crowd went wild with cheering before it had risen even an inch. The air was raw with energy, and Maia felt a shiver go down her back. The screams deafened her. She watched with relief as the portcullis lifted and then the yawning chasm of the doors parted and opened.

The first people who emerged were Dodd and Suzenne, hand in hand, grinning at her triumphantly. Maia almost wept with the joy of seeing them together and hale. Behind them was the Earl of Caspur, a limping and bruised Captain Carew, and several other nobles who doffed their hats and joined in the cheering. So she had supporters within the castle as well. Her heart felt ready to burst.

Maia kicked away from her stirrups and was about to jump down when a soldier rushed up to help her dismount more gracefully. Along with the mayor, who had also climbed off his horse, Maia strode forward to greet her friends. She hugged Suzenne fiercely, blinking back tears as Dodd grinned like a fool at her from over his wife's shoulder. His only obvious injury was a mottled bruise on his cheekbone, and Suzenne looked well behind the haze of sleeplessness.

"You *are* alive!" her friend whispered in her ear. "We feared it was a trick!"

Maia hugged her even tighter before pulling back and greeting Dodd with a hug.

The Earl of Caspur gave them a moment before stepping forward. He dropped to one knee and gazed up at her.

"Lady Maia, Your Majesty, I thought if your friends were the first people you saw, it would help you understand the truth of our allegiance." Captain Carew also dropped to one knee, though he grimaced with pain at the effort. Soon the entire group before her had dropped to their knees, her dear friends included. Hearing a flutter of motion, she turned to see the entire courtyard was now kneeling before her. Tears swam in her own eyes as she beheld her people.

"The city is yours," Caspur continued in a hoarse voice. "The kingdom, you must fight for, but we stand with you, my queen. We are yours to command."

Maia's heart nearly burst as she continued to stare at the courtyard, at the tears streaming like rain from the faces of her people. Even the mayor was tear stricken. She felt their fresh hope, their imploring looks that begged her to change things for the better. Her throat was swollen, and she did not know if she could speak. She only knew she must.

Maia faced the courtyard, her heart brimming over. Then she sank to her knees before them. There was a gasp of surprise as she did so.

"I am your servant," she called out as loudly as she could. As she knelt there, she felt the presence of dozens of Leerings within the castle. Some were in the kitchen for heating and cooking food for the castle. Some were for water. Some made light. She felt them all at once, a combination of usefulness—each one carefully sculpted and carved to serve a purpose. And in that moment she invoked them and summoned the Medium through them. All she wanted was to give the people a taste of it, a chance to feel what she had so enjoyed upon arriving in Muirwood.

Welcome, she bade them to say. *Welcome home.*

Maia rose and turned to the Earl of Caspur. She did not know where his loyalties truly lay. He had been part of her father's Privy

Council. He owed his wealth and station to her father's whims. Yet when last they had met, she had seen something in his eyes.

She put her hand on his shoulder. "They are hungry," she said, gesturing back to the crowd that had assembled behind her. "Open the larders and start feeding them."

He looked at her in confusion. "All of them? There are too many."

"As many as you can," Maia said, patting his shoulder.

***

It was the strangest experience of her life. Maia had often walked the halls of Pent Tower during festivities, but in those days, she had been a shadow, a pariah, earning looks of sympathy and sadness. This day could not be more different. The castle was buzzing like a hive of bees as her servants strove to fulfill her first order—to feed those who were gathered outside. Bread was baking in the many ovens. Casks of wine and cider were being carried from the cellars. The butchers were hard at work, and everyone was occupied in a task.

In the midst of all this activity, Maia gathered in the throne room with all her supporters. She wanted to be seen, wanted to do things out in the open. The doors of the castle were being kept open, against the advice of the mayor, to allow the people to come and go freely.

"What happened to you?" Maia asked Suzenne, gripping her hands and pulling her down onto a bench situated near the dais and throne. Dodd hovered nearby. "When the kishion pulled me into the fog, Trefew used you to protect himself. I was so worried!"

"You were worried?" Suzenne said in wonder. "Maia, you were taken away by force and vanished in that stinging smoke! You were the one we feared for! Trefew let me go as soon as the kishion fled. He was only concerned for his own skin."

"I was safe," she answered, keeping her explanation simple for the moment. "Now tell me what happened here."

Dodd interrupted. "Let me tell it," he said, his eyes gleaming with excitement. "There was a little war between Chancellor Crabwell, Forshee, and Caspur. Forshee hoped to fulfill the chancellor's orders to execute you, knowing they would all lose power if you rose. Caspur did not support either of them, but without enough men to openly defy them, he felt he could not act. As soon as Forshee witnessed your abduction, he fled the city by boat, and Caspur's men joined forces with Captain Carew to defeat the chancellor's personal guards, led by that villain Trefew. We tried to arrest Crabwell, but he went into hiding. The search goes on to find him. Caspur made sure Suzenne was safe and then came to the dungeons to free me and your other supporters."

"Where did you go?" Suzenne asked.

Maia shook her head, refusing to disclose that information publicly. "I went to an inn for safety," she said. "The mayor met me there and helped rally the people. Who is on our side?"

"It does not matter right now," Dodd said, beaming. "When word spreads of this, supporters will come flocking to you. I would count on Norris-York. But watch out for the south. Kranmir escaped, and is no doubt bound for Augustin to cause trouble."

Maia frowned.

Suzenne nodded. "He was one of the first to flee. I am sure he intends to wait out the storm at his abbey. You hold the capital city, Maia, but how you fare with the rest of the kingdom depends on how many earls support you and will fight for you."

The mayor waved his hand. He pitched his voice lower so that the bystanders would not overhear. The commotion in the throne room would have made it difficult anyway. "Forshee will try and rally the people in his Hundred, but they will not fight for him when Dodd Price is standing near you." He grinned mischievously. "He will be an outcast in his own lands, but then he was always an insufferable braggart and a cockroach. You will enjoy squishing him. Caspur is gambling on your weakness right now. You need allies, and he needs patrimony. He will watch the winds, though. You must be careful of him."

"I am not my father, Justin," Maia told the mayor. "I will rule by law and reward those who are obedient. I believe in forgiveness, and will give all of them a chance to prove their loyalty."

The mayor's eyebrows twitched. "Even Forshee?" he asked.

"Even him," Maia replied. "You see, they were only doing as they had been rewarded for doing. My father did not value the truth, so he attracted liars. I am different, but I am also just."

The mayor looked her in the eye. "Your father put me in my current position," he reminded her.

She reached out and took his arm. "I have not forgotten that you served him. Nor will I forget the service you did me today."

The Earl of Caspur strode into the throne room, flanked by several guards. He looked a bit nervous and pale as he approached her and made to kneel, but Maia waved off the gesture.

"Are the people being fed?" she asked him.

He seemed surprised that it was her first question for him. "Yes, my lady. The preparations in the kitchens are all underway, and the staff is working hard. It will take some hours before they are fully ready, but the commands have been given."

"See that they are obeyed," she said. "Thank you. That is my highest priority at the moment. It will be dark soon, and the people thronging the castle need to eat. What else do you have to report?"

He chaffed his hands together. "How will this . . . generosity be paid for?" he asked.

"The city can levy a one-time fee," the mayor said offhandedly. "No need to worry about that, Caspur."

"No," Maia said, shaking her head. "My father has a treasury, does he not?"

"A substantial one," the mayor replied. "It is spread throughout the realm and guarded to prevent any one cache from becoming all-important. I do not know the amount, but I have heard it is sizable." The mayor scratched the strip of hair below his lip. "He hoarded wealth, my lady. He was loath to spend his own coin, and always asked others to pay."

Maia nodded. "Then I understand your question. I will pay my obligations," she said. "The cost for the food will come from the royal treasury. Who has the keys of the Exchequer? Crabwell?"

"Yes, my lady," Caspur said.

"Has he been found?" she asked.

"Not yet, my lady. He was not seen leaving the castle. I have had guards placed at every door to look for him. He is skulking somewhere, and we will find him."

"I want Crabwell found and brought to me," Maia said with determination. "He is not to be harmed. If he surrenders now, he will be pardoned. I do not seek his blood."

Caspur balked. "My lady, he—"

She gave him a stern look and he clammed up. "Go on, my lord," she said softly.

"Well, I can see by your expression that you are prone to be merciful." He shook his head. "He ordered your execution *after* your father was poisoned. If any man deserves to be punished, it is he."

"I must say I agree, Your Highness," the mayor chimed in. "Crabwell was chancellor of the Exchequer, but he took more authority upon himself than his station permitted. I understand he had men tortured into confessions. That is why he hides from you, my lady. He has committed a myriad of crimes, and he fears being held to account for them. Do not be rash in pardoning him."

Maia sighed. "I will be merciful," she said simply. "Sometimes we commit acts that we regret. That does not mean we do not live with the consequences of those actions. But I do not seek his death. I have always felt that mercy and patience are as important as justice. These first days will be critical in persuading people whether they will follow me or no." She also secretly feared that the reason he had not been found yet was because the kishion might have gotten to him first.

"My lady, I agree," the mayor said, his teeth grinding. "But if you are too lenient, they will rebel against you. You must make examples to win men's obedience."

She smiled at him. "That is the way things have been for many years, my lord. I prefer to *be* an example, rather than make them. My father would have rebuked you for contradicting him. But I value your counsel even if I choose not to heed it."

Just then, Collier entered the throne room with a girl at his arm. Maia squinted and saw that it was Jayn Sexton. As soon as she too registered the girl's identity, Suzenne gasped and rushed across the room to embrace her longtime friend. Maia smiled at Collier and nodded. She had not needed to ask him to find the other woman—he had guessed at her wish.

"Find Crabwell," Maia told the mayor and Caspur. "But have no fear," she said with a small smile. "He will not be *my* chancellor."

CHAPTER EIGHT

Privy Council

W hen they did find Crabwell, it was at the bottom of Pent Tower, dead.

The next morning, Maia listened with a queasy stomach as the lord mayor recounted the news to her in the throne room. The hall was empty except for Justin and Suzenne and a pair of guardsmen posted by the door. Although Maia was exhausted, she dared not sleep. As soon as she had dozed off the night before in her room in the palace, a feeling of blackness had seeped into her, accompanied by frightening whispers. She had summoned Suzenne for company, and the two had walked the palace all night, fighting to stay awake.

"Are you feeling well?" the mayor of Comoros asked her, pausing in his narrative of Crabwell's demise. "You look as if you did not sleep soundly last night."

"I did not sleep at all," she replied. There were so many ghosts in this palace still, so many things that reminded her of her father.

Many of the Leerings, she had discovered, especially in his personal chambers, had been chiseled from the walls or defaced so that they would not work. Almost as if he had been unable to bear them looking at him. "Go on, Justin. I am sorry."

"What I was saying is the evidence of what happened is unclear. Was Crabwell pushed off the tower, or did he jump? There was a hastily written confession that implies he killed himself, but that could also have been forged. Or he may have been duped into writing it."

Maia sighed and glanced at Suzenne. Her friend frowned, indicating she too had trouble believing it was a suicide.

"So there is no evidence he was murdered or by whom?" Maia asked.

"None," the mayor replied, shrugging. "My lady. Let me say this delicately. People feared Crabwell. No one loved him. I really do not think it worth the bother of an inquest. No one cares how he died, only that he is no longer the chancellor. It is a relief that he met his end by a hand other than yours, and will not oppose your coronation."

Maia gave him a stern look. "But should we not order an inquest into the murders, Justin? My mother, my father, and the chancellor have all died in rather short order. If we do not follow due process, someone may one day try to assign the blame to *me*."

He looked shocked. "No one would dare accuse you!"

"I told you this earlier. Lady Deorwynn, I understand, was the one who hired a kishion and allowed him to enter the realm. He then was the headsman at her own execution. I want him found, Justin. If not for him, my bones would be moldering in an ossuary right now. He will never meet his fate by my hand, but I cannot permit a kishion to defend my throne. He is acting on his own motives, I believe. I would send him away in peace, and with my gratitude, but he needs to go if he will not abide by the laws and rules that govern my life and my reign. I fear it will be difficult to hunt him." The thought of losing such a staunch ally and friend grieved her, but she was determined to see her purpose through to the end. Of course, exiling such a wily predator would not be easy, and she knew it.

He frowned, looking at her seriously. "My men are frightened," he said softly.

She nodded. "They should be. He is dangerous, but he is only a man."

There was movement at the head of the hall as one of the soldiers responded to a knock on the door, and to Maia's immense relief, her grandmother came striding into the audience chamber. Maia broke away from the mayor and Suzenne and rushed across the hall to pull her grandmother into an embrace.

"I am so grateful you are here!" Maia said, nearly bursting from joy and relief. "Word arrived that the refugees from Assinica have come to Muirwood. I had hoped to visit you there tonight through the Apse Veil."

Sabine clung to her for a long moment before pulling back and tipping Maia's chin up with her finger and thumb. "You are exhausted."

"Sleeping here is dangerous, I have discovered." Maia shuddered involuntarily. "Suzenne kept me company all night, but it is taking its toll on her."

"What about Gideon?"

Maia winced at the pointed question. "He does not want the people to worry he is controlling me, so he has been giving me room to rule. He is making arrangements to return to Dahomey by ship. There is trouble in his kingdom, incursions by Paeiz and now Mon. We have not seen as much of each other as I would like. He does not stay in the palace at night."

Sabine gave her a weighing look. "He is your husband, Maia."

She nodded. "I know. You can understand that this entire situation is rather unusual." She smiled wryly. "My husband holds my heart, but there are so many problems pulling us in opposite directions right now. Would that we could both escape somewhere and spend time alone."

Sabine hooked arms and led her back to the bench near the throne, where Suzenne was dozing.

The mayor stepped back and bowed. "High Seer, greetings. Your arrival was unexpected." He scratched the little strip of beard on his bottom lip and then snapped his fingers. "I will summon some refreshment for you. Cider and cheese?" He clapped his hands, motioning for a servant lingering in the doorway to approach.

"Thank you, Lord Mayor. I came to speak to my granddaughter."

"Of course," he said, and excused himself with a gracious bow. Suzenne, who had gathered her wits, rose to greet Sabine, though she seemed uncertain of how formal their greeting should be. They had all been on familiar terms at Muirwood, but it was different at the palace.

Sabine reached out and took Suzenne's hands, smiling at her. "Thank you for your loyalty to my granddaughter. Please stay with us."

Suzenne returned her smile. "She is my friend, and now she is my queen. She will always have my loyalty." The three women sat down on the bench for a quiet conversation.

"Yes, my dear," Sabine said. "Now what news, Maia? How can I help?"

Maia shook her head. "Tell me of the refugees? How many are there? Where are they?"

"I brought them all with me to Muirwood," Sabine said. "Most of the families were originally from Comoros and Pry-Ree. Some of those with Pry-rian roots are already asking to travel across the Bearden Muir and start for home."

"I imagine Jon Tayt has volunteered to guide them, by Cheshu!" She smiled as she thought of the abbey hunter and his pointed beard.

Sabine smiled. "Of course. There are thousands of refugees, Maia. We knew they were coming, and still we were not prepared for the numbers. There are tents and supplies enough at the abbey to support them for the moment, but they cannot all stay in Muirwood Hundred. As you can imagine, they are nervous and anxious."

"How many children? I worry about the little ones. They will not understand what has happened. How can I help them?"

"I think seeing you would be a blessing, not just for the children but for all of them. It would help calm their disrupted lives a little," she answered. "I was hoping to persuade you to come back with me for a time."

"Yes!" Maia said with a grin. "I would see them. Do they have a ruler?"

"I was wondering that as well," Suzenne said with curiosity. "We have been separated for so long. How different are their traditions?"

"They have no kings or queens or earls. There are no ranks among them. They have Aldermastons, as we do, and they are considered the rulers. The chief among them is a wise Aldermaston named Wyrich." She paused, and Maia could tell there was more she wished to say.

"Tell me," Maia said, taking her grandmother's hands. "Please."

"Aldermaston Wyrich is strong with the Medium," Sabine said. "I do not know how it will work, but I feel quite impressed that he should be an Aldermaston here in Comoros. The people look up to him and follow his example." She paused, considering. "I can *feel* that these people have many Gifts of the Medium, Maia. They have lost everything, yet they do not brood on it. They are anxious to help, asking always for ways they can serve us. They consider themselves indebted to this kingdom for preserving their lives. Such meek people. In all my journeys throughout the realm, I have found few who could equal them. They are a worth more than treasures or ransom."

Maia nodded, anxious to meet them herself. "Grandmother, I wish to discuss something with you as well. Actually, several things." The servants arrived with trays of food, which they arranged in a sumptuous array. Maia nodded to dismiss them once they were finished, and after the throne room doors closed behind them, she quickly related the story of how she had come to Comoros in an attempt to stop Lady Deorwynn's pending execution. She described the upheaval in the government and the many nobles who had clawed at each other's throats as their ship sank.

Sabine's countenance changed as she shared the story, her look darkening.

When she was done, Maia said, "I need your counsel. I need the Aldermaston's counsel! I cannot rule this great realm by myself. From morn to dusk, I am beset by people seeking my direction and approval. I need a chancellor who understands the way I think, one who will act on my behalf and help restore faith in the Medium in Comoros. When my father drove the Dochte Mandar from the realm, he did nothing to fill the void they left. Even the Dochte Mandar believed in the wisdom of the maston tomes. Even though they did not fully understand our ways, they attempted to live by that wisdom and to live by virtue. When that virtue was removed and replaced with the immoral sycophants favored by my father, it drew the Myriad Ones upon us like a plague." She pressed her lips together and shook her head. "Grandmother, I would like Richard Syon to be my chancellor. I know I can trust his guidance and integrity."

Suzenne looked shocked by the suggestion. This was not a secret Maia had confided in anyone but Collier. She had wanted to determine her grandmother's willingness first.

As ever, Sabine's expression was more difficult to read. "No Aldermaston has ever been chancellor before, Maia."

"I know," Maia replied. "And no queen has ever ruled Comoros either. I can tell the mayor wants the position. He has not asked for it yet, but every day he assumes more and more authority and seeks to insinuate himself with me. His help has been invaluable, and yet I am not willing to choose him for the job. The chancellor will lead my Privy Council. The only other person I would trust to do it is yourself, and you are the High Seer."

Sabine smiled at the compliment and cupped Maia's cheek.

"Must I persuade you?" Maia said, wringing her hands in her lap. "I truly feel it is the Medium's will."

Sabine looked over at Suzenne, who was listening to them with great interest. "You agree, Suzenne?"

She nodded vigorously. "I have the utmost respect for Aldermaston Syon and his wife, Joanna. I have secretly mourned the thought of leaving Muirwood to begin my life anew. To have them here at court would be a comfort. And a constant example of honor. The people here would respect them. They have no false humility."

Sabine nodded in agreement. "Truly, you could not have named two more capable people. While Richard would be an admirable chancellor, his wife's counsel would be valuable as well. And since the Ciphers are spread throughout the realm, they are very well informed about the realm and its needs. They are wise without being cunning, and they will be a help to you." She stroked Maia's arm. "I have also felt the Medium prompting me. Now I can see why. As you know, Aldermaston Kranmir must be replaced. Augustin will be without a ruler, and it is close to the port city of Doviur, which is one of the greatest centers of commerce in the realm. It is a proud abbey and needs to be chastened with a gentle hand. When I met Wyrich after crossing over to Assinica, I felt strongly that he should become the Aldermaston of Muirwood. There is much unsettled land in the Bearden Muir. It is a swamp that can be drained. Muirwood would remain the seat of the maston order in Comoros, but under Wyrich's gaze. I would make Richard and Joanna the Aldermastons of Augustin, with Joanna fulfilling the majority of the abbey duties so that Richard could serve you. That abbey is closer to Comoros, and he could travel by Apse Veil between the two places to perform his dual roles. Yes, and there is wisdom in not having your chancellor also be the highest Aldermaston of the realm. While I do not believe Richard is corruptible, it is better not to tempt a man when you can avoid it. He is getting older, so it will be hard on him. But he could at least serve you until you are established."

Maia clung to her grandmother again, smiling. "Thank you!"

"It is the Medium's will," Sabine said, nodding. "I can feel it now. Who else do you hope to have on your Privy Council?"

Maia glanced at Suzenne before returning her attention to her grandmother. "Suzenne and Dodd. I plan to invest Dodd as the Earl of Forshee. The incumbent has fled to the north and must be dealt with in due course. I have promised him a pardon if he surrenders, but word has likely not reached him yet. I was also planning to name my husband as Earl of Dieyre, of course."

"Naturally," Sabine said, nodding in agreement.

"I seek to reward the Earl of Caspur for his loyalty, and I was also going to name Lord Paget of Bridgestow. He served in my grandfather's Privy Council, and I knew him when I lived in that city. He was one of my most trusted advisors."

Sabine nodded. "I know him well."

"And I plan to include the mayor of Comoros. He played a crucial role in supporting me when others sought my death."

Sabine smiled. "He is self-serving, to be sure. But it is not unwise to align his interests with yours. Who else?"

"Anyone you would recommend?" Maia asked. "I am still learning a bit about the existing power structure. I do not intend to strip all of my father's supporters of power. That would doom me before I start."

"It would. You can always make additional selections after your coronation, but you should announce your choice of chancellor after you have spoken to Richard so that word can go out. Let your enemies consider their position before you bring them to heel. And you must set the date of your coronation immediately. Once you are the anointed queen, it will change the nature of their defiance."

Maia smiled. "I am so grateful you are here. Will you stay in Comoros?"

Sabine shook her head sadly. "I cannot. After I make the changes we discussed, I must go to the other realms and continue to open the Apse Veils in those abbeys. I will do what I can to win support for you and help your cause. But you are the ruler of Comoros, Maia. Not I."

It made her cringe to think of her grandmother leaving again so soon. She had hoped at least to have her company and guidance for a few months. Having the High Seer as an ally would make all the difference to her rule. Her father had flouted his relationship with the mastons. Maia would need it in order to survive.

"How much time do I have, Grandmother?" Maia asked.

Sabine did not need to ask what she meant. "Not long," she whispered. She took Maia's hands again, kneading the knuckles with her thumbs. "In a few months, your kingdom will be plunged into war. The Victus will try to unite all the others against you. Pry-Ree will help defend you. Trust that. With Dahomey on your side as well, we have a chance. But if all the other kingdoms do join forces against us, we will fail. If we can persuade one more to join . . . just one, it may help tip the balance." Her look was grim. "That is what the Victus fear. They have conspired to hold our kingdoms in subjugation. They do so with cunning and wealth. Breaking their grip on our necks will not come without bloodshed. I believe we have years of war ahead of us. You will not have much time to prepare, I am afraid. Even if the other kingdoms learn the truth about Assinica and the fate the Victus has planned for them, they may look only to protect themselves."

Maia sighed deeply, and was about to speak, when the main door creaked open. Turning, she noticed Collier pausing in the archway, watching them. He had a grim look on his face. A *restless* look.

She reached out her hand to him, inviting him closer.

Breaking his pose, he rushed to her side as if physically drawn there. Suzenne squeezed Maia's hand and rose to leave, making room for him.

"Good morning, Gideon." Sabine smiled at him, but he did not return her smile.

"What is it?" Maia asked, staring into his troubled eyes.

He gave a little bow to Sabine. "I did not expect to find you here, High Seer. You returned from Assinica?"

She nodded. "I did. The refugees have come."

"I will have ships brought to Muirwood if any would like to settle in Dahomey."

"That is kind of you. Your kingdom is already constrained in land. Your people would not give it up willingly."

"They will if I persuade them," he replied. "I must return soon. It . . . presses on me." He looked at Maia, his gaze dark and brooding. "I heard you were up all night."

Maia sighed. "I cannot sleep here. But I will return to Muirwood and get some rest. I plan to offer Richard Syon the role we discussed, and I would like to spend some time with the Assinicans."

"A wise choice," Collier said. He fidgeted, which was unusual for him, and looked as if he felt uncomfortable in his own skin.

"What is it?" Maia asked again, reaching out to touch his arm.

"You are not safe here," he whispered curtly. "And though it is not what I want, the Medium tells me to leave you." His jaw clenched and he stared down at the floor for a moment. "I have Simon inspecting the palace. There are secret doors and hidden passageways throughout. I am surprised the walls themselves do not crumble." Collier scratched his neck. "The tunnels even lead to your chambers, Maia. You are not safe *anywhere* in this place."

Maia stared at him. "I do not think he intends to harm me," she said softly, for she knew he spoke of the kishion.

He pursed his lips. "Oh, I agree. But what *does* he intend after you become queen? He has brought down his fair share of rulers in this kingdom."

"You are shrewd to be concerned," Sabine said softly, her eyes narrowing. "Maia, the tomes describe people such as the kishion. The records are full of warning. When men hire other men to kill for power, it grieves the Medium. It cannot abide murder, especially when it is done so deliberately. When murderers are permitted to operate within a kingdom, it will always bring a Blight. The tomes warn of this. It will not be easy to . . . *evict* him."

Maia looked down at the ground. "I do not believe he is working for hire, Grandmother. And he has saved my life more than once. I doubt the Victus—or anyone else, for that matter—control him anymore."

She stiffened. "What do you mean?" she asked apprehensively.

Maia looked at them both, feeling at once confused and anguished. "I think he . . . cares for me."

***

The sun lowered across the horizon, drawing shadows across the pathway ahead as Maia and Collier walked hand in hand down the steps leading into the palace gardens. It was a place where she had sought refuge more than once in her life. Large pots full of flowers and Leerings of various sizes and designs brightened the grounds.

"I prefer Muirwood," Collier said, squeezing her hand. "That place has many tender memories. I am afraid my memory of your castle will always be of me wishing that wall would collapse so I could be the one to rescue you. I have to admit I am still bitterly jealous that it was the *kishion* who saved you." His frown clashed with a smile, and he shook his head. "I am struggling to cope with it."

Maia sighed, swinging his arm as they started down the path into the gardens. She smoothed some hair over her ear. "Do not be angry with him for saving me," she chided.

"Not for saving you. I owe him a debt for that. But you are my wife, and it is my privilege to protect you. I would have gladly faced off against Schuyler and Trefew. Five at once, even. It would have been a feat for the minstrels." There was some levity in his voice, but she could tell his own helplessness in the situation had left a wound.

"There is a little fountain over there," Maia said, tugging on his hand. "Follow me."

They passed a Leering with a sun-faced visage. She remembered brushing her hand against it on her last visit to the garden. The dusk of night had faded from the area around the light Leering in an instant. After walking a little farther, they reached the circular fountain with the fish Leering spouting water in the middle. The joyful pattering sound helped mask the tumult of the city noises beyond the wall.

She sat on the edge of the fountain's stone railing, and Collier stared at the fish, a far-off look on his face.

"What is it?" Maia asked him.

"Another memory," he said, then shook his head to brush it off. "You like this garden?"

She shrugged. "The last time I was here was the night my father summoned me to go to the lost abbey." She clasped her hands together and pressed her thumbs against her lips. "We argued, of course. I came here afterward to think about what he had said. It was a strange night. That was right before I first set foot in *your* kingdom." She put her hands down on the stone and looked up at him. "Before you deceived me." She gave him a wry smile.

Collier did not look chagrined. He folded his arms and put one boot up on the railing next to her. "I do not recall you confessing who *you* were either. I hope you do not regret that I took the liberty of dancing with you at the Gables?"

Maia smiled with pleasure and shook her head. The sinking sun made the shadows lengthen. She needed to cross the Apse Veil back to Muirwood to get some rest. Unfortunately, Collier was not yet a maston and could not travel there with her.

"You look bone weary," he murmured softly. "The noise from this fish Leering is going to lull you to sleep."

She started to rise, but he reached out and took her hand, helping to draw her up. She nestled against his chest, drawing her arms around him tightly. She felt his hands gently smooth her hair.

"I wish I did not have to go," she murmured.

"I wish I could go with you," he said darkly. "Soon, my love. Once the Paeizians are subdued, I will do my best to pass the maston test quickly. One cannot rush the Medium, I believe, but if it is at all possible, I will try."

She lifted her gaze up to his face, saw the tender look there. "Will you walk me to the abbey?"

Collier nodded with a pained smile. Then he smoothed a lock of hair over her ear. "He does not care for you . . . as I do," he whispered thickly.

Word has reached me that Lady Marciana will shortly be crowned Queen of Comoros. She surrounds herself with mastons, and listens only to their whispering in her ear. This will upset those in the realm who have betrayed the order. Her own people may topple her before the fleets even return. Then we will crush them all to cinders.

—Corriveaux Tenir, Victus of Dahomey

CHAPTER NINE

Wyrich

She awoke to darkness. Her heart tremored with fear, for the kishion had haunted her in her dreams. With a thought, she summoned light from a nearby Leering, and was startled to discover she was back at Muirwood in the room that she and Suzenne had once shared. The familiarity of the beds, changing screen, and even the tub in the corner by the fire Leering brought her comfort and helped dispel the gloom of her night terrors.

Because the room had no windows, she did not know what time it was or how late she had slept. Her body was sore and weary, but ever since she had arrived back at Muirwood, she had felt gloriously free. No longer was she subject to the oppressive taint of the Myriad Ones. All was peaceful, except for her own turbulent thoughts. She knew that she could not forever return to Muirwood to sleep at night, but until she found a way to rid the palace of the Myriad Ones and their influence, she needed to avoid the possibility of being overwhelmed by them.

Sitting up and rubbing her eyes, she remembered the look on the kishion's face. The look that had told her more clearly than any words that he cared for her.

What a contradiction he was—the severed portion of his ear and his many scars were a gruesome reminder of his bloody deeds and dark past, of how ruthless and remorseless he could be. Yet she remembered sharing strawberries with him in the gardens of the lost abbey and seeing him smile. And he had saved her life twice. Still, it made her shudder to imagine him roaming through Comoros unchecked. Though it would seem he was not a danger to her, he *was* a danger. The knowledge that he would not abandon her willingly weighed on her. And she knew he would kill any man who tried to uproot him.

She straightened the blankets on her bed and quickly splashed water on her face to help wipe away the remnants of sleep. Then she hurriedly dressed in a simple gown and unbolted the door.

The Aldermaston's manor was thrumming with activity. People scurried around everywhere, carrying crates and boxes, and the halls were filled with a veritable crowd of newcomers she did not recognize. Most wore simple clothing, not of any particular style—the men were in ribbed shirts the color of fleece, covered by leather vests with simple decorations along the fringes, and the women wore unadorned dresses and girdles of various colors, their hair partly concealed beneath simple scarves.

Maia was ravenous, so she left through the rear of the manor and headed to the kitchen where she and Suzenne had shared so many meals. It was no surprise to find Collett there, but in addition to the two kitchen helpers—Davi and Aloia—there were at least a dozen other young girls punching dough and stirring soups. There was bread baking in the oven fires, and meat was sizzling on spits near the ovens, at least ten hens with flakes of spices sticking to their glistening skins.

"Well, my lady," Collett said with her usual sternness, "you find us much changed. Both of the kitchens work night and day now, and the menfolk are constructing two more kitchens over by the fish pond."

"Poor Thewliss," Davi said with a grin. "He cannot abide the crowds!"

Maia smiled and greeted the girls and quickly committed the new girls' names to memory while Aloia fetched her something to eat. The kitchens were usually a place of quiet solitude, but she realized things had been changed permanently. With so many refugees from Assinica, the grounds of Muirwood Abbey would never be the same.

"You were born for such a challenge, Collett," Maia said. "I do not know anyone else who could handle it."

Collett gave her a small smile, but she was too proud of her humility to allow more of a reaction. "We all do what we can, thank the Medium. I am certain you have cooks aplenty in Comoros now. Many are thinking about following the Aldermaston to Augustin Abbey, but I am not such a fool. Muirwood is my home and ever it shall be." Seeing the startled look on Maia's face, she continued. "The High Seer announced some changes this morning while you were abed. Seems that we have a new master to serve." Judging from her tone, she was a little unsettled by the idea, but she bore it stoically.

Maia sat on a stool and ate the salty soup Aloia brought her, relishing every bite. She dipped an end hunk of bread into the leftover broth and ate it more slowly.

"You have met the new Aldermaston then?" Maia asked.

Collett sniffed and nodded. "He is quite tall compared to our former master," she said. "I must get used to his tastes and preferences. He is a good man, but we will always honor and respect Richard and Joanna Syon here." She looked over Maia's shoulder, her expression changing.

With the noise and clatter of the kitchen, Maia had not heard the doors open. She turned to see that the Aldermaston and his wife had entered, bringing with them another man who also wore the gray cassock of the order.

"Aldermaston Wyrich," Maia said, bowing her head to him and rising. She set the soup bowl down on her seat.

He was tall and strongly built, and she was immediately struck by his sense of presence. He was a handsome, grandfatherly man, with cropped gray hair with a spike of white at the front. His natural, effusive smile and good-natured aura indicated he was at complete harmony with the Medium. When he saw her, he came forward and knelt in front of her, then reached out and took her hands.

His voice was heavily accented, reminding her slightly of the dialect of Hautland. But he spoke articulately in her language, and she realized that he had been Gifted with Xenoglossia. "Your Majesty, it is an honor and a privilege to finally meet you. We are ever your most devoted servants and friends." He smiled at her—a smile that somehow touched his every feature. "You are the one who opened the Apse Veils again. You saved us from death at the hands of our brothers."

Maia felt her cheeks flush to be on the receiving end of such attention and heartfelt gratitude. "Please," Maia said, interrupting him. She helped him stand. "I am your fellow servant, Aldermaston. Do not kneel before me. It is my understanding that in Assinica, there are no rulers?"

"That is correct," he said, each word richly accented. He smiled warmly. "But we understand the traditions here are different, and we will adapt to them. We have enjoyed a long season of peace, but that season has ended. It is the way of the world. It is we who are *your* humble servants, my queen."

"You have left everything behind," Maia said sadly. "It must be difficult for your people."

"We left trifles behind, my lady. What we brought with us cannot be taken away. We bring our covenants. We bring our knowledge. We bring our empathy. I hope all will be useful to you, my queen. We have come to serve."

Maia shook her head. "Please, call me Maia as *my* Aldermaston does," she said, walking over and taking Aldermaston Syon by the hand. She turned back to him. "Do you have a wife?"

"I do indeed," he answered. "She is helping in the laundry at the moment. She will wish to meet you. Her name is Frances."

Maia turned her gaze back to Richard Syon. "Aldermaston," she said softly, her eyes looking into his. It was always difficult to meet his gaze, for it was always so penetrating and deep. He looked troubled, his face suppressing very clear feelings of mourning. He loved the abbey. He loved Muirwood with all his being. Asking him to leave it was like asking him to stop using one of his hands. But he did not murmur or complain.

"Maia," he breathed softly, his compassionate smile twisting his sad lips upward. His eyes twinkled with affection for her. His thick hands squeezed hers. He was not tall or handsome. He was a doughy man with large ears and thinning hair. But he was also the most patient and kindhearted person she knew.

"I know your heart will always be here," she said tenderly. "As will mine. But your kingdom needs you, Aldermaston. Your queen needs you. If we are to restore the people's faith in mastons, there will need to be a period of revival, of reawakening. As you taught me yourself, the word repentance means to change our thoughts, our hearts, even our breath. I need you to help breathe new life into this kingdom. If we cannot spark their belief in the Medium strongly enough, we will be made void when the Naestors come. I wish you to be my chancellor. My advisor. My friend."

The Aldermaston's lips pursed, his jowls quivering. "I do not seek this office," he whispered.

Joanna's expression was equally serious. Where once she and her husband had shared constant companionship, they would now often be parted. But Maia could see the encouraging look in her eyes. Despite the difficulties such a change would pose, she wanted him to accept the office.

Maia put her hand on his shoulder. "For that reason, I give it to you."

He frowned, weighed down by his emotions. "It is the Medium's will," he said, choking. "I will do it, however it pains me to accept it."

Maia put her arms around him and then pulled his wife into the embrace. She stared at them with joy. "Thank you. I know that with one choice I get you both." After squeezing them tight, she pulled away and turned back to Aldermaston Wyrich. "I need your help, Aldermaston."

"Anything," he replied, folding his hands in front of him.

"The coronation will be in Comoros," Maia said. "Not Muirwood. All the people must see the queen anointed by an Aldermaston. This has never happened before. But it must be clear that the authority of the Crown is below the authority of the Medium. I depend on you—" she nodded to Richard—"to help him understand our rituals."

"There is a tome where the rituals are engraved," Richard said.

"The anointing will happen at Claredon Abbey in Comoros. I have this information and will share it with Aldermaston Wyrich." He gave her a grave look.

"What is it?" she asked him. He gestured that he would not speak of it then.

"The plans for the coronation are well underway," Maia said. "When will the two of you join me in Comoros?" she asked.

Richard looked at his wife. "We were planning to cross the Apse Veil today. Your grandmother has already consecrated us as the Aldermastons of Augustin. We planned to return with you to the palace."

"If I may make a suggestion," Aldermaston Wyrich offered.

Maia looked at him expectantly.

"I am unfamiliar with the city of Comoros. But the records have taught us that even in Lia's day, the city was corrupted."

"And it still is," Maia said. "One of the first things I plan on asking the chancellor to do is to prepare the city for the coronation. If I could summon a storm, I would. Shovels and rakes will have to suffice."

Wyrich beamed. "Excellent. I will send a few through the Veil to assist with the cleanup. I also have charged a goldsmith with making a crown for your coronation. If you will visit with him before you leave, it can be sized appropriately. I have tailors working on clothes for you as well. I understand that you prefer more simple designs?"

Maia smiled at him. "Indeed."

"I am certain we will come up with something you like. My people are at your disposal, my lady. Over the years, we have invented many interesting devices that will be useful to your people. Have you considered what music you would like for the coronation assembly?"

Maia stared at him.

"I thought not," he replied with a wink. "Leave that to us as well. I will go find Frances. She will want to greet you personally, and I am certain there is much you must discuss with your new chancellor. Excuse me."

He bowed meekly and strode out of the kitchen. Maia noticed that the additional kitchen helpers from Assinica had all been staring at him in respect. Upon his departure, they immediately went back to work without a reminder from Collett.

"What troubles you?" Maia asked the Aldermaston, who still looked grave.

He glanced at his wife, who nodded and approached closer. "What Richard is loath to speak, I will," she said in a hushed voice. "This is not about serving you, Maia. Please believe that. We are humbled by your faith in us. The city is much in commotion, we hear. There may be rioting the day of your coronation. But that is not the concern. Richard looked over the tome containing the coronation ritual. Clearly some of the words need to be adapted, but a certain practice has been in place for centuries."

She frowned. "Maia, the anointing of a king or queen is called the Chrism. It is holy oil. It is to be anointed on your shoulders, breast, forehead, and temples."

Maia blanched. "I did not know this."

Richard nodded sternly, his voice too low for the others in the kitchen to hear. "It is clear that the tradition is in place to prevent an Aldermaston from unknowingly anointing a . . . hetaera."

"The ceremony is usually performed inside the abbey walls, but it is done in front of a few witnesses," Joanna continued. Her look darkened. "Changing the ritual drastically will only attract more attention. And it would not be honest to do so."

Maia felt the wrenching anguish again, and tears swam in her eyes.

The Aldermaston reached out and took her arm. "I feel the Medium has forgiven you, Maia. You would not have been able to open the Apse Veil otherwise. But consequences are still being meted out, dram by dram. We will ponder this situation. Do not be grieved by it."

"How can this not grieve me?" she said. She kept her voice low so that the kitchen helpers would not hear. The weight of the past threatened to crush her, and she felt miserable. "Before Crabwell tried to execute me, he sent Aldermaston Kranmir to talk to me. I was forced to show him my shoulder. He already knows." She was starting to tremble and could not quell it. "He is going to try and use that knowledge to unseat my grandmother. And you. He is already calling himself the High Seer."

The Aldermaston and his wife shared a grim look. "He may try to discredit you. But he will only invalidate his own authority," Richard said. "When we go to Augustin, we will go with the full authority of the Medium. The Leerings there will no longer obey him. He may have deceived himself and others, but he cannot fool the Medium."

Worry welled in Maia's stomach. "I have the shadowstain on my chest," she said with a groan. "And the mark on my shoulder. I do not see how this can stay secret. It is my sin. It is my offense. As long as the Chrism is anointed inside the abbey, the Myriad Ones cannot overwhelm me. They nearly did in the palace. But the witnesses will all know something is wrong."

She felt the Aldermaston's wife put an arm around her shoulder. "Perhaps it is time for the binding sigil to be broken," she whispered, squeezing Maia.

CHAPTER TEN

Coroner's Inquest

E
ven though the sun had long since set, many people still wandered the corridors of the castle, trying to complete the work of the day. Another day had passed since the news of the new chancellor had been announced, in which time Richard had been installed in the tower and his wife had taken up residence at Augustin Abbey. Kranmir had fled with some of his loyal supporters, but his whereabouts were still unknown. As Maia walked toward the chancellor's tower, she was met with startled looks and quick obeisance as her subjects recognized her and the guardsmen escorting her. Light streamed down from several Leerings, and she saw it reflected in the glossy polish of the tiled floor. There were hardly any floor rushes and a host of servants swept the floors clean each day. Maia even saw a little drudge with a rag kneeling and scrubbing at the seams, and she frowned, knowing the little girl should be abed already.

When she reached the tower, she turned to face her escort.

"Wait for me here if you must, but I would prefer that you retire for the night. It has been a long and busy day."

"We will wait," said one of the men without affection or warmth. The two positioned themselves on either side of the doorway. Maia sighed and then started up the tower steps.

As she walked, memories flowed back to her in a rush. She grazed her fingers along the stone of the stairwell, recalling the many times she had intruded on Chancellor Walraven as a child. When she was little, this turret had seemed monstrous in its size and filled with mystery and wonder. It had been a refuge for her, a place where she had met with her mentor and learned to read. The ban on girls reading was a law she planned to remedy. All in its proper time.

The steps were steep, but she found the exercise invigorating, and after all, she had once made a habit of crossing mountains. She smiled wistfully as she took the steps one by one toward the chamber at the top.

The door to the chancellor's office was open, and inside she saw her chancellor, Richard Syon, bent over a scroll at his desk. He still wore the gray cassock, but a ceremonial stole of his new office had been added to his attire. His hair was askew, reminding her of the lateness of the hour and also of her old friend Walraven. There was an inviting scent in the room, which made her pause at the threshold, and then she noticed the tied clumps of purple mint hanging from racks on the walls. There were other subtle changes as well—vases of flowers, a small basket filled with Muirwood apples, a warm blanket folded on the window seat where, as a child, she had enjoyed sitting and gazing out at the city.

"Your Highness," Richard said with surprise in his voice. "If you wished to see me, I would have come to you willingly. It is your right to summon *me*."

Maia smiled and entered the chamber. "I have many memo-ries of this tower," she answered, walking up and putting her hand on his shoulder. "I am also younger than you, Aldermaston, and more accustomed to climbing stairs."

He gave her a knowing look, his penetrating eyes meeting her own. Turning in the chair, he clasped his hands over his girth and waited for her to speak.

Maia saw a small sculpture of Muirwood Abbey on the desk and wandered over for a closer look. "This is amazing," she said, admiring the intricate craftsmanship.

"Joanna is thoughtful," he replied, his voice full of endear-ment. "She knows I love the mint, the apples—the things that remind me of home when I am here." He smiled with obvious tenderness.

"She is at Augustin tonight?" Maia asked, and Richard nodded.

"It is getting late, Maia. I had assumed you had crossed the Apse Veil to Muirwood already. Truly, I would have come if you had called for me. I have several reports if you would hear them before the Privy Council meeting tomorrow?"

She nodded and went over to the window seat and sat down.

"First, Lady Shilton has asked for custody of her grand-children—Murer, Jolecia, Edmon, and little Brannon. They have all been traumatized by the events of these past weeks, and the grandmother seems to be the right person to care for them. Do you have any objections?"

"None at all," Maia replied. Though she never wished to return to that manor house again. It held too many dark memories.

Richard turned to the desk and fetched a parchment from a stack. His countenance rarely showed displeasure, so Maia was alarmed by his scowl. "Ely Kranmir," he explained.

Maia let out her breath. "What news?"

"There are several reports now. He is traveling from abbey to abbey, trying to denounce you and repeating his claim that he is the new High Seer." His jaw clenched slightly, then relaxed. "I fear the Medium may punish him for such an affront. He may be winding his way north to seek refuge with the renegades there. He had much to gain from your father's rise to power . . . and much to lose. The reports I have received say he is maligning your reputation as much as he can."

Maia pressed her lips together. The memory of how he had insisted on examining her and Suzenne still rankled. "Is all the news this cheery, Richard?"

"I am afraid so." He tossed that one down and drew another. "This one is from Willem Bend, the court physician."

"I know him," Maia said. He had examined her after she was poisoned at Lady Shilton's manor, and had reported the incident to her father.

"He is a trustworthy man," Richard said, scratching his earlobe. "Let me summarize it for you. Your father's lips and stomach revealed the presence of poison. Doctor Bend believes the poison used was *strychnos nux*. It was a painful, slow death. In essence, he was strangled by convulsions."

A chill shot down to Maia's very bones as the words were spoken. She blinked back tears, unable to help imagining her father twitching on the ground, trying to breathe. In spite of what he'd done to her—what he'd been willing to do—the thought horrified her and made her cold and nauseous.

"That is terrible," she whispered, choking on her words.

Richard nodded compassionately. "It is clear he was murdered, Maia. The kishion admitted it to you, so I think there can be no doubt as to why. As we both know, you would not have survived if he had stayed his hand. It seems, from the witnesses' statements I have read today, that once your father passed orders to execute you, the kishion infiltrated his personal chambers and poisoned his wine cup. He has been impersonating the king's headsman for several executions, including Lady Deorwynn's and, fortunately, your own. I do not believe he means you harm, but it pains me that we have still been unable to locate him. The hunt continues."

Maia felt herself trembling, but she nodded in agreement. The kishion needed to be found.

"What about Chancellor Crabwell's death?" Maia asked. "Any news there?"

"Yes," Richard replied thoughtfully. "Doctor Bend also examined his body. When they found it broken on the ground by a turret, it at first appeared he had killed himself. But the doctor found a knife wound in his back. It was a killing blow that punctured several major organs and severed part of his spine—crippling him. There is no way he could have climbed over the stone railing, my lady. He was *helped* off the wall. The wound was caused by the kishion's preferred weapon—a sharp knife. Crabwell would have died from the stabbing in a day or two anyway. It was a mortal blow. The fall did not kill him initially, but he died shortly afterward from the tremendous shock to his body. It was a cruel death. The facts confirm what you said."

Maia felt herself turn dizzy.

"I am sorry to trouble you with such a grisly report, but I thought it best to prepare you before the rest of the council hears it tomorrow."

"Thank you," Maia gasped, feeling her stomach wrenching. He had done this for her, to remove the power of those who would rather end her life than allow her to challenge them. The guilt of that was a heavy burden.

"Are you unwell?" he asked softly.

"A moment," Maia said. She hated to see anyone suffer, no matter how they may have deserved it. She tried to steady herself, grateful to the Aldermaston for having delivered the shocking news to her now rather than in front of her Privy Council. Before them, she would look strong. "Thank you, Richard, for telling me. In spite of everything, I did not seek my father's death."

"I know," he answered kindly.

She bit her lip. "I am sure the High Seer showed you my mother's tome, so you know that she forgave my father."

"She died in her sleep, and we found her with a peaceful look on her face. She did not suffer. I did read the last words in her tome," he admitted. "I consider your mother a woman of true virtue. I knew her for many years, Maia. It was not easy for her to forgive your father, but you can rest assured in the knowledge that her feelings were sincere. There is magic in forgiveness."

Maia swallowed. "I only wish my father knew it . . . before he died."

Richard's eyes were full of compassion, and he nodded.

"The kishion must be found," Maia said with an ache in her heart. "I do not want it said that I resorted to murder to claim my father's crown. Or condoned his murder by letting his killer serve me still. Where can he be hiding?"

Richard nodded at her. "It will not be easy to find him anywhere in the city, Maia. Even the palace has many hiding places. As he has shown, he is a man who knows how to live in the shadows. I have asked your grandmother to lend the support of several Evnissyen to help in the search."

She smiled. "I saw Jon Tayt working with the Assinicans at Muirwood. Maybe he could be summoned to help? He knows the man we are seeking. His scars make him distinctive enough.

Hopefully that was the worst part of your report," she said with a weak laugh. "What else will you share with the Privy Council on the morrow?" She touched the soft fabric of the blanket next to her on the window seat.

He scratched the fleshy part of his throat and nodded. "Chancellor Crabwell kept meticulous records. He had underservants, mostly lawyers, who kept detailed records of the Crown's expenditures and taxes. As you know, the treasury is not located in one place, but the men holding the keys have all been summoned, and I have met personally with several of them. Others have yet to arrive. From what I understand, Maia, you rule one of the wealthiest kingdoms. Comoros has not been involved in any wars for several years, and yet your father continued to raise taxes every year." He turned and pulled out a wax tablet covered in markings. "The earliest estimates show you have in excess of five hundred thousand marks and that is conservative."

"Oh dear," Maia said, blinking quickly.

"It rivals the treasury of Hautland and Mon," Richard continued.

"What about the money already seized from the abbeys?" Maia pressed.

He shook his head. "I did *not* include those treasures, Maia, as you instructed that they should be returned to the abbeys for reconstruction. If your father had claimed them all, it would have nearly doubled his holdings."

Maia stood and began pacing, her mind afire with ideas. "Unbelievable," she whispered.

"Your father was a shrewd man," Richard said. "He was lavish with his spending, but very disciplined, and more apt to spend another man's coin than his own. He also was wise in his trading agreements and sold more than what he bought. He has been positioning Comoros, you see, as a place where luxuries are valued."

"Yes, I should say so," Maia agreed, still pacing and struggling with her feelings. She turned to the Aldermaston eagerly. "Richard, all this wealth has been accumulated and increased but to what purpose? You have *seen* the throne room?"

"I have," Richard replied, his look darkening. "There is hardly a suitable word to describe it."

"Opulent," Maia suggested. "The amount of gold decorations, the marble tile on the floor, the cushioned seats and benches. Every time I walk into it, I feel the Myriad Ones snuffling about like rats. I think my father had two lions chained as pets! It was all for show, all to flaunt his wealth and power in front of visitors."

"Yes," Richard agreed. "My understanding from the men with the treasury keys was that your father's intention was to provide a show of power and strength that would prevent other kingdoms from attacking Comoros. Yet he built his kingdom on the backs of the poor. Those who could not pay his taxes were forced into prison."

Maia gritted her teeth. "That is unjust!"

"It is, Maia. This is what we must discuss at the Privy Council tomorrow. The tax collectors are still at work. The prisons are overcrowded. The poor are hungry, living in the streets, and we are selling bushels of apples and cider overseas."

She sighed and wrung her hands. "I see now why the people were nearly ready to revolt. Why have they not acted yet?"

Richard smiled at her. "What choice did they have? The earls control the knights and soldiers. The king controlled the coin and could summon mercenaries if there was an uprising. The people have grown used to the depravity. As you have said, they have forgotten what the Medium feels like."

Maia stopped pacing and stared at him. "I grew up always wanting to *be* a maston. But over the years I never truly understood what it meant. It is time we set a proper example. It is time we stopped crushing the poor. I want a kingdom the people will want to fight to preserve. I do not want to hire mercenaries who defend us for a fee. If we are to survive the Naestors' incursion, it will not be because of the size of our army or navy. We cannot hope to match what they will send against us."

She walked toward him, her eyes afire. "My grandmother told me that when an apple barrel is corrupt, it must be cleansed on the inside first. We must clean the kingdom before another Blight descends upon us. We do this, Richard, by first cleansing the streets. Every day people are walking in mud and muck to and fro to do their business. I want the streets cleaned. I want every window to be washed. Every house painted. When I went to Rostick in Hautland, I saw a city much larger than this one in which every paving stone was swept clean. The people wore tidy, clean frocks and coats. The coronation gives us the excuse to rally the people to help cleanse our city. Use the treasury, Richard. Be generous with those who will work hard. When people arrive for the coronation, I want them to *feel* the difference."

A smile quirked on Richard's mouth. "Yes, my lady. I think they will."

She walked over and knelt in front of his chair. "When I was coming here, I saw a child cleaning the corners of the corridor at this late hour." She shook her head. "No more. Children are children, not slaves. I will be inspecting the kitchens and the stables and all the places where the lowest live. If I could make this city into a replica of Muirwood, I would. I want children chattering and laughing, like Aloia and Davi, while they work. The Medium will not grace us if there is so much suffering in this place. This is what I want, my lord chancellor. This is why I chose you." She gripped his arm and saw the tears in his eyes.

"As you wish, my lady," he answered softly. "It will take time."

Maia shook her head. "That is not a privilege we have. The Naestors will come here first. They will try to ruin the symbol of my father's power. We must be ready and waiting when they do."

She rose and then smiled fondly at him. "You must get to sleep yourself. It is late."

He chuckled softly. "I will, Maia. You can expect delegations from the other kingdoms to start arriving after the coronation. There is much to do."

He smiled and nodded and turned back to his desk as she briskly descended the stairwell, full of energy and hope. She had to prepare herself to face the Privy Council on the morrow. She knew many would be resistant to her new ideas. It would take repetition and determination to change the standards of her father's court. What had once been acceptable would now be eschewed.

It begins with a thought.

Maia smiled and startled when she saw both her guardsmen were gone. Collier leaned against the wall, arms folded, head cocked at her.

"You surprised me," she said, brightening. The sight of him sent tingles up her spine, as ever it did.

"I must go," he said.

Her heart sank. "When do you leave?"

"With the tide tomorrow on one of Simon's ships," he answered. He reached over and took her hand, rubbing his thumb across her knuckles.

"I was going to return to Muirwood to sleep," she said, glancing down the hall. They were truly alone. "But I want to be there ere you depart."

"Stay then," he said, smiling in his roguish way. He squeezed her hand. "I will watch over you while you sleep." His other hand came up and grazed her temple, smoothing hair over her ear.

"I . . . was hoping you would stay until after the coronation," she stammered.

He shook his head. "If Dahomey is going to stand with Comoros when the Victus comes, we need to be at our strongest." He brought her hand up higher and stared down at it as if he were going to kiss it, but he did not. "I must go tomorrow. But I do not want to."

Fear of death is a terror unequaled. That is why we created the threat of the Void—the extermination of every man, woman, and child. The Medium uses it to enforce obedience. The maston saying is true. Men are swayed more by fear than by reverence.

—Corriveaux Tenir, Victus of Dahomey

CHAPTER ELEVEN

Parting

Maia trudged through a dense forest, cold and shivering. There were little cuts from the branches across her skin as well as spider bites that itched mercilessly. A chill, rank mist clung to the treetops, sending feathery tendrils down. The crunch of boots against foliage and the short huff of labored breathing filled her ears. She was cold, weary, and weighed down with heavy sorrow, sorrow so thick she could hardly breathe through it.

Flicking her eyes up, she saw a figure before her, swathed in a tattered cloak. It filled her with dread. The march halted at the edge of a clearing. She heard someone else's voice, a voice with a whine to it, but the words were garbled and impossible to understand. Staring ahead, Maia saw a field of bones and a Leering crowning the heap.

She started, remembering the place vividly. The hooded man turned and she saw the torn ear, the scars. The kishion looked at her knowingly, sharing her remembrance of the place.

Fear shook her to her core. She wanted to flee, to escape, but

THE VOID OF MUIRWOOD

somehow it was impossible. The mist was raining down upon them. She could see the puffs of breath coming from the kishion's mouth. *I am asleep. This is a dream*, she told herself. She wrestled against it, trying to rouse herself. Terror and sorrow battled for domination in her mind. If she were truly asleep, did the cogent quality of the dream mean she was once again being controlled by Ereshkigal? Before, the Myriad One had controlled her while she slept, controlled her while she revisited her most painful memories in her sleep. With anguish, she fought to surface from sleep.

Her eyes blinked open, her heart shuddering beneath her ribs. Cold sweat clung to her skin, and she shivered beneath a thick blanket.

A warm hand touched hers and she flinched, jerking away in fear until she distinguished her husband's face in the dim light of a small Leering. A spasm of relief flooded her. She looked around, recognizing the room as her private chambers. She was on an elegant four-post bed draped with simple white veils. There were wardrobes and chests and a slightly crooked mirror in the corner. A deep bath was by the wall next to a water Leering. She filled her senses with every small detail, grounding herself in the reality of the place, the moment, and the nightmare slowly faded.

"Was it a dream . . . or something worse?" Collier asked her tenderly, his look serious and intense as he sat at the edge of the bed.

"Hold me," she whispered, opening her arms and pulling him close. The terror and sadness of the dream still wrenched at her heart. She felt as if she had lost someone dear to her. Her memory raced to find a source. Was she grieving her mother's death? Her father's? So many conflicting, tangled emotions writhed inside her.

Collier held her close, wrapping his arms around her and softly stroking her hair. She felt the first sobs bubble up and tried to choke them down.

"Ssshhh," he soothed, stroking her. "I am here."

"But you are leaving," she said with distress. "I want you to stay."

He sighed. "Believe me, this is painful for me also, Maia. Your kingdom is so vulnerable right now. *You* are vulnerable. I want to be here for you. To help you take your first steps as the ruler of Comoros. But it is as I told you. You are the heir. It is yours to rule by right, not mine. Simon will help you. He will deliver my letters to you."

"You will write to me?" she asked, pulling away and looking up at him hopefully.

"Every day," he replied. He stared into her eyes, his face full of shadows. Stubble covered his chin and jaw. She realized he had not been sleeping; he had watched over her during the night.

"I could come to your realm through the Apse Veil?" she suggested. She was aware of the warmth coming from him. Aware she was wearing a thin chemise and he was still dressed in his clothes—his disguise as he prepared to cross the sea to Dahomey in one of Simon's cargo ships.

He pulled her cheek against his chest and then started stroking her hair again. "I will be at war, not near the abbey. What were you dreaming about, my love?"

She scrunched her face at the memory. "It was awful."

"Tell me," he said soothingly.

She could hear his heartbeat beneath the padded shirt. It was soothing, repetitive. "I was in Dahomey."

He grunted. "That does not sound terrible to me," he joked.

"It was the cursed shores. Spider bites and ticks."

"Ah, yes. That is not a place where I intend to build a palace for us. Go on."

"There was a place there. A place full of bones, topped with a Leering. A graveyard, really. We found it while we were looking for the lost abbey. My heart was heavy . . . so heavy. It felt like I was drowning in sadness." She shook her head a little, pressing her nose against his shirt. "It was terrible. The kishion was there." She shuddered, grateful for the comfort of Collier's presence.

"Him again. Was it a dream?" he asked her.

"I thought not at first," she replied. "I was afraid that falling asleep in the castle had doomed me. To be truthful, I do not even remember falling asleep."

She heard the chuckle in his breath. "It happened quite quickly, I assure you. You are exhausted, Maia. You changed into your chemise and were asleep within moments of lying down on the pillow. You tried to talk to me at first, but I could see it was pointless."

She smiled in embarrassment, hiding her face further. "I am sorry. I do remember that. I so wanted to talk before you left. Have you been awake all night?"

His hand rested on the back of her neck. "It is night still," he answered. "Though I was going to wake you soon, for I must leave. You were sleeping peacefully, Maia. It was only at the end that you seemed disturbed. I enjoyed watching you sleep."

She pulled away, brushing some hair behind her ear, and looked into his piercing blue eyes.

"You do not understand, do you?" he said wryly. "You are beautiful, Maia. I could watch you always and never grow tired of it."

There was a burning feeling in her chest, one that throbbed with happiness, and it extinguished the fear and sorrow that had clung to her from her dream. She let herself bask in the feeling for a moment, but only a moment.

"I have never fully trusted handsome men," she confided. "I will not always be young. My father's behavior taught me that most men cannot be trusted." It was a fear she had held in her chest ever since she had admitted to herself that she loved him.

His look grew serious. "A fair accusation. Considering how we met and my . . . disposition at the time, I have given you reason to think your fears are justified. At the time, I was not a man worthy of your good faith." He had the good grace to look abashed and she loved him all the more for it. An uncomfortable silence hung between them, but then he looked up and gazed into her eyes. "But I am not that man anymore."

She licked her lips. "You have changed, Collier. So have I." She swallowed, summoning her courage. "I want this to work. Between us. I am still . . . fearful, but I trust you."

"Do not prove me by my words," he said seriously. "Prove me by my actions. You are a treasure to me, Maia." He slid his fingers into her hair gently. "You are worth more than a ransom to me."

Her heart felt like it would burst. "Come back to me," she whispered, taking his other hand in hers and squeezing his fingers. "Please come back to me!"

A small quirk twisted on his mouth. "With such an incentive, I pity the King of Paeiz. He will regret the day he chose to invade Dahomey. I will do my best to defeat him and perhaps even win him to our cause. You will not stand against the Victus alone, Maia. Neither storms nor gales will keep me away."

She reached out and hugged him around the neck, savoring the feeling of his hands, his arms.

The door rattled and opened and Suzenne entered, catching them midembrace. "Forgive me!" she gasped with shock, blushing. She hurried to leave, but Maia called her back.

"It is all right, Suzenne. Please stay."

There was a splotch of crimson across Suzenne's cheeks as she reluctantly returned to the room. Collier laughed at the look on her face and stood, pulling Maia up with him.

"I thought you had returned to Muirwood last night," Suzenne stammered. "I was coming early to light the Leerings and get your gown ready for the Privy Council meeting. I am sorry—"

"Do not apologize," Collier said offhandedly. "If there is one thing I have come to learn as king, it is that privacy is a rare gem, and as such, must often be stolen." He switched his language to Dahomeyjan. "I depart with the tide for my kingdom. Look after my lady while I am gone."

Suzenne did a formal curtsy and replied in the same language. "I will, my lord." She turned her back on them and started fussing with Maia's gown for that day, giving them a moment without being observed.

Collier walked over to the window and parted the curtain. "It is time. Simon will be anxious to have me on board. He is the type of man who will tell you the truth, even if you do not want to hear it. Such a man is worth fifty thousand marks."

"I will heed him then," Maia replied, following him to the curtain. "Safe journey, Husband."

Collier smiled when she said it and pulled her into a final embrace. "I like the way you say that," he answered, toying with the earring in her earlobe. He had given them to her before her journey to Muirwood, and she had worn them ever since. "Rule wisely, my love. May the ancient enmity between our kingdoms and our Families finally be healed."

"Make it thus so," Maia whispered in benediction as he left the room with a final backward glance.

***

Maia and Suzenne walked arm in arm down the corridor toward the private room that had been chosen for the Privy Council's meetings. Out of the endless array of gowns at her disposal, Maia had chosen a simply designed cream-colored gown. It had a woven sash bedecked with beads around the front and a fur-lined robe that fastened with a royal brooch. It was one of the simplest gowns that had been sent to her, and she had chosen it in the hopes of setting an example for the court. Suzenne had helped to arrange her hair in a simple yet comely design. It was the kind of elegant look that Sabine favored.

The corridor was decorated with polished bronze torches. The ground was capped in smooth stone tiles inlaid with gold. The workmanship was exquisite and ostentatious and it made Maia shake her head with anger. The people starved in the streets, yet she and her courtiers trod on gold.

At the end of the long hallway, she could see Captain Carew waiting outside the new council room.

"I am sorry," Suzenne whispered again in her ear, "about interrupting you this morning."

"You are my friend as well as my chief lady-in-waiting, Suzenne. I am certain there will be other embarrassing occasions in the future."

"I know. But if someone had walked in on Dodd and me, I would be mortified."

Maia reached and squeezed her hand. "Let us not talk of it again. I am so pleased to have both of you on my Privy Council, you know. You are the first woman to be invited. Please do not be daunted to give your advice, Suzenne. I will expect you to speak your mind. You must speak for the women and the children of the realm."

Suzenne paled at the thought, but her expression was determined. "It is a privilege, Maia." She squeezed her hand in return.

Maia nodded to Captain Carew as they neared him. "Good morning, Captain!" she said cheerily.

"Your Grace, good morning," he replied, stiffening to a bow. His injured leg had been healing well, and he no longer winced when he put weight on it. "Your first Privy Council meeting is underway. They await you." He opened the handle and invited her inside.

In keeping with rules of rank, Suzenne fell several steps back so Maia could enter the room well before her. Designed as a half circle, the enormous room was dazzlingly appointed. Rings of stuffed leather-and-wood seats were arranged in concentric rows around a carved, polished throne chair stationed before several enormous stained-glass windows. The rich wainscoting on the walls was a buttery brown color that shimmered with bronze and gold touches. A large chandelier hung over the center, and Leerings for light had been fixed into pillars along the walls. The workmanship was more than fine—it almost assaulted the senses with its lavish detail. It reminded her of the Rood Screen of Muirwood, only more luxurious and costly.

The members of the Privy Council rose as she entered and made her way down the center aisle toward the throne. She received nods of attention from the Earl of Caspur, his graying hair and pointed beard dipping dramatically as he bowed to her, as well as the mayor of Comoros, Dodd Price, and several others whom Maia had appointed to the council. The first seat was taken by Richard Syon, of course, and she noticed that her old friend looked about as comfortable with the setting as she was.

She could feel their eyes on her, weighing her choice of gown, the simplicity of her style. They were all careful to guard their expressions, but she could sense a growing unease in the room. This was the first time a woman had ruled Comoros. She was intruding on a lair that had been dominated by men for centuries.

They were all watching her. They were all curious to know how she would react. She felt a flush start to rise on her cheeks, and her stomach clenched with nervousness.

Maia paused before the throne at the head of the room, unable to mount the steps to the seat. It would put her above everyone else around her. Her father had done that deliberately, she knew. She turned and faced them from the floor, feeling the strangeness of the moment as a physical weight. The others awaited her signal to sit. She acknowledged that by nodding for them to seat themselves.

Memories began to unwind in her mind. Years ago, Chancellor Walraven had arranged for her to be sent to the borders of Pry-Ree to settle land disputes. She had seen a functioning Privy Council before. She knew how to rule. But she also realized that what she did outside this chamber would have more meaning to the people than what she did inside it. It was how she chose to treat her servants, down to the lowliest ones, that would matter most. Still, she needed her councillors on her side. How best to approach the situation?

If Collier had been there, as Earl of Dieyre, it might have been different. People would have looked to him, a king in his own right, to lead the conversation.

She folded her hands in front of her, still standing before the throne chair without sitting in it. She looked at each of those assembled, one by one, gazing into their eyes and nodding to them. She tried on a smile, which felt a little forced. "There is a saying in Pry-Ree," she began. "*Os nad iditch in gweebod forth, certheth in araf.* If you do not know the way, walk slowly."

Some of them chuckled nervously.

Maia then sank to her knees before them. "I cannot walk slowly, so I must kneel and beg your help. I am here before you reluctantly. I am young and inexperienced with the ways of men.

We have a foe who seeks our eternal destruction. A foe that is even now summoning their forces to crush us, to destroy our beliefs, to make the rest of the kingdoms cower in fear and obeisance." She shook her head slowly. "I do not know how long the Medium will have me be your queen, but I know there are enemies in our realm that we must face together. There is distrust and rancor amongst our people. It is the duty of every leader to protect her people, even at the risk of her own life and comfort. It is my solemn intention to carry out the task the Medium has given me to the public good and to the benefit of all of my subjects." She sighed deeply. "I have entrusted my affairs and myself to you, my councillors, and I urge you to be faithful to the oaths you have sworn. To be loyal to me as your queen. To follow the example I give you, I who am only following the examples of others greater than myself."

When she looked up at their faces, she was surprised to see tears in their eyes, especially Lord Paget of Bridgestow, whom she remembered of old. Her Pry-rian words had touched his heart for certain. They were staring at her in amazement, as if they had never seen or heard such a thing before.

"I will give my last drop of blood to save our kingdom from the Naestors," Maia vowed.

CHAPTER TWELVE

Coronation Day

I t felt to Maia as if the entire world had filled the streets of Comoros. The sound of the crowd was as deep and penetrating as the rush of wind in a storm. The noise of the congregation could be heard within the palace walls, and when the outer doors opened, it flooded into the bailey and made several of the servants gasp with shock.

The procession was long and solemn, its order and scope prescribed by the traditions of her people. The front was led by the gentlemen of the realm, or at least those who had left their Hundreds to support the anointing of the new queen. Hailing from obscure Families as well as famous ones, there were easily two hundred of them. They walked in rows, two by two, either flanked by a spouse or one of their fellows. They were followed by the knights of the realm; the city ealdermen of Comoros; and the mayor, who walked with his head held high and a jubilant smile on his face as he waved to the assembled crowds.

The streets had been shoveled, broomed, brushed, and scrubbed in preparation for this day, all of which had tamed the fetid odors. The windows had been cleaned and polished, besides, with fresh paint or lacquer applied to the beams and struts of the houses and gutters. Fragrant garlands hung from the maypoles, and the streamers shimmered in the air. There would be dancing after the coronation. The faces in the mob were eager, the short straining against the tall to get a better view. Every window was jammed with people on every floor, and some brave souls even strutted up on the rooftops for a better vantage point. They murmured and talked as the procession marched solemnly past, walking along a carpet of blue cloth that had been laid from the marble porch of Pent Tower all the way to Claredon Abbey.

Maia's stomach twisted with nervousness, and though she tried to steady herself, to feel the subtle impressions of the Medium, she could not. Sabine stood at her elbow, her presence a comfort. Of course, it would be Aldermaston Wyrich, the newly appointed Aldermaston of Muirwood, who performed the ceremony, not her grandmother.

"It is normal to be nervous," Sabine whispered in her ear. "I would entreat you to enjoy the moment, but I know you will not. I am always uneasy in crowds."

"I did not know so many people could even fit in the city," Maia answered, her voice strained.

Sabine smiled. "They have come from all the Hundreds, dear one. All who wanted to come. Some have been walking for days. A coronation does not happen often in a lifetime. The coronation of a woman to rule? Never."

Maia sighed as she watched the Privy Council join the procession next, led by Richard Syon. He looked grave and dutiful, a sharp contrast to the flamboyant mayor, Justin, who had worn his finest tunic, cape, and gloves. The Privy Council was followed by three knights who carried the naked blades of their maston swords, representing justice, the Medium, and mercy. They were followed by Captain Carew, who bore the sword of state. He too wore his most outlandish fashions, and she noticed an earring in his ear.

Maia swallowed—it was nearly her turn. She pursed her lips, trying not to be sick.

She dreaded what was coming. Part of the ritual involved her removing her gown down to her chaen. A canopy would be held around her to preserve her modesty, so only a few select individuals—those closest to her in the procession, meaning all those who were currently a part of her Privy Council—would witness the moment when the Aldermaston anointed her with the Chrism oil. Those few would see the brand on her shoulder; they would see the kystrel's stain on her breastbone.

"What if they reject me?" she whispered to Sabine, her voice throbbing with suffering.

"I removed the binding sigil," her grandmother replied, "so we can explain the situation to those who do not know. You are a maston, Maia. You made your oaths to uphold the Medium's will. The symbol of the chaen is a more sure witness to who you are than the hetaera's marks. If we sought to change the ceremony, to conceal the truth, it would only create more suspicion and doubt. Aldermaston Wyrich already knows the truth. So will the Privy Council. They *must* know it, and they *will* support you."

Maia felt a little faint as she watched Dodd begin to march. As the new Earl of Forshee, Dodd carried the velvet pillow with her crown. Richard Syon's wife, Joanna, carried the Cruciger orb on another pillow. The Earl of Caspur bore the scepter, which was made of solid gold, wreathed with ornate designs, and topped with enormous sapphire gems.

And finally it was her turn. Sabine squeezed her arm one last time and let her go. She would follow in the crowd behind. The High Seer was not part of the ceremony, her position being dominant over all the rulers of the realms.

Maia sucked in her breath and started to walk. Her royal gown was simple and beautiful, but it would be changed once the anointing was complete. Another gown awaited her at the abbey. Her train was carried by Suzenne, the Countess of Forshee, and they were followed by the other ladies-in-waiting whom Maia had chosen to serve her.

As she trod on the rumpled blue cloth, gazing straight ahead with as much dignity as she could muster, there was an audible sigh from the crowd, and a hush quickly fell across those who had assembled to watch the auspicious occasion. She saw men doff their hats and crush them against their shirts. Women bowed and curtsied as she passed by them. Though she longed to stare at her people, Maia maintained the tradition and kept her eyes fixed on the abbey spire. There was a tradition that queens be carried in a litter—that was the way Lady Deorwynn had insisted upon—but there was also another tradition for going on foot, which Maia preferred. Her hair was down and full, decorated with no braids or ornaments.

The procession to the abbey was not long, but to Maia it lasted an almost unendurable time. She had never been the focus of so many eyes. She wondered, darkly, if the kishion was among those who watched her. She did not doubt that he was, and the thought caused a chill to seep into her bones. She wished Collier had been able to attend the occasion. She knew from Simon that he had landed safely in Dahomey, but that was all she had heard.

The abbey grounds had been decorated for the occasion, but her heart was beating hard in her chest and she barely paid attention to her surroundings as she entered the main gates, glancing up at the tall archway and blinking back at the bright sunlight. A large platform had been erected in the middle of the courtyard where the ceremony would take place. She saw the canopy screen being held in the ready. On each side of the courtyard, benches had been constructed, and the choir from Assinica had assembled, a group of at least a hundred men, women, and even children.

She saw Aldermaston Wyrich awaiting her at the head of the platform, a tall, stately figure. His hands were clasped in front of him, and he stared at her with a peaceful, reassuring look, as if he saw her fears and concerns and hoped to soothe them.

The constant regret of what had happened to her in the lost abbey pressed down on her more than ever. But she marched forward, determined to face her humiliation with as much dignity as possible.

The inner courtyard was teeming with the nobles of the realm. Flags fluttered in a small breeze. Those bearing the royal regalia mounted the steps in front of her and arranged themselves around the Aldermaston. Maia came forward and then knelt on a cushion in front of him. He gave her a warm smile and winked affectionately, a final attempt to calm her.

The Aldermaston turned to those assembled. "My friends, here present is Marciana, rightful and undoubted inheritrix by the laws of maston and man to the Crown and royal dignity of this realm of Comoros. This day she is appointed by the peers of this land for the consecration, inunction, and coronation of said most excellent Princess Maia." He smiled benevolently, his voice easy and unpretentious, his accent only adding to the richness. He was an excellent speaker. "Will you serve, at this time, and give your will and assent to the same?"

Maia trembled on her knees, waiting to hear her people's pledges. They came in a rush of sound, filled with enthusiasm and forcefulness.

"Yeah! Yeah! Yeah!"

The sound sent shudders jolting through her, and she felt, for the first time that day, the whispering of the Medium. It brought a feeling of warmth, of approval, and most importantly, of peacefulness. Within the grounds of Claredon Abbey, she had found the reassurance she had not felt in the palace. She closed her eyes as the Aldermaston laid his hand on her head.

"Please close your eyes," he instructed those assembled. She sensed him raising his hand in the maston sign.

"Marciana Soliven, by Idumea's hand, I Gift you on this, your coronation day. I Gift you with the wisdom to rule and lead this mighty people, to defend your realm against its enemies. I Gift you with patience and understanding, so that you may judge not after the manner of men, but in accordance with the will of the Medium. I grant you a feeling of peace on this day and with . . ."

His voice dropped off. Maia felt a prickle of unease. A strange darkness settled on her soul as he started to speak again, his voice choked with emotion. "Maia . . . I Gift you with . . . hope. When the storm comes. When night shrouds this land and your heart. When you are at the brink of utter despair, I Gift you with hope that will see you through." He forced the words through his teeth, his turbulent feelings clearly roiling beneath the surface. "Even the darkest night will give way to the dawn. Remember this, Maia. Remember this, our queen. Make it thus so."

The words he spoke sent a pall over those assembled. He lowered his arm from the maston sign, and Maia opened her eyes and looked up at his face. Tears coursed down his cheeks as he stared down at her with deep sympathy, and she shuddered at what it meant. What had he seen as he had performed the Gifting? It was clearly a premonition of something horrible.

Aldermaston Wyrich extended his hand to help her rise. As she came to her feet, the choir from Assinica began to sing.

It was a sound unlike anything she had ever heard before.

The voices were strong, skilled, and perfectly blended. It was not a song with words, just a series of chords and strains. There were no instruments to accompany them, but their voices replicated the sounds of a full orchestra, some low and throbbing, some high and piercing. It was soft, lilting, and the force of it grew and grew, swelling like a rainstorm of sound that washed across the courtyard of the abbey, ascending over the walls and into the streets. Maia could hear the sounds of the little ones, the children, among the others, and it stung her eyes with tears.

The choir's music built and then ebbed and then built again to a crescendo more powerful and affecting than anything she'd ever heard. With the sound came the Medium. It was as if the singers had ensnared it with a spell, their voices a supplication that could not be denied. Maia stared at them in wonder and awe, experiencing a flood of unexpected emotions. The gathered crowd was mesmerized too, she could tell. The choir's song had stilled the enormous city as if it were a child too wonder-struck to breathe. The feeling of the Medium permeated the throng, spreading to every soul who could hear the singing.

Maia glanced back at the Aldermaston, who beamed with pride and approval at those who were singing the coronation anthem. She stared at him in disbelief, understanding anew the importance of these people they had saved from destruction. She could not imagine what would have happened if the Victus had gotten to them first, silencing their music, art, poetry, and craft forever.

The choir finished singing, the end of their performance leaving pricks of gooseflesh down Maia's arms. The Aldermaston smiled at the choir. There was no clapping or cheering. Praise would only have defiled such purity of music.

Aldermaston Wyrich gestured for her to kneel again. She did and lifted her face to him.

"Will you, Lady Maia, pledge to defend your subjects, maintain peace, and administer justice throughout the realm?" He smiled at her again, but now there was solemnity in his expression.

"Yes," she answered boldly.

"Will you promise to the people of Comoros, your realms and dominions, to keep the just and licit laws and liberties of this realm and your dominion?"

"Yes," she said. Now was the time. She shuddered with anxiety, but the dread in her heart had vanished.

Once she had risen from the pillow, the Aldermaston escorted her to the canopy held by four men who were part of her Privy Council—the mayor, the Earl of Caspur, Dodd, and Richard Syon. Suzenne waited behind them to help her disrobe.

She trembled with cold as Suzenne helped strip away her gown, leaving her in her chaen and chemise. She saw the men's eyes widen as they took in the sight of the kystrel's taint rising from beneath her bodice. Even Dodd's mouth firmed into a small frown. Maia breathed deeply and then knelt once again before the Aldermaston.

Aldermaston Wyrich turned to the four men, his expression grave. "We allow you knowledge of this," he said softly, "so that there be no deceit in the realm. The marks of corruption you see on her body were not chosen willingly; they were offenses done against her. She passed her maston oaths at Muirwood on Whitsunday. She *is* a queen-maston, *not* a hetaera."

As he spoke, the force of the Medium jolted through the group, as palpable as it had been during the choir's performance. Maia saw those holding the staves start to tremble, as if the meager weight of it were suddenly too heavy to bear. Tears trickled down Caspur's cheeks. With a look of astonishment, the mayor flushed and turned away his gaze. Dodd continued to look at her for a moment, his expression changing to wonderment, and then shifted his gaze to Suzenne, as if to ask if she already knew. Suzenne nodded and smiled knowingly.

Richard Syon, who had long known the truth, gave Maia a look of tenderness and encouragement that warmed her heart and emboldened her. He was the one who had helped her the most. He had sustained her, taught her the ways of the Medium, and enlightened her with wisdom and the tomes of the ages. She respected him as a father.

Aldermaston Wyrich took out a small delicate vial topped with a jeweled stopper, which he unsealed. "The Chrism oil," he said. Then he dipped his smallest finger into the vial and anointed her forehead, temples, shoulders, and breastbone with the pungent-smelling oil.

The wetness and warmth of the oil felt strange against Maia's skin, yet it did not burn or hurt. It did not mark her as something counter to the Medium. "This coronation ritual has existed for centuries," the Aldermaston explained. He spoke louder, his voice carrying past the curtain for the crowd to hear. "This oil is pressed from fruit in a certain garden in Idumea. The Garden of Semani. Called the Chrism oil, it is used to anoint Aldermastons. And in this case, a queen. I bestow upon you the rights and stewardship of the kingdom of Comoros as sovereign ruler. May you keep and preserve your oaths as you defend this people."

"Amen," uttered the four men holding the canopy. As she looked at each of the men holding the canopy, she saw nothing but respect and loyalty. She felt their support and was silently grateful.

Suzenne then opened a wardrobe chest and removed the queen's regalia, a gown befitting Maia's rank, though one that was less adorned than the ones Lady Deorwynn had favored. She quickly helped her dress, covering her from the sight of the men who now knew her secret. With the binding sigil removed, they would be free to speak of it with others. She silently hoped that they would not, that the power of the Medium they had felt would be enough to silence their tongues.

Once she was dressed in the ceremonial gown, they lowered the covering and revealed her to the rest of those assembled in the courtyard. The Aldermaston then summoned the implements of her authority—the sword of state, which he girded around her waist as if she had been a king, the scepter of power, and the Cruciger orb. Then in front of everyone assembled, the Aldermaston put the coronation ring on her finger—marrying her to the kingdom—and the crown on her head, giving her full authority over it. This finalized the ceremony.

As she felt the metal of the crown weigh down her hair and press against her temples, the choir of Assinica started to sing again, and this time their anthem was more festive and celebratory. Their song signaled to the crowds that the coronation was over, and the cheer that began outside the walls shook the very platform on which Maia stood. People on rooftops visible over the abbey walls waved hats and screamed her name. There were so many people in the street, on porches and verandas and roofs, it was almost a riot. She would have to pass through them to get back to the palace, and the very notion of doing so was daunting.

The choir continued to sing as the procession began to return to the castle, leaving in the same order that it had entered. The sea of onlookers strained against the wall of pikemen who had formed to prevent the people from converging on the street.

"Are you relieved it is almost over?" Suzenne whispered from behind her.

"Over?" Maia asked, straining with a smile and twirling the scepter as she waited for their turn to walk. "My troubles are just beginning."

***

The coronation was celebrated with an enormous feast at the palace that evening, though Maia felt disgruntled by the mood of revelry in the hall, by the freely flowing spirits. But she had harkened to the lord mayor's counsel not to change the tradition. Doing so would have risked offending the nobles *and* the common people, who expected to celebrate such occasions. The audience hall had been turned into an enormous banquet—after removing the benches, the palace servants had brought in tables and arranged them in a giant square. Now Maia sat on a raised dais with her councillors. Her seat, by tradition, was higher than all the rest. She had eaten sparingly, still nervous about the first official day of her reign. Part of her poor mood had to do with her father. She could not stop thinking about how he had managed to convince himself that the authority invested in him by an Aldermaston could be superseded by royal decree. It was unthinkable. The solemn occasion had touched her deeply, and she felt the marks of the Chrism oil almost as if they were a palpable burden laid on her by Aldermaston Wyrich. How could her father have deceived himself and bucked the traditions of the realm so completely? Another qualm she felt about the celebration was that this display of wantonness, greed, drunkenness, and celebration did not seem to acknowledge the true state of the kingdom. They were on the verge of being attacked by the Naestors and their limitless cargo of bloodthirsty warriors, who hoped not just to steal their treasures, but to put every one of their victims to death.

She stared at the throng around her, at all of the courtiers imbibing and eating, feeling anxious for the demonstrations of wealth, wine, and feasting to end. The people, she had heard, were carousing in the streets. They had ripped down every decoration to keep as souvenirs and had already filled the gutters with debris and muck. Maia had told Richard that she wanted the streets swept again that night so they would be clean in the morning.

"My lady, a word?" came a voice at her ear, and she turned to find the mayor, Justin, standing nearby with a wine goblet.

"Was is it?" she asked him, her brow crinkling under her brooding thoughts.

"You do not look as if you are enjoying this celebration."

She shook her head. "I am not. The people appear to have forgotten the danger we face."

He frowned. "No . . . they celebrate, which does not happen often enough. I wondered if you had considered what to do with the Rundalen estate?"

"Please, Justin," she said, waving him off. "I said I would make all such decisions in the presence of the Privy Council after taking some time for deliberation. This is not the place."

"Very well. I beg your pardon." He sauntered off, stopping to bid a servant to fill his cup. She frowned after him, missing Collier so much it hurt.

"What did the lord mayor want?" Suzenne asked, approaching Maia from behind. It was an immediate comfort to have her close.

"What they all seem to want right now," Maia replied with disappointment. "Money and power. It will not be easy to change the temperament my father instilled at court. All this celebration is making me ill. Can they not appreciate that danger and doom are almost upon us?"

Suzenne rested her hand on Maia's arm. "You have seen the armada, Maia. They have not."

Maia watched a married man flirting with a younger woman. The sight sickened her. "Where is Jayn?" she asked.

"Over there," Suzenne responded. "Talking to Joanna. Jayn is grateful for you, you know. If things had gone differently, she would be sitting in your chair right now. She dreaded it."

Maia suppressed a smirk. "I would almost welcome a reprieve. I am glad she is staying on as a lady-in-waiting. She must be very overwhelmed by all the sudden changes. I am sure we all are."

There was a commotion at the entrance to the great hall, and a rider appeared, bringing his stallion into the assemblage. He wore the royal colors, and Maia recognized him as Captain Carew, her champion. This was part of the ritual as well. The crowd of feasters stopped talking as the horse clomped in, snorting roughly at the mess and crowd. The tables were lined around in a giant square, leaving an opening in the middle. Carew's steed trotted to the center. He wore ceremonial armor, gauntlets, and had a sword belted to his waist.

"Who dares to affirm that this lady is not the rightful queen of this kingdom? Who dares it?" His voice bellowed out to those assembled in mock sincerity. Maia saw he was a good actor. He looked both menacing and handsome as he stared into the crowd. "Who challenges her right to rule Comoros? Come forward and I will show you the truth! Come forward and meet your doom! Who here challenges her right to rule?" He flung down one of his gauntlets, which clattered in the middle of the hall.

Maia cocked her head toward her friend, dropping her voice to a whisper as she felt the sudden stillness of the room. "Suzenne, would you remind me tomorrow that—"

"I do!"

Maia stopped, blinking with surprise. A voice rippling with challenge and menace sounded in the crowd. The ceremonial utterance of the threat had never before been accepted in all the history of the realm.

A man wearing a chain hauberk beneath his tunic strode forward. He was young, with long dark hair and a white-and-black cape. He was barely half of Carew's age, but he looked both fit and strong.

"My name is Hove," the young man said with a sneer. "Sworn man of the *true* Earl of Forshee and the *true* Aldermaston of Muirwood, who even now ride from the north with an army to topple this pretend queen." He walked up to where Carew had thrown down his glove and picked it up. "This woman is no queen. She is but a vessel of evil sent to deceive us. May the Medium prove my words to be true."

And then he drew his sword.

CHAPTER THIRTEEN

Walraven's Dagger

Corriveaux heard the steps coming down the darkened hallway, but the Leerings had already warned him of the visitor's approach. He waited in the darkness, past the curtain of light that spilled down on the stone plinth in the center of the room. He was nervous. Even though Walraven was an old man, he was cunning and would not be taken off guard easily. Corriveaux knew he could best him in a battle of strength, but this would be a battle of minds.

At last, he could see Walraven in the shadowy corridor. The older man's mass of gray hair was wild and unkempt, his figure more gaunt than before. There was a haggard, weary look on his face. The walk down the steps into the dungeon had fatigued him, which showed in his labored breathing.

Walraven paused in the threshold of the room, his eyes scanning the darkness.

"You sent for me, Corriveaux?" Walraven asked mildly, still not entering.

"Come in, old friend," Corriveaux greeted. He kept perfectly still.

Walraven's expression tightened somewhat as he shuffled into the chamber. "My joints have been aching lately. Is there a Leering for arthritic joints, I wonder? It would be a helpful invention."

Corriveaux was not fooled. That declaration of weakness had been a purposeful attempt to seem more vulnerable. He was sharp, the old man. The truth was, Corriveaux respected him immensely. Walraven scratched a patch of gray hair at the back of his head and scrunched up his face, his eyes still probing the dark.

"What is the report from Comoros?" he asked the old man. "What have you heard from your man Fox?"

He asked the words deliberately, studying Walraven's face for a reaction.

The older man rubbed his throat. "Mayhem, as you can expect. Deorwynn was executed and the old king poisoned. The kishion is being hunted, but unless we send another to find him, he will likely remain beyond our power. The girl is taking the throne."

Corriveaux smiled darkly, bridling his fury. Walraven did not use Maia's name, he noticed. Their humiliation at losing her and the High Seer together was still a festering sore. They had been outmaneuvered by an old woman from Pry-Ree, one who continued to meddle with their strategies.

"The installation of a new queen is perfect for our plans," Corriveaux said. "The people will be unruly for a while. She will seek to change things, which will only add to the confusion."

"Have you had word from the armada?" Walraven asked with unconcern. "When will they arrive?"

"Why do you wish to know?" Corriveaux asked pointedly.

"It is no matter," Walraven said with a shrug. "Only curiosity. This may interest you, though. There appears to be a schism among the mastons in Comoros. The incumbent Aldermaston of Augustin . . . the one known as Kranmir. You know of him?"

"I do not. Dahomey is my specialty. Augustin is one of their wealthier abbeys, if I recall."

"Indeed. The former king had positioned Kranmir to assume command of Muirwood. Kranmir and some of the king's loyalists are starting a civil war. They mean to challenge the girl for the throne."

Corriveaux snorted. "So if we do nothing, they may kill each other for us? How foolish of them. That kingdom has always been fractious. But it does not change our plans. Let them howl and stab each other. When the armada arrives off its shores, they will learn the true meaning of the Void."

"Yes, I am sure they will. I told you about Kranmir because I believe we would be better served to strike the south first. You do not know the earldoms as I do. The north is controlled by a disgruntled man named Kord Schuyler, who ran the earldom of Forshee and murdered his predecessors."

"I recall that," Corriveaux said.

"He is acting with Kranmir, and they have summoned an army to march on the capital. It will leave the south undefended. Just a suggestion, my friend, for the next time you contact the armada commander by the waymarker."

Corriveaux narrowed his gaze at Walraven. He slowly walked around in the darkness, his footfalls muffled by Leerings that had been installed for that purpose.

"Put your dagger on the plinth," Corriveaux said softly, his own drawn and gripped tightly in his hand.

Walraven's neck muscle twitched. "If you feel it is necessary," he said with nonchalance. He walked into the room, bathed with light from the Leering in the ceiling. He reached into his robe and withdrew his dagger, the symbol of his membership in the Victus. Any Victus who refused the call to put his dagger on the plinth would be hunted down by a kishion and killed. Setting down the dagger also made a man vulnerable, which was just what Corriveaux wanted.

Walraven stood there for a moment, his dagger clutched in his hand. Then he gently reached out and set it on the plinth.

"You killed Gastone," Walraven said simply, stepping away from the plinth.

"I did," Corriveaux answered.

"You thought he betrayed us?" There was a curious tone in his voice, but still . . . he sounded almost indifferent.

"No. I thought *you* betrayed us, my friend."

Walraven's brow crinkled and then smoothed. "Ah. I see."

"I knew you would," Corriveaux said, moving closer to the older man, watching him for any sign that he would flee or snatch back the dagger. He was preparing himself to plunge his own weapon into Walraven's back. He knew just where to stab him. "I watched your movements after Gastone's death. You knew I would do this, Walraven. You knew I had to kill you. I thought you would flee on a ship."

Walraven bowed his head, as if anticipating the blow that would come.

"I know," the old man said softly. "First the Hand. Then Gastone. I knew it was you, Corriveaux. Yet I still came here, into the bowels of the fortress." He turned his head slightly, angling it toward where Corriveaux lurked in the shadows.

"You did not run."

Walraven coughed and chuckled. "I am an old man, Corriveaux Tenir. Running is no longer an ability I possess. I do not wish to rule the Victus as you do. You impressed me from the start with your ambition and—"

"Do not *flatter* me!" Corriveaux seethed. "One of the Victus betrayed us. It is no accident that the High Seer and the girl escaped. They must have received help from within. It was you or it was me. No one else was around."

"Have you not considered that it may have been the Medium?" Walraven asked with a hint of challenge in his voice.

Corriveaux frowned, his feelings churning uneasily inside him. "I do not believe that."

"Of course not, or I would not be standing here in front of you about to be murdered."

Corriveaux lunged at him. He wrapped his arm around the old man's neck, jerking him off balance. Though he grunted with pain and toppled backward, Walraven kept his hands open and spread, not resisting the crushing force around his neck. Corriveaux jabbed the dagger blade against the old man's spine, but still he did not resist. Instead, he hissed through his teeth and sunk to his wobbling knees, his posture still submissive.

"Do you not want to live, Walraven?" Corriveaux whispered in his ear.

A pent-up breath was released, followed by a twisting sigh of pain and discomfort. "I am old, my friend. If it would make you feel better to kill me, go ahead. You can summon my spirit into the dark pools if you have any questions. I told you already, I do not seek your place and never have."

Corriveaux hesitated. It would be so easy to finish it now. A dagger thrust would kill Walraven and end his worries. This had long been the way of the Victus. But what if Walraven were not a traitor? He would be executing a man whose wisdom and connections would benefit him later, especially in a battle with Comoros.

"I should kill you," Corriveaux whispered.

"If I have ceased being useful to you."

Slowly, Corriveaux released the grip around Walraven's neck. He let the old man slump to the ground, breathing in heavy gasps to return the air to his lungs.

"Give me your signet ring," Corriveaux said.

Still wheezing and breathing hard, Walraven eased himself up on his knees. He twisted the ring off his finger and reached out to hand it over.

"I suppose we will see if you are right," Corriveaux continued. "If the Medium is what rescued the High Seer and her blighted granddaughter, you will be vindicated if it saves them again. For now, I will hold you prisoner until this is over and Comoros is left desolate. I will send word in your name," he continued, holding up the ring. "And we will see how your servants respond. Let us see . . . I believe I shall summon the High Seer to meet you in Hautland. If she comes, then I will know you are in league with her. I will command Fox to do mischief as well. We will see whether or not he obeys." He smiled darkly. "I have already dispatched a second kishion to Comoros."

Walraven's bleary eyes widened slightly. "You did?"

"Yes, of course. The renegade must be destroyed. But I also sent a kystrel with him. The *girl's* kystrel. He will give it to someone who can carry on the work we started. Someone we have already prepared. When the armada arrives, Comoros will be so fraught with discord they will be unable to defend themselves against us. They will distrust each other so much even the Medium will forsake them. The Void will destroy Comoros, Walraven. And we will usher it into being by destroying the High Seer herself."

Walraven's countenance slowly calmed and took on a more placid look. "Thank you for sparing me, Corriveaux. Let me assist you, to prove my loyalty to the Victus. I will write the letters as you instruct. They will come from my hand and bear my symbol. You only need to tell me what you wish me to say."

"You would cooperate?" Corriveaux said with surprise, looking askance at the man crumpled on the floor. "After the way I have treated you?" He knew that when a man was threatened with death, it scarred him for life. The trust between them was shattered.

"I must prove myself to you," Walraven said.

Corriveaux shook his head. "No, my friend. From this day forward, we must ever be enemies. You will not relish being in the dungeons. But it is better than being a corpse."

Pulling his boot back, Corriveaux kicked Walraven in the ribs, hard enough to snap the bones. The older man gasped with pain and crumpled over, writhing on the ground. Turning the dagger over in his hand, Corriveaux slammed the hilt down on Walraven's skull. The action filled him with a sense of power. He could feel the Myriad Ones filling the chamber, snuffling around the body prostrate on the ground. A madness seized him then, an irrepressible madness to hurt and destroy.

***

When the guards later dragged Walraven's body to the dungeon cell, they wondered how the crushed old man was even breathing.

I must often remind myself that my enemy is a young woman not even twenty years old. All people are corruptible if the right device can be employed. We have tempted her with riches, and she rejected them. We have tempted her with love, and she demurred. But I recall now the wise words of one maston. Youth is easily deceived because it is quick to hope. We will tempt her with hope, and then we will crush it.

—Corriveaux Tenir, Victus of Dahomey

CHAPTER FOURTEEN

The Champion of Comoros

The words of the challenger stilled all conversation within the hall. Maia stared at the young man, who was probably just a slight bit older than she was. He had a solemn bearing, his eyes near glowed with anger, and he had drawn a maston sword, which he held purposefully before him. She saw the glint of the hauberk beneath his white-and-black tunic and cape, and his hair was dark, like Collier's, only longer.

Carew kicked off the stirrups and landed with a clatter of the spurs on the paving stones. His own sword rung clear of his sheath. He was larger and more intimidating than the young man, although he had recently been wounded.

Maia stood at her table suddenly, feeling the thick tension fill the hall like haze.

"What abbey do you hail from?" she called out to the young man, who had declared his name Hove.

The look he gave her was dark and distrusting, and his gaze almost immediately returned to Captain Carew. "I passed the maston test at Augustin. You will not deceive me with your words as you have these others. Speak no more, woman. I will not hear you."

"She is your queen," Carew said angrily, closing the gap between them.

"I will have no bloodshed in my hall," Maia said with firmness in her voice, though she felt her knees trembling at the prospect of the coming conflict. "Captain . . . disarm him."

"It will not be difficult," Carew said with a chuckle.

"So said the giant before he fell," Hove retorted. He fell into a battle stance, guard held high, eyes focused on Carew.

The more seasoned soldier grunted with mockery and rushed at him with a flurry of blows. Maia remained on her feet, unable to feel the Medium at all amidst the drunkenness and frivolity of the coronation celebration. She had not expected Kranmir to challenge her right to rule so openly, at least not yet. As she heard and saw the two swords clash, she tried to understand the rogue Aldermaston's motives. Why would he send a stripling, one who had passed the maston test at his own abbey? Certainly, the young man would be totally loyal and obedient, sharing the same regard for him as she herself felt for Richard Syon, but did that explain it?

She glanced over at her chancellor, who had a wrinkled frown on his face as he stared at the spectacle playing out in front of them.

Carew locked hilts with Hove and used his size to drive the young man back, but suddenly the young man dipped and hammered his gauntleted fist into the captain's leg. Carew's face twisted with pain, and Maia realized the blow had been delivered to his injured leg, the one that had been wounded in the battle of Muirwood. Carew crumpled and sagged onto one knee, but he countered with a punch to Hove's ribs. The two men wrestled a bit before separating, both wincing and breathing hard.

"A cruel trick," Carew sneered.

Hove saluted him with his sword and delivered a mocking smile before coming at the captain again, more vigorously this time. Carew struggled back to his feet, but he was limping now, and Maia felt a trembling of dread that her drunken champion was about to fail.

There were sparks as the blades met, and although he was younger and less experienced, the boy's passion helped close the gap created by Carew's skills and size.

"I do not like this," Maia seethed, watching helplessly as the two men fought. A dark feeling wriggled inside her heart. She felt certain that she needed to stop the conflict. If she did not succeed, something dreadful would happen.

Carew pivoted and folded in, trapping Hove's sword arm against his body. He snapped his head forward against Hove's forehead, aiming for the boy's nose but glancing his cheekbone instead. The young man's head whipped back in a daze, and Carew twisted him around and threw him to the ground.

Maia saw the look of rage and fury in Carew's eyes as he went after the young man, his sword raised to deliver a blow.

"Stop!" Maia shouted at him.

Carew ignored her and rushed up to kick the young man in the ribs. Prepared for the blow, Hove caught Carew's leg before it landed and hoisted it up. Carew tottered and slammed down on his back, hard. There was a gasp from all who were assembled as the captain choked for breath, writhing on the ground. He clenched his stomach, trying to breathe, and Hove got to his feet and kicked the other man's sword away. He looked down at the fallen captain with triumph, his sword at the ready.

"It is over!" Maia shouted. "Leave him be."

The white-and-black knight gave her a rebellious look, his cheeks flushed, his breathing hard, but it was clear he had won. He said nothing in reply, but she could see by his look that he would defy her. He adjusted his grip on his sword and prepared to plunge it into Carew's stomach.

"You may be brave, but do not be a fool."

Maia turned and watched as Dodd strode into the center of the tables, a battle-axe gripped in one hand. Next to her, Suzenne sucked in her breath, clearly terrified to see her husband join the fray.

"The queen said no blood would be spilled in her hall this night. Stand down," Dodd said.

The feeling of dread intensified in the room as Dodd purposefully closed the distance separating him from the other men. If Hove struck down Carew, it would leave his back exposed to Dodd. The young knight seemed to realize the dilemma.

"And who are you?" Hove said derisively. "Another lackey sent to challenge me?"

"I am the Earl of Forshee, whom you claim to serve," Dodd replied, his voice and temper controlled. "Lay down your arms. You won the duel fairly. I will grant you that, even if Carew had too many cups. Put down the sword, man."

"I serve the *true* Earl of Forshee," Hove said angrily, stepping away from the writhing captain and facing Dodd with a martial stance. "Our true king to be. The Medium has chosen him to rule over us, and he will purge the realm of traitors. The coronation today was a sham. Our true king comes even now."

Dodd met him in the center, holding his axe blade down and away. "You are deceived, friend. The true ruler of Comoros is the king's heir, his lawful daughter. Kranmir overstepped his authority, so the High Seer has deposed him. You know not what you are doing."

Hove's face twisted with resentment and anger. "The High Seer? She is corrupt. She has fallen into the shadows."

Dodd shook his head. "She is the true High Seer. If you would meet with her, you would—"

"Risk being deceived myself?" Hove challenged. "I pity your lord father and brothers, Dodleah Price. Truly I do. But they died in accordance to the laws of the realm. You cannot wrest my lord's earldom from him out of revenge."

The young man's words pained Maia. She could see he was sincere. He truly believed she was a hetaera, controlled by a being beyond her. He had come into the heart of Comoros to challenge her right to rule, knowing that he would likely be killed. Perhaps Kranmir had even knowingly sent him to his death in the hopes it would help support his cause. The machinations of men sickened her. Hove did not look malicious, she thought, but he was clearly proud. His views were probably much like his tunic and cape—he saw things in black and white. He trusted his Aldermaston and obeyed him. She had to respect him for that, even if he had been misled.

The pressure on her heart grew stronger. Something was going to happen, something awful. She sensed it, though she did not understand what she should do to stop it. She only knew that the young maston should not be killed in the great hall on her coronation day. That would be awful. It would grieve the Medium further.

"I do not wish to fight you, but I will if you force my hand," Dodd said, still keeping his axe pointed away.

Hove brushed his arm against his mouth, wiping away the sweat. "How gracious of you," he said with disdain.

"We are brothers," Dodd said, opening his arms wider. "We are both mastons. Cannot we resolve this peacefully?"

"You, a true maston?" Hove snorted. "I heard you were allowed to pass the test so you could remain sheltered at Muirwood instead of facing your fate with your father as a man." His words were meant to provoke.

Dodd frowned, but his expression was smooth. "Well said. You will not yield then. I arrest you in the name of the queen. Lay down your arms or I will compel you."

"There is no Queen of Comoros," Hove replied bitterly. He struck out at Dodd, slashing his sword down and across in a series of swooping circles.

Dodd did not retreat from the slashes. He brought up his sturdy axe haft, using it to block the attack, and then kicked Hove hard in the stomach. Hove was knocked backward, but he recovered quickly and started a series of feints and thrusts toward Dodd.

It was axe against sword.

Maia squeezed Suzenne's hand and reminded herself that Dodd had been trained to use an axe by Jon Tayt, who was an Evnissyen—the royal protectors of Pry-Ree. They were cunning in battle. Lia's group of protectors had disarmed Maia's father and all his men with efficiency. She felt a spark of hope, but it did not counter the feeling of doom that had seeped into the hall.

Dodd whipped up the flat of the axe head and blocked a blow and then jabbed the butt of the axe into Hove's chest. The two continued to strike at each other, but the effort was mostly one-sided. Hove kept pressing the attack; Dodd kept defending against it. When an opening came, he took it and delivered a kick or an elbow to the other man, but he never used the axe blade itself for harm.

Before long Hove was panting with the exertion, but although Dodd's brow glistened with sweat, he did not look winded at all. She realized now that all the hours he had spent chopping wood by Jon Tayt's shed had served more than one purpose. He had a familiarity with the axe and he had the endurance to outlast his opponents. Dodd was not trying to hurt the black-and-white knight. He was wearing him down.

Those in attendance gasped and cheered every time a blow was dealt or missed. The emotion of the moment seared into the onlookers, making the fight at the center of the room the focus of all eyes. Some cheered when Dodd landed a blow against his enemy. Others booed at Hove, the sound rising and growing louder and louder.

Hove's face grew more frantic as his strength ebbed and the crowd began calling for him to fall. Every thrust, every move was easily countered. The two were not the same size—Dodd was bulkier than his adversary, his arms more accustomed to the rigors of labor. He had a solemn look on his face, even as a ball of sweat dropped from the tip of his nose. Hove's attacks were growing less and less intense, his legs starting to tremble as he shuffled one way and then the other. Carew had scuttled away from the fray, and now he stood watching the fight with some of his guardsmen on the fringe. His eyes were savage and full of hate toward the intruder, but she detected some grudging respect for Dodd. The captain held a bloody napkin to his nose.

"Are you getting tired yet?" Dodd asked the boy with a chuckle. "It looks like you would use a little rest."

"You mock me," Hove snarled. "If you were a man, you would fight me truly and end this!"

Dodd smirked but said nothing. The provocation clearly had not moved him.

Even though Dodd was winning, Maia still felt a growing sense of foreboding. She glanced at Suzenne, whose lips were pursed, her eyes riveted on her husband.

Hove stabbed at Dodd's foot suddenly and then rushed forward to tackle him. Dodd planted himself firmly, legs bent in a low stance, and bore the brunt of the collision without giving ground. Hove heaved against him, trying—and failing—to throw Dodd down. Catching Hove's foot with his own ankle, Dodd levered his adversary backward and slammed him into the ground.

Though Hove bucked and tried to get up, clawing desperately at Dodd's shirt collar, Dodd easily shrugged off the blow and encircled the young man's neck in a chokehold. Maia's heart tremored with worry as she watched the boy's legs thrashing.

"Enough! Dodd, enough!" she shouted as she finally pushed away from the tables and rushed off the dais to reach the center of the room. Gooseflesh crawled down her arms as she watched Hove's eyes roll back in his head. He went limp and blood trickled from a cut on his forehead.

Dodd released his grip and rose, fetching his fallen axe. The hall erupted with cheers, and people surged to their feet, stamping their heels against the ground and thumping the tables.

Kneeling beside the unconscious young knight, Maia searched his sweaty face and saw the smudges of bruises already forming on his cheek.

"Fetch a healer," she called, waving Suzenne over to join them.

"I did not kill him," Dodd whispered with concern. "You knew I would not, Maia. He will be fine."

"It is not that," Maia said, hovering over the fallen knight. She felt the pressure around her heart releasing, the danger passing. Noise echoed throughout the hall, so she could not have heard anything. But she *sensed* it . . . a presence in the hall. Looking up, she slid some hair behind her ear and looked to the wooden struts and rafters supporting the roof of the hall. She saw him there in the shadows—the kishion—and his crossbow was aimed right at her.

For a moment, her heart spasmed with fear. He slowly lowered the crossbow and looked down at her, frowning with disgust at her efforts to save the very knight who had threatened her authority. She realized then why the Medium had been warning her. The kishion had planned to kill Hove regardless of the outcome. He would always eliminate anyone who threatened her. It was a loyalty she did not want.

"Dodd," she breathed, trying to find the words, though they were slurred. "Dodd, he is here!"

The kishion slung the crossbow around his shoulder and then gracefully strode down the wide beam toward one of the upper windows in the hall. No one else had seen him. All eyes had been fixed on the struggle down below.

"Who?" Dodd asked. Maia shook with fear and dread as she watched the kishion slip away.

"Nothing," she whispered. She knew he would be gone without a trace before she could even summon her guards. And most of her guards, she realized angrily, were probably drunk.

"Take him to Pent Tower," she said, wiping some of the blood from the young knight's temple. "I will send Richard Syon to speak to him. I think he can help the young man understand his misconceptions about the Medium. Thank you, Dodd." She rose and took his hand. "You are my new champion."

She raised his hand in the air, and the hall thundered once more with cheers and applause.

CHAPTER FIFTEEN

Rebellion

A s soon as she crossed the Apse Veil the next morning after
spending the coronation night in Muirwood, Maia was
greeted by the Aldermaston of Claredon, who awaited
her on the other side with Richard Syon. Claredon's Aldermaston
was a portly man named Dower whose crest of snowy hair ringed
a gleaming bald head. A warmhearted man, he always had a smile
and a kind word for her. Richard looked as if he had not slept at
all the night of her coronation. The undersides of his eyes were
puffy and shadowed, but he stood at attention, waiting for her to
finish greeting Aldermaston Dower.

"Good morning, my dear friend," Maia said to Richard, taking his arm and leading him briskly away. When they emerged
from the abbey, she realized what a beautiful day it was in
Comoros, with a sunlit sky as bright and clear as any she had
seen. A few birds bickered and chased each other from the steeple. He guided her toward the outer walls of the abbey, the one

that connected with the street rather than the gate that separated the abbey from the palace grounds. She looked at him curiously, wondering at his choice.

He said nothing, only gestured as the porter wrenched on the bars of the gate and pulled it open. The street was crowded, as ever it was, but when they entered the flow of traffic she immediately noticed that the streets had been meticulously swept during the night. There were no broken flasks of wine, no debris to clog the gutters.

Maia stopped in place and stared down at the clean streets. The people in the street were noticing too, she realized. Some stopped to stare at a clean window, looks of mild surprise on their faces. She also saw a good many smiles on passersby. Maia was not dressed as a queen and earned only a few pointed stares, mostly from men who were blatantly admiring her. Without a crown or a scepter, she was unlikely to be recognized and could maintain a disguise not unlike Collier's.

"Thank you, Richard," she said. "This is *exactly* what I had hoped to achieve. Every day, we must start again with clean streets."

He patted her arm. "There is no shortage of men looking for work. They are joined by the masses from Assinica who insist on working for nothing. They want to help wherever and however they can. It is not just the part of the city near the palace that looks like this, either. All the streets do."

Maia beamed at him and then followed him to the palace wall. They headed to the secret corridor Maia had used to escape the castle not so very long ago, and were able to silence its power, to create fear, and pass. Due to its special ability to repel trespassers, the alley was as empty as ever it was. When they reached the end of the wall, Richard knocked on the door, which was opened by a member of her guard.

"Your Majesty." The young soldier greeted her with a salute.

Maia asked him for his name and tried to memorize it as they continued across the greenyard toward the palace, walking quickly.

"What did you learn from the young knight in Pent Tower?" Maia asked. "I believe Hove was his name."

"Yes. He hails from Augustin Hundred originally, but he was recently knighted by Forshee for his willingness to challenge your champion. He believed he risked his life and was surprised that we did not lock him in irons and throw him into the dungeons."

"Thank you for not doing that," Maia said. "What did he reveal to you?"

"I tested him on his maston training," Richard replied. "He is one, truly. We had an excellent conversation. He was so fearful that I wondered if he would even be able to feel the Medium at all. But after some assurances and gestures to lower his defenses, I learned that he is well intentioned. He is ambitious, to be sure, but that is normal for young men his age. After the intensity of the moment ebbed, he looked younger and younger and began to worry more about his parents and what they would think of him."

Maia nodded to the pikemen guarding the palace doors, winning surprised looks of gratitude from both of them, before she and Richard entered.

"Did you tell him the truth about me?" Maia asked.

"I told him just enough to explain, no more. An Aldermaston cannot deliberately lie, so the boy trusted what Kranmir told him explicitly. I explained to him the doctrine of investment and how Kranmir's actions have forfeited his right to govern an abbey. It is troubling indeed that Kranmir is spreading gossip and lurid misrepresentations about you, which will only fan the flames of distrust in ardent young men like this one, who do not understand that something can be untrue without being fully a lie. I am being brief, of necessity, for we must meet with the Privy Council, but I believe the youth is no longer our enemy."

Maia nodded in agreement. "What do you believe we should do to him?"

"I would like to release him at once."

She smiled. "Good. That is my will also. Have him set free immediately."

"I will," he said, returning her smile. "I am glad to see we think alike on this matter. I had the sense you would not want to keep him incarcerated, but I wanted to leave the judgment to you."

"Thank you, but you have my authority to act on my behalf, Richard. I trust your wisdom in matters such as this."

"Very well," he agreed meekly.

As they walked toward the council room, Maia was aware of the attention, the stares and whispers, of the people they passed. Even the lowliest servants were marking her, recognizing her, and watching her with interested eyes. They seemed . . . eager and most were busy with some kind of work. She remembered that she still wanted to visit them in their places and get to know them. But with the threat of rebellion hanging in the air, that would have to wait.

The mayor of Comoros was pacing outside the council chamber, his eyes bloodshot and haggard from the past night's festivities.

"Good morning, Your Majesty." He greeted her with a bow and opened the door.

She entered and found the full Privy Council in attendance. Bristling tension hung in the air, and a few of the council members bore angry looks, including Dodd. She sensed the shift in mood, the repelling of the Medium as she crossed the threshold. Suzenne looked at her with a small, tight frown, as if in warning.

"Good morning," Maia greeted, walking in quickly, a little out of breath from the brisk walk from the abbey. Strange how she had broken her fast with Davi and Aloia in the kitchens of Muirwood not long ago. Just an hour prior, she had been trying to coax a conversation from the quiet Thewliss, the gardener whose wife ran the kitchen. Now that Maia was a queen herself, he had regressed back to his former silence.

She motioned for Richard to begin the meeting as she paced along the front aisle of the room. She hated seeing that tall, carved throne on the dais and could not picture herself ever sitting on it, gazing down at her council members from its imperious height.

Richard walked to the front seat and desk next to the throne, which was piled with stacks of scrolls, parchments, and even a gleaming tome. He paused for a moment and took a long look at those who had assembled before him. Even that was enough to make the dark mood in the chamber wane. With a stern look on his face, he cocked his head slightly and pointed to a spot on the tome with his thick finger.

"It is said in the tomes that anger is a choice. It is a decision. One wise maston once said"—he looked down at the golden page, his voice slowing deliberately to articulate the quote—"'There are two things a person should never be angry at. What they can help. And what they cannot.'" He smiled at the saying and lifted his hand. "In a word, let us try to banish anger from these meetings. It is entirely possible for wise and educated persons to disagree about points of fact. But facts are stubborn things. Whatever may be our wishes, our inclinations, or the dictates of our passions, they cannot alter facts and evidence. We must strip away the rest. The happiness of the people is the aim of any good government. Now for the reports."

He turned his gaze to the lord mayor of Comoros. "Justin . . . the streets of Comoros were exceedingly clean and passable this morning. Maia is pleased and commends you for your attention to detail. Do you have anything to report? Any difficulties faced?"

Justin shook his head. "It is interesting, Your Highness—I mean, Maia—what this change has already wrought in the city. There are some enterprising individuals who are looking to make a business of street sweeping. They are taking the coin paid to them and using it to pay the youth—younger men and girls—some small wages to help sweep and tidy the streets. They are making a profit while ensuring that the job is done and done well. If it works, I thought we might save money by hiring the children ourselves."

Maia smiled and shook her head. "Do not rob these men of their initiative. If they earn a profit by influencing others to work for less, then we should not punish them for their enterprising spirit. Only intervene if they exploit the children. I will not have that."

Justin bowed gracefully. "Very well."

Maia continued to look at him. "Have rumors of the rebellion spread in the city?"

Justin shook his head. "Not yet, but there were many witnesses last night. Some of them were even sober," he added with a self-deprecating chuckle. "We cannot contain the news for long, but we will try. The people are used to the threat of danger. They will not riot. They will stand behind you, my lady."

Maia smiled and continued to pace. "What protections does the city have?"

"My lady, we have—"

"Do not let him fool you," the Earl of Caspur interrupted. "Comoros cannot withstand an army of knights and mercenaries. Forshee has considerable power, and he will bring it to bear. The threat is very real."

162

The anger in Justin's eyes was unmistakable, and she could tell he was not just peeved at the rude interruption. There had been arguments about this very matter before she arrived. She clasped her hands behind her and glanced at Richard, saying nothing.

Richard spoke up. "Everyone will get a turn to speak. We are peers here in this council. I do not condone interrupting a person before he has finished making his points. Proceed, Justin. What defenses do we have?"

Justin smiled with satisfaction; Caspur glowered at the gentle rebuke. "I believe the city can withstand a sizable force."

Richard frowned. "Before we seek your opinion, we need facts. What defenses does the city have? When were they last inspected?"

"I see what you mean," Justin replied, nodding. "The city watch, first of all. I have nearly a thousand men, in watchman uniforms, who can help defend the city." Caspur snorted, but then waved off the attention when he realized the others were staring at him. "There are twelve gates that can be barred and shut. We have access to the river as well. The Stews, as you know, is across the river. There are fewer defenses there, but the river becomes a natural barrier. There are four bridges that span the river and each has a gatehouse and guard."

"How much food do we have stored?" Richard asked next.

"Enough to last a siege of six months, maybe more, but I will be cautious in my estimate. We have been expecting the armada to strike, remember, and—"

"King Brannon had abandoned Comoros to destruction," Caspur interrupted again. "I served on the previous Privy Council, Maia—what he tells you is not fully true."

Maia gave Caspur an even look. "I told all of you that I expect you to speak your minds," she said, keeping her voice very low and controlled. "I appreciate that. But it seems to me that this is the type of debate my father permitted. Each man speaking over his neighbor. Arguing and wrestling. My lord, that will prevent the Medium from helping us. Each must be given a turn to speak. You will be given yours. Please . . . do not interrupt him again."

"Thank you," Justin said, squaring his shoulders. He gave Caspur a sharp look, but he continued with good humor. "As I was saying, we expected the armada to strike. We have chains in the river ready to hoist up and help bar the fleet from sailing into the city. Comoros was designed to withstand a sea attack. Pent Tower was specifically built to prevent the city from falling prey to such a tactic, and walls and barriers throughout the city provide rings of defense. It would take a sizable force, and by that I mean ten thousand men, to force entry. I do not believe Forshee has that many."

Maia looked at him. "Justin, you forget that the Earl of Forshee is sitting here among us. Let us call the man by his true name. Kord Schuyler. He is no longer the Earl of Forshee. Indeed, he is in open rebellion against the Crown. Are there any other defenses to use for the city? How can we evacuate the townspeople?"

Justin wrinkled his brow. "Why would we do that?"

Maia glanced at Richard, and was relieved to see he understood.

"Because she is not only considering the threat of this rebel army," the chancellor said. "The Naestors' armada is on its way. She has seen the size of the fleet. They will have more than ten thousand soldiers. They may have ten times that amount."

"A hundred thousand soldiers?" Justin asked, his mouth gaping open as he considered the number.

"Indeed," Richard said. "What is the evacuation plan for the city?"

The mayor looked completely unprepared to answer. "I . . . I do not have . . . well . . . what we could do . . ."

Richard shook his head. "Facts, Lord Mayor. It is clear that we do not *have* an evacuation plan for the city. Please work with the ealdermen to prepare one. This is important. It may help us during the rebellion, but it will certainly be necessary once the armada comes." He turned to Dodd.

"Lord Price, what have you learned about Kord Schuyler's power? When your father was Earl of Forshee, how many men could he bring to bear?"

Dodd looked much calmer than he had appeared at the beginning of the meeting, and he seemed almost pleased by the question. "I have spoken to the court historian. Kord had assembled three earldoms under his command, two in the north and one in the south. Combined, they give him the right to call fifteen thousand men, if all will heed and serve him. I have already been approached by many of my vassals, who have pledged their support to me. I believe five thousand will come if I call. More may rally, but that is my best information for the moment. My understanding is that Billerbeck Hundred is faithful to my Family. They are assembling soldiers even now."

Richard nodded. "How long would it take to march them here?"

Dodd frowned. "It may be a fortnight."

Shaking his head, Caspur murmured to himself but did not address the group.

Richard nodded. "How long will it take you to reach that Hundred and determine whether you can raise that many?"

"I planned to take the Apse Veil to Billerbeck Abbey today," Dodd said, giving Maia a quick smile. "That saves me two days of riding."

Suzenne beamed as he said it, and Maia could not help but smile with them. "The situation has indeed changed," Maia said. "The full rites of the abbeys have been restored. That will hasten this work. Thank you, Dodd. You have my leave to go whenever you are ready."

"Thank you," he said, grinning. She saw him sneak his hand under the table to clasp Suzenne's.

Richard fumbled with some of the scrolls on his desk. "Ah, this is it," he said, withdrawing one. "Lord Caspur, you gave this to me last night. Your earldom is still intact. Please educate the council on your situation."

The earl rose swiftly, brushing his hands together. He was struggling to control his expression, for Maia could see the admonishment he had received was difficult for him to endure. "I beg your pardon. We need to act swiftly, so forgive my agitation. I had hoped to be on the saddle already and riding for my domain. I cannot . . . use the Apse Veil, as Lord Price can, so I must be away and quickly. Schuyler had the largest domain in the realm. He is a formidable enemy, Lady Maia, and tested. Your father made him warden of the army, and he was quick and ruthless with his power. He has men like Trefew serving him. While some of his soldiers may be inclined to serve Lord Price," he added with a subtle urgency in his tone, "he will execute any man who flees his camp. Your Highness, a rebellion gains size the longer it lasts. He strikes at you now because he knows you are at your weakest. If you would appoint me to be the warden—"

Maia's brow furrowed. "Please . . . before we discuss that, help me understand how many soldiers you can muster and how soon. It sounds like you still need to summon them."

"Yes," he said through clenched teeth. He was fidgeting, which Maia did not like. "If you insist on the formalities, so be it. I can bring nine thousand men from the west. If we march to Comoros, we can be here in five or six days. But I suggest you send me to face Kord Schuyler directly. It would be wiser to fight a battle *before* he reaches the city. If I can bar his way, then Lord Price can attack him from behind while I serve as a wall in front and"—he clapped his hands—"we have him defeated! He is your biggest threat at the moment, Maia. If it is quick and decisive, you will put down the rebellion."

Maia did not feel right about his words, which were delivered too quickly, with a manic sort of energy. She wondered at that.

Perhaps her doubt showed. Richard said, "My lord earl, I feel *uneasy* about your assessment."

Caspur glowered. "And what would an *Aldermaston* know of armies and soldiers?"

The deliberate barb struck Maia, and she felt her anger stirring, but she tamped it down with effort. This was how her father used to run his Privy Council. She could see the tension in Caspur's eyes, the eagerness for . . . for what?

Glory.

She felt the sudden urge for Jon Tayt's counsel. Thinking of him almost made her smile. Back at Muirwood, her dearest advisors and friends had all believed as she did and held the same intentions. As she gazed at her Privy Council, she realized it would take much longer for this group to reach a conclusion.

"That is why I chose him, you see," Maia said softly, looking at Richard Syon with a growing heart. She trusted him. She respected him. Having long ago learned to master his anger, he was not ruffled by the earl's provocation. Once the very man they discussed, Kord Schuyler, the former Earl of Forshee, had come to Muirwood to threaten him. He was unflappable. "Please, Lord Caspur. Be more civil."

Caspur's face mottled with rage and he clenched his jaw, clearly struggling to accept the rebuke of a young woman. His voice was almost a low growl when he next spoke. "Maia, I have risked everything siding with you. If Schuyler is not stopped quickly, he will not only take your crown, but also my head. Forgive me if I am impatient, but I know what to do. I have a force strong enough to challenge his, especially if Lord Price's force joins us from the north. Do not fight him so near the city. A river gains strength as it flows down from the mountain. Do not let him become a flood." He raised his hands and shrugged. "You do not have a seasoned battle commander, my lady, except for me. Give me this charge, and I will bring the rebel to heel."

And it was his lack of humility that made Maia realize she could not trust him with that authority. But if she did not, who would stand against her enemies?

He who is to be a good ruler must have first been ruled. Men must be trained to obey and obey absolutely. Fear is education. Peril is persuasion. We dreaded the return of the mastons from Assinica. As we look at the plunder we have harvested from their lands, we marvel at the strangeness of their creations. Musical instruments never before devised. Gears and pulleys and levers melded into new creations we do not yet know how to use. These people are geniuses. It will take a lifetime to unravel their mysteries after they have been destroyed.

—*Corriveaux Tenir, Victus of Dahomey*

CHAPTER SIXTEEN

Counsel

There was no unity among her council members. Maia saw open distrust and hostility in Justin's eyes as he glared at the Earl of Caspur. With such a threat looming against them, it was no wonder. And yet she would not allow herself to be bullied into giving Caspur his way. That would not bode well for the future.

"I have not heard from you yet, Lord Paget," Maia said, turning to her old advisor from Bridgestow. He was the most quiet member of the council, and she had come to learn he rarely spoke unless addressed specifically. "What is your counsel?"

Lord Paget had gray-blond hair that receded up his hairline and a darker goatee sprinkled with white. Clearly surprised to be addressed so pointedly, he sat up and began to fidget. Caspur looked at the man with growing disdain, as if annoyed someone who lived on the borders of the realm had been allowed to join the Privy Council. But Maia knew that he had served on her grandfather's council in the past.

He looked full of unease as he spoke. "Your Majesty, it is a difficult problem, to be sure."

Caspur sniffed and cleared his throat, his expression growing more impatient by the moment.

"I would value your counsel," Maia prodded.

The man looked a little flustered by Caspur's impatience, but his voice grew strength as he spoke. "It is easy, in my opinion, to start a rebellion. And yet it takes fuel to feed it. When men grow hungry or are unpaid, they turn fractious. Kord Schuyler seems to be hoping for a quick victory. The longer you stay on the throne, my queen, the more his supporters will dwindle. He is risking much, to be sure, but his march on Comoros is an attempt to make you act rashly." At these words, he gave Caspur a pointed look. "Two forces of unequal size can be mitigated across a battle-field, depending on who has the more favorable ground. I learned from my dealings with the Pry-rians that a smaller force can easily repel a larger force if sitting in a defensible position, be it a river at their back, a fenland on their flank. I cannot think of a more defensible position than a walled city."

Justin flashed the man a smile, looking pleased at his assessment. Caspur just glowered, clearly more angry than ever.

"So you would suggest we let him come to us," Maia said.

Paget nodded quickly. "Any delay benefits you, my lady. An army needs supplies. It runs out of food quickly. Hot passions begin to subside. Defend the heart of your realm, and you preserve the core."

Caspur looked impatient to speak.

"Yes?" Maia asked, turning to him, thankful he had not interrupted.

"While I applaud Lord Paget's words, I would challenge his experience. Have you ever led soldiers into battle, my lord? From whence comes this knowledge? There has not been war with Pry-Ree for centuries."

Paget stiffened, his look darkening. "I have read a good deal . . ."

"Books," Caspur snorted with derision.

". . . and I assisted the chancellor's office in outfitting and supplying the king's armies." He gave Richard Syon an imploring look.

"That experience may prove useful," Richard said, nodding his head. "I may call on you."

There was a sudden shift of tension, and Maia felt certain in that moment that her council was not behind Caspur's ideas.

"I would hear from everyone," Maia continued. "Suzenne?"

Her friend looked flustered. "I have no experience that would be helpful," she said, her cheeks flushing.

Maia gave her an encouraging nod.

After wrestling with herself for a moment, Suzenne finally said, "What of the children? The families to be displaced? If there is to be a siege of the city, they will suffer. I agree that we must have a plan to evacuate the sick, the young, and those who cannot defend themselves."

"Thank you," Maia said. "Please work with the lord mayor and offer your suggestions to him. Consider where they may be moved and how to supply them with their needs."

Caspur wrung his hands, clearly sensing he had lost the room. "Lady Maia, I *insist* that you hear me out. I have more experience than all the rest of these council members combined. Put me in charge of your army, and I swear to you, by Idumea's hand, I will put down this rebellion and bring Schuyler before you in chains for punishment. Marching my army to defend the city would mean leaving my own lands unguarded. I know what Paget meant by choosing good ground. This realm is more familiar to me than it is to most, as I have holdings throughout. I would choose a battlefield that would give us a sure advantage. Why trouble the citizenry at all, Your Grace? Give me the command, I implore you!"

Maia could almost *feel* his desperation for glory. That would lead to foolish decisions. Her trust would be earned, not taken for granted.

"I *have* heard you," Maia said, staring into his eyes. She shook her head, using that gesture to begin communicating the news that would disappoint him. "Comoros is a vast city, split by a river. Losing control of it would be disastrous. These are my instructions. Dodd—bring as many forces as you can and march them quickly to Comoros. If you raise your banners, you may draw some of Schuyler's soldiers away. Do not engage with his army. Lord Mayor, prepare to defend the city. Have your watchmen trained and keep them sober, my lord. Will a curfew help you maintain order?"

Justin beamed. "It would indeed. With your permission?"

"You have it." She turned to her chancellor. "Richard, see that the order is written and affix it with the seal granting authority." It was only then that she turned back to the Earl of Caspur. "Bring your army to Comoros to defend us. You have the largest force and the most experience in battle. Some of the vigor being used to challenge us may wane in time. It will give us more options if we force Schuyler to react to us rather than reacting to him. Do not engage his army, my lord. Bring your army here."

His jaw quivered with disappointed rage, but though his eyes burned with enmity, he gave her a curt nod and made no comment.

"Go make your preparations," Maia said. "Report back to the chancellor regularly. Keep him informed of your progress."

She dismissed the council.

***

The rest of the day was long and wearisome. Being a queen, Maia discovered, was replete with commitments and obligations. It seemed every person in the realm wanted to see her, speak with her, implore her for a position or a favor. Thankfully, her chancellor controlled access to her during the formal times of the day. Only in rare moments could he travel back to Augustin to see his wife and assist her with her duties in the abbey, and Maia hurt for them, knowing the separation was painful.

Suzenne served the same gate-keeping function during Maia's private hours. The two were enjoying an elaborate meal in Maia's private chambers. Her other ladies-in-waiting, including Jayn Sexton, were also there, helping to arrange an assortment of gowns, traveling clothes, blankets, and household items that she had found herself owning without knowing how. Many of the pieces, she learned, had belonged to her mother before being usurped by Lady Deorwynn. After Suzenne, Maia was closest to Jayn and appreciated her quiet ways and thoughtfulness.

Maia's appetite had waned with the threat of rebellion, but the soup was good, and she nibbled on the loaf of trencher bread.

"I miss the Aldermaston's kitchen at Muirwood," Maia said to Suzenne.

Her friend smiled and nodded in agreement. One of the other girls had picked up a lute and had begun plucking simple chords from it—the sound a lovely accompaniment to their meal.

"What did you think of the council meeting this morning?" Maia asked.

Suzenne fidgeted with her spoon. "Caspur looked quite . . . displeased, but I do not know what else you could have done. He seemed determined to get his way. I am glad you did not give in. He made it very uncomfortable, though."

"He did," Maia agreed. "It will take time before the council acts in harmony. I confess, it is difficult to discern the motives of every person. Caspur means well, I think, but he is very ambitious. His need for glory clouds his judgment."

She continued to eat the soup. A dish of spiced fish was nearby, and she plucked a few flaky crumbs from it with her fingers. The cooks always insisted on bringing her a variety of dishes and had tried to learn about her favorites. She had admitted to a fondness for Pry-rian cooking, which had upset the head cook very much. She sighed aloud. It was just too difficult to attempt pleasing everyone.

There was a short knock at the door, and Suzenne sighed and pushed away from the table to answer it. Maia did not feel like seeing visitors. In truth, she yearned to don a simple disguise so she could leave the palace grounds to visit the people and learn firsthand about their troubles and the mood—much as her own husband did on occasion in his own kingdom. She did not want to rely solely on the lord mayor's telling. Suzenne's expression changed quickly, and she turned aside to admit Sabine and Simon Fox.

Smiling eagerly, Maia rose to greet them and rushed to embrace her grandmother. "Have you eaten yet?" Maia asked her. "We have more than enough. Come share with us."

Sabine smiled and patted her back. "I had a meal already, but thank you. If we could speak privately?"

Suzenne nodded and quickly dismissed the ladies-in-waiting, who left the chamber from a back exit without even a murmur. Jayn Sexton paused in the doorway, looking back to see if Suzenne would join her, but Sabine gestured for her to stay. When her private chamber was private once more, Maia gave her grandmother a worried look. "What is it?"

Sabine's expression was thoughtful, pensive. "I know about your troubles, Maia. I have heard about the rebellion. But I must leave Comoros again almost as quickly as I have arrived."

Maia's heart sank. "I know I should not strive to keep you here longer," she said, taking her grandmother's hands and squeezing them tenderly. "But it pains me to be apart from you. You are my only Family. Where must you go next?"

Sabine shook her head sadly. "I still have duties to perform, dear one. I must continue to open the Apse Veils throughout the realms. I have already opened one each in Avinion and Mon. I go to Dahomey next and then Paeiz." She glanced at Simon. "There is troubling news, Maia. I must go to Hautland as well."

Maia stiffened. "But they are loyal to the Dochte Mandar," she said.

Sabine nodded. "I know. Simon received word from the Hand of the Victus. The Hand is the one who directs them. The person in that position is given his title because of the saying, 'the hand directs the knife.' The Victus, as you know, employs various machinations throughout the kingdoms. They are behind Paeiz's attack on Dahomey. They seek nothing but turmoil and conflict; their aim is to pit each kingdom against the other. Obviously they want to embroil Dahomey in a war with its neighbor to prevent your husband from defending Comoros when the armada comes."

Maia's heart wrenched at the mention of her husband. She missed him dreadfully and had not heard from him since he had sailed from Comoros.

"What news have you received then?"

"The Hand communicates throughout the realms through waymarker Leerings they have stolen. One of the properties of Leerings is to bind two points that are distant, allowing individuals to touch minds and speak to each other."

Maia knew about this phenomenon already, having experienced it in the cursed shores of Dahomey. She had touched a

Leering to summon water and had found herself ensnared in a duel of wills with Corriveaux and another Dochte Mandar.

"Yes," Maia said, revolted by the memory of wearing the kystrel, "I have used a Leering that way in the past."

Sabine turned to Simon. "Tell her the rest."

She had not seen Simon for several days. His dark eyes were even more brooding than usual. "The Hand of the Victus has changed. I normally would not mention something like this to you, except you know the man who now leads them. His name is Corriveaux, from Dahomey."

Maia felt a cold shudder at the mention of his name. He had hunted her throughout the realms, conspired to make her the queen of the hetaera. The Medium had saved her from him in Naess, where she had feared her journey would end.

"You told me of him," Suzenne said, touching Maia's arm. She looked grave. "He was in authority with the Dochte Mandar in Dahomey. He hunted you."

"And he leads them now?" Maia asked, new fear blossoming in her heart. In all the times she had faced him, his power of will with the kystrel had exceeded her own. And yet now she served the Medium without using some trinket to control it. Surely that would make a difference.

"Indeed," Simon said. "I received word from my master that Corriveaux suspects him of betraying the Victus. He believed that Corriveaux would test his loyalty." He looked so dark and serious, and every word he spoke carried a weight. "He will very likely test my own loyalty as well. Walraven would like to meet Sabine in Hautland to discuss recent events. He seeks her wisdom and input on how to proceed. It may be time for Walraven to come out openly against Corriveaux."

Maia felt a warning throb from the Medium. "I do not like this," she whispered.

"Nor do I," Sabine replied. "Messages delivered through Leerings are troubling because you do not always know the identity of the sender. There are Dochte Mandar throughout each major city of the realm who transcribe and transmit these messages. So while the message Simon received claims to be from Walraven, I have my suspicions."

"I felt a warning from the Medium," Maia said.

Sabine touched her arm. "As have I," she replied. Suzenne's expression was grave as she listened.

"What will you do?" Maia asked.

"There are abbeys under construction throughout the realms," Sabine said. "I plan to go to Hautland to open the Apse Veil in Viegg anyway. But the Cruciger orb tells me Walraven is still in Naess. I will check it every day. If he stays in Naess, then I know it is a trap from Corriveaux. But if the Cruciger orb shows him in Hautland, then I will know it is possible to meet him there. I trust the Cruciger orb will guide me to him. I will take some Evnissyen with me, of course. But I am concerned about Walraven. I have an uneasy feeling whenever I think about him."

Maia frowned—the disquiet inside her had not abated. "I will worry about you, Grandmother," she said. "I could not bear it if anything happened to you."

Sabine smiled and smoothed Maia's cheek. "We have an advantage the Victus do not share. With the Apse Veils restored, we can send mastons across the kingdoms very quickly. As I travel from realm to realm, I will ask for help to join you in Comoros. You have the support of Pry-Ree and Dahomey. We must negotiate the support of other kingdoms so we can wrench loose the yoke of the Naestors completely." She sighed. "How I wish I had

Lia's Gift of Seering. Instead, we must stumble ahead through the fog, not knowing the way. But the Medium will guide us."

Maia felt pain in her heart at the thought of not seeing her grandmother for a while.

"There is more," Simon said, reaching into his tunic and withdrawing a sealed letter. "I have not read the contents."

"From my husband?" Maia asked eagerly.

Simon smiled and handed her the letter. It bore the royal seal of Dahomey. "It came a short while ago. I am told he arrived safely."

Maia broke the seal and opened the letter, her heart filling with giddiness at the prospect of seeing her husband's words.

The first thing she noticed sent a stab of terror through her heart. It was the signature at the end. *Corriveaux.*

Greetings, Queen Maia of Comoros

Knowing full well that you can read, I address this to you personally. If my will has been done, this note has reached you through the hand of one of my loyal supporters in your realm. I congratulate you on your coronation. You will not long wear your crown. When you betrayed us and refused to lend your support to our cause, do not suppose that I would let you claim a crown without my consent. I hereby warn you, Marciana Soliven, that I am coming for you. I will strike the heart of your realm first. Your heart, to be precise. You will suffer greatly for your arrogance and conceit. What you have been given can be ripped from you. You will watch your people be murdered. Those you have sheltered from Assinica will curse your name in the end. You will learn firsthand the consequences of defying me. Yes, I am coming for you, Maia. Be warned.

Corriveaux

CHAPTER SEVENTEEN

Uprising

Corriveaux's message served its intended purpose. Though Maia's grandmother had warned her that the message's intent was to cause fear and worry, the very emotions that would repel the Medium's assistance, in the days following her receipt of the note, she often found herself ruminating over it.

It did comfort her to hear directly from Collier not long after she received her enemy's ominous missive. Her husband had scrawled a quick note confiding his plans to bring the Paeizians to heel. She could easily imagine him in the costume of Feint Collier, dashing around the countryside on his cream-colored horse, and she secretly wished she could join him. In her darkest hours, she could not help but worry for him; Corriveaux had threatened her heart . . . could he plan on attacking her husband? She was anxious for Collier to pass the maston test, but it had taken several months of study for the Medium to permit her to take it.

Her days were no longer full of meetings, as her council was busy implementing the plan they had adopted. She had not inspected the city's defenses yet, but the city watch was on patrol. Maia had no recent word from Caspur, increasing her sense of dread, but a note had arrived via courier from Dodd that he had three thousand men marching day and night from the north.

Reports indicated that Kord Schuyler's army was moving slowly, gathering more volunteers each day, but it was still two days from Comoros. Maybe three.

In the late afternoon, she was speaking to Richard in the chancellor's tower when they were interrupted by the sound of boots rushing up the stairwell. Maia was poring over rosters of provisions and inventories of weapons and hastily set them down, alarmed by the sound. Comoros had a sizable armory and there were plenty of spears, swords, chain hauberks, helmets, shields, arrows—enough to outfit a sizable army . . . if only they had the soldiers to use them. The city blacksmiths were hammering all day long as well, repairing broken weapons and armor and manufacturing new ones.

"I feel comfortable," Richard said, glancing at the doorway, "that we have enough provisions for a month, maybe two if we ration. I advise using the river to ferry in new supplies from around the realm. If there is a chance the city will be under siege for some time, we will do better to be prepared."

Simon Fox appeared on the stairwell, his face flushed and pale. He was normally very calm, so the extent of his agitation was alarming in itself.

"What is it, Simon?" Maia asked. The chancellor just stared at their visitor in concern, his brows knit together.

"My lady," Simon said, almost out of breath. "Pardon . . . but as soon as I found out, I ran all the way from my shop."

"Speak," Maia implored, feeling a well of darkness open up beneath her before he even explained the situation.

"Caspur has betrayed you," Simon said curtly, beginning to pace.

"Oh no," Maia whispered. "What has he done?"

Simon ran a hand through his hair and continued to walk the room. "When you told me how insistent he was on leading a force against Schuyler's, I sent some of my men to follow his movements. My lady, he raised a force of ten thousand from his domains. He was urgent in his preparations, acting as my men thought one in his position should. He started them marching almost immediately. That was four days ago. I thought all was well until his army suddenly veered to the north to intercept Schuyler's."

Maia closed her eyes, feeling the terrible moment keenly.

"It is worse, my lady," Simon said vehemently. "By design or not, I do not know, but when Caspur's army closed with Schuyler's, the two were camped near each other. In the morn, his men joined Schuyler's."

Richard's expression was even more grave, if that were possible. "They joined, Simon?"

The Dahomeyjan spymaster nodded vigorously. "My lady, combined, they are nearly unstoppable. Even if Lord Price gets here in time, his troops will hardly make a difference. My lady, you are betrayed. Schuyler's army is also much closer than you realize. The outriders will reach the city limits sometime tomorrow."

Maia felt light-headed as she turned to look at her chancellor. "We have more money and resources, but we lack time to summon them. My husband is caught fighting his own war. My grandmother left for Hautland, and even if Pry-Ree were willing to offer their support for our internal war, it would take too long for their troops to arrive."

Simon scratched the back of his head roughly. "This is a peril-ous hour. I came straight here. No one else knows. If the city finds out, there will be a panic and an exodus."

"*When* they find out," Maia corrected him. "This is not a secret we can keep." She sighed in despair. "Should I have given him the command after all? I did not believe him capable of such treachery. He and Schuyler are rivals. Caspur stands more to gain if he supports me than his enemy. I am hurt, but I am also astonished. I truly did not believe him capable of such a betrayal."

Richard stared solemnly at the floor for a moment and then lifted his gaze to her face. "I also did not expect him to betray the Crown. He threw in his lot with you when your father was murdered. Speaking of which, the interment of his body was supposed to happen tomorrow. I suppose that must be altered. Our options, it seems, are few."

Simon folded his arms. "Fight, flee, or fail. There are truly only three choices. By fail, I mean capitulate . . . surrender. You do not have enough troops to fight. If you flee now, you will lose your throne forever. Taking back a lost throne is almost impos-sible. And if you surrender . . . I cannot imagine Schuyler will show you mercy. He was only too eager to behead you when you were your father's prisoner."

Maia started pacing. "There is only one choice," she said, shaking her head firmly. "We must fight with whatever force we have available to us. The citizens must help . . . and to help, they must be told. We do not have time to waste. Richard, sum-mon Justin and any available Privy Council members. We must share this news immediately. I will not be returning to Muirwood tonight."

"But my lady," Simon implored. "Are there no mastons we can summon to aid us?"

"We must and will summon every ally we can," Maia said. "I will meet you in the council room. I had promised to inspect the kitchens this afternoon. I will do that now while you gather the council. I need a moment to think and prepare. Tell me as soon as everyone has been summoned."

Richard nodded and rose quickly from his desk. Simon looked greensick with worry as he unbolted the door. Collier had left him to advise her, a task that had to seem futile at the moment. She could see that he was determining the possible outcomes, and all of them looked equally bleak.

"Courage, Simon," Maia said, resting her hand on his shoulder. Though she addressed the words to him, she knew she was really telling herself.

***

Maia wrung her hands as she walked down the hall toward the castle kitchen. Dinner was underway, and she could smell the scents of baking bread and sizzling meat. Normally it would have made her mouth water, but her knowledge of the impending attack had buried her appetite. The kitchen worked day and night to feed so many, and Maia was concerned that young children were being worked too hard or treated with excessive harshness. She loved visiting Muirwood's kitchen, but the castle kitchen lacked any kind of hominess. Here there were ten chimneys, dozens of tables, two larders, a pen holding animals to butcher, and cellars stuffed with sacks of vegetables and grains.

It would be difficult to explain the situation to the Privy Council. She wanted to trust that the Medium would lead them to victory—that Dodd's three thousand men could come out ahead just as Garen Demont's small force had done at the battle of Winterrowd. And truly she did trust that the Medium would protect them from Kord Schuyler, a man who denigrated others and scorned Aldermastons. But the struggle before them still terrified her, and she could not forget how many lives she carried in her hands.

The thoughts made her frown with anger, and she noticed several servants were gathered outside the kitchen, staring at her with concern. She turned the frown into an apologetic smile and continued toward the kitchen door. One of the servants bustled up to her, his look nervous.

"Your Majesty, we knew you were coming, but there is a problem in the kitchen. We need a few more moments before your visit."

Maia did not slow her stride. "Unfortunately Solomon, I do not have time to delay. I must be at a Privy Council meeting shortly. I will not stay long."

He seemed desperate to persuade her otherwise. "Well, it is just that there is a *situation* and I had hoped it to be resolved already, but it is not."

Maia raised her eyebrows. "What do you mean?"

The servant looked flustered. He was tall and lanky and very proper. Her father had given special uniforms to the court servants denoting their place within the hierarchy. While Maia cared nothing for such matters, she was trying to learn the various protocols of the lower staff. Her hunch would be that this fellow ranked highly.

"Well, Your Majesty instructed us to feed any vagrant who entered the castle hungry. One arrived earlier this afternoon and . . . well, he has not only eaten a fair amount, but he has also rattled the cooks with his advice about how to cook properly."

Maia's eyes widened with surprise. "I wish to meet him at once," she said, hardly daring to hope.

"Well, if you insist," Solomon said bleakly, wringing his hands. The doors opened and as Maia entered, she heard Jon Tayt's voice ring out with a laugh.

"The entire kingdom of Dahomey eats cheese this way, by Cheshu!" he roared. "Melted! Little metal skewers dipped into bowls. It burns your mouth at first, but if you add the right spices to the cheese . . . oooooh, I tell you there is no finer feast than this."

Maia's heart nearly burst when she saw Jon Tayt slouched over on a barrel, his belt stuffed with throwing axes, his cloak askew off one thick shoulder, his coppery hair ruffled from the journey. He looked over his shoulder at her when the door opened, and the warm smile he gave her made tears sting her eyes.

"Ah lass," he said, leaning forward and grunting as he stood. "Made queen at last. What a kettle of fish." There were crumbs in his beard and grease stains on his shirt front, but he looked and smelled and laughed like Jon Tayt, and she had never been so happy in her life to see someone.

Maia shocked the entire kitchen when she rushed forward and gave him a fierce hug. The dawning realization that this opinionated traveler was a *friend* of the Queen of Comoros seemed to stun the kitchen staff into silence.

Jon Tayt put a meaty arm around her shoulders, its very weight and heaviness a comfort. "I was attempting to explain to these skillful cooks the finer points of Dahomeyjan culture. I think I may have offended several, but I was only trying to help them impress you for dinner by bringing you something you would enjoy." He cast his gaze around the kitchen, raising his eyebrows mischievously. "Mayhap next time you will heed my counsel," he said to a few frightened-looking chefs clustered at a nearby counter. "The meal, which was delicious, I thank you for. I am pleased to see, my lady, that you insist on feeding travelers."

He patted his belly with satisfaction. "Satisfying my appetite took some doing, by Cheshu."

"What are you doing here?" Maia gasped with delight. She stroked some hair behind her ear and pulled Jon Tayt away from the kitchen staff. She gave a nod to Solomon to indicate all was well and she would escort him from the kitchen so they could continue their work. She took Jon Tayt back into the hall and started toward the council room.

Jon Tayt smiled and fingered one of his axe blades. "I suppose you could say the Medium bade me to come. Or you did. To be honest, I have not been my normal cheerful self lately. It is not enough to only see you in passing now and then at the abbey grounds. I am not a maston, of course, so I could not cross the Apse Veil. But word came from Aldermaston Wyrich. He said there was a pressing need . . . that you were in danger and needed protection. He sent me three days ago and I just arrived. What is amiss?"

A flushed feeling of warmth came into Maia's heart. Jon Tayt was one man. But he was her friend, her traveling companion, and—additionally—an Evnissyen. Members of his family were traditionally advisors and protectors of the rulers of Pry-Ree, and her grandmother had sent this man to Dahomey to watch and wait for her. She felt Jon Tayt had been aware of her for her entire life. The relief it gave her to be in his mere presence was staggering. She had thought of summoning him to help track down the kishion, but events had overwhelmed everyone, and the message had never been sent.

She quickly shared the news from Simon Fox, warning him of the implications. If they were in the middle of a civil war when the Naestors posed their invasion, they would provide an easy target.

Jon Tayt rubbed his nose as they walked, listening carefully to her. "You would be amazed, Maia, at how few it takes to conquer many. I know this problem is urgent and difficult, and I assure you it will not be easy. But consider how Pry-Ree fares beside such a large and violent neighbor. We have tactics for occasions such as this one. There are ways you can mislead another army into thinking you are bigger than you are. If Schuyler believes he is marching into a trap, he will be hesitant and overcautious."

Maia felt a ray of hope brightening inside her. She could not help but grin at him. "Are you telling me, Jon Tayt, that there is a proper way to defend a city during a siege?"

"My lady, there is only one *proper* way to defend a city or fight a war. And it just so happens that I know the secret. It is simple. Be wise and always do the unpredictable. We will make those false earls believe we have ten times our number. Once a Pry-rian captain ordered his men to run through the woods in circles to make them look mightier . . . and it worked. It is not a hopeless situation, lass." He hooked his arm around hers. "Let me tell you a little story while we walk."

If fear is pain arising from the anticipation of evil, then we must unleash the anticipation of the most evil possible. Fear chases away the Medium. It leads to doubt and then despair. Fear will win us this war.

—*Corriveaux Tenir, Victus of Dahomey*

CHAPTER EIGHTEEN

Ludgate

It was past midnight, but no one in the castle was asleep. Maia and Suzenne sat near each other on a comfortable couch, their hands gripped together. Their last report from Dodd revealed that he was pushing his men to exhaustion, but they would still not arrive at the city for several days. They would arrive well after Schuyler's force. Meanwhile, reports that Schuyler's army had reached the outer villages surrounding the capital had unleashed a mass panic in the city. Curfew was being enforced, but some families were trying to slip away and flee into the countryside in the night. The gates were closed and under constant watch, but much of the city had been built up outside the walls. The citizens were rightly terrified.

"And I thought I felt ill at ease the night before Whitsunday," Suzenne said, pressing her other hand against her forehead. "Will these pangs of dread never leave us, Maia?"

The other ladies-in-waiting were gathered with them in Maia's chamber. All of them wore nightgowns and shawls, but everyone was too nervous to sleep. Maia had another reason to fight sleep. Every time her eyelids grew heavy, a dark feeling fluttered in her heart—anxious, watchful, waiting . . .

"We have no army," one of the girls, Raquelle, said nervously, wringing her hands and fidgeting. Her lashes were wet with tears. Jayn Sexton walked over and put an arm around her. Maia appreciated how calm and collected the other girl appeared to be, and she herself tried to radiate that same comforting presence.

Maia patted Suzenne's hand. "Much of my life has been spent in dread. I suppose I am used to it."

There was a series of loud noises, followed by the solemn pounding of boots in the corridor. Maia released Suzenne and stood just as the door was thrust open and armed men burst into the chamber. Jon Tayt was at the front, wearing a chain hauberk. His left arm was enclosed in metal—bracers, gauntlet, ribbed shoulder guard. He looked like a ferocious man—half metal, half beast—and the look in his eyes frightened half the girls out of their wits.

"Who is that! Will they kill us!"

"Do not harm us!"

Raquelle shrieked hysterically, which made many of the others rise up and turn as white as their chemises. Jon Tayt frowned in annoyance and marched up to Maia, trailed by Richard and by Maia's personal guard. Simon Fox slipped in at the end of the small procession.

"*Chut!*" Jon Tayt barked curtly as if he were trying to silence Argus. It both made Maia smile and hurt her heart. The hysterical girls quieted, but they still shivered fearfully.

"Please," Maia said. "Settle down." She turned back to her advisors. "Where is Justin?"

"At Ludgate," Jon Tayt said with a sniff. He hooked his gloved hand around the axe head wedged in his belt. "We need someone with authority there in case the force strikes before dawn. That gate is the closest to the palace and the abbey. If it falls, the city falls with it." He wiped his nose and gave another sharp look at the whimpering girls. Suzenne and Jayn were trying their best to soothe their fears, but the ladies-in-waiting were clearly unsettled by the presence of armed knights and soldiers in the queen's chamber. Undoubtedly it did not help that they were still in their nightclothes. Appearing to sense that it would be next to impossible to calm the girls, Suzenne and Jayn began to lead them out of the room.

Richard pulled out a long parchment scroll and swept his hand across the nearest table to clear away the trays and chalices. He unrolled the scroll, revealing it as a marked-up map of the city.

"Maia, access to the city is controlled by twelve gates," he said in a somber but unhurried tone, his thick finger quickly identifying each of them. His tone was as even and measured as if he were explaining a favorite quote from his tome, rather than the approach of an enormous army. "Ludgate is the closest to the palace, as you see. Most of the citizens have moved inside the walls, but a third or a quarter of them will probably choose to remain outside and ride out the storm of uncertainty."

"Attempting to guard twelve positions will divide our defenders too much," Maia said.

Jon Tayt sniffed. "I was getting to that," he explained. "You are right, Maia, we cannot guard all twelve gates at once. The Aldermast—I mean, the chancellor—told me about the armory within the city. We have been rounding up able-bodied men to stand watch at the gates. They are dressed in the royal uniforms and carrying spears, but though they *look* like an army, they are about as disciplined as a litter of hungry pups. They will run at the first sign of trouble, by Cheshu, but they are stationed at these other gates to make it seem as if we are heavily fortified."

"How much did you have to pay them?" she asked.

Richard waved away the question. "They are brave enough to *stand* there, but little more. No amount of coin is worth their lives. I agree with Jon Tayt . . . they will flee rather than fight for you."

"Which brings us to Ludgate. What makes you so certain they will strike there?"

"I am no longer the Aldermaston of Muirwood, my dear," Richard said. "But I respect that position and sought counsel from my superior. I asked Aldermaston Wyrich which gate Schuyler's army would attack first."

Jon Tayt grinned wickedly. "It is cheating, in a way," he admitted gruffly. "But knowing where they will strike allows us to shore up this position with the majority of the city watch there." He laid his fat finger on the point. "My lady, Ludgate is also a prison. This is where your father and his ilk imprisoned those who could not afford his taxes and those who refused to sign his acts. The nobles were sent to Pent Tower of course, but not the commoners or the merchants." His wicked grin broadened.

"With your permission," Richard said, "I would like to offer clemency to those still imprisoned in Ludgate. There are easily several hundred men in there. Most of them have no love of Kord Schuyler. They may even be willing to fight for you. It is not much, but it will help if they agree. I was hoping that you could come to Ludgate and pardon the prisoners at dawn. If you gave a speech, even a short one, to the city watch who will defend us and the ealdermen, it would rally their spirits."

It did not escape Maia that they were putting all their trust in the intuition of Aldermaston Wyrich, a man who had visited the city of Comoros only once, for her coronation. If Schuyler attacked any other gate, the defenses would crumble. Adhering to this defense required her to pour all her trust and confidence into the Medium.

"We will be ready at dawn," Maia said firmly.

***

The sound of Maia's stallion clopping on the cobblestones brought eager eyes to every window down Fleet Street. She wore her full regalia, including the gown she had worn on her coronation and her filigree crown. The reins were decorated with sashes of color, and the saddle skirts matched her own. Captain Carew and his knights rode behind her, leading a procession of soldiers toward Ludgate. The dawn air was spiked with cold, and she tried to quell the urge to tremble. She had to appear strong and formidable to her people. They needed to believe their queen would defend them. Her father may not have been loved, but he was a soldier, and no one had questioned his ability to fight or to lead a battle. She knew she would have to prove herself.

Her stallion snorted as it climbed the gentle incline toward Ludgate. The gatehouse was three levels high with a wide arch and portcullis in the middle bottom level. Two smaller arches festooned either side, each containing an iron postern door. The gate was wide enough to permit a vast flow of traffic, which would normally start streaming in and out of the city when the gates opened at dawn. But the gate remained shut this morn. The second and third levels had square windows, barred, which clearly belonged to the prison Jon Tayt had described to her. She could see faces behind the bars. The second two levels had some stone pillars set into them, holding up a stone façade. A cupola crowned the top of Ludgate, and she could see members of the watch gathered along the top of the wall, holding spears and flags bearing the royal colors of Comoros.

As she approached the gatehouse, she sensed something familiar about it. It took her a moment to realize that there were

Leerings set throughout the pillars and the stone façade. As she approached, she *felt* them, almost as if they were reaching out to her. Her heart began to pound with excitement, and she felt a small smile creep across her mouth.

And what purpose do you have? She asked them in her mind as each one revealed itself to her.

The Leerings were part of the city defenses, she realized. The city had been rebuilt when her ancestors returned from Assinica to reclaim it, so these Leerings were not as ancient, but they still served a purpose. A thrill shot through her as the Leerings whispered to her. They had not been used before to defend the city because of the weakness of Comoros's mastons. Their purpose was to repel attackers, to cast a sense of foreboding and fear upon any force attempting to attack the gate, similar to the Leerings defending the abbey doors or the one guarding the passageway leading to the castle. She suspected that each of the other gates were protected by similar Leerings—Leerings *she* could activate.

She nearly burst with excitement and hope. Here was another way in which the Medium would defend them. As she rode up to the edge of Ludgate, she caught sight of Jon Tayt, Richard, and the mayor, who were clustered with the leaders of the city watch and the ealdermen. She could see the puffs of steam coming from their mouths in the cold morning air. The soldiers stared at her—no, *gawked* at her—their eyes growing wide with either fear or respect. She had looked at herself in the mirror before leaving her chambers. Suzenne had woven her hair into an elegant yet fierce style that made her appear more regal.

Trying to subdue her nervousness, she leaned forward in the saddle and lifted her voice to address her city's protectors. She had been grasping for the correct words to say since Jon Tayt left the castle a few hours earlier. In an instant, her thoughts were suddenly clear. It felt as if the Medium were guiding her mouth.

"At my coronation, I was given this ring." She raised her hand, almost as if she were making the maston sign, and let the sunlight play off her glittering coronation ring. "I am now wedded to the realm. This ring has never left my finger since that day, and it never will. I am the trueborn daughter of King Brannon and Queen Catrin." She lowered her arm and leaned forward, her hands resting on the saddle horn. "And you are my people. I do *earnestly* and *tenderly* love you, as a mother loves her children. I will not abandon you, as I was abandoned. I will not punish you, as I was punished. I will defend you, even if only a few will stand with me. I will give *my last drop of blood* to preserve your lives." She swallowed down a swell of emotion as she stared down at them. Some of the men had tears in their eyes, and everywhere she looked there were expressions of fierce determination. "My father imprisoned those who did not obey his unjust laws. Let the prison doors be opened this morning. Some of you have committed crimes for which you ought to be punished. Some of you are here because you could not deny your conscience. Today, I pardon you *all*. You have a new chance at life. A new chance to serve your kingdom and your queen, to defend your realm from injustice. On my word, I promise to pardon you this day. Come and stand tall in defense of your queen. I am your servant, and you are my family."

She felt tears moisten her eyes, but they did not fall. A cheer went up from Ludgate. The lord mayor was staring at her, she noticed, tears streaming down his cheeks. He gave the order and the watch began to open the prison doors.

There was an audible sigh from the crowd as men began filing through the inner doors of the gates. Men dressed in ragged clothes, some showing purple disfigurations from recent beatings.

Some bore scars from torture. Her heart clenched with pain as she watched them file out . . . some barefoot, some with tattered shoes. Richard and Jon Tayt awaited them with chests full of clothes: tunics, boots, liveries with her colors. Some of the ragged men had long beards and hair, their faces tight and drawn with suffering. Some were bone thin and weary and had trouble even walking. Some were proud and defiant. One thing united them . . . and they came to her in droves.

Captain Carew brought up his soldiers to shield Maia, but she waved his men aside and allowed the former prisoners to approach her. Men shuffled toward her to give her some form of salute, whether a nod or a humble bow. There were even a few women who had chosen to suffer in prison with their husbands rather than be parted from them. Some kissed their own hands and then gestured toward her, as if they were too ashamed and rough to kiss her coronation ring. Her heart welled with compassion for these suffering people. The numbers kept pouring forth, dazzling to behold.

One man in the crowd particularly caught her gaze. She recognized him from her coronation day. The knight named Hove who had challenged her right to rule. She noticed him because he was replacing his black-and-white tunic with a royal one. It made her smile. It made her hope.

Suddenly, a shout sounded from outside the crowd, and a rider came charging down the far side of Fleet Street, moving toward the portcullis. He was shouting as he rode at breakneck speed. He dismounted when he reached the gate and the lord mayor met him on the city side of the gate.

"The army is behind me," the rider panted. "Schuyler's army. They are marching toward Ludgate this instant!" His eyes flew to Maia, still mounted on her horse, then to the crowd behind the gate. He did a double take when he realized the numbers of their force had perhaps doubled. "By the Blood, where did all these come from?"

Jon Tayt and Richard pushed through the crowd to reach Maia's side. "Get back to the palace," the hunter growled. "The fighting is about to start. You will get word on what happens here. Go."

Maia looked down at him and shook her head. "No, Jon Tayt. I must stay." She leaned down in the saddle so that they both could hear her. "There are Leerings on the walls. They are part of the city defenses. They will help repel Schuyler's army." She reached down and clasped Richard's shoulder. "Send Suzenne, Jayn, and all the mastons you can find to the city's gates. Have them start summoning the Leerings to protect us. I will invoke these."

A confident smile stretched across Richard's face. "As you command. But what about you?"

"There may be mastons in Schuyler's army. A few, probably. I will stay in case they try to silence the Leerings. I think we all know we will fail if we do not hold Ludgate."

Richard shook his head in wonder. "I do not think the Medium will let us fail. There is a certain feeling . . . yes, I do not think we need worry about failure."

She felt the shuddering of the cobblestones beneath their feet. The men milling around the gate yard felt it too, and everyone began to turn. Jon Tayt gave her a crooked smile and drew two of his throwing axes, one for each hand. He looked . . . frightening . . . in the armor, helm, buckler, and blades. Without another word to anyone, he marched back toward the gatehouse.

Maia looked up and saw the front ranks of Schuyler's army of thousands as it began to march toward Ludgate.

CHAPTER NINETEEN

Remorse

A rough hand suddenly gripped Maia's arm, and she looked down to see the lord mayor's eyes gazing up at her. "Back to the castle, Your Majesty. You are vulnerable here. We will face this rabble."

Maia shook her head sternly. "They will fight harder if I am here. Patience, Justin. The battle begins."

He shook his head worriedly. "It may take them several days to breach Ludgate." The street was full of men who were hastily donning armor and weapons, as well as members of the city watch, who were already prepared for the coming battle. Archers lined the battlement walls, waiting for orders to fire down at the crowd. Beyond the gates, Schuyler's army was assembling, filling the air with their chants and cheers. The air was fraught with anticipation.

"When it begins," Justin said with emotion, "it cannot be controlled. There will be death and blood on both sides, my lady. Go back to the castle! Captain Carew, help me persuade her!"

Maia watched as the captain's stallion nudged its way through the floodwaters of people. His eyes glinted with dark emotion as he stared at the army massing beyond the wall. "He is right, Lady Maia. The streets will be difficult to cross, especially if the men flee."

Maia shook her head. "It is you who do not understand." She wished Richard was still with her, but she had sent him to summon the other mastons. "A moment longer, please. You will see."

"A moment longer," Carew said, "and someone may throw a rock at you and knock you from your horse. You just unleashed all the prisoners in Ludgate. Many are violent men who may not have fancied your pretty speech."

It was getting more difficult to hear his words above the shouting. The prisoners-turned-soldiers were up near the front of the gate, jeering and yelling at Schuyler's troops on the other side. Jon Tayt was among them, trying to keep them in check, but the situation was growing more and more precarious. There was wisdom in the idea of retreating to safety, but she could not abandon her people. She had seen bloodshed before. While it sickened her, she did not think it would overwhelm her.

"Lady Maia, please!" Justin implored.

"No," she stated firmly. "The gatehouse has more protections than you know. I am here to invoke them. How much of the army do you think has arrived?"

Someone jostled her horse accidentally and the animal snorted and stomped. She nearly slipped off the saddle before she managed to right herself and calm her horse.

"Only the first half," Carew said, gazing from his perch over the heads of the men. "They will not need the full force to—"

"It is enough then," Maia said, interrupting him. "I am going to invoke the Leerings on the gatehouse. They are waiting to help us. The Medium is on our side, gentlemen."

She closed her eyes, trying to drown out the ruckus closing in on her and calm her thoughts and mind. She felt the Leerings embedded in the gatehouse thrum to life. It was as if a deep horn blew from the midst of a vast lake, sending ripples throughout the water. The horn was not a physical sound . . . it was something that echoed inside her heart and throbbed within her bones. She felt it to her core. With her will, she directed the force of that power outside the gates, thrusting the power at Schuyler and his army. When she finally looked at them, the eyes of the Leerings burned white-hot with heat and intensity.

The chanting and jeering subsided immediately, as if a clap of thunder had come from a clear sky. Maia could tell that even her own soldiers felt the power of the Leerings, although it was not directed at them. They stood at the gate in mute wonder, weapons held at the ready, as they watched the impact on their adversaries.

The Leerings blasted into the thoughts of the opposing army, filling their minds with dread, fear, and hopelessness. There was confusion on the other side. Then the army started to peel away, shrinking and shriveling before the mental blasts like children afraid of the dark. One by one, the soldiers who had been rushing against the gates began to fall back, their eyes white with terror.

The soldiers loyal to Maia began to stomp their boots in unison. It started with a few men and then spread to others. Maia shut her eyes once more and gripped the reins of her horse, feeling the weight of controlling so many Leerings at once. But they continued to respond to her, obeying her summons to defend the city.

The tempo of the stomping increased. Then a chant began, voices low and rough but growing in volume and energy.

"Long live Queen Maia. Long live Queen Maia. Long live the queen!"

Soon everyone in the street with her was echoing the chant. She opened her eyes, feeling the edges of her vision blur under the force of the power she was channeling. Pressure built in her skull. It felt as if a mountain were perched on her shoulders, but somehow she had the strength to keep it there.

She glanced down at her defenders, at their beards and scars, their crisp dark uniforms and tattered rags. It was a motley force, but she felt their willingness and enthusiasm.

There was shouting at the gates. The opposing force continued to melt away before their eyes, but the men who were trying to flee were blocked by the men arriving. It was a jumbled mess of limbs. Through it all, the Leerings from the gatehouse continued to blast their chords of fear into their minds.

The shouted words began to register, and Maia realized the speaker was Kord Schuyler himself, mounted on horseback. "It is only a trick!" he shouted at his soldiers with obvious fury. "Back, I say! Back to the gate! There is nothing to fear!"

Maia could barely make him out, but she could see well enough to know his army was disintegrating before his eyes. A sudden burst of hope swelled in her breast. They were outnumbered fifteen to one. Yet Schuyler's army was fleeing before the first blows had even been struck. Perhaps it would be possible to weather this storm without blood pouring into the streets.

"Back, you cowards!" Schuyler screamed. "It is your minds that are weak! Fight! You must fight! Kranmir! Kranmir! Where are you! Do something!"

Maia felt a gentle push against her will. Another mind was trying to silence the Leerings. She felt the weight of the opposition, but that opposition could neither sway her, nor force her to release her dominion.

I will not yield, Ely Kranmir, Maia thought angrily. *You must bend me. If you can.*

She could sense slivers of Kranmir's thoughts in the bursts of effort he sent toward the Leerings. But it was like a child pushing against an adult's hands. Kranmir, with all his years and experience, could do nothing to make the Leerings obey. The Medium would not heed him. It would give him no notice whatsoever. She felt his heart quail with dread as he realized she was not forcing the Medium through a kystrel. She had submitted to its will, and it opposed Schuyler and his army. It opposed Kranmir. She felt his mind buckle under the terrible realization.

The pressure stopped abruptly as Kranmir yielded to the impulse to flee. In her mind, she could see him whipping his horse, nearly trampling the soldiers around him as he tried to escape.

Maia fixed her gaze on Schuyler through the gates. "Lord Mayor!" she called out in a booming voice. "Order the watch to open the gates. After them! Do not let the leaders escape!"

Justin's eyes blazed with triumph. He could feel the victory in the air, even though a single blow had not been struck. With a whoop of delight, he shouted to his captain to fulfill the order. A hurrah broke through the chanting, and the hinges and chains of the portcullis began to groan. The men strained with impatience, especially the newly released prisoners.

Maia watched Kord Schuyler wheel his horse around as the gates opened. As soon as the jagged teeth of the portcullis had lifted enough to provide them with an exit, a flood of prisoners and watchmen spilled into the street.

Schuyler slapped his stallion's flanks and joined the ranks of his fleeing men.

***

Before the day was done, the people had named it the Battle of Ludgate. Stories spread through the city like wildfire, each telling more exaggerated than the first. Maia had to wonder what the wise Maderos would write in his tome about it—she herself had already heard a half dozen conflicting tales. She sat in the same main audience hall in the castle—the very same cavernous space where she had sat restlessly through her coronation dinner not long before. A constant influx of soldiers and guests arrived at the hall throughout the day to pay homage and respect to her as their queen.

By midafternoon, Dodd arrived with his army, having pressed them hard enough to cover ground faster than the wind. They reached Comoros just in time to see Schuyler's army disperse and to capture the opposing force's fleeing leaders. Dodd found himself surrounded by men once loyal to his father, who begged him to pardon their offenses and accept their undying loyalty. His army tripled in size amidst the chaos.

Maia set down her goblet and watched as Suzenne and Dodd, seated to one side of her, stole a lingering kiss. Though she was happy to see her friends reunited, their simple display of affection loosed a twinge of bitterness in her heart. She would never be able to kiss Collier that way. Her curse prevented it.

The city was ebullient with the unexpectedly quick and relatively bloodless victory, which was unprecedented in the kingdom. Only eighty men had died in the melee, seventy-five of them from Schuyler's side . . . and a third of those slain by Jon Tayt alone. The freed prisoners had followed Jon Tayt into the thickest ranks of their foes and bludgeoned the fleeing soldiers into submission. The city watch had used their knowledge of the streets to hem in the escaping men. Soldiers had quickly stripped away their tunics and tried to disguise themselves, but the locals all knew each other, so the defecting soldiers found no shelter amid the populace.

Kord Schuyler had been found with a bruise on his head, wandering aimlessly in a nearby street outside a brewery. He had been brought in chains to Pent Tower. The leaders had all been seized— not a single one had escaped into the woods. The enemy soldiers, upon hearing Maia's orders to seize the ringleaders, had turned on their masters and voluntarily brought them to the watch.

Aldermaston Kranmir had been caught as well and suffered a similar fate, and though Maia intended to let her grandmother devise his punishment, she asked that he be brought to her.

Sitting in her audience chamber, on the throne, Maia watched as Kranmir was delivered in chains. His gray cassock was smeared with mud, and without his mushroom-shaped hat, his dark hair was disheveled. There was a puffiness around his eyes, a pallor to his cheeks, but his lips still quivered with defiance and hatred as he gazed up at her. One of the soldiers who escorted him looked affronted that he did not kneel, and nudged the back of his legs with a poleaxe.

"Do not force him," Maia said, giving the soldier a subtle shake of her head. She fixed her eyes on Ely Kranmir and waited for him to speak.

Richard approached the throne from the nearby bench, arms clasped behind his back. He looked stern but not angry. He positioned himself close to Maia, as if he were ready to personally defend her from an attack.

"What would you have me say?" Kranmir asked in a challenging tone.

"Only the truth," Maia answered. She could sense the conversation would not go well. She had hoped to find him repentant.

"The *truth*," Kranmir said with a half chuckle. "Oh, I speak the truth. I am an Aldermaston after all. And I wear chains." He rattled them mockingly. "You have authority, Lady Maia, but you are not my queen."

Richard took a step forward. "Do you intend to continue speaking out against Her Majesty's right to the throne?" he asked in a formal, neutral tone. There was no hint of anger or resentment at all in his countenance. "I have had reports already that you have not been silent about your perceived injustices."

"Perceived, Richard? Perceived? My domain has been stripped from me. I have been hunted by the royal wolves and treated with indignities unbecoming of my station. But so suffered the martyrs of the past as well. Yes, Richard. I am an Aldermaston, and I will continue to speak the truth about what this girl really is. I will tell the world what I have *seen* with my own eyes! You are the imposter, Richard. You are her pawn. I pity you. There will come a day when everyone will know that Comoros's queen is nothing but a—"

"Be silent," Richard commanded in a firm, powerful voice. "By the Medium, I revoke your power of speech. I strike you with palsy in your hands. You will neither utter nor write another word until your heart is sufficiently humbled. You have forsaken the ways of the Medium, Ely. Her Majesty has decided that the true High Seer will oversee your punishment. Take him away." He gestured to the guards.

Maia watched as Kranmir's eyes widened with shock and terror. His jaw moved, his mouth opened, but no sound came out. A rattling noise followed, and she watched his hands begin to tremble uncontrollably. She turned to Richard, whose face was firm and unyielding, yet free of any rage. He gestured for the guards, and one of them grabbed Kranmir by the arm and escorted him from the audience hall.

"Richard," Maia whispered in awe.

He looked at her mildly and shook his head. "It was not my will, Your Majesty. Even the Medium grew weary of his disrespect."

***

Later that evening, Maia rubbed her finger along the rim of her goblet, feeling a sense of peace and wonder. Another disaster had been averted. Another danger faced and met. As she watched her friends and supporters mingle in the hall, she thought of the armada that was even now on its way to Comoros. Knowing about Ludgate's defenses had helped her preserve the city. But she knew she could not count on them against the Dochte Mandar. Even with all her strength, she knew she could not overcome the combined will of so many men empowered with kystrels. While those around her were celebrating her triumph over her foes, she could only brood about the worse danger that was still coming.

Suzenne touched her arm. She had not seen her friend approach. "Look, Maia," she whispered.

Maia turned and gazed at the men who approached her seat. Richard Syon was escorting the Earl of Caspur, whose head was hung low with apparent shame. His hands were worrying each other and were not in chains, which surprised her. Each of the others had been brought forward in shackles before being escorted to the dungeons of Pent Tower. She noticed the difference and gave Richard a curious look. Rather than reply, Richard gestured for Caspur to speak.

Never had she seen him appear so pitiful. She narrowed her eyes at him, wondering what he could have to say. Dodd coughed into his fist and leaned forward for a better look.

Caspur struggled to find his voice. She could see the wretchedness on his face, the misery. The humiliation. She waited patiently.

"Your . . . Your Majesty," Caspur said chokingly. He struggled to master himself. Menacing and hateful looks narrowed in on him from around the room. He was a proud man, and his arrogance had alienated many. His courage quailed, but he persisted. "I . . . I know you will not . . . likely believe me. And if you send me to Pent Tower . . . I will accept it. But I wanted you . . . nay . . . I *needed* you to know that although I disobeyed you"—he paused again, struggling to contain his surging emotions—"I am not a traitor . . . as you may suppose me to be." His hands formed into fists, the knuckles white, the tendons straining.

"Tell me why not," Maia said calmly, giving him an encouraging look and a gesture to continue.

He glanced at her, seeming to be stung by her open look, and lowered his gaze again. His hands were all knotted up. "I disobeyed you. I thought . . . I thought your decision foolish and . . . too risky. I wanted to prove myself to you. I wanted . . . desperately . . . for you to value me and my counsel. I . . . my lady . . . I went to face Kord Schuyler to defeat him, not to join him." His voice gathered strength. "When our armies were nigh each other . . . his captains seduced mine. He offered them rewards I could not match, and the men defected against my orders. I fled to warn you, but I was captured. When you routed them this . . . this very morning . . . I was able to escape and make my way back to the city. I met with your lady . . . Lady Suzenne . . . at the gate. She heard me plead my case and sent for the chancellor."

With trembling knees, the Earl of Caspur knelt before her chair. "I beg your forgiveness for my pride." Tears trickled down his wrinkled cheeks. "I deserve your punishment. I submit to it with no conditions. My actions can clearly be construed as treason. I swear to you . . . on the soul of my father . . . that I never intended to betray you. I disobeyed you, for which I am truly and deeply sorrowful. Had I heeded you, there would not have been such a panic . . . in your household . . . and I regret that most ardently. I await your judgment and beg your compassion." He bowed his head before her.

Maia's heart was moved at his speech. Could he be dissembling? Possibly. But he looked so beaten down, so humiliated, so sincere. She surmised that Richard trusted his repentance was genuine, else the earl would have been brought before her in chains. Suzenne had not forewarned her of this, for whatever reason. She glanced at her friend, and from the look of sympathy on her face, Maia could tell that she too believed Caspur's tale.

The Earl of Caspur was one of the wealthiest men of the realm. She could almost sense the courtiers staring at her, eager to feast on the carcass of his possessions, which would be stripped away from him. He could lose everything, including his life, for what he had done.

Maia rose from the chair and approached the kneeling man. She knelt herself and took his hands with hers. The knots of sinews and tendons were still blanched and straining. She rubbed her palm across his knuckles to soothe him.

"My lord earl," she said, drawing him to his feet. "I believe you, and I forgive you for your trespasses." She clenched his hands and gazed into his eyes. "Come, dine with us."

Maia signaled for a server to bring him some of the meal. She glanced at Richard, and the look of approval and respect she saw in his eyes put a lump in her throat. She escorted Caspur to an empty seat.

A murmuring sound filled the hall as the witnesses of Caspur's reprieve began to talk and gossip and speculate about what they had just witnessed. Maia patted the earl's shoulder and took note of the beads of sweat on his brow.

"I did not . . . I did not expect this," he said to her, his voice low and unguarded.

Maia smiled at him. "I know what it means to be forgiven," she answered.

"Well . . . yes," he said, shaking his head. "But what I did was unpardonable. You could have stripped everything from me. I would have deserved no less."

Maia left her hand on his shoulder and kept her voice low. "My lord earl, then what use would you have been to me? You just had a life-altering lesson in loyalty and obedience. I trust you more now because you had the courage to return and confess your folly. I do not believe you will ever disobey me again. And to prove my trust in you, I wish to keep you on my Privy Council. For I will need you and your loyalty to face the dangers ahead. I cannot spare men nor train new ones in the short time left to us. And I believe you fully when you say you will never do this again."

He stared up at her eyes, his look soft and compliant. "I swear it on my soul." He gritted his teeth. "When your father died, lass, you may have been the only one left in the kingdom who still loved him. I can tell already that your rule will be quite different from his. I will serve you to my dying breath, my lady. My queen."

Maia smiled and patted his shoulder before returning to the celebration. Her heart was suddenly heavy. For though she had been able to pardon this one man, she knew she would have to deal with the traitors to her realm much differently.

We are Naestors first and foremost. We live in a land dominated by night, cold, and darkness. We have learned to be hard like ice, and that ice is strong enough to shatter mountains. There is great subtlety in how water destroys things, drip by drip. The first Victus taught his followers that to fight and win every battle is not a matter of supreme excellence. Supreme excellence consists of breaking the enemy's resistance without fighting. Break their will before you break their bodies.

—Corriveaux Tenir, Victus of Dahomey

CHAPTER TWENTY

Warning from Doviur

O f all the duties that Maia performed as Queen of Comoros, the one she enjoyed the most was done in disguise. It was Suzenne who had started the scheme. The ladies-in-waiting would each take turns leaving the palace to visit the poorest quarters of the city, distributing alms, baskets of food, and visiting the poor and the sick. They were not to use their names or wear fancy gowns. If asked, and only if asked, they would merely identify themselves as servants of the queen. It was not uncommon for little beggar children to approach two cloaked well-wishers—they always left as companions—and receive silver pence in recompense. What the little children did not know was that Queen Maia herself was often one of the cloaked young women. After learning of what her friend had instigated, Maia was determined to take part.

At first, some of the ladies-in-waiting were reluctant to carry out this particular duty, but Suzenne led by example and always brought a different girl with her. The undercover visits were useful in another way—it helped Maia learn how her people felt about her and their city. Suzenne made the assignments and received the reports on who her ladies had visited and what they had learned.

Maia enjoyed making these jaunts into the city herself. One day she was walking through the city streets with Jayn Sexton after a particularly enjoyable visit with an old widower named Albert. Maia had wanted to meet him herself after learning about him from a previous report. Though he was in his nineties, he had been known for helping his friends and neighbors with everything from clearing leaves from the gutters to giving children rides on his cart, until an apple cart struck him and broke his leg.

"I hope Albert recovers from his injury," Jayn said as they walked through the crowded streets.

"I expect he will be climbing ladders again before long," Maia said, smiling. The street was shadowed because of the high roofs and dormer windows, but it was clean, and she saw a little girl pick up some debris that had been blown in by the wind. She paused to thank the girl and give her a silver coin.

"Will you report to Suzenne?" Maia asked Jayn, linking arms with her again. "I need to see Simon on the way back."

Jayn's face fell a little at the mention of Suzenne.

"What is it?" Maia pressed.

"It is nothing."

"You looked sad for a moment. What is wrong?"

Jayn offered a guilty smile. "You are very observant," she answered, swinging her arm a little. "I have been worrying about Suzenne, that is all."

Maia wrinkled her brow. "Tell me, Jayn." She had noticed Suzenne seemed more tired lately, but there had been no other signs to give her concern. "Is she unwell?"

"She is unhappy," Jayn said with a sigh. "I am sure she would not want me speaking of this to you."

"What has she not told me?" Maia asked, growing more concerned.

"The separation from Dodd," Jayn said.

Maia felt as if the sunlight had pierced the clouds. Understanding flooded her. "She misses him." He had been in the north, preparing to defend their borders from the armada.

Jayn nodded, trying to keep her expression neutral. Over time, she had come to know Jayn better and had learned that she was very discreet. She did not flaunt her emotions for all to see. She was private and reserved and a loyal confidante, so it was natural that she was struggling with how much she should reveal.

"I see I have made you feel compromised," Maia said, squeezing her arm. "Let me try and guess, then you can rightly say I have needled the truth out of you, loosening stitch by stitch. It has been several weeks since Dodd has been to court, as he is securing our northern borders. I know he has been on the saddle a great deal and has amassed a considerable army to help defend Comoros. But the two are newlyweds, so it is natural they miss each other." She nodded to herself and then patted Jayn's arm. "I shall contrive an excuse for her to join him. She can cross the Apse Veil to Billerbeck and spend a few days with her husband. Do you think that will ease her spirits, Jayn?"

Jayn nodded eagerly.

"Why did she not *tell* me?" Maia said, feeling a little exasperated.

Jayn gave her a serious look. "How could she?" she replied earnestly. "*You* have been separated from your husband for even longer. Yours is across the sea. She felt . . . how could she complain to you when you have suffered more? She was determined to bear it, truly. She will be upset to learn that I have told you."

The reminder was like a knife in an old wound. She missed Collier desperately and treasured the messages he sent to her through Simon Fox, reading each one over and over. They were like a bridge that spanned the time and distance separating them. She wanted so much to be with him, to walk with him as they had done in Muirwood, holding hands and finding quiet amidst the apple trees or in the shelter of the walled garden. Her cheeks flushed with the memories. It had been over a month since he had left her to protect his own kingdom. It had been a month since Corriveaux had threatened her heart. She worried about Collier. If anything happened to him, she could not bear it.

It was the nervous tension on Jayn's face that made her realize she had been silent too long—lost in thought. "You were right to tell me," she said, patting her arm. "I will not reveal that you confided in me. But I am grateful you did. You are a loyal friend to her and to me. I treasure you both."

Jayn gave her a dimpled smile in response. "I will always be grateful to you for saving me," she said. They both knew what she meant.

They made a turn, and Maia spied Simon's shop. Maia glanced back a moment later and saw their escort round the corner. He was one of Simon's men—Piers. She gave him a smile and a wink, acknowledging that she knew he had been shadowing them. While Maia did enjoy the freedom to roam the city in disguise, Simon's spies were always nearby, both to deliver messages and to ensure she was safe. Piers scowled at her for breaking protocol by greeting him, and she and Jayn entered the wine merchant's shop.

As they stepped through the door, it occurred to Maia that this is where she had come that long-ago day after the kishion saved her life. So much had changed since then. There had been no reports of the kishion since Schuyler's rebellion had been squelched—perhaps because there was no current threat to her life. Her enemies were under guard at Pent Tower awaiting trials, which Maia was in no rush to pursue. With their capture, all resistance to her authority had crumpled. Comoros was truly hers.

Maia patted Jayn's arm one last time. "Tell Suzenne to expect me shortly. I will need to speak to Richard about the progress with the river defenses."

"I will," Jayn replied. She gave her hand a grateful squeeze and then turned around and left, followed by Piers, who would escort her back to the castle.

The merchant's shop was always bustling, but one of Simon's men recognized her and nodded for her to follow him back to Simon's office. He was a complex man who constantly walked a tightrope. Besides being a spy, both for her husband and as a double agent for the Victus, he was also an unofficial member of her Privy Council. He would often come to the castle after dark and meet with her and Suzenne, discuss the affairs of the day, and pass along any news he deemed worthy of her attention. She trusted him implicitly.

The servant shut the door, leaving the two of them alone.

"Good morning, Simon," she greeted. Excitement shot down her spine when she noticed the folded piece of paper in his hand. "Is that for me?"

He nodded and handed it to her, his look guarded.

Maia felt a twinge of disappointment. "He rejected the idea," she said with a sigh. In her last message to Collier, she had offered to cross the Apse Veil to Lisyeux Abbey to see him, in the hopes he could spare time from his war with Paeiz to meet her there.

"You think I would read your private messages?" Simon said, giving her an unruffled stare.

Maia smiled slyly and hurried to open the note. She normally would have waited to read it back at the palace, but today she could not bear it. His words were charming, as always, but he did not think it would be wise to meet her at Lisyeux. Still, he promised that if all went well, he would soon join her in Comoros with his army.

Patience, Wife, he extolled her. *As I used to say to my steward Jeremiah, 'patience is for those who have nothing better to do with their time.' But I have since learned that it is truly a virtue the Medium rewards. I beg you to forgive me, my dove. I long for nothing more than to see you again and to hold you in my arms. I will come to you.*

It was strange to feel disappointment and love at the same moment. She gently folded the paper and slipped it into her girdle to read again later. She sat down on the cushioned chair near Simon's desk.

"How goes his war?" she asked, confident that he would tell her true.

Simon shrugged slightly. "War is unpredictable. But he is motivated to win it and win it quickly. Still, these things take time, my lady."

Maia sighed, trying to sort through the feelings in her tumultuous heart. "I sent an ambassador to Paeiz to sue for an alliance," she said. "I have not heard back from him yet. Maybe I should heighten the rhetoric. By attacking Dahomey, he has also attacked Comoros."

Simon winced, though only slightly. "You have enough troubles of your own, Lady Maia. You have only been queen for a month. It takes time to see results."

"Speaking of abbeys," Maia said with a twinge of impatience. "My husband has not yet taken the maston test at Lisyeux. If this war does not end soon . . ." She gritted her teeth, unable to finish the thought. She wanted so much to marry him by irrevocare sigil. But he needed to be a maston first.

She looked up and caught a peculiar look in Simon's eye. "What is it?"

"What is *what*, my lady?"

"What does that *look* mean?" she asked, trying to rope him in. "Is there something you are not telling me?"

Simon smiled demurely. "There is always *plenty* I am not telling you. Insignificant trifles."

"I know that," she said with a hint of exasperation. "I mean about Collier. If something happened to him, you would tell me?" She looked at him seriously. "Simon? You *would* tell me, correct?"

Simon drummed his fingers on the desk. "I will always be honest with you, my lady."

She hated it when he was evasive. "That comforts me. Is my husband well? He has not been injured, has he?"

Simon shook his head. "No, he is quite hale."

She furrowed her brow. "There is something you are concealing from me."

He pursed his lips and said nothing.

"Simon," she prodded.

"Yes, my lady?"

She was growing more and more uneasy. "Please tell me."

He studied her closely. "I know my lord's reasons for not granting your wish to meet him," he said in his most diplomatic way. "I know him very well. It is nothing that should alarm or concern you. You must understand, he is *very* busy and has much to accomplish. He has a hard time sitting still, as you well remember. He was *flattered* by your offer to cross to Dahomey, and it took immeasurable self-possession on his part to refuse your offer, but he does not want you to come now. He wants you to come over for your coronation. First, he hopes to subdue his enemies and present you with an attractive alliance. I will say no more, because I was commanded not to speak on the matter." Simon leaned back in his chair and scratched the corner of his eyebrow. "You are tenacious, my lady. I must never forget that."

Maia smiled at the compliment and felt a measure of relief. But it troubled her that Collier was keeping secrets from her and that he had commanded his spy to do the same.

"I will prod you no more," Maia said. "Any word from my grandmother? She went to Hautland and then to Mon. Is she still there?"

"I believe so," Simon replied. "Word can travel slowly, and she often changes her mind about where she is going midcourse. My understanding is that the Apse Veil is now open in Hautland. Her visit was well received, and she was treated with great honor and respect. She left for Mon a fortnight ago, but I have had no word since her arrival there."

"Any word from Walraven?" Maia asked.

Simon nodded. "Yes, he revealed that the Naestors still intend to attack the city of Comoros itself as soon as the armada arrives. Corriveaux has contact with the fleet captains through waymarker Leerings, you know. It takes sixty to eighty days to make the voyage to Assinica. He said it will be at least another month before they arrive. Which is why spending time preparing the defenses is wise."

Maia sighed. "I do not want to abandon the city," she said restlessly. "But I do not see any way we can withstand such a fleet and survive. The Leerings cannot defend us against the Dochte Mandar. We have been gathering food and supplies either for a siege or to flee. But the people will need a safe haven. Muirwood is the only place that makes sense to me," Maia said. "It is surrounded by the Bearden Muir. It will be a difficult Hundred to invade, especially by sea. If the other kingdoms do not come to our aid . . ."

Simon nodded in agreement. He was also convinced that only the combined might of all the kingdoms could save them from the fury of the Naestors.

A firm rapping sounded on the door, breaking Maia from her reverie.

Simon rose and answered it. A flushed man came in, his eyes wide, his cheeks pale. He was trembling.

"What is it?" Simon asked curtly. "Have you received a message from the king?"

The man shook his head. "I came from the castle," he said, out of breath. He looked at Maia. "My lady, you must come at once! The Privy Council is gathering."

Maia bolted from her chair. "What has happened?" The painfully familiar feeling of dread fused her bones and heart together.

The man mopped his brow. "Ships were seen from Doviur," he said. "White sails. They bear the flag of Hautland. They passed the port of Doviur and have been seen sailing along the coast—directly toward our city. The message came from the chancellor's wife, Joanna, who saw them near Augustin. A maston just came through Claredon with the news. My lady, it could be the armada!" He looked panicked as he gripped Simon's arm. "We thought we had another month, but the ships will be here by nightfall!"

CHAPTER TWENTY-ONE

Prince of Hautland

The city trembled in suspense as Maia prepared to give the order to evacuate. Plans had been developed; the city watch was trained; and wagons, teams of horses, and provisions had been assembled. But the appearance of ships off the coast caused a panic. Some of the citizenry bolted, and Maia had to give the order for all the gates save one to be shut. Ludgate was calmer, it being garrisoned by a company of prisoners-turned-soldiers whom Jon Tayt had been drilling and shaping into warriors. It was the only gate that she allowed to remain open. Mastons traveled through the Apse Veils to offer warnings and to prepare the armies of the Earls of Caspur and Forshee for the coming invasion.

Maia paced in the solar, thronged by her ladies-in-waiting and a few members of the Privy Council. She had assigned the lord mayor and her chancellor to prepare the city for attack and she waited to hear from them with keen anxiety. Suzenne looked greensick with worry. Jayn plucked chords from a lute to try to soften the mood, but it did nothing to dispel the oppressive feeling in the room.

A knight from her guard bounded up the steps and rushed into the room, face dripping with sweat. Everyone was on their feet in a moment. Maia stared at him as he hurried and knelt in front of her. She cared nothing for such formalities. She wanted only to hear his news.

"My lady, I was told to bring you word. The ships arriving bear the royal flag of Hautland. The lead ship flies a truce flag. The lord mayor has ordered the men to hold their crossbows at the ready. Three ships approached the harbor, but only one docked."

Maia looked worriedly at Suzenne and Jayn before returning her attention to the knight. "A truce flag?"

"Yes, my lady. The chancellor is talking to the ship's captain even now. I was sent to apprise you of the situation. Another knight will be sent soon to bring you more news."

"Thank you," Maia said, increasingly perplexed. She began pacing again as soon as the knight left.

"It could be a trick," Suzenne said, hurrying to her side. "They know we are expecting an invasion. Maybe they wish to see our defenses before they attack?"

"It feels strange . . ." Maia mused, shaking her head. "But I trust Richard's judgment. He is an Aldermaston and will not easily be fooled."

Maia pressed her fingers against her mouth, trying to listen for the whispers of the Medium to guide her. Soon it would be nightfall, signaling the start of curfew, and hopefully the people who were still attempting to flee the city would return to their homes. However, waiting for dark to attack would be a wise tactic for the armada because it would make it more difficult for her guards to see the approach of the invading ships. She felt a surge of wariness engulf her.

More time passed, filled by Jayn's music, and then another knight arrived in the solar, a different man than the first. With no preliminaries, he walked up to Maia and nodded in deference. He looked harried and did not kneel.

"My lady, the chancellor requests your presence immediately. I am to escort you."

"What is going on?" Maia demanded. "What news?"

"I was not given information to relate, my lady," he answered. "Only that the chancellor must speak with you privately. There have been discussions at the wharf between the captain of the Hautlander ship and the chancellor. I know not what was discussed, I only know I am to bring you at once to counsel with Master Syon."

"I will go," Maia said. She turned to Suzenne and gripped her arm. "Stay here and try to keep everyone calm. If I do not send word back to you within the hour, order the evacuation of the city."

Suzenne blanched and then nodded dutifully.

Maia followed the knight out of the solar and easily kept pace with him down the long corridor. A detachment of Carew's guard awaited her below, sword hilts in hand. By the time she reached the courtyard, a horse had been saddled for her and brought to the front. Captain Carew was already mounted, and his horse stood next to hers. He had a grim, distrustful look. A groom helped Maia mount, even though she did not need the assistance. It was a warm summer's eve, and the air was warm and pleasant.

Captain Carew brought his mount up next to hers. "I do not know what the fuss is about, Lady Maia. But I do not trust Hautlanders. Be on your guard."

"I have been to Rostick, Captain," Maia said simply. "Believe me, my trust must be earned."

They rode at a quick pace to the rear of the castle grounds, where the royal wharves had been built. When they arrived, she found Richard waiting on the planks by a skiff full of armed men equipped with breastplates and poleaxes. Richard looked very grave and troubled, his eyes brooding and dark as he watched her dismount and make her approach.

A few torches hissed and sputtered in iron sconces fastened to the edge of the dock. The waters from the river lapped against the dock posts. The peculiar smell of dead fish lingered in the air.

"I do not like that look," Maia told him. "What is it, Richard?"

He gestured for her to draw in next to him, and he walked a few paces away from her escort and the other men. He gave her a pitying look that made her heart darken with apprehension.

"Tell me!" she pleaded, unable to withstand the suspense.

She could tell it was painful for him to share whatever dark truth it was he knew. His look softened to one of great compassion.

"Maia," he said gently. "It is not the armada. They are mastons, primarily. I have tested them to be absolutely certain. On board is the chancellor of Hautland, who seeks a truce and a treaty with Comoros. They wish to defy the Naestors and help defend us against the coming invasion."

Maia stared at him, trying to understand why his look did not match his words. "It is likely a deception, a trick," she said, shaking her head. "But you already know this. What troubles you so?"

He bowed his head and let out a deep breath. Then he met her gaze again, his eyes full of sadness. "The Prince of Hautland is on board the vessel. I met him as well. They are very wary of our intentions and do not want their heir captured and held hostage. But I did speak with him in our language. They desire a truce with Comoros and will join their power with ours *if* you agree to marry the Hautlander prince."

Maia stared at him in confusion. "I am already married, Richard," she said.

He sighed again and then reached out and gently touched her arm. "The chancellor has told me that the Dochte Mandar have invalidated your marriage to King Gideon."

So *that* was the blow he had feared delivering. It felt as if a knife had been thrust into her stomach and twisted. Her strength seemed to drain from her, and her head began to buzz like a beehive. She felt sick with despair and racked with anguish.

"How can they do that?" Maia said, shaking her head. "It was performed by a Dochte Mandar surely, but there were witnesses. It was a legal marriage. Even my grandmother admits as much."

"Yes, I know," Richard said sympathetically. "But by whose authority was it conducted? The Dochte Mandar, and they are not recognized in this kingdom. I am sure this is intended as a way of sowing confusion and enmity, a way of further distancing us from the Medium. Did not Corriveaux say he would strike at your *heart*? By the decree of the High Scribe of the Dochte Mandar, your union has been annulled. The writ claims there was no consummation of the wedding, that you were abducted and forced into the marriage against your will, and that they revoke the decree performed by the presiding Dochte Mandar in Dahomey. Legally, they *can* do this, Maia. You are no longer his wife."

Maia felt spasms of pain in her heart. She wanted to weep, but the surprise was still so fresh, it was hard to even draw breath. What would Collier think when the news reached him?

"This was announced?" Maia asked wretchedly. "This knowledge is spreading through the kingdoms?"

Richard nodded. "There is more."

"Please, Richard, I am not sure I can bear it," she said, stifling a moan. She hated that there were so many witnesses. Though she had learned not to bury all her emotions, it still shamed her for others to see her tears. She wanted to cover her face.

"You must," he implored, squeezing her arm.

"Tell me," she whispered.

"The Prince of Hautland speaks our language in a broken manner. He has been studying our speech for many months, and I can understand him passably well. I was given to understand this first by the chancellor, but I needed to hear it said by the prince himself. He claimed to already know you."

Maia's head jerked up. Memories she had long since suppressed came bubbling into her mind. There was a snowstorm. An avalanche. She and Jon Tayt were crossing the mountains into Hautland when they were trapped by soldiers and Dochte Mandar. There had been no choice. In her mind, she could hear the noise of hunting horns, she could feel the kystrel in her hand as she summoned an avalanche. All was white and chill after the snow took her. She remembered a rider crushing through the snow. A man in a tunic. He gripped her hand and helped pull her from the drift.

Richard's eyes had wrinkles on the edges. "The prince's name is Oderick. He claims that he met you during your excursion into Dahomey when you crossed from Mon into Hautland. He took you on his horse to Rostick and cared for you when you were delirious and sick. He locked you in the room of an inn to bring you help, but you managed to escape out the window."

"Yes," Maia said. "Yes, it *is* true. I did not know . . . I did not know who he was. I was not . . . myself . . . at the moment. I . . . oh, Richard! What does this mean? I feel as if my heart will burst."

A few tears trickled down the old man's cheeks. "The prince is in love with you," he said hoarsely. "He has thought only of you for these past many months. He began his search for you when you were taken away on a Dahomeyjan ship. Only when news of your coronation arrived did he understand that the girl who had bewitched him was now the Queen of Comoros. He is the heir of Hautland. He is a maston, Maia. He seeks to marry you by irrevocare sigil immediately and bind your kingdoms together in power. He has the strength to blunt the attack on Comoros. In truth, Gideon does not." Richard looked at her gravely. "This is a terrible decision you must make, Maia. I cannot make it for you."

"But he is still . . . my husband," Maia said, thinking again about what this news would do to Collier. She had felt herself shackled by marriage at first. It was not what she had wanted. Since childhood, she had wished to be a maston and to continue the tradition of her ancestors, binding her Family to the Medium more strongly by marrying another maston. It grieved her that Collier had chosen to deliberately fail the maston test when first he took it, but she knew he hoped and strived to pass it now—not only for her, for himself. Right now he was embroiled in a fight with Paeiz, defending his kingdom. What would he do when he learned their marriage had been invalidated?

She had betrayed and abandoned him before. She could not betray him again, no matter what the cost.

"I had not expected this," Maia said, her voice catching on her emotions. "I am bound to him, Richard, and by more than any mere decree. I *love* him. I do not even know who this Hautlander prince really is . . . He is a maston, you say? You tested him?"

"I did."

Maia shook her head. "Does he know about my past? If he did, he surely would not want me."

Richard rubbed her arm and then patted her back. "No decision needs to be made this evening, Maia. We thought these ships were part of the armada . . . the beginning of the invasion. They may be potential allies, regardless of your decision. They still await us in their ship at the trading wharf. The skiff is here to take me back there to continue the discussion. Do we allow them to come to the palace as welcome guests? Do we accept and honor their truce flag?"

"Of course we do," Maia said with concern. "They must be made welcome. We will discuss this on the morrow. Until then, we cannot lower our guard. This may still be a *feint* . . . a diversion." Just saying the word "feint" reminded her of him, of the name he used when he posed as a commoner. She needed to get word to Simon. She needed him to tell Collier that she remained true to them and to their relationship.

Richard nodded his head.

"What does the prince look like?" Maia asked, hoping there was perhaps a mistake. She dreaded meeting this nobleman from Hautland. She dreaded it with all her broken heart.

Richard nodded sagely. "He is about thirty years old. He is short—about my own height, though more trim and fit. His eyes are blue and his hair is a cropped brown, which seems a dark gray in the light. I checked his palm for the mark and he had it. He is a maston, child. He was most ardent to see you and was able to describe you perfectly, down to the dress you wore when he found you in the avalanche."

"So you did not tell him?" Maia asked, her heart still throbbing with anguish. "He does not know what I am?"

Richard shook his head no. "That is your secret to tell," he replied gently. "But do not believe it will dissuade him. One of the reasons a kystrel is so dangerous is how vividly it invokes feelings. Feelings create memories, and the stronger the feeling, the deeper and more life-changing the memory. He appears to be truly besotted with you, my dear. And most enthusiastic to see you again."

That only made it worse. A kystrel had done this to his heart. Maia had no idea what Ereshkigal had said to him while she was unconscious. What promises had been made? At the very thought, Maia's shoulder began to burn. She realized that her suffering was drawing the Myriad Ones to her. It was opening an old wound that would fester.

Maia squeezed her eyes shut, feeling the darkness awaken inside her. Small whispers susurrated in her mind, sibilant and eager.

"I am truly sorry to be the one to bring you such ill news," Richard said. "I wish Joanna were here. She is much better at offering comfort than I am."

"You do well enough," Maia said with a forced smile. No matter what complications it created for her kingdom, she would not marry this Hautlander prince—not for gold or jewels or armies. More than anything else, she wanted Collier in front of her, she wanted to be able to hold him and promise him that she would not betray him again. If they were not married in the eyes of the Dochte Mandar, then they would be married by an Aldermaston in an abbey. She would give everything, including her crown, for that privilege. Her heart throbbed with anguish.

But a new feeling smoldered in her heart. She felt the yellow, fiery glare begin to crack through the crust. The hatred she felt against Corriveaux surprised her with its intensity.

And it delighted the Myriad Ones snuffling around her on the wharf.

There is a graveyard of bones and moldering armor on the cursed shores of Dahomey. I myself have trod that unhallowed ground. There is a Leering amidst the heap. It is a stark reminder that even the dead can speak to us. They can whisper from dust. They warn us not to trod on the same path that led to their fate, that created the Void. Annihilation is the ultimate mark of failure. We will leave no living person in Comoros. The ruins will be a stark reminder to the other kingdoms that supplication is the only answer. It will be a graveyard too. And then none of the other kingdoms will dare resist the authority of the Dochte Mandar. The deaths will begin one by one, a steady drip. And then they will come as a flood.

—Corriveaux Tenir, Victus of Dahomey

CHAPTER
TWENTY-TWO

Queen's Garden

Maia walked forlornly in the Queen's Garden in Muirwood, hidden away from the prying gazes of those who
would seek her out. The sun had just risen, and her
stomach growled for breakfast, but she walked amidst the rows of
flowers and fruit trees, watching the buds begin to open to the light.

After the dreadful news from Richard, she had summoned
Simon in the hope she could confer with him before leaving
for Muirwood, but he had not come. She stopped by one of the
benches where she and Collier had spent time together. A pang
of wistfulness struck her heart. She wished there were a way to
summon him, to draw him from the battlefields of Dahomey to
join her in this quiet garden. A few birds trilled from the upper
branches, their tiny bodies and fluttering wings the only noise,
and the perfume from the flowers lifted her spirits. She made a
mental note to thank the old gardener Thewliss for his patient
care of this secret place. A feeling of dread waited beyond these

walls, as she knew she would need to return to the city to face her would-be suitor. And she would need to do so with a calm mind and a sturdy heart.

The familiar squeaking of wheels on axles sounded from beyond the wall, and Maia walked over to the Leering that protected the door and invoked it. After opening it, she saw Thewliss tugging the cart and greeted him with a smile. But over his shoulder, Maia saw an approaching figure—Suzenne, her shoulders swathed in a shawl, a look of determination and worry on her face. Her friend would not have sought her out here unless something important had happened, and Maia felt a swell of panic as she left the arch of the garden door and met her friend on the lawn.

"What has happened?" Maia said, reaching out and seizing her friend's arm.

Suzenne looked stricken. She blinked rapidly, clearly trying to calm herself before speaking. "The chancellor sent me right away. Maia," she shook her head. "Simon was murdered."

A pit of pain opened in Maia's stomach. "Simon Fox?"

"Yes," Suzenne said in a shaky voice. "He was discovered before dawn. There was no sign of a struggle. He was stabbed in the back, crippled, and then left to bleed to death from a cut on his throat." She covered her mouth, her face growing white.

Maia's heart hammered in her chest and dizziness overtook her body as she imagined the scene. "Sweet Idumea."

Suzenne shook her head. "The coroner is examining the body for details, but Richard sent me right away to warn you. Why would the kishion do this? He has only acted in support of you . . . why kill someone who was helping you? I do not understand it."

Maia drew in a shuddering breath. "It may not have been him."

"What? How can you doubt it?"

"Because a ship from Hautland just arrived," Maia said. "The timing, Suzenne. The chancellor of Hautland may have brought another kishion to Comoros unwittingly. The Victus would not want to leave a kishion loose to betray them." She pressed her fingers to her lips, trying to quell the revulsion. "Poor Simon," she whispered. "Corriveaux is behind this, I have no doubt of that. He is preparing his invasion. The delegation . . . the prince . . . this is all a ruse. He will attack soon, and by killing Simon, he has disrupted our ability to get news. I must go back to the castle at once." Maia started for the abbey, no longer hungry.

"Is that wise?" Suzenne asked, keeping up with her. "If there is *another* kishion, he may also try to kill you. You would be safer here at Muirwood."

"I will not abandon my people," Maia said firmly, "but it is vital that I have no set routine. Have my chambers emptied. I do not want any of my ladies-in-waiting to be at risk. Remember when they marched us all over the palace the night before our execution? That is what we must do. If we do not stay in one place for long, then it will help safeguard us while Richard investigates the murder. A new kishion will not know Comoros. I will tell Justin to have the city watch on the lookout for him. Asking questions. Hurry, Suzenne, there is much to do."

***

The caretakers of Claredon Abbey were used to Maia's sudden arrivals, and there was usually an escort waiting for her to bring her back to the palace through the gate it shared with the abbey.

She went straight to the chancellor's tower and found Richard in deep conversation with the lord mayor, Justin. The two men had formed a strong partnership over the past month, much to Maia's satisfaction.

"Ah, my lady," Justin said, bowing gracefully. "Ill news, I fear."

Richard nodded somberly. "I just received the coroner's initial report if you would like to hear it."

"Thank you," Maia said with a curt nod, and took her place at the window seat where she had often sat as a child. Suzenne had gone to warn her ladies-in-waiting about the plan to move and change locations frequently. Sorrow burdened her now that she had the opportunity to absorb the news. She had valued Simon's frankness and had come to rely on him for quick information from Dahomey.

"Simon's body has been moved to the castle," Richard began, leaning back in his chair a little, locking his fingers and resting his hands on his stomach. "The murder was similar to the other suspicious deaths we have seen, including Crabwell's. The position of the knife wound on the spine was almost identical. He was rendered helpless first, but would have survived for hours with only that injury. The neck wound was done deliberately so that he would die quickly. He bled to death, my lady. They are still cleaning up the mess."

Maia shuddered, feeling her stomach twist. "Were there any witnesses?"

Richard shook his head. "Just the ones who found the body this morning. Nothing unusual happened during the night. There were no signs of force . . . no broken latches or windows. The door was unlocked. It seems Simon greeted the man and allowed him in. There were no signs of a struggle." He stared into her eyes before continuing. "Do you think . . . was it the kishion who saved you?"

"I do not think he is the culprit," Maia said. "Why would he do such a thing without cause?"

"He had plenty of cause," Justin said, moving toward her. He did not look the least bit squeamish. He had dealt with plenty of murders as lord mayor of Comoros, and it had hardened him.

"Simon was helping us hunt him down, per your orders. Maybe one of Simon's men got too close?"

"True," Maia said, nodding thoughtfully. "But there is also the fact that the Hautlander ship arrived yesterday. A man could easily have slipped into the waters in the dark. All our attention was on the ship and its passengers. One of them could have been another kishion. It makes sense that they would send one to stop him if he no longer follows their orders."

Richard furrowed his brow. "I do not think my counterpart in Hautland would have permitted it. Such an action would have put him open to retaliation."

"Precisely what Corriveaux may have intended," Maia said. "I have a dreadful feeling that this Hautland commission is nothing more than a distraction to us. Treaties take time, anyway. Perhaps Corriveaux seeks to lull us into inaction with the futile hope of preventing an invasion." She shook her head firmly. "The Naestors are coming. I have no doubt of that."

"Will you still meet with Prince Oderick?" Richard asked.

"I must. If only to disabuse him of the idea that I will marry him. I gave this much thought last night while I paced. My mind is unchanged—I will not abandon my true husband. Yes, the Dochte Mandar may have invalidated the marriage, but that can and will be rectified. Do we know how Simon sent messages to Dahomey?"

Richard looked to Justin and both shrugged. "We are not certain," the chancellor said.

"Find out. But send a royal message to King Gideon at once to inform him of Simon's death. I am sure Simon's people have already done that, but I want one sent with my extreme condolences as well. I wish he were here. I feel certain the attack is coming soon."

Richard nodded in agreement. "I feel it as well. Like clouds in the distance threatening a storm."

"This is unlike any storm we have dealt with before," Maia said. Then she rose from the window seat. "I will speak with Prince Oderick immediately. Much better for me to rebuff him quickly and firmly. I do not wish to be alone with him. Richard, can you arrange a visit in the solar? I would like Captain Carew and you to be present. Also the chancellor of Hautland. This is to be done in the open. If things become . . . awkward . . . I will end the conversation quickly."

"We will make the preparations right away," came his answer. His approving smile gave her some vastly needed comfort.

***

Maia was restless by the time the meeting had finally assembled. How she longed for this embarrassing meeting to be behind both of them. She was careful to select a plain gown—one that was no more formal than what her ladies-in-waiting wore. It had taken several hours to communicate the breadth of the situation to the Hautlanders and they, of course, had tried to bargain and wheedle for more time with her instead of a curt interview.

Instead of the solar, it was agreed that the prince and Maia would walk together in the royal garden, accompanied by their chancellors and full retinue. It was all quite exasperating, even down to the points of who would arrive first and how the greeting would take place. Ceremony was important to Hautlanders, it turned out, and the notion of an informal event made them uncomfortable. Among other demands, they had insisted trumpets play a fanfare before the meeting took place.

The day was warm and pleasant, and several pavilions for shade had been strewn around the lawns, between the fountains and manicured hedges. There were short tables laden with fruits, various cheeses, and other fare the cooks had devised to appeal to their guests. Maia was more nervous than hungry, and felt she would be ready for a feast when this ruse was over and she could finally relax again.

As she and Richard left the palace and approached the meeting point together, arm in arm, to the accompaniment of the trumpets, she caught sight of the Hautland delegation, dressed in opulent finery that made her own humble costume seem like a pauper's rags. The prince was a little shorter than her, with a wide black felt hat with several plumed feathers. He had a restless, eager look, as if he could hardly bear to wait for her to make her approach. He broke decorum by pointing her out to the white-haired man beside him, whom she assumed was the chancellor. The prince was wearing a ribbed green vest, a shirt with puffy sleeves, and a cape that glittered with small gems. A jeweled sword was belted at his waist, and his collar was thick with insignia and necklaces. He was well groomed, well proportioned, and had a confident if not slightly arrogant stance.

He also made no pretense of hiding his adoration for her. His smile seemed to quiver with pent-up emotion as she and Richard came nearer. His hands trembled, and he began to fidget excitedly. Even though he was at least a decade older than her, he actually looked like a young man in the throes of love for the first time.

"Why am I doing this?" Maia muttered with despair, quiet enough for only Richard to hear. He just squeezed her arm and kept leading her forward.

"Chancellor Vorstad," Richard said with a polite nod once they stood in front of the Hautland delegation.

"Chancellor Syon," the white-haired man said, his speech

heavily accented but properly enunciated. "Your Majesty, let me introduce you to Prince Oderick, heir to the throne of Hautland! He is most gratified to meet you."

Oderick's eyes were wild with enthusiasm as he came forward and took her hand and then bowed deeply, bending at the waist. His touch was surprisingly light. She had worried that in his enthusiasm he would crush her hand in his.

"Thank you for coming," Maia said.

"Your Majesty, it vis my graat priwilege," Oderick said in a heavily accented tongue that was not as precise as his chancellor's. He straightened, bowed again, and straightened once more. He offered her his arm and gestured that they should take a walk in the garden, as had been arranged.

Maia sighed and took his arm, feeling awkward and uncomfortable. She wished again, hopelessly, that Collier were there to rescue her from this situation.

"I hef attempted, dear lady, to conform my tongue to your langwage," he said with an attempt at gallantry. "I hef failt miserably. But I am persistent. Qvite persistent. You speak my tongue werry vell."

"I do not speak your tongue at all," Maia said. It was necessary for her to end this farce.

He looked at her oddly. "Ah, yes. Vell . . . I have hurt you."

"You have hurt me?" Maia asked, confused.

"Hurt? Oh, my pardon. Heard. Speaking your langwage . . . I have only started to learn it since ve met. You remember? When *we* met?"

Maia stopped and put her other hand on his arm. "I do, Prince Oderick. But I must confess something to you. You are mistaken about me."

He frowned slightly as he met her eyes. "Perhaps. Perhaps not. I . . ." he swallowed nervously, "I . . . believe . . . I truly believe you *verr* a . . . a hetaera. Not so now." He looked at her seriously, with a look of affection and great earnestness. "Hmmm? You have no kystrel?"

Maia stared at him in surprise. "No," she answered, feeling strangely guilty and relieved. "I do not have a kystrel. Though I bear the marks of the hetaera, I am not one." She looked at him pointedly. "This was not the case . . . when we first met."

"Yah!" he said, his eyes glittering with enthusiasm. He gestured toward a bench in the park, and they sat down next to each other. She was aware of the eyes of all the bystanders watching them. They were not close enough to overhear what was said between her and the prince, but they could witness everything. She was grateful for that.

"So you knew?" Maia asked, looking at him worriedly.

"Yah," he replied, nodding vigorously. "You said . . . I save you. You said . . . take to Rostick. I did. I knew . . . vhat you verr. But you took me . . ." He clustered his fingers together and then tapped his own chest. "Here. You took my hurt. My *heart*. So difficult. I will keep trying. When you fell sleeping . . . I saw no kystrel. Medium said . . . help you. Get help. I vent to find Aldermaston of Rostick. You verr gone when ve returned. Rope of sheets . . . hanging from vindow. Ve searched for you. Vanted to help you." His pronunciation deteriorated as he tried eagerly to get out the long-withheld words.

Maia felt a prick of tenderness in her heart at his story. She had wondered why she had awoken in a locked bedroom rather than a prison cell. She had no memory of that night or of what she had said to Prince Oderick. His face was familiar to her, but it was as if she had seen it only through a sleepy fog.

"Help you," Prince Oderick continued, taking her hands with his. "The Victus . . . they threaten my people as vell. Cannot fight them . . . alone. They gather ships . . . many ships. An armada to destroy Comoros. They wish to bring the Void." He shook his head firmly. "Fight them together. You and I." He began bobbing his head excitedly. "Maston and maston. Queen and prince. You and I!"

He looked at her imploringly, and Maia felt her heart throb with sympathy. She pulled her hands away from his. "No," she answered, shaking her head. "No, I cannot."

He stared at her seriously, as if deciphering her words. "Dahomey," he said. "You love . . . Gideon of Dahomey." He stifled a chuckle. "Handsome. Proud." He shook his head with determination. "Not for you. Many vimen. Many, many vimen."

"Women?" Maia asked.

"Yah. *Wimen*. Not for you. Not maston. Puny kingdom. Not like Hautland. Ve crush Dahomey like . . . fig. Comoros strong. Hautland strong. Good match." His attempt to persuade her made his words more choppy and curt. He snapped his fingers a few times. "Dochte Mandar annulled marriage. Not your husband. You are free."

Maia felt the pain of the moment keenly and knew she needed to end their conversation at once. "But my *heart* is not free," she answered and started to rise.

"No, no, no!" he implored, seizing her hands and pulling her down again. *"Ach, dizeng!"* he muttered under his breath. "More thing! More thing." He begged her with his eyes to stay. "I study tomes. Tomes . . . yah?"

Maia looked at him in confusion. "The maston tomes?"

"Yah!" he said, bobbing his head. He moved closer to her. *"Zurit.* Ach, no . . . pardon. Kiss. Maston tome say kiss of hetaera . . . umm . . . poison. Yah?"

"Yes," she said, nodding in agreement. "What do you mean? You have a tome that speaks of it?"

Prince Oderick nodded vigorously. "Yah! Tome says there is cure."

Maia stared at him in disbelief. "No, there is no cure," she said, shaking her head.

"No, no! Tome says cure! Hetaera forsakes kystrel. Cure. You give up kystrel. Cure."

A wrenching feeling twisted Maia's heart within her chest. "No," she said, shaking her head. How could she explain to him that she had spoken to Lia Demont herself, the woman who had put the curse on the hetaera's Leering . . . and bound it by irrevocare sigil. The curse would last forever. "The tome is wrong," Maia said, shaking her head. She looked over at Richard and gave him a miserable look, silently begging him to rescue her. He nodded and started to walk over to them.

"Not wrong!" Prince Oderick said vehemently. "Show you."

Maia turned to look at him when his face suddenly collided with hers. He had released her hands, and he seized her neck as he pressed his lips to hers. She recoiled with utter horror and tried to shove him away, but his grip was strong.

She did not return the kiss.

It did not matter. The brand on her shoulder began to burn with fire, and she felt a tingling feeling pass from her lips into him as a Leering far distant was invoked.

Maia finally wrenched away from him and shoved him hard with her hands. "No!" she shouted, wiping his spittle from her mouth. He stared at her in confusion, a look of growing dread haunting his eyes as he touched his lips.

It was as if the kiss had burned him.

CHAPTER
TWENTY-THREE

Captured

Maia stood from the bench, her eyes wild with accusation and horror. She wiped her mouth repeatedly, trying to understand what madness had driven him to kiss her. Richard Syon rushed to her side.

"He kissed me," Maia said shakily as she took a step back, watching the bewilderment in Prince Oderick's face. He seemed to be realizing that what he had done would have terrible consequences.

"I saw it," Richard said. He stared down the younger man. "Prince Oderick, what possessed you to take such a liberty with *any* woman, let alone the Queen of Comoros?"

Prince Oderick's face was flushed, his eyes worried. He gestured for the Hautland chancellor to join him. "I vas told . . . by Aldermaston Breinholt . . . I saw his tome!" He gave Richard a look of desperation. "He vould lie to me? *Sprechen gaffin!*"

When Chancellor Vorstad arrived, the prince spluttered a series of coarse words at the older man and jabbed his finger at Maia.

Maia's stomach shriveled into a prune. She felt sick at heart. Both her grandmother and Lia had warned her never to kiss anyone. Oderick had completely startled her with his action. She had not expected it, and while there had been nothing she could do to stop him, she regretted it immensely.

The Hautland chancellor gave the prince a worried look and then turned to face Richard. "I myself spoke with the Aldermaston of Viegg Abbey not four days ago," he said. "He showed us the tome that said the hetaera's curse would lift if the kystrel was forsaken. The High Seer herself assured me that the queen had forsaken it!"

Maia stared hard at the man. "The High Seer is my grandmother," she said, her voice trembling. "She would *never* have said it was safe for him to kiss me, Chancellor. Watch your words with care, sir. What precisely did the High Seer say?"

The man looked truly concerned and baffled. "I saw her in person, my lady. She came to Hautland to open the Apse Veil and arrived in Viegg . . . the oldest abbey in the realm. I counseled with her regarding your status, because the prince *believed* you were a hetaera and wanted to rescue you. The High Seer told me you had been deceived by the Victus, that you did not choose to bear the brand on your shoulder. Is this not true?"

"That part is true," Maia said, nodding gravely. "What else did she say?" Maia glanced at Richard, whose face was twisted with concern.

The chancellor coughed and put his hand on the prince's shoulder, almost as if to steady himself. "She said that you were married to King Gideon of Dahomey by the rites of the Dochte Mandar. After I informed her of the marriage's invalidation, she told me she needed to depart immediately. The Aldermaston of Viegg offered to escort her back through the abbey himself. They went with some of his servants, as I recall. When he returned, he said she had crossed the Apse Veil to Mon. He then told me that the High Seer had mentioned a passage in the Aldermaston tomes . . . the tomes we are not allowed to read. He showed us the page . . . I saw the words myself, my lady. It said if a hetaera surrenders her kystrel, the Medium will not suffer her kiss to cause harm. The prince wanted to prove this to you. Upon my honor, my lady, this information was given to us by an Aldermaston."

Maia stared at Richard again, her stomach dropping to her feet. "My grandmother went to Mon?" she asked. His report matched what Simon had last told her.

Except Simon was now dead.

Richard's frown was severe. "Perhaps . . . she did not make it to Mon safely," he said softly in her ear.

Maia felt a sense of deep dread inside of her. She knew her grandmother. Sabine would have sent word right away—she would have warned Maia of the Dochte Mandar's decree. Sabine sought to rally the kingdoms to help Comoros defend itself against the armada. She was a natural target for the Victus.

Maia stared at Prince Oderick and then at his chancellor. "You have been tricked, my lords. There is no cure for the hetaera's curse. It was bound by irrevocare sigil. When the prince . . . kissed me, I felt it invoke the Leering. He will become very sick." Maia's heart anguished for the man. "Oderick, if you leave, you will only infect others. If you return to your kingdom, you could be the very means of destroying it." Maia shook her head in frustration. "The Victus sent you here to *die*," she said angrily.

Chancellor Vorstad's eyes widened until nearly all the whites were showing. He took an involuntary step away from the prince, his lips quivering with horror.

"I cannot let you leave," Maia said, staring at the prince. "Think of the deaths you would cause. The plague strikes quick and hard. By tomorrow, you will learn for yourself that my words are true." She reached out and touched the prince's arm. "I am sorry. I would have prevented this if I could have."

The prince stared at her, his face miserable. Then he shook his head. "I am not your hustage," he said. He tried to smile, but his mouth could not work that way. "I am still your guest. You are right, my lady. I must not infect the others." He turned to the chancellor. "Ven it is clear that my death is close, you must return to Hautland. You must abolish the Dochte Mandar from Hautland. I order this, Chancellor. In my father's name. I order this."

***

It was after dark and most of the castle had gone to bed. Maia walked with Richard toward the chancellor's tower, where her aging friend would yet spend a few more hours reading correspondence that had arrived in the middle of the crisis. Richard walked with a slight limp, one hand on his hip as if it pained him, but he never said a word about his suffering.

Maia's heart felt as if it had been trampled on. "How do we fight such cunning?" Maia said as they walked slowly, passing the Leerings that illuminated the way. "First Simon. Then Oderick. Now my grandmother," she said, her stomach clenching with dread. "I fear for Dahomey next."

Richard sighed deeply, his exhaustion evident in his voice. "The role of the High Seer is crucial. If they kill her, then a convocation must be called. A new High Seer will be chosen from amongst the Aldermastons. That process takes . . . months." He breathed out sharply. "The war will be over before then." He gave her a grave look as they walked. "When the Naestors come, they will come quickly, and they will come with fire. We must gather all our people together, Maia. We must congregate them into a place where they can be defended."

"No town is large enough," Maia said. "No castle could fit everyone."

Richard shook his head. "A castle could only defend us from battering rams and catapults. What they are attacking is more than carved stone. They are attacking our very belief, our faith in the Medium. They are attacking our minds." He bowed his head low as they continued to walk. "I have felt the stirrings of the Medium growing," he said softly. "Aldermaston Wyrich has felt this as well. This brooding of the Medium."

He cocked his head at her.

"We must gather at Muirwood now," Maia answered. The words came to her the moment before she said them, and the gush of warmth in her heart and the spark of light in her mind told her they were true.

"Yes," Richard said, nodding. "The abbey will shield us from the Naestors. You know the legend of the Tor, do you not?"

"I know it well. An Aldermaston dropped the hill on a marauding band of Naestors that had invaded the shores of that Hundred."

Richard looked troubled. "What is lesser known is that a village was massacred first. The Naestors plundered it, killing every man, woman, and child."

"A Void," Maia said darkly.

"Maia, the word means empty, unfulfilled. A garden can be rendered void. So can a contract between two merchants. It is as if the contract was never there in the first place. What I do not know, Maia, is how many lives will be lost before the Medium is stirred to defend us."

She swallowed, feeling a bottomless pit in her stomach as she thought of her people—the poor, the powerless, the refugees from Assinica. All of them would need to keep faith in the Medium.

"I believe it will," Maia said, putting her arm around his shoulder and giving him a small hug. "The Medium drove our ancestors away to flee the Scourge. It has brought us back together again to defy those who seek to enslave us. I agree with you . . . there will be a toll of blood to be paid. That has always been the case." They reached the door arch leading to his tower. Several guards were posted there. "What I fear, Richard, is not that the Medium will *not* defend us. What I fear is what it will do to our enemies." She shook her head uneasily. "It is not their fault that they are so bloodthirsty and vicious. This is the way they have been taught since their infancy. I would turn them to our side, if I could."

He gave her a somber look. "You are kind and wise. I only wish more were like you."

Maia smiled and then turned to face the guards. "See that he is kept safe," she instructed. With her hand on his shoulder, she looked into his eyes. "I could not bear it if I lost you. May the Medium protect and guide you, Richard."

"And you, my queen," he responded, his eyes moist and tender.

She paused before leaving. "A question. Have you been shielding me from certain reports? There used to be stories each day about horrific acts people had done to one another. I have not heard of any recently, but I wonder if it is because you have kept the stories to yourself."

He looked at her sadly, his eyes weighed down with sorrow. And she had her answer in his silence.

"Will you return to Muirwood tonight?" he asked her.

Maia nodded. "Have Doctor Bend summoned to examine the prince tomorrow."

"It will be done."

She turned to leave and watched the two guardsmen escort Richard up the tower steps. She had made arrangements for his increased protection with Captain Carew earlier in the day. But the comfort it provided was illusory. If a kishion were determined to kill him, only the Medium could save him. She had to trust in that. As she walked away, she heard the boots trailing behind her, and when she glanced back, she saw two more guardsmen were following her at a respectful distance.

She thought wearily about the events of the day, feeling exhausted, but also restless. So the mere act of touching her lips was enough to invoke the hetaera's Leering. It was not just in the intent. She cupped her mouth, overcome with horror by the thought of what would become of Oderick after his fatal mistake. He had not been driven by logic and reason to seek an alliance with her. His very heart had been tampered and toyed with by their shared enemies. His emotions had been cruelly manipulated. What he had believed to be the Medium truly was not. She knew what it was like to be so deceived, to be so surrounded by lies it was impossible to discern the truth. She walked steadily, heading toward the corridor that would lead her to Claredon Abbey. She wanted to counsel with Aldermaston Wyrich. Perhaps one of the healers from Assinica would know a way to ease the prince's suffering. Besides, she needed to tell him all that had happened that day. He was probably still awake, awaiting her arrival. He usually did that to offer his encouragement and counsel.

The castle was quiet and still, and the empty click of the guards' boots and her scuffing shoes were the only sounds that pierced the night. As she turned the corner, they encountered several other patrolling guards who nodded to her as they passed.

"Good evening, my lady," one of them offered.

She smiled wearily and continued onward. As she turned the final corner, she began to feel almost unbearably fatigued. Two guards stood at the end, blocking the passage.

When they were halfway down the hall, the Leerings extinguished, plunging her into blackness.

An instant sense of dread and fear crawled into her heart. She invoked the Leerings and felt something heavy pressing against them, blocking her power.

Down the corridor, a set of silver eyes began to glow in the dark, and Maia's heart quailed.

She heard the noise of boots coming from both behind and in front of her.

"My lady?" one of her guards said worriedly.

"Call for help—" Maia started to say, and suddenly her tongue was swollen in her mouth, her words choked off. She felt as if a hand were squeezing her throat, but it was no physical hand.

The glowing eyes approached faster, and she began to make out a face. A somewhat handsome face, with brownish-gray hair and a close-cropped beard. She recognized him immediately.

Corriveaux.

She panted, struggling for air. The guards continued to approach from behind, and suddenly a wave of panic and terror blasted from the man's kystrel, knifing through her—and the men behind her. Maia felt her knees buckle, and she dropped to the floor, still struggling to breathe. Her shoulder burned giddily in response to the kystrel's magic. She felt a sense of triumph and delight that clearly was not hers.

One of her guards was trying to speak, perhaps to yell for help, but his voice was strangled and small. He could not utter any words of warning. Both men behind her collapsed and began gibbering in fear.

Maia could almost *feel* the abbey beyond her enemy, a mute witness to her struggle.

"You have become too predictable," Corriveaux said smugly, drawing nearer. The man in the shadows behind him was a brute. They were clearly in this together. Both wore tunics stolen from her guardsmen. She remembered how the Victus liked to impersonate authority. She fought against the surge of panic and fear that engulfed her like drowning waters. She tried to sit up and force her thoughts to obey her.

"But always you flee to the abbeys. When will you learn that they are not a haven for you? A kystrel has more power than a maston could . . . more power than even an abbey. You know *that*. I saw what you did at Cruix. I admired your . . . handiwork. Did you really think stone walls could protect you from me?" The sheen of light from his eyes revealed the stark lines of his face as he moved toward her.

Maia thought of her grandmother. She thought of their walks in Muirwood. She had many more positive memories to draw on now. She had her friendship with Suzenne. Her tender relationship with Richard Syon, which she cherished. There was Jon Tayt, the faithful hound Argus. Her love for Collier. She summoned the memories, and with them came power. The Leerings in the hall began to glow once more, and Maia pushed herself up, wrapping herself in the warm feelings like they were a cloak to protect her from the cold.

Corriveaux frowned when the Leerings began to glow, and she felt his will slam down on her like a steel bar.

"You challenge me still?" he said, fury smoldering in his voice. "When you wore your kystrel, you were *almost* a match for me. But even a maston must yield to a stronger power," he said. "Kishion, *kill* her."

The man next to him, the brute, moved forward, and a dagger appeared in his hand.

Maia gritted her teeth and pulled on the power of the Leerings, trying to make them flare too bright to see. She felt the weight of Corriveaux's will crushing down on her, but she was managing to slowly lift it. The Leerings grew brighter still, their eyes glowing with molten heat. The corridor began to shine.

"You will obey *me*," Corriveaux snarled. His eyes were like fires themselves, only cold and silver.

The edges of her vision began to unravel in black flakes. Maia slumped to the floor, unable to bear the strain. Her heart pounded so loudly in her ears she could no longer hear the thud of the boots approaching her. She fell into the blackness.

The King of Dahomey is a cunning young man. He slips through his kingdom in a disguise—an identity he forged while a prisoner in Paeiz. He is known to us as Feint Collier. A feint is using trickery to mislead your opponent. By focusing Comoros on defending their capital, we misdirect them to our intended aim. If you destroy the pillar, the house will crash down on its own.

—*Corriveaux Tenir, Victus of Dahomey*

CHAPTER
TWENTY-FOUR

Lady Shilton's Manor

Maia dreamed of an abbey burning. She could smell the cinders in the air, feel the waves of fire dance across the stones. At first she thought it was Cruix Abbey, that this was a buried memory that had finally resurfaced. But this abbey was taller and broader—a formidable presence that blazed in the night sky as it went up in flames. She was awed to see it so consumed. A wicked sense of delight made her shudder.

Slowly the edges of the dream faded, and she became aware of a jostling motion. She was being carried. She wondered if the dream had merely changed and she was now back at Muirwood, trussed up in a canvas bag by the sheriff of Mendenhall. But this felt different. She experienced the sensation of being carried up steps. She could hear the hiss of torches and the soft clip of boots against stone; she could smell a musty, earthen odor. If this were a dream, it was an uncommonly vivid one.

Too weak to move or struggle, Maia drifted out of consciousness again and dreamed nothing at all.

She awoke facedown on a pallet.

Her eyes blinked open, her mind snared in a haze of fog. A scratchy wool blanket chafed her face. Stretching her limbs, she discovered she was not bound in ropes or chains. She pushed herself up and discovered the small rectangular pallet where she lay was inset on a series of bed beams and poles. Light streamed in from a tall, narrow window, the glass so thick and treated that it distorted the view outside.

Hearing a subtle cough, she turned her head and found *her* kishion sitting on a stool near the window, using gut thread to sew a knife wound on his upper arm. His shirt was stripped down past his waist, and his muscled back was riddled with scars. He jabbed a needle through his own skin without even a flinch and continued to work. A bluish paste was in a grist bowl next to him, and a pestle lay beside it on the windowsill.

Maia sat up, her heart shuddering as she tried to remember how she had gotten there. It was a small cell, sparsely furnished. There was a wooden bench with several trays containing vials and powders. An executioner's axe hung on a peg on the wall near the only door.

When the kishion finished stitching the wound, he bit off the thread end with his teeth and then cleaned his hands on a rag. He turned and finally noticed her staring at him.

His cheekbone was puffy and bruised. His lip was split with an angry red slash, but the blood had already been mopped up. His nose was a little crooked, and one of his eyes was swollen.

Her heart reached out to him as she realized he had once again saved her life.

"Where is Corriveaux?" she asked, but it came out as a croak. She coughed and tried to swallow, earning a familiar mocking smile from her protector. He grabbed a leather flask from nearby and tossed it to her.

"Across the river by now," the kishion said curtly. "I almost went after him and finished it, but I could not leave you there unprotected." He quickly donned his shirt, stretching his wounded arm and wincing slightly.

Maia stared at him, her feelings conflicted. How many times had he saved her? She had tried to banish him, to rid him from her kingdom, but he was as elusive as smoke.

"Where . . . are we?" she asked, looking around the isolated chamber.

"A secret place." He nodded to the door. "It is pretty thick. It would take a large axe to break that one down. I needed to bring you somewhere safe until you woke." He gave her a pointed look. "Did you . . . *dream*?"

She knew what he was asking her. During their journeys together, she had become possessed by the Myriad Ones at night-fall and would often do or say things she could not remember in the morning.

Maia could almost smell the burning stones of the abbey. "Yes," she answered guiltily. "I did."

He shrugged his unconcern and then fetched a bloodied rag to dab his split bottom lip. "I killed the kishion who was trying to murder you. I did not have time to move his bulk, so he bloodied up the corridor. My apologies for the mess."

"An apology is hardly necessary," she said. "Are we still on the castle grounds?" she persisted, seeking an answer.

He nodded subtly. "But nowhere your people will look. Lady Maia, the spiders are crawling all across the webs, and you do not even see them. The kishion I killed for you? He murdered your spy-master on Flax Street. They sent three others to kill me, you know.

I have dealt with the first, but there are two more. If you stay here, they will murder you. You have no idea what is truly happening."

Maia suppressed another shudder as she stared into the eyes of her menacing companion. The look she saw there frightened her . . . yet she knew she somehow had power over this man. "Then tell me," she offered, sitting on the edge of the bed.

"Before I killed the first man who tried to murder me, I kept him alive and . . . gained some information from him. Corriveaux is intent on unleashing a Void on Comoros. You remember that little village in the mountains?"

"Argus," she said, nodding curtly. Her heart panged her as she remembered the faithful boarhound from which the town had taken its name.

"He and the Victus plan on doing that and worse in Comoros. They wish to make it uninhabitable. Your people are going to die. All of them."

Maia frowned, but she did not look away from him. "We will fight him."

He snorted with laughter. "It would take the combined strength of all the kingdoms to prevent it. No one will leave their own land undefended to come help a pretty young lass new to her throne." His voice was deadly earnest when he continued. "I will not allow them to destroy you."

The look he gave her was suddenly . . . tortured. Clenching his jaw, he glanced away from her and hurled the rag onto the window-sill by the pestle. "You need to leave the city, Maia. The spiders are crawling everywhere now. They have been sneaking in for days."

"Who?"

"The Dochte Mandar!" he said gruffly, giving her a scowl that softened quickly. "Hundreds. There are too many for you. They do not just wish to subvert you, Maia; they want you dead. They will kill you and lead the people to their slaughter." He looked pained by what he said. She could see in his eyes he was utterly convinced of her danger.

She imagined her Privy Council was desperate to find her. By now, they must know about the attempted attack in the castle. "Will you let me go?"

He gave her another scowl and muttered something under his breath.

"You *must* let me go," she pleaded.

"I will on one condition," he said, folding his arms over his chest.

"What is that?" she asked.

"Call off your hounds. I am weary of being hunted. I know you ordered them to find me. Stop it. I am trying to help you. I am loyal to you, Maia. Only to you."

Maia frowned at him. "You murdered my parents."

He shrugged, looking unconcerned. Then his gaze sharpened. "Your father was going to murder you. I could not allow that. I *would not* allow that."

"I will abandon the search for you," she said. "I promise. Right now, it is more important to begin evacuating the city."

"To where?" he grunted contemptuously. "Muirwood? That place is even more vulnerable than the palace. True, the swamp will slow Corriveaux's army down, but the outcome is inevitable. They will bring enough drunk Naestors to do the job, my lady. They will not give you a *moment's* reprieve. I have fought in a war band. That is how I got this," he said, gesturing to his severed ear.

Maia did not want to confirm his hunch, but she sensed he already knew. "The abbey will defend us," she said firmly.

He bit back a laugh. "As you say. Now for my second condition. You are not safe. Corriveaux is determined to butcher you. If you fall, so does the realm. Your guards could not protect you from me, let alone another kishion sent to murder you. I want Tayt by your side during the day. Do not *leave* his sight. I will guard you at night. We will take turns watching over you, as we used to do. No more hiding in Muirwood at night." He leaned back against the wall by the window, folding his arms. "Those are my demands. I know you will keep your word if you promise me something." His lip quivered with a suppressed smile.

Maia knew she did not have time to argue. Besides, what he said made sense. "You will go with us when we abandon the city?" she probed.

He nodded. "You do not always see me when I am near you, Maia."

She felt a mix of dread and reassurance at the thought. He had been part of her life for a while now. They had shared many experiences. Despite her complete disapproval of his choices, she cared for him as a friend. Still, she was concerned about the look she saw in his eyes when he looked at her. She thought about Collier, so very far away, and wished again that she could see him.

"Very well," she said, wondering if she would come to regret her decision.

***

Maia found the palace in an uproar. Every guardsman, servant, and guest was frantically searching the grounds for her. When she was discovered walking in from a remote part of the castle, there was a gush of relief. Suzenne, who had taken part in the search effort all night, burst into relieved tears upon seeing her. No one from Claredon had seen her enter the abbey the previous night, and concern for her had risen to a fever pitch when a man was found dead in the corridor connecting the palace with the abbey wall. Maia called an emergency meeting of the Privy Council and explained exactly what had happened and her new understanding with the kishion. She would not go back on her word.

The lord mayor was ordered to summon the city watch and begin a manhunt for Corriveaux. Searching both sides of the river—as well as every boat in the harbor—would be arduous, and Maia was far from certain Corriveaux was still in the city, but she did not want to make it easy for him to walk into her kingdom with impunity. After all, the Dochte Mandar had been expelled from the kingdom, which was one law of her father's she did not plan to change. She warned Justin that Corriveaux had a habit of traveling with men who impersonated soldiers from whatever realm he was infiltrating, and requested that a watchword be created to help identify friend from foe. She also sent word to Muirwood to summon the Aldermaston's steward to Comoros. The Privy Council would prepare to implement the evacuation plans immediately.

It was a long and difficult day, and Maia could not banish the kishion from her thoughts. She had summoned Jon Tayt after the council meeting to tell him what the kishion had demanded of her. Jon Tayt had frowned fiercely, and his anger toward the kishion had barely cooled by nightfall. He insisted on going everywhere with her, and she found his constant companionship a reminder of the voyage they had made together.

Later that day, as Maia ate in her private chambers, Suzenne arrived with Doctor Bend to report on the condition of the Prince of Hautland. The night before, Prince Oderick had come down with a mild fever. During the day, the fever had grown rapidly, and other symptoms had manifested themselves. He was isolated from all but his most loyal servants, who refused to leave his side but still pressed linen napkins to their mouths whenever they stood near him. The doctor's report made Maia cringe, and she found she could not finish her meal. Jon Tayt happily devoured it.

As soon as the doctor had left, Suzenne came over to her and whispered in her ear.

"I know you are tired, Maia, but there is one person who came after nightfall for an audience with you. I tried to find out what she wants, but she says she will only tell you." Suzenne pulled back and looked into Maia's eyes. "It is Maeg Baynton. She claims it is important Cipher business."

Maia looked at Suzenne in concern. She had not given much thought to her erstwhile enemy Maeg, who had tormented her while they were studying at Muirwood together. She was the daughter of the dead sheriff of Mendenhall. Maia had heard nothing about her since they had both left the abbey—she had been too consumed with the troubles of her kingdom to worry about a girl who could not stand her.

Maia felt an oncoming sigh. "She will not tell you?"

Suzenne shook her head. "Should I have her wait until tomorrow?"

"No," Maia said, touching her friend's arm. "Send her in."

After Suzenne left, Maia shot a worried glance at Jon Tayt.

"I remember the lass," he said candidly. "Pretty face. Mean as a cat whose tail was run over by a cart."

Maia stifled a smile as the door to her private room opened and Suzenne ushered Maeg inside. She shut the door after the girl, leaving her alone with Maia and Jon Tayt.

The gown Maeg wore was instantly and painfully familiar. It marked her as one of the servants of Lady Shilton. Maia herself had eventually been given a gown after the same fashion. She had worn it on the *Blessing of Burntisland*. She had worn it while facing the lost abbey. She had worn it across Dahomey and into Mon. Seeing Maeg wear a similar gown made her draw up short.

"You serve Lady Shilton?" Maia asked in surprise.

"Yes," Maeg said, fidgeting with her skirts. She looked uncomfortable . . . no, she looked terror-stricken. Her eyes were haunted.

"What is it?" Maia asked, rising to her feet and walking toward the other girl. "What has happened?"

"I tried to come earlier," Maeg said, her voice low and soft. She glanced around the room surreptitiously. "We are truly alone except for the hunter?"

Maia felt a spasm of fear. "Yes. Suzenne said you wanted to tell me something. Why could you not share the truth with her?"

The suggestion made Maeg look even more miserable, if it were possible. "Because it concerns her as well, and she was my friend once . . . before she was yours."

"Tell me," Maia said softly, stroking the girl's arm. "I am not your enemy, Maeg."

Maeg tried to laugh but could not. She sighed, mastered her emotions with apparent difficulty, and continued. "I did find a position after Muirwood," she said. Smoothing the skirts of her gown, she continued, "with Lady Shilton. Aldermaston Joanna . . . she encouraged it discreetly, believing it would help you to have a Cipher in that household." She paused and stared down at the ground for a moment before speaking again. "My apparent dislike of you, Your Majesty, actually helped me earn the position."

Maia tried to listen patiently, but she could sense the news would be terrible. "Go on."

"Just before the Hautlander ships arrived, a ship from Dahomey came." Maia's heart flinched, and she tried to keep her expression guarded. "Secret visitors entered Lady Shilton's manor. One was a man, a Dochte Mandar. He bore a Dahomeyjan name . . . Corriveaux . . . and he seemed to know Lady Shilton." Maeg swallowed, fidgeting more. "There were other men with him . . . dangerous men. Men that made me shudder. They guarded the house, and no one was allowed in or out during his visit. They gave something to Lady Murer. At first I thought it was just a necklace . . . but Maia, it was a *kystrel*." Fear flashed in her eyes. "I watched her summon its power. Her eyes glowed silver. I have never been so frightened."

"By Idumea," Maia whispered in horror.

Corriveaux had taken from her the kystrel that Chancellor Walraven had given her. It was full of Maia's memories and fears and emotions. She knew, without being told, that this was the same kystrel he had given to Murer.

"That was before they took Lady Murer," Maeg added.

"What? They took her?"

Maeg's fidgeting worsened. "I know where they went. Lady Murer . . . you should have heard her boast of it. As soon as she put on the kystrel, she changed. She had been miserable since losing her position. She would mourn and then rage about it often. Once she had the kystrel, she became imbued with power. She wants revenge against you and anyone close to you." Maeg gave Maia an imploring look and took her hand. "Murer went *north*. She is going to destroy Dodd's army and burn Billerbeck Abbey. And she plans to ruin your relationship . . . with the King of Dahomey. She left two days ago. I tried to escape, but the house has been guarded until today. Corriveaux returned this morning, alone, and took the others with him and fled the city. I cannot go back there, Maia. They will know I betrayed them. They will kill me."

Maia stared into the other girl's eyes, into the well of conviction and despair she saw there, and then looked over at Jon Tayt.

"Your strongest army is in the north," he said, his own gaze full of wrath. "He will hold his own, by Cheshu. He better."

But Maia could not bear to tell him what she knew about the powers of a kystrel. And if Murer's goal was to travel to Dahomey, it meant only one thing.

Her stepsister Murer was turning into a hetaera.

CHAPTER TWENTY-FIVE

Burning

It was nearing midnight when Lady Shilton and her household arrived at the palace under guard. Maia was weary, but she dared not sleep. Guards roamed the corridors and the city was restive and uneasy. Some families had abandoned their homes during the day, and more were beginning to trickle out.

Maia waited impatiently in the solar with Jon Tayt as her silent companion. It was the room where she had met her father the night he had sent her to seek the lost abbey. It was full of memories. She was heartsick from the knowledge that her impulsive, selfish stepsister was on the loose . . . and that she was likely wearing Maia's former kystrel. The power the kystrel contained was enormous, and she had no doubt that Murer would not exercise the restraint Chancellor Walraven had always encouraged in her. After Maeg left, Maia had shared her news with Suzenne. The look on her friend's face would haunt her nights for weeks to come. Suzenne trusted Dodd's integrity, but she did not trust him completely against the power of a kystrel wielded by a jealous woman. While Lady Shilton had never implied Dodd would be a target for revenge, Maia and Suzenne knew the ways of the hetaera. With a face chalk white with dread, Suzenne had begged to go to Claredon Abbey to travel by Apse Veil to Billerbeck to warn Dodd about the invasion. She had left hours before, and there was still no sign of her.

The guards at the door announced the arrival of Lady Shilton. Richard had already interrogated her in his tower, and he accompanied her now. The woman looked frightened, her nerves frayed. Dark smudges marked the flesh under her eyes, and there was a guilty look about her.

Maia's mind swarmed with memories of the hostility and abuse she had received from this woman. It nearly overwhelmed her, and she could not keep a disapproving frown from her mouth. She reined in her feelings, knowing that the dark memories would only foster more ill will between them. Instead, she forced herself to remember the night Lady Shilton had at last showed her compassion by giving her a new gown and trying to help ease her pain. Of course, Maia had been poisoned that same night, but she had survived that ordeal. She reminded herself that this woman's daughter had been executed. The fall from grace must have been painful.

"Your Maj . . . esty summoned me," Lady Shilton said in a tremulous voice.

Maia had been fidgeting all night and could not bear to sit down. Anxious to keep herself moving so fatigue would not drag her down, she approached her one-time jailer. "Lady Shilton," she said with a nod. The woman looked haunted . . . fearful.

"I wish to plead for a life," Lady Shilton said, coming forward and dropping to her knees. "You may do what you will with me, but I *beg* you to spare my granddaughter."

Richard stepped forward and put his hand on her shoulder. "Before you beg for mercy, Lady Shilton, it would be best if you shared with the queen what you confessed to me this evening."

Lady Shilton trembled and looked at the hand on her shoulder with abhorrence. She twisted her neck to gaze up at Richard Syon.

It did not escape Maia's notice that Jon Tayt seemed about ready to spit on the hem of the woman's dress. He sat by the window seat, holding a mug, and sipped from it slowly. He remained quiet and unobtrusive.

Lady Shilton wrung her hands.

"Please," Maia said, reaching down and helping the older woman stand. "Sit at the table. Would you like something to drink?" The main table had plenty of empty chairs. Jon Tayt sat by the window overlooking the black night sky.

The woman allowed Maia to help her rise, and she cringed at the compassion being shown to her by the girl she had so mistreated. "Nothing," she answered, shaking her head curtly. She retreated to the offered chair and sat, tucking some stray wisps of hair behind her ear. Her face was lined from age, but she still tried to maintain the illusion of youth through the fashion of her hair and the rouge on her cheeks.

Maia sat adjacent to her and then took her hand and patted it comfortingly. Richard sat in a chair opposite her and folded his hands on the table before him. He watched her sternly.

Lady Shilton trembled. A few fat tears pooled in her eyes. They quivered and hung on her lashes, and only did not fall because of the great force of her will. "I am guilty," she whispered hoarsely. "I have always . . . hated you. Because you were so good. I thought you would succumb. Even a dog flinches from its master if it is beaten enough."

Jon Tayt stifled a grunt, earning a look of misery from Lady Shilton.

"And yet you persisted despite my efforts to humiliate and destroy you. I . . . I am a traitor to Comoros. I deserve to die. But I am still a grandmother, and I love my own family." She looked down at the table, trying to master the courage to speak. "I was a maston, you know. I studied at Billerbeck, but was not allowed to read. I was always so tempted by the forbidden knowledge. I did everything I could to steal glances at tomes. I was ambitious, so I resented the Aldermaston who prevented me from learning. I knew that the Medium brings you your thoughts. If you want it enough. If you demand it." She hung her head. "I was a fool."

Richard cleared his throat. "The hour is late, Lady Shilton. Tell her."

Maia stared at the older woman curiously, wondering what dreadful secrets were finally releasing from her scabbed heart.

"I began to befriend some of the Dochte Mandar," Lady Shilton said. "I wanted to know why women were forbidden to read. They toyed with me. Toyed with my emotions, I think. They told me I would be taught if I gave up my child to learn as well. I was married by that time, joined to a man I did not love. Deorwynn was our only child. When she came of age, I was told to send her to Dahomey for her maston training. They promised me that one day she would become queen. I thought perhaps they meant she would be Queen of Dahomey, but I realized later that it was Comoros she was fated to rule. She was taken in by a strong-willed man, a man whom I later realized was a Victus. His name was Corriveaux Tenir. They became lovers. He inspired her with ambition. He corrupted her heart as the Dochte Mandar had corrupted mine. She ruined your father, who was a faithful maston at the time."

Maia's heart burned with anger. She thought of Collier and found it difficult to keep the look of fury from her face.

"Your daughter was loyal to the Victus," Maia said. "That I know. What of Murer?"

"She was to become a hetaera if you failed to *become*," Lady Shilton said, her voice low. "They were grooming you, you see. There is power gained in suffering, and after a time, I realized the Victus were using my family to shape you and make you strong. I feared what you would do to us when you came to power. But I was too compromised. And you failed to accept the fate they had fashioned for you. That left me with the hope that the Victus would choose my granddaughter to fulfill your destiny. Not just to become Queen of Comoros, but to become *empress* of all the kingdoms. You see, Murer is Corriveaux's daughter. She is strong willed and subtle, like her father. She is wiser than her own mother, always playing the innocent. In truth, she knew Deorwynn was losing her station, and she did not want to lose her own in the rubble. Murer came to me after your coronation. She has been secretly communing with her father through a Leering in my manor house." Lady Shilton started to wring her hands again. "He arrived and gave her your kystrel. For a hetaera to achieve her greatest power, she must first betray someone she loves. She was interested in the King of Dahomey and he spurned her. For *you*. Murer will seek your lover in Dahomey, but first she will burn Billerbeck Abbey. That will be the signal for the armada to land in the north and begin the invasion. As you send your troops there to fight, the second wave of ships will strike in the west, in Caspur's Hundred. Their goal is to trap you in Comoros before you can flee to Muirwood with your people."

Lady Shilton seized Maia's wrist, her look desperate. "I have confessed all of this without torture. I deserve to perish and will gladly face the headsman's axe. I *implore* you to spare my granddaughter. She was corrupted and twisted as a youth. She was never even given the chance to study at an abbey or become a maston. She has not been hardened by suffering as you have. Please spare her life, Your Highness. I beg of you!"

Maia felt the strain on her wrist from the old woman's fingers. She glanced up at Richard and saw the displeasure rife in his face.

"There is a saying from Ovidius," Maia said, wresting her hand away from Lady Shilton's grip. "What is allowed us is disagreeable, what is denied us creates intense desire. You were a maston and you knew you sought a forbidden path." Maia slowly rose from her chair. "Your daughter was executed because of what she learned from your example. And now your granddaughter seeks to destroy the kingdom—nay, the realm—because of her ambition." Maia tried to feel compassion, but it had withered away. "What did Corriveaux promise, I wonder? That he would spare the kingdom if you succeeded in killing me?"

Lady Shilton's tears trickled down her cheeks. She shook her head. "He will not spare Comoros," she said, grieving. "Only the lives of my Family. Everyone else will be destroyed. Including you."

"I am sorry for the choices you have made," Maia said, folding her arms. "But you made them willingly. You knew exactly what you were doing. Richard, have her sent to the dungeon. Her servants must be questioned as well. If any knew and did not tell, they will share her fate." Maia stared down at the woman, her enemy. The door opened and in walked Suzenne, her face gray with pallor. She looked on the verge of despair.

"Take her away," Maia whispered.

"Your Majesty, I beg you!" Lady Shilton shrieked.

Maia shook her head. "You could have come to me sooner, Lady Shilton. You could have exposed this threat to my kingdom, and I would have pardoned you. An earlier confession would have saved you, and it would have saved your granddaughter." She repressed a shudder. "Do you know what Corriveaux has done to *my* grandmother?"

Lady Shilton's face crumbled. "They have brought her in chains to Naess. She will be executed."

At that, Maia nodded to Richard to have the woman removed. Lady Shilton began choking down sobs as the guardsmen took her away.

From the expression on Suzenne's face, Maia feared the worst. She closed the distance and hugged her friend fiercely, smoothing back her golden tresses and feeling her repressed sobs in the movement of her back.

"Billerbeck Abbey has burned," Suzenne whispered in a quavering voice.

"No!" Maia groaned, shaking her head and feeling tears threaten her. So many years had been poured into rebuilding it. Now it was gone . . . like Cruix Abbey. And it was the signal that the armada would strike her realm. The flames would summon the fleet like vicious moths. She remembered her dream from the previous night. A dream about an abbey burning and the joy and delight felt while watching it.

And she knew in an instant that Murer had done it. Maia could feel the connection between them. She knew that if she delved into that buried part of herself, she would be linked to Murer's mind. She could learn about her enemies, know their plans. But it would require her to sink back into that terrible abyss. It would allow her to be sucked into the Myriad Ones' web.

Maia pulled away, cupping Suzenne's cheek. She rubbed one of her friend's tears away with her thumb. "What else did you learn?" she asked.

Jon Tayt rose from the bench and came forward, his expression intense and furious.

Stifling a sob, Suzenne folded her arms across her bosom. "I thought it was my fault, at first. That the Medium would not work for me because I was too anxious. I could not cross the Apse Veil myself. But the Aldermaston sent for his steward, and he could not cross it either. So both of us traveled to Muirwood, and it worked. They have also been unable to contact Billerbeck Abbey today. The nearest abbey to that location is Sempringfall. I crossed with several others and discovered they had just heard of the abbey's destruction. A short while later, word arrived of the armada's landing at Billerbeck. There are riders coming to warn you, Maia, but the Apse Veils were faster." She wiped her eyes. "Forshee Hundred has been invaded. I have no word from my husband. I do not know if he is even alive. Or where he is right now."

Suzenne's face crumbled and she started weeping violently. Maia hugged her close, feeling her own heart breaking.

***

Maia sent for Jayn Sexton to help comfort Suzenne and take her to bed. Soon Jon Tayt and Maia were left alone in the solar again. The night was dark and oppressive, and Maia found herself staring at her own reflection in the glass window. A panel in the wall opened in the reflection, and she whirled around to look. A moment later the kishion stepped through a gap.

Jon Tayt's neck muscles tensed as he saw the other man enter the room.

The kishion sauntered over to a tray of leftover food and began nibbling on a piece of meat. He fetched himself a goblet and poured some cider.

"What do we do now?" Maia said. She heaved a mournful sigh and folded her arms in front of her.

Jon Tayt rose from the window seat and hooked his thumbs in his belt. "It is a fine kettle of fish," he said with clenched teeth. "How much did you overhear?" he asked the kishion.

The man grunted as he swallowed a mouthful of food, then scooped up some roasted nuts and munched a few. "All that I needed to hear," he said enigmatically. He gave Maia a probing look. "Spiders, as I warned you. Corriveaux fled, but you can be assured he left others in the city to work his mischief."

The bruise on his cheek had turned purple, she noticed, and there was a brownish-red clot of blood on his split lip. He seemed to enjoy the nuts and took another scoop.

"We must evacuate the city immediately," Maia said. "It will take a lot of time to move so many people."

"To Muirwood?" the kishion said with a disapproving grunt.

Maia nodded. "That Hundred is our most defensible position. They cannot attack it by sea. The Bearden Muir will slow them down and give us time to call for aid."

The kishion looked smug and shook his head with barely concealed mirth. "You believe that if you wish, Maia. Dahomey is locked in battle with Paeiz. It is deliberate, I assure you. Prince Oderick of Hautland is retching violently and sick with fever. Even *I* know he will not recover from his illness, and it is no poison of mine that afflicts him. So will Hautland come to your aid? I think not. That leaves . . . Mon? You burned *their* main abbey, if you remember. Besides, getting word to them will take time, and time you do not have. That leaves Pry-Ree and Avinion, the two smallest kingdoms. And your grandmother has been imprisoned. Do not think the Victus will not use her as leverage to prolong the ordeal. They will kill her, you can be certain, but not before they use her to get what they want. Avinions can carve gems and catch fish. Perhaps one of those skills will be useful to you." He laughed heartily and took another fistful of nuts into his mouth and chewed them noisily. "Believe me when I tell you that the Naestors have enough men and enough axes to cut down every stunted oak tree between here and Muirwood Abbey. And *that* will provide the kindling. They are going to unleash a Void. The sooner you accept this truth, the better."

Maia felt anger stir at his hopeless appraisal of the situation. "I will not abandon my people. I trust the Medium will assist us."

At those words, the kishion sneered. "Very well. Let the Medium save you. But when you learn to your grief that it obeys whoever *forces* it to obey, you may remember what I have told you. You have always had a soft heart for your people, Lady Maia. But they will forsake you in the end. Especially when Corriveaux promises to spare their lives if they give you up." He gave her a stern look. "You know as well as I do that he is a liar. He will dangle hope and then crush it under his heel. Even Lady Shilton is a fool for trusting his promises. Men like him know only how to burn things."

He tipped his goblet toward her. Then he looked at Jon Tayt. "It is my turn to guard her. Off with you now."

Jon Tayt's eyes burned with anger. He sat rigid, his curly coppery hair glinting in the light. In that moment, he looked like a man prepared to fight to the death.

Maia approached the hunter and put her hand on his shoulder. "Good night, Jon Tayt. I will stay in the castle tonight." She gave him a gentle nudge. She could not bear to lose him too.

I perceive that the kishion loves her. Or he feels what he esteems to be that emotion. Truly, the powers of a kystrel are penetrating. Her short time with him managed to overcome even the most arduous training a man can endure. One is brave who overcomes his desires—not just his enemies. The hardest victory is always over self. If Maia can vanquish a cold-hearted killer, then I imagine my daughter will make far easier sport of her victims. She wants to seduce Dahomey's king for revenge. We should have unleashed Murer with a kystrel earlier. Then Comoros would not have needed to be destroyed.

—Corriveaux Tenir, Victus of Dahomey

CHAPTER TWENTY-SIX

Forgetting

In her dream, she was floating. There was a subtle bob and sway, the shifting groan of timbers. She was at sea. It was not the *Blessing of Burntisland*. It was the *Argiver*. Looking down at herself, she saw she was wearing a rich gold gown, a costly dress from the master seamstresses of Dahomey. It fit her well, hugging her hips and draping featherlight against her skin. How strange it was that she could remember even the smallest details, the intricate seams and beaded designs woven into the fabric. It was the gown of a queen, and she had not worn its like since abandoning her destiny as a hetaera.

Maia rubbed her arm, feeling the smooth fabric there. It was so real. Were dreams normally this vivid? Collier had left her to change, she remembered. Her husband then—but no longer. Her stomach was worried, wrought with the anticipation of his return. Maia needed to tell him something. What did she need to tell him? Her mind was a syrupy fog. She had to confess something.

When she had married him, she had not been herself. The urge to speak the truth to him burned on her tongue. She had to confess herself, had to give him the chance to cast her aside. He would show her a box of jewels. In her mind's eye, she could see them.

No, they were in a box on the table in front of her. The wooden box with velvet seating was open, and she saw the lustrous baubles wink up at her. She remembered the stones . . . gems that were bluish green . . . the color of her eyes, he had said. Her hands moved of their own will as they lifted the necklace and fastened it around her neck, her skin feeling the poke of the little hasps as she arranged it. The necklace was made of gold and stunning gems, and she could feel its weight just beneath her kystrel.

Confusion warped Maia's mind. No, Collier wore her kystrel. And yet she could feel the medallion nestled against her bosom. It was warm, almost burning. Her breastbone was stained with creeping, ivy-like tattoos. They were small, like a tiny budding flower. A taller wave made the ship lurch, and Maia gripped the table and watched the jewelry box slide. The swell ended and then she reached in and took the bracelets, sliding them onto her wrists. There was a spot for earrings, but they were missing. She would have to wait for them until Maia was dead.

The thought sent a spasm of alarm through Maia. She was asleep, yes, but this was not a dream. She was leagues away, on a boat. As she tried to clear her vision, she saw that she was not in the *Argiver* at all. This was not the captain's quarters, but a lush room fit for a ruler. There was an enormous canopied bed, and gowns had been tossed hither and yon. There were still more hanging from wooden pegs and stacked on chests. The room was rife with the smell of the sea as well as the overpowering smell of cider.

On the far wall, there was an oval mirror. Maia was certain she was in someone else's body . . . and she thought she knew whose. If the woman would only look at herself in the mirror, she would know for sure.

As if in obedience to the thought, she felt the woman rise.

So you wish to see yourself? Very well.

The mirror showed a shaft of light as the door opened and a man drew in his head. He had a pointed beard, a thick muscled chest, and a rakish look. There was a sword at his hip. He was easily forty, and sweeps of gray meshed with his dark locks. He was unfamiliar to Maia.

"You look . . . dazzling," the man said in a thick accent, absorbing her with his eyes. Maia felt the pulse of the kystrel and could sense that it inflamed the man's passions even more. He stared at her, his eyes hungry, his mouth slightly open as if he were dumbfounded. Maia could sense his desire and passion as a physical force.

Maia saw all of this through the reflection in the mirror. The door was somewhere behind her, but the mirror revealed it. And then another image blocked her view. The woman herself.

Murer. Maia recognized her haughty face, but she saw in her eyes a vengefulness that looked both cruel and alluring. It was like looking at herself, and Maia's senses reeled from the sight. Murer was wearing a wig, the hair a deep brown to match Maia's own locks. The gown, the jewels, the hair. A sickening horror spread through her.

Ah, you understand at last. I am you, Maia. I am what you should have become. And he will mourn the day he spurned me in that dance. He will beg for my mercy and forgiveness, but he shall not get it. They are coming for you, Maia. I will claim the crown you stole from me after all your bodies are burned.

"Where are we, Captain?" Murer asked the man with the pointed beard, smoothing the fabric of the golden gown seductively, knowing he could see her reflection in the mirror.

"We have arrived at the riverhead, my lady. We will be docked within the hour at Lisyeux." His voice throbbed with emotion. He could hardly keep his composure.

Murer smoothed some hair over her ears, a small frown forming on her face when she did not feel earrings there. *Ah, but you have them, Maia.*

"I have the cloak for you, my lady," the captain said, entering with a deep velvet shroud. "You wished to be seen arriving from the abbey. There will be a coach brought straightaway."

"Very well. That is all," Murer said, waving him away with a dismissive look.

"Is there *another* way I may serve you?" he asked pleadingly.

"Be gone," she said curtly, but gave him a sly look as he shut the door.

Maia struggled to force herself awake. She shook against the grip that held her and felt her left shoulder burn. The pain, oh, the pain—

"Wake up! Maia, wake up!"

She could almost hear the tinkling sound of Murer's laughter as she was ripped away from the vision. *Men are easily seduced, Maia. They never cease craving with their eyes. They want to yield to us. Even the mastons. You had your chance. Now it is my turn.*

The vision broke apart and Maia found herself being shaken violently. She was in her nightclothes, in her bed in the palace. The blankets were tangled and askew. Strong hands gripped her shoulders, clenching hard enough to hurt.

"Please, wake up!" the kishion said with desperation. His fingers made the brand on her shoulder burn and she knew that if she had not been wearing the chaen beneath her chemise, the Myriad Ones would have already infested her. Even with it, she could feel them mewling around her, hissing.

Her eyes snapped open, and she saw the kishion's face, a look of worry and fear mingling with his scars. His eyes were wide and sincerely concerned.

"I am well, let me go!" she said, realizing only then she was trembling, and pushed his arms away.

Looking relieved, he released his hold on her shoulders. She could feel the marks where his fingers had pressed and was very aware of how close he was and the smell of him, and a spasm of fear shook her.

Maybe it shone on her face. His look hardened, turning in an instant from concern to spurned anger, and he rose and stepped away from the bed.

"It was another nightmare," he said, almost defensively. Frail light seeped in through the parted curtains. She saw him walk to the table and grab a goblet. He raised it to his lips and gulped the liquid inside down quickly, muttering something to himself she could not make out.

Maia ripped away the bed sheets and blankets. It was dawn, just as it had been in her dream. That meant Murer had already left Comoros by ship and sailed across the channel to Dahomey. It was not a great distance to travel, and in good weather could be done in less than a day. She strode over to the changing screen, snatching one of her gowns on the way.

"What is it?" the kishion asked her gruffly. "In a hurry to leave me?" He scowled, as if already regretting the choice of words.

"Thank you for watching over me," Maia said, holding the gown in the crook of her arm and pausing before the changing screen. "It was not just a dream . . . but a vision of sorts. I must go to Dahomey. Right away."

"What?" he asked with a perplexed chuckle.

Maia summoned light from the Leerings in the room, and they

dispelled the gloom and shadows, revealing her private chambers. None of her ladies-in-waiting were present, since Suzenne had ordered them to move around to various chambers to protect them and conceal where Maia slept. She quickly removed the nightgown and then pulled on the other gown, trying to hurry for fear someone would enter and find her alone with the kishion.

"You must *go*," she said, struggling to fit her hands through the sleeves. The impatience to be gone was frightening.

"You are *not* going to Dahomey," he said angrily. "What was this dream? Tell me."

Maia repressed the urge to scream at him and the gown in frustration. "It was not a dream, it was a vision. I was in a ship . . . no . . . I could *see* a ship heading to Dahomey. My stepsister was there."

"Murer," said the kishion knowingly.

Maia finished putting her arms in the sleeves, only to belatedly realize that the gown laced up in the back. She did the first of the lower strings, but she knew she could not finish it herself. Her cheeks burned with embarrassment; it galled her to her core to have to ask *him* for assistance.

She straightened the skirts and pulled the strings as tight as she could manage. Gritting her teeth, she rested her head on the wooden frame of the changing screen.

"Can you . . . help me?" she asked in a small, defeated voice.

He had a quiet step, and she barely heard his boots on the floor, but he approached the screen.

"What is it?" he asked.

Maia sighed, smothering her pride, and stepped around so he could see her. "I cannot do the lacings . . . by myself," she said. "I should have chosen another dress, but I was not thinking."

He gave her a curious look. "For a moment, I thought you had discovered a tick and needed me to fetch a hot needle." A low smile came to his mouth as he brought up their shared memory of the cursed shores. He shrugged as if it were no matter to help a queen with her gown and quickly cinched up the lacings and tied the string off deftly.

"So Murer is headed to Dahomey," he said.

"I have to warn my husband," Maia said, fidgeting.

"But he is *not* your husband," he reminded her. "You fear his faithlessness so much? I am not surprised," he added with a chuckle.

"I do not fear his faithfulness," she said, perhaps too hotly. "But Murer is a hetaera . . . or nearly one. And she has *my* kystrel. That is why I connected with her so easily. It was like I was inside her mind."

The kishion frowned. "Was she aware of you?"

Maia nodded, folding her arms over her chest to quell the heaving of her stomach.

"Then there is likely a trap waiting for you," the kishion said. "They are luring you away."

Maia stared at him, not wanting to believe what he said, but seeing the truth in it.

"You doubt me," he said, snorting. "I am no Victus, Maia. But I have worked for them long enough. What does a fisherman use? Not just a hook. He uses bait. Corriveaux tried to murder you in person. Now that you have not complied with his will, he wants you out of the way. If he cannot come to you, then he will make you come to him."

"But I can travel through the Apse Veil," Maia said, growing angrier by the moment.

"And do you not suppose that they are watching the abbeys on that side as well?" He folded his arms and gave her an imperious look.

"I must at least send him a message," Maia conceded, "with someone I can trust."

The kishion nodded. "I knew you would think of it once you had calmed down. Good lass."

She was about to storm to the door, but he caught her sleeve. "Brush your hair first. You are a queen."

***

There was so much to do that Maia did not have time to eat. The lord mayor announced the evacuation of Comoros that morning, and the plans they had formed over these last weeks were put in place immediately. The city would be abandoned quarter by quarter—those closest to the river first, followed by those on the outskirts. The city watch roamed the streets and manned the gates, helping the carts and wagons as they began to trundle toward Mendenhall castle, leagues away, where the citizens of Muirwood Hundred would be gathering before trekking into the Bearden Muir.

Sempringfall Abbey still stood, but reports had streamed in throughout the night confirming that Billerbeck had been razed and the armada had arrived. There was still no word from Dodd or his army. The Naestors had brought both horses and foot soldiers, and they had pillaged Forshee, driving the inhabitants from their homes in fear and terror. Refugees were arriving in hordes from the north, heading toward safer ground. Word had been sent to Augustin and Ceaster Abbeys in the south and west, warning them that the invasion had begun. Fishing boats were being used to ferry people from Caspur Hundred to Winterrowd, where they would walk on foot to Muirwood. The Earl of Caspur had sent word that his army stood ready for Maia's orders. Should he come to the capital and help with the evacuation? Or defend the southern borders should the second attack arrive as predicted?

After counseling with her advisors, Maia had ordered Caspur to hold the south and slow any advancing army to buy time for the people of Comoros to flee. If Lady Shilton's warning bore weight, it would be the most useful position for him . . . and it would help trump the Victus's plan.

What surprised Maia was how many people were refusing to abandon the city. According to the lord mayor, at least two in ten households desired to remain behind and ride out the storm.

"They would rather linger here and *die*, Justin?" she asked him, shocked. She cast her eyes around the mostly empty council chamber, shaking her head in disbelief.

He tapped his goatee and pointed at her. "You would be surprised how many of them have never left the city before. They feel safe behind these walls, even though they *know* the walls cannot protect them from the Dochte Mandar. They just do not believe that the Dochte Mandar would murder them all. Some say you are fearmongering."

"I cannot understand," Maia said, shaking her head. She glanced at Suzenne and Jayn, who sat close to her, to see if they shared her incredulity. "We have been planning this for several months, Justin. Why are they balking now?"

"Some people will not believe in a danger unless they can see it with their own eyes. There are undisputed reports that the Naestors have arrived . . . in force." He puffed out his breath. "I think our estimates of the size of their army may have been too hopeful. Tens of thousands have disembarked on the first day alone. They are coming ashore on canoes and skiffs. Some of our people want to trample each other to flee. My question for you is this, my lady—should we force everyone to leave? And what about the prisoners being held in the dungeon?"

Maia gave him an icy look. "Send them in barred wagons to the dungeon at Mendenhall castle. They will not be left to face Corriveaux's questionable mercy, but they will not be freed. They have had second chances enough, and will face trial when this war is over."

The door to the solar opened and Richard strode in with a tall man wearing a hooded cloak. The man was gangly and tall and unfamiliar, but his clothing was Dahomeyjan. Her pulse quickened.

"What do you think of those who will not leave, Jayn? Suzenne?" Maia asked, looking to her friends.

"Two in ten is significant," Jayn said. "But can we truly force them to come? The Medium resists compulsion in any form. They cannot be persuaded to see reason, Lord Mayor?"

Justin threw up his hands. "It is a simple enough argument. If you remain in the city, you will die. We thrust out the Dochte Mandar, if you remember. I imagine they will not be friendly when they return on warships. I do not know how much more motivation I can offer them!"

Maia turned to glance at Suzenne.

It seemed as if they shared the same thought, for suddenly Suzenne quoted the maston proverb that had been running through Maia's mind. "A gentle answer turns away wrath. Harsh words stir up anger."

Maia smiled and nodded to Richard. "That is one of the Aldermaston's favorite ones. I remember it well. Justin, you have done all you can. Continue to oversee the evacuation. This city must be deserted when the Naestors come. Suzenne, Jayn. Gather my handmaidens. Go out into the city and seek to persuade the families to leave. Especially the elderly and those with little children. If their parents will not leave, coax them into letting us help their children escape. This would ease my burden greatly."

Jayn and Suzenne both rose, holding hands to give each other strength. "We will go," Jayn promised, and Maia loved her for it.

She had entrusted a message for Collier with Richard and begged him to send someone loyal and reliable to deliver the missive to her husband. She had not expected an answer so soon, as she knew Collier was likely riding with his army against Paeiz rather than waiting behind in Lisyeux. The man next to Richard was almost twice his height, a scarecrow of a man.

"Maia, this is De Vere from Lisyeux Abbey. He is the Aldermaston's steward."

The man lowered his hood, revealing a head of close-cropped hair that was pepper colored and well spotted with white. He was lean and long, his complexion weather-beaten, as if he had spent his entire life out of doors instead of inside an abbey.

"My lady," the man said with a crooked bow and a thick accent. He had a gouty hip joint as he bent and winced. "I bring this from my master, the King of Dahomey. He gave it to me himself and requested that I entrust it to no hand other than your own. As you and I have never met, he bade me to ask you a password to confirm. He asked for the name of your favorite hound." He gave her a pleasant smile and awaited her answer.

"Argus, who shared a name with a village in the mountains south of Roc-Adamour." Maia replied softly in Dahomeyjan, smiling warmly at him.

The maston's face crinkled into a delighted grin. "You do justice to my mother tongue, my lady," he said jovially. "I heard that you did. You are our true queen, Lady Marciana. If you will have us." He extended to her a small folded card, sealed with wax.

"Is this an answer to my warning?" Maia asked, taking it with trembling fingers. She could not believe Collier had responded so quickly.

"No, my lady," De Vere answered. "I was with him this morning and saw him write with his own hand. What warning?"

Maia's stomach wilted and she broke the seal. As she opened the paper, a tiny blue flower nearly tumbled out, and she caught it before it could flutter to the floor. It was a small flower with dainty blue stems.

My love please wait

Word reached me that the Dochte Mandar annulled our marriage and suitors from Hautland have come seeking your hand. I will not rage against fate or the Medium. I know you have longed for freedom. To marry who you choose by irrevocare sigil. I know you have always desired to marry a maston, and Prince Oderick is truly one. It is my belief that he is sincere. That the alliance with Hautland is real. Simon is dead. I do not trust the messages I am getting about you. Rumors that the Victus are preparing to wage war against all of us. It may last for years. Having Hautland as an ally would be a blessing. But please, my dearest love, please wait for me. Do not decide rashly. Do not promise yourself yet. Wait for me. I will come for you.

Ne-mou-blie
Ne-mou-blie
Ne-mou-blie

Her throat caught with anguish, and tears stung her eyes as she stared at the little flower in her palm.

Forget me not.
Forget me not.
Forget me not.

CHAPTER
TWENTY-SEVEN

Invasion

The fire Leerings burned so hot in the sickroom that sweat trickled down Maia's forehead, back, and ribs. The days were a jumbled heap in her mind, difficult to sort out. She dipped a cloth in the warm water, sopped it, squeezed out some of the excess, and then gently patted Prince Oderick's feverish skin. Despite the oven-like temperature in the sickroom, he shivered and convulsed. His lips were chapped and peeling. His skin looked sunken against his flesh. He was shriveling before her eyes, his throat and cheeks pocked with lesions. After six others attending him had fallen victim to the symptoms as well, there had been no other visitors. No one except for Maia.

Doctor Bend was terrified of coming down with the plague sores himself. No one knew how it was transmitted. Each victim suffered agonizing coughs that spewed spittle into the air. Then there was sweating and shaking and, earlier this morning, the prince had begun bleeding from his eyes. It was a grotesque suffering.

"I beg you . . . forgive . . ." the prince wheezed. His eyes were haunted, delirious.

"Forgive? Forgive what?" Maia asked, bathing the water-sodden cloth against his forehead.

His weak hand trembled and then touched her arm, as weak as a puppy. "Forgive . . . me. I was fooled . . . by the Victus." He blinked, seized by a contortion of pain. "Hautland will revenge. My people . . . will know . . . you tended me. When I was sick." He doubled over and coughed, moving away from her and hacking violently.

Maia's heart ached to see him in this state. She did not fear the disease that ravaged those in the palace's sickroom. Though she tended them all, she had a calm sense of assurance that she, as the originator of the illness, could not be harmed by it.

He lay panting after the cough, his breaths coming in deep rugged gasps. His jaw locked and he began to seize. And then suddenly, he was still, his final breath ebbing from him like a punctured water skin. Maia bit her lip as she watched him die. It was strange to see, almost as if his skin was sloughing something off. A part of him was gone. The wasted flesh remained behind, but something greater lingered in the air around her. She felt tears prick her eyes, not of sadness, but of relief.

An invisible hand seemed to rest on her shoulder as she closed her eyes, feeling her heart brim with emotions. A brightness illuminated the room.

"Farewell, Prince Oderick," she whispered through her tears. "Until we meet again . . . in Idumea."

She felt a trembling feeling of warmth and appreciation glide across her shoulders. Who he was . . . the essence of his being . . . was not lying still and crumpled on the bed—she *knew* it. It was like staring at a rumpled shirt on the floor—evidence of the man who had worn it, but not of the man himself.

Thank you, my lady. The thought-whisper was so faint, she almost missed it.

Drenched with sweat, Maia rose and extinguished the blazing Leerings all at once with a final thought. She dropped the cloth near the dish and then walked to a wash basin near the door and rinsed her hands with lye. She lingered a moment, realizing with a mixture of pathos and horror that the others so infected would likely die that day as well.

Then she opened the door and walked out. The corridor was heavily guarded, preventing passersby from straying near the sick and dying men. Maia found Richard, his gray hair askew, conferring with the Hautlander chancellor. Both men looked at her with imploring eyes. She nodded to them.

"The prince is dead," she said softly. A hush fell over those crowding the hall.

Captain Carew strode up to her. "Your Majesty, you *must* abandon the city. The armada could be here any moment. You must go!" he said, his voice burning with impatience.

"Walk with me," Maia said, heading toward her personal chambers, where she could change.

Richard and the Hautlander chancellor followed as well, and the crowd parted for them to pass.

"How many are left in the city?" Maia asked, keeping a brisk pace.

"One in ten," Richard answered. "Your ladies persuaded half of those who refused. They are still out there trying. I think they should be summoned back to the palace."

Maia nodded her head. "Absolutely. Have them evacuate

through the Apse Veil to Muirwood immediately. Tell them I will meet them at the abbey."

Richard gave her a confused look. "You are not coming with us through the Veil?"

Maia shook her head. "I will not abandon the people while they trek across the kingdom to safety. I must lead them to Muirwood. Richard, I want you to make sure Aldermaston Wyrich sends supplies, carts, horses . . . anything he can muster to help us."

She saw Jon Tayt approaching out of the corner of her eye. "The first ships have been spotted," he shouted. His eyes had a wild look about them.

Richard took her arm. "The palace is near the river. They will land here first. You *must* leave!"

She looked at Captain Carew. "Ready my horse!"

He looked at her as if she were crazed. "My lady, the road is no place for a queen right now. The people are desperate. They—"

"They need to see me, Captain," Maia said firmly. "I have slept in the woods many times. Jon Tayt has already agreed to see me to Muirwood safely. Get my horse ready."

"Already done," Jon Tayt said with a smirk, closing the gap between them. "I would trust no other to do it right, by Cheshu. We leave through Ludgate. The guards will hold that gate until the very end, then retreat after us, forming a defense for the refugees when the Naestors attack."

"You are utterly foolish," the captain said with a snarl. "You could be in Muirwood within the hour!"

She put her hand on his arm. "And leave my people to be slaughtered?" She looked then at Richard. "Has Joanna evacuated Augustin and Doviur?"

"Yes," he answered. "She shut the abbey and sealed it from within. I received word she arrived in Muirwood this morning."

Maia smiled with relief. "Tell her I look forward to greeting her. We should arrive at Muirwood in two days' time." She looked around. "Where is Justin?"

"Leading the evacuation. He has not slept in two days," Richard answered with admiration.

Maia turned to look at the Hautlander chancellor. "My lord, you are coming with us to Muirwood?"

"I am, my lady," he said, wiping perspiration from his forehead. "My ship is sailing around to Bridgestow. If it makes it, then we will depart from there for Hautland. I fear treachery on the seas if the armada has formed a blockade. I have an able captain, my lady. I have sent a messenger through the Apse Veil to Viegg with a warning and orders to summon soldiers to help fight the Naestors. It will take time, but we will assist you. You have treated our prince with the greatest courtesy and compassion. It will not be forgotten."

Maia was grateful for the words, but she worried the assistance would not come in time. "Thank you, Chancellor. I did what I could."

They reached the outer doors of the palace and quickly descended the steps to a courtyard teeming with horses. Her spike-haired groomsman, Jacobs, stood holding the reins of her palfrey. "Up you go, Your Majesty," he said with a grunt, helping her mount.

As soon as she settled into the saddle, Jon Tayt inspected the girth straps to make sure nothing had altered.

Jacobs looked affronted. "No one touched her, Master Tayt," he said with a snort. "I assure you, I *too* know how to saddle a horse properly!"

Maia was grateful to be mounted and ready to depart. She saw a hand reaching up toward her and noticed Carew was handing her a hooded cloak, a simple riding cloak, nothing to mark her as nobility. She accepted it and fastened the clasp.

"She looks like she can run quite a ways," Jon Tayt said, slapping the horse's flank affectionately. "A sturdy girl. I like her."

"Thank you," Jacobs said with barely concealed annoyance. "I am pleased she earns your approval."

Jon Tayt adjusted the strap of the shoulder armor he wore. He looked like a bristling hedgehog of weapons. Arrows fanned out from his back like turkey feathers. Several throwing axes were stuffed in hoops in his belt and a large battle-axe was strapped to a piece of leather on his shoulder. He was equipped with shooting gloves, dirks, and even a gladius for close combat. A shorter pony was waiting for him, and he quickly mounted up with a jangle of his weapons.

"Your Highness!" shouted a voice.

A herald wearing the livery of Caspur pressed through the swelling crowd. Maia waved for him to approach and he rushed over and quickly dropped to one knee in front of her. "My lady, my name is Collin, herald of the Earl of Caspur."

"What news?" Maia asked, seeing the man's nervous look.

"There has been a battle," he said, coming up close. Richard Syon sidled up on foot, his face grave.

Maia frowned, trying to keep her restless horse still.

"The Naestors came inland and started killing stragglers. The earl could not abide the slaughter and led his men against them. It was a trap, and we were quickly outnumbered by reinforcements."

Maia closed her eyes, dreading the news.

"The fighting was fierce, my lady. The Naestors are bloodthirsty and savage, but the earl's men were not cowards. Though we were outnumbered, we fought them off. They went back to the ships to fetch more men and are coming at us again. The earl bade me to tell you that we are retreating as you ordered and will slow the Naestors' advance as best we can. We lost many good men in the battle. But he wanted you to know they fought bravely. They fought for you." He mopped his mouth on his glove. "He did not bade me to say this, but I will say it all the same. He rallied the men with a speech, my lady. He sang your praises to the skies. That you were a true queen-maston, that the Medium would deliver us from our enemies if we believed in you as he does. The men fought like lions, my lady. Even out-numbered as we were."

Maia felt a rush of pride and appreciation for the Earl of Caspur. "Well done, my lord," she said, grinning down at the herald. "Thank you. I have full confidence in your master. How many did you lose?"

The herald gave her a hard look. "Three thousand men," he said chokingly. "But they lost six . . . maybe eight thousand. There was no time to count the corpses."

"How many more do they have attacking from the south?" Maia wondered aloud.

The man looked at her fiercely. "It matters not. We will hold them, my lady. We will hold them all for you."

Maia gave him a grim smile and then regarded Jon Tayt as he brought his mount up next to hers.

"A fine kettle of fish," he said with a crooked grin. Despite his pointy beard, he almost looked like a boy on the eve of his name-day celebration.

One more time, Maia looked back at Richard. "We will see each other again in Muirwood, Richard. We are coming *home*."

He gave her that look again, a fatherly look of tenderness and affection she had not seen from her own father since she was a small child. Although he would not say it, she knew that even though he worried about her, he was proud of her decision to stay with the people.

As her retinue rode out of the courtyard and into the deserted streets, she saw with amazement that the streets had been swept clean. The people began to cheer for her long before she reached Ludgate. As she rode through the gate on the palfrey, the roar became deafening.

***

It was well past dusk and Maia was exhausted. Servants had ridden ahead and set up pavilions and a camp for her host along the road leading to Muirwood. She was still waiting for word of the Naestors arriving at Comoros. Though the sun had set hours ago, she believed the ships would have arrived by now. Men had been left behind to watch what happened and bring her news as soon as it was available. She wandered the camp, stopping at cook-fires to visit those who were traveling. Word spread quickly where the queen had camped, and well-wishers came in a continuous stream to seek her blessing or pay their respects.

While the rest of the ladies-in-waiting had gone on to Muirwood, Suzenne had ridden hard to catch up with Maia. Unaccustomed to hard riding and camping, she looked haunted and completely out of her element. Maia wanted desperately to comfort her friend with positive news about Dodd, but no word had come during the day. His fate—and his army's—was a complete mystery, adding to their many worries. With no news, she did not know how she could best console her friend. Upon Suzenne's own insistence, she was overseeing the preparations for the pavilion where Maia would sleep that night—a task with which she felt more comfortable—while Maia visited with her people.

"We made good time today," Jon Tayt said, approaching her with a sniffle as she walked back to her pavilion. "Another hard ride tomorrow and we may even see the Hundred."

Maia watched the different passersby, looking for a sign of the kishion. She had no doubt he was somewhere in the camp. The flickering lights from torches and campfires would make it easy for him to skulk and hide among the travelers. She had a feeling he would come to her tent that night to watch her, and the thought made her feel a mixture of dread and relief. In truth, she was afraid of falling asleep, afraid of what visions her dreams would bring.

As she and Jon Tayt wove through the maze of campfires, she fell silent, reminded of the night she had learned Collier was the King of Dahomey. She had been captured by his soldiers and brought to his command pavilion. There had been an element of fear in the air that night as well, but nothing like what she had experienced amidst the Dahomeyjan soldiers. The people were worried about the Naestors who had invaded. They were worried but not panicked. She could see their confidence in their eyes, their trust in her.

As she approached her tent, which was smaller than Collier's, her thoughts continued to cling to that night . . . the night she had learned about the brand on her shoulder. Collier had insisted on seeing her shoulder, and eventually she had relented.

The memory brought a queasy, guilty feeling to her heart. A chill rippled through her back, her vision began to fray at the edges, and she started breathing hard. The whispers of the smoke-shapes began to hiss sibilantly around her. She struggled to control her thoughts, to bring them toward cheerier domains. It was night. Was it nearly midnight? She could not tell through the web of trees above.

Maia.

She immediately recognized Murer's voice in her mind. Panic and fear followed fast behind. In her mind, she began summoning images of Muirwood, of her mother's garden. She thought of Thewliss and his white mustache and soft-spoken ways. She thought of Aloia and Davi in the kitchen, imagining them prattling and teasing each other.

"Are you all right?" Jon Tayt asked, nudging her elbow.

I thought you would wish to know where I am right now.

Murer's voice sliced through her thoughts. She began to feel what Murer was feeling. A giddy anticipation of triumph. The desire for revenge. Part of her vision began to slough away, and Maia could see through Murer's eyes. Her stepsister was also walking in a camp of soldiers. It was night. The same moon hung in the sky.

And then Maia saw Collier's tent, stiff and impassive. It was dark, and there were soldiers guarding it.

As she approached, one of the guards held out his hand. "The king is asleep," he said gruffly in Dahomeyjan. "Begone, strumpet."

Murer hit him with a blast of fear and desire, and the hand instantly dropped. He backed away, looking at her with astonished amazement. "Your . . . Your Majesty!" he whispered in shock. "I . . . I beg your pardon! I thought you were another camp follower!"

"He will wish to see *me*, I think," Murer said with a seductive purr, in flawless Dahomeyjan. Maia could feel the heat radiating from her bones. Tongues of fire licked at her insides—fire that consumed and would never fail to burn.

"Yes, yes at once!" the guard said, holding open the tent flap. It was dark within, but Maia could just make out the familiar scene. She had been there herself, after all.

Yes, child, murmured Ereshkigal. *All men submit to me. And you will watch it. This is* my *revenge on you as well.*

"Maia!"

Firm hands grabbed her, and the vision shattered. She was back at her camp, crouched at the door of her pavilion. She had swooned, and Jon Tayt had caught her. The force of the hetaera's thoughts thudded against her mind.

"Help me," Maia whimpered, and Jon Tayt led her dazed into the tent. Suzenne was waiting in there, and her eyes grew huge with concern. But it was impossible for Maia to process what was going on around her. She felt the tears squeeze through her lashes as she trembled and shook. *No, not Collier, no . . . please!* Her heart burned and ached, and she wanted to scream out in rage and desperation.

"What is it?" Suzenne asked, rushing to her side. "She looks awful. What happened?"

Maia covered her face and started to weep.

Quickness is the essence of war. Strike where you are least expected. Overwhelm with terror and force. The resistance will shatter, and your enemies will flee. It is easier to destroy a man who is running away. It has been many years since the full force of the Naestors has been used. The kingdoms we have long enslaved will remember this Void for years to come. They will remember it, and they will fear us. I write these words from the Privy Council chambers in Comoros. We have destroyed the northern army. We are forcing Caspur's army to retreat. From our station in Comoros, we will lead the assault into the hinterlands and destroy the young queen at Muirwood.

—*Corriveaux Tenir, Victus of Dahomey*

CHAPTER
TWENTY-EIGHT

Defenders

I t was midnight. Suzenne sat with Maia, a tome spread on the table before them, and she read from it softly, using the words to drive away the terrors of the night. Maia shuddered helplessly, feeling her enemies prowling around her, seeking to stave their way into her mind and crush her. The soothing words from the tome provided just enough sparks of light to keep the darkness at bay.

"You should sleep," Jon Tayt said, offering her a cup of valerianum tea. Even though it was midnight, the camp was still noisy with crackling and snapping fires and the soft coughing and murmuring of the populace around them. The scent of smoke lingered in the air.

"I will," Maia said, patting his hand. Her heart was heavy with the knowledge of what Murer was doing in Dahomey. With Suzenne's help, she had been able to keep the evil from intruding on her thoughts again, which at least meant she would not have to witness the horrible scene herself. "You must get some sleep as well. I will need you tomorrow. You must teach people to cover our trail, to make it difficult to find us."

Jon Tayt scratched the back of his neck. "We're leaving marks a blind man could follow," he said with disgust. "I will do my best."

The chair the hunter sat on creaked as he rose and then shuffled from the tent.

Suzenne paused from reading the tome, her eyes red and shadowed. Their fingers entwined, and Maia squeezed firmly. "Thank you," she whispered. "You helped me get through the worst of it. At least I *hope* that was the worst of it." She stared down at the gleaming aurichalcum page and traced one finger across the engravings. "I cannot help but think that the men and women who carved these tomes must have faced the same impossible situations and heartaches we do. And these very words helped them endure it."

Suzenne nodded and stroked Maia's arm. "To endure suffering patiently. It is no easy thing."

Staring into her friend's sad eyes, Maia said, "Do you fear the worst about Dodd?"

"That he is dead?"

"No . . . that he betrayed you."

Suzenne's lips tightened into a small frown. "I do not believe he is dead. I think I would *know* that, somehow. But do I think he succumbed? At first I could not bear the thought. But . . . I see now that it is possible. A kystrel is so powerful. You know that for yourself. The maston test warns us to beware them. If he did, I am sure he feels . . . racked with shame and guilt. He may be afraid to come to me. To face me with that stain." She sighed and looked down. "But I love him, Maia, and I fear what it will do to my heart to learn the truth. It is a difficult burden. Each day I have not heard from him is a dagger in my breast. I long to see him again. To forgive him if he is contrite. I hope he is not wounded, languishing somewhere all alone."

Maia squeezed harder, trying to communicate comfort through her touch. She had to believe the same about Collier. When she had approached his tent those many months ago, he had been expecting her to be a hetaera and to use her kystrel against him. He had seemed to relish the notion, in fact. But his shaming of Murer and Muirwood came at a cost. The girl would be revenged on him. The notion made Maia sick inside. The fact Murer was only now traveling to Dahomey told her something else—her stepsister was not a full hetaera . . . yet.

There was a rustle from the tent wall, and the kishion slipped inside. In his presence, the small comfort she had derived from the tome faded. When Suzenne saw him, she grew pale with fear and the tendons in her hands stiffened.

The kishion looked from the two of them to the tome, and a smirk hovered on his mouth. He looked restless, full of energy. She had not seen him throughout the journey, but she had sensed he was there, lurking in the shadows. Always just out of sight. Always watching her.

"Out," he said dismissively to Suzenne.

She did not move, her eyes staring into his cold ones with fear *and* resolve.

"I wish her to stay," Maia said softly, firmly, keeping her grip on Suzenne's hands.

"If you wish her to hear what I have to tell you, so be it," he replied with a scowl. "It matters not."

"Say what you must," Maia sighed, forcing herself to be patient. She stared up at him, feeling the mood in the tent shift. He looked edgy and nervous. He kept glancing back at the tent door as if he expected soldiers to come rushing in.

"We should go. Tonight," he said to her.

"Where?" she demanded. "To Muirwood?"

He snorted with laughter. "Do you really think an *abbey* will save you? Of course you do, look at that tome." He scrubbed his gloved hand through his mass of hair, as if trying to scratch a violent itch. "The end is nigh, Maia. The Naestors are almost here, and they did not leave their victory to chance. They will not stop until you are dead and your people are murdered. I know you cannot abide this thought. That you cannot dwell on the fact that so many will be slain in cold blood. But believe me, I know these people. *I* am a Naestor."

Maia had rarely seen him so emotional. "I know what they intend. I believe you."

"Then come with me!" he seethed, stepping forward. Suzenne looked shocked, her face struggling to conceal her revulsion. "They are encircling you. Like hunters cornering a deer. They send the dogs to flush you out. But soon it will be spears and arrows. It is almost too late. Once the circle closes, it is over." His eyes were wild with intensity. "These are not your father's soldiers . . . they are not knights. They do not fight with honor, but with ruthlessness and savagery." He stepped back from her, his voice low and compelling. "Each man has multiple weapons. Spears, throwing axes, battle-axes, and swords. Each man carries a shield, which they will wedge together to create a wall. Throw a man against that wall and he cannot break through. Throw a dozen men and they still will not manage to budge it. Then the soldiers will jab at you with their spears. They will hook you with axes. The wall will advance and advance and advance, and you will have no way of stopping it. Not with arrows. Not with a battering ram! They are trained like this. Each unit travels with a Dochte Mandar to keep fear away and to embolden the men to murder. They are connected like a hive of bees, and they swarm and sting. Maia, your knights have never faced this sort of enemy before. Naestors are quick, they are fearless, and they are numberless. It is not an army. It is a horde."

Maia stared at him, her mind full of the sight and sound of clashing men, screaming in guttural tones as they slew their enemies. She closed her eyes, quelling the violent thoughts. Then she opened her eyes and stared at him with as much serenity as she could muster. "The Medium *will* deliver us."

He looked at her with disdain. "I knew you were going to say something *trite* like that." He grunted with ill humor.

Maia shook her head. "The Medium can be forced, it is true. But do not be deceived. That is not the true order of things. If we trust it and if we believe in it, the Medium can save us. All you do is *poison* my mind with your words. The Medium is not warning us to flee these shores. It commands that we gather together, that we summon our wills together to withstand the Naestors."

"They will make you *watch*," he said in a low, strangled voice. "You do not understand the violence of which these men are capable. I have trained with them, Maia. I have fought alongside these war bands, seen them destroy villages and raze cities!" His jaw quivered. "I cannot bear to watch them destroy you too. Come with me. Tonight!"

His thoughts were so powerful, his will so strong, Maia felt a trickle from the Medium nudge against her. Part of his mind opened to her in that moment. Just a flicker of insight, a flash of intention. He was not trying to deceive or trick her. He was a desperate man who had never felt love in his life until now, and the object of his secret, sacred feelings was about to be butchered and massacred in a way that would devastate him. He was trying to protect her, not just from death, but from witnessing the savage atrocity of his people. He had absolutely no doubt that Corriveaux would win.

Maia rose from the table and approached him deliberately, using her force of will to counter his. She stared into his eyes, watching his look turn pained. As if being too near her hurt him.

She reached out and took his hand between hers. His heavy, gloved, murderous hand. She watched as his neck muscles stiffened at her touch. He stared at her in confused amazement.

"I know your *heart*," she whispered to him. "But I cannot give you what you seek. I love another."

He frowned at the words. A cold and chilling frown. "He is a dead man. Everyone you love will be taken from you."

"Even so," Maia said, holding him fast. "I will not surrender. I will not abandon my people. If they are to die, if it is the Medium's *will* that we perish, then I will perish with them. Do not ask me to go with you. I cannot forsake my people. And the Medium will not forsake those who *believe*."

He stared at her, his eyes brimming with doubt. "You are a fool," he whispered. "The Medium did not save you from your father. *I* did."

"Then it *used* you to save me," Maia replied.

When she said that, she saw something flash in his eyes. His mouth parted, but he said nothing. Turning, he stalked back out of the tent and vanished into the night.

***

Maia rode on her palfrey, the air hazy with dust from the exodus to Muirwood. On horseback, they passed several small wagons and carts trundling toward the land ahead. Very often she would hear her name called from a little child waving up at her. And Maia would smile and wave back, wondering how she had been recognized without any of her royal finery. Word had undoubtedly spread through the camp. The queen rode with them. No one could harm them so long as the queen was there. If only that were true.

The day was dusty and hot. Riders coming back and forth to scout for the Naestors would pass her, for she kept an easy pace, not a breakneck one. They rode toward Mendenhall, a castle where she would spend the night on the last leg of the journey before reaching Muirwood. Her prisoners had been moved to the dungeons there. It made her think of Maeg's father, who had been the last sheriff of Mendenhall. She found herself wondering where Maeg had gone after issuing her warning. When all this was done, Maia would reward her for her loyalty. If Maeg had not come forward, Corriveaux's plan would have undoubtedly prevailed. She would need to seek Suzenne's counsel on how best to honor the other girl.

One of her knights came from the road ahead at a gallop and reined in when he saw her. The horse was frothing at the mouth and the knight looked grizzled and intense. "My lady, a column of soldiers is coming toward us from Mendenhall."

Maia looked at him, confused. "All the soldiers were assigned to protect the exodus. Who is it?"

"I know not, but they wear the colors and fly the banner of Comoros."

"Dodd's army?" Maia wondered in surprise.

"It could be a trap," the knight warned. "Captain Carew has gone ahead to challenge them, but we may need to flee, and quickly."

The line of wagons and carts that strung out before and behind her was utterly defenseless. She had her household knights, but they would be insufficient against a sizeable force. Then she saw Jon Tayt's pony coming from ahead, and he looked calm and easy in his saddle.

She tapped the flanks of her horse and hurried to meet him. "What news?" she asked worriedly.

Jon Tayt looked dumbfounded. "My lady, it appears you have another army."

She looked at him with concern. "Who are they?"

"The young lads from Assinica," Jon Tayt replied. "Nary a one is older than you, my lady. They have never fought before. But they are dressed in hauberks and shields. They have spears and maces . . . some have maston swords . . . and they are marching to aid Earl Caspur in his retreat. They heard he is losing men every day, so they rallied to come shore up the retreat."

It was Maia's turn to look surprised. She caught sight of the advancing columns through the haze of dust—ten men deep, they held spears and banners fluttering with the insignia of Comoros. She could feel the shuddering of the ground as they drew near.

"And who leads them?" Maia asked in wonder. She saw a man on horseback in their midst, the sunlight gleaming off his helm and shield.

"You will see," Jon Tayt said with a gruff smile.

Maia led her palfrey into a canter and approached the advancing column of soldiers. Their tabards were brown with dust from the march, but the young men looked sturdy and strong. These were blacksmiths' sons, the children of artisans, stonemasons, and musicians. As they approached, she noted the look of calm and steady dignity in their faces. Though they had never fought before, they were now marching to war in a land they called home.

To Maia's surprise, Aldermaston Wyrich rode amidst the first ranks of the soldiers, wearing armor. A flanged mace hung from his saddle strap. He wore a gray tabard over his hauberk, reminiscent of his Aldermaston robes.

"Aldermaston Wyrich," Maia said with a surprised greeting. "What have you done?"

He smiled warmly at her. "I intended to stay and supervise the defenders of Muirwood at the abbey, Your Majesty. But these lads insisted they could not wait to defend the walls while so many in your army were dying. They wanted to help bring the Earl of Caspur's troops back safely. Until then, their posts are being held by the city watch of Comoros under the lord mayor's charge. They wish to face our enemies, my lady. I could not oppose them."

Maia glanced behind and around him. These were all very young men, as Jon Tayt had warned her, but she saw a seriousness in their eyes.

"They are mastons?" she asked.

The Aldermaston nodded approvingly. "Each one is. They fight to defend their families, the abbeys of the realm, and they will defend your crown, my queen."

"How many are there?"

He looked at her seriously. "Just over a thousand. They do not fear death, Your Majesty. They believe the Medium will save them as it did Garen Demont at Winterrowd. They asked if I would lead them," he said in a humble voice. He gripped his flanged mace, his look serious and imposing. "And so I have agreed. The Medium bids me to rescue the Earl of Caspur's men and see them safely to Muirwood. I have asked Richard to stand in on my behalf."

"Then you must go," Maia said. She felt her throat tighten as she glanced again at the column before her. She lifted her hand in the maston sign, and the soldiers stopped and bowed their heads. "Young men of Assinica, I Gift you with courage and strength," she said in a clear, calm voice. "I Gift you with obedience, that you may fulfill every command and charge given you. Go forth, defenders of Muirwood. The Medium will go with you, as will this blessing. Make it thus so."

She heard a rippling murmur through the ranks as she lowered her arm. They were so young. As Aldermaston Wyrich nudged his horse and the march continued, Maia waited until the last row passed her, staring into their faces, seeing their determination. Her heart clenched with heaviness as she wondered how many of them would return. These were unseasoned, untrained young men, and though she had not heeded the kishion, his words had penetrated. The enemy was fierce.

As the dust from their marching began to settle, she could just make out the form of Mendenhall Keep in the distance. Behind it stretched the tangled woods of the Bearden Muir.

CHAPTER
TWENTY-NINE

Refuge

Though Maia had visited Muirwood Abbey almost nightly for the past months, she rarely left the abbey grounds, so what she found outside its walls startled her. Since Whitsunday, the village of Muirwood had expanded to the size of a town. She could not believe how many houses and homes had been erected in so short a time. They were fresh and new, with timbers hewn from the mighty oaks surrounding the grounds. There were several grist mills, and she heard the constant clanking of blacksmiths' hammers and smelled sawdust and pungent dross. Little shops teeming with crafts and art had been assembled along the main roads. There was music amidst the pounding, the trill of flutes and the melodic tones of harps and dulcimers.

There were also hundreds of tents and pavilions within the bounds of the woods, and Maia watched with fascination as the citizens of Muirwood—particularly those from Assinica—warmly greeted the refugees from Comoros. Each cluster of tents had Leerings for fire and water, and everywhere there were cakes sizzling on pans, dishes being scrubbed in tubs of water, and other chores underway.

As Maia rode her palfrey down the main street, she was greeted warmly by smiling, tranquil faces that seemed more as if they were preparing to celebrate Whitsunday than for an invasion.

"My lady," said a woman who reached up from the street and handed her a honeyed cake. Maia thankfully accepted it and took a bite. It was stuffed with sweetened berries that made her hungry for more. Each shop was small, and they were bunched tight together with the living quarters perched above. The shingles were fresh and still smelled pleasantly of the wood that had constructed them. The streets were cobbled, which amazed her, and the stones were flat with gentle rounded edges, which reduced the noise from the clatter of wheels and hooves.

She craned her neck, marveling at the progress their cousins from Assinica had made in establishing a thriving community in the swamp. There were dikes and ditches draining away the swamp water, and she could discern large swaths of fields that had already been plowed and seeded. The woods were thinner now, but the land surrounding the abbey was still lush and thick with greenery. In the distance, she could see the tower on the Tor rising above it all, and the glint of metal-shod soldiers marching up and down the stone steps. From that vantage point she knew they would be able to see the oncoming armies well in advance.

Maia rode next to Jon Tayt as they approached the abbey walls. As soon as they entered them, it felt as if a soft blanket had been tucked around her shoulders. She tugged gently on the reins, bringing her faithful mount to a stop as she breathed in the scents of home and felt the weariness drip away from her soul. This was a bastion, a refuge, a place of peace.

"I have almost grown fond of this muddy place, by Cheshu," Jon Tayt drawled. He sniffed and wiped his nose on his glove. "It is not Pry-Ree, mind you, but it will do in a trice. Ah, there is the Aldermaston again in his gray robes. Richard Syon looks like a content man at long last. Being here has lifted years from his gray head."

Maia saw Richard and Joanna walking toward them, both dressed in the gray cassock of the Aldermaston order. Richard also wore the chain and stole of his office as chancellor, but she knew he would not feel comfortable being on the grounds of Muirwood in his typical court attire.

Maia quickly dismounted, and Jon Tayt took her reins and began to lead the horses to the paddock. The grounds were crowded with families, and everywhere she looked, there were people doing chores. She had never seen it so busy.

"Welcome home, Maia," Richard said. "It is good to be back."

"How I have missed the abbey," Maia said, giving Joanna a hug first. "Not long ago I was sneaking into the cloisters before dawn to read the tomes. I would give my crown to return to that simpler time."

Joanna hugged her back affectionately. "I have missed seeing you, Maia. Augustin has changed, but I must confess to feeling a partiality for Muirwood. It may not be as grand, but it is home." She took Richard's hand and squeezed it. It was clear that their forced separation had taken a toll on them both.

"I was grateful to learn that Aldermaston Wyrich put you in charge of the abbey again," Maia said as they began to walk back to the manor house together. "He has turned soldier, it seems."

"There are many cases of Aldermastons stepping up to combat in the past," Richard said. "I will admit that it gratifies me to be steward of Muirwood while he is gone. Refugees continue to arrive every hour, every day."

"Is there enough room for the entire kingdom?" Maia asked him thoughtfully, gazing at the Cider Orchard. She saw Collier's smile as he had watched her bite into a Muirwood apple—a memory that pierced her soul.

"Yes, truly," Richard replied. "There are settlements from here all the way to the Tor. We keep people working, and everyone is willing to help. You can imagine what it takes to feed such a mass. The kitchens we have are running night and day, and several larger ones are being constructed. You should know, my lady, that aid has come from our allies. Some of your people in the north are being sheltered by Pry-Ree. They have already welcomed many from the Hundreds that have fallen up north. We have received word from the Earl of Forshee."

"Dodd!" Maia exclaimed. "Poor Suzenne. She went on ahead to make sure we would be settled."

"I have already told her," Joanna said. "She was grateful to learn he is well. His army was trampled by the Naestors, but they have since regrouped and are now joined by Pry-rian archers. They travel behind the northern army invading our land and harry them with raids and attacks on their supply wagons. Their efforts have slowed the Naestors down somewhat and forced them to increase the numbers of soldiers guarding the wagons. He sent a message to his wife, which I am certain she will share with you." Joanna paused, her look wise and thoughtful. "His force is no more than a tenth of what the Naestors are bringing down from the north, but he is doing what he can to make them pay for their progress."

Maia sighed with relief at the news that he was alive. "I am so grateful to hear that," she said. "Not knowing what had become of him was the worst part of Suzenne's torture. Thank you. What else have you heard?"

Richard pointed to men hoisting large crates and boxes full of vegetables and sacks of grain. "The men unloading the wagon. That food comes from Avinion. They have been sending ships to Bridgestow loaded with provisions under Lord Paget's leadership. He controls our supply lines and is quite organized. They know we are gathering our people into one location and they want to make sure we do not go hungry. It is risky because the armada is blockading the sea, but the Avinions sail wide to avoid them. Bridgestow is crowded with ships right now. It will not be long before the Naestors realize this and blockade that port as well, so we are gathering as many supplies as we can. The armada's ships will prove harmful to us still."

Maia looked at him with concern. "Ships can navigate the river, I know that, but they cannot land here in force, can they?"

"Let me explain," Richard said. "The rivers can be navigated by individual ships, as you well know, but not enough to bring in a fleet. Still, the Dochte Mandar know the history of this abbey. They know about its defenses. If blood is shed on the grounds, the Leerings can summon waters to flood the lowlands. When that happens, the rivers gorge with water and the sea comes in. Muirwood has become an island in the past. I believe that is the Naestors' strategy, Maia. If they bring in their army close enough, they will attempt to massacre enough people to trigger the abbey's defenses and provide a path for their ships."

Maia stared at him in surprise. "I had not realized that, Richard. Flooding the valley will save us from the army, but it will make us vulnerable to their ships. That would hurt us both, I think."

Richard looked at her sternly. "Remember, they seek to *force* the Medium to do *their* will. What they cannot comprehend is that the Medium will not harm us if we are faithful. Their efforts will only lead to their own destruction." He put his hand on her shoulder. "I have no doubt the Medium will deliver us from the Naestors, Maia. The Covenant of Muirwood has been fulfilled. Yes, abbeys are being razed across these lands, but we have not been commanded to flee as we have been in the past. Sometimes the Medium gathers the wicked in one place to destroy them." He frowned. "I only wish we could save everyone . . . including our foes. Before it is too late."

Maia glanced at Joanna, and saw the same look of compassion in her eyes. The Tor was a witness to the Medium's power to crush enemies that would not relent. Her heart grew heavy. She did not want to destroy all the Naestors.

She frowned, anguished by the knowledge of the violence that would come. "The Void is not about us," she said softly. "If they press on, they will bring it on themselves." She winced, feeling torn by conflicting emotions. Her people were being murdered by the Naestors and the Dochte Mandar. That made her angry. Yet they were being manipulated from within by the Victus, by years of ill-begotten convictions. "How can we prevent them from creating their own doom?"

Richard stared at her solemnly. He did not have the answer.

***

Maia needed time to think, but she was anxious to see Suzenne and hear the news. She found her friend unloading chests brought from the palace, and the two quickly embraced.

"I was relieved to hear that there has been word from Dodd at last!" Maia said, gripping Suzenne's shoulders. She searched her friend's face, trying to determine whether the news was hopeful or discouraging.

Suzenne squeezed her eyes shut, and then opened them and gave Maia a dazzling smile that sent relief rushing through her.

"Oh, I am almost too overcome to speak." She put a hand on her heart. "The news is good, Maia. I was so worried, and with good cause. Murer arrived under the cover of darkness, seeking Dodd's help. He felt . . . wary when his steward told him she had arrived and asked to see him. The steward was excessively agitated, which gave Dodd a bad feeling. The Medium warned him to flee. He has always been sensitive to the Medium, Maia. He recognized the warning for what it was, even without knowing all the reasons. He left without even taking his cloak. Fetched his horse and rode to camp. Murer abandoned his manor and went to Billerbeck Abbey that night and burned it."

Suzenne lowered her head and sighed with gratitude. "His army tried to halt the Naestors, but they were outnumbered and overrun. His force has been trapped behind our enemies, but he managed to get some Pry-rian hunters through with a message."

"Thank Idumea," Maia breathed. "If Murer had gotten him alone."

Suzenne nodded. "Dodd felt the same way. He felt the temptation . . . the prideful conviction that he could handle her. I am grateful he heeded the Medium's warning instead. He has been wounded in the fighting with the Naestors, but he promises it is nothing serious." She screwed up her confidence. "I should not have doubted."

"I am relieved." The two friends embraced again.

"Have you had any word from Gideon?" Suzenne asked.

Maia knew that her own dark expression revealed the truth.

***

Maia spent the rest of the afternoon walking the abbey grounds, seeking the Medium's guidance and direction as she went. She wished her grandmother were there so they could walk together as they had in the past. Whenever she thought about Sabine, a gnawing dread filled her stomach. She had lost her parents. Now she was about to lose her grandmother too.

"What would you have me do?" Maia whispered as she walked through the rows of purple mint, hearing the droning bees among them. Her thoughts were interrupted when she walked past a stranger. Maia returned the nod of the young fellow, who did not appear to realize who she was.

Wanting to be left alone to her brooding, she retreated to her mother's garden. After opening the door with the Leering, she shut it behind her and leaned back against it, closing her eyes. There was solitude in this garden, yes, but there were ghosts as well. She remembered seeing the white lily amidst the crown of blue flowers. And the dazzling mix of forget-me-nots summoned Collier's voice again and again in her mind. She sighed deeply and stepped away from the door so she could walk past the accusing plants and wander the rest of the garden.

Earlier that afternoon, she had used her Gift of Invocation to study all of the Leerings she could find on the grounds and learn their purposes. Even now, she felt the power of the abbey Leerings pressing at the edge of her awareness. They would obey her in unison, she knew. She could sense the water Leerings that would summon the rivers to flood the lower valleys of Muirwood Hundred in case of emergency. The last time those had been invoked was when Lia had used them to defend the abbey against the Queen Dowager, a hetaera.

Maia folded her arms tightly around herself, feeling a chill in the shadows of the garden. It was getting late and her stomach growled for supper. She pictured Collett and Thewliss, the two kitchen helpers Aloia and Davi. It had been several days since she had seen them. The little kitchen had become such a tranquil escape for her.

She heard the squeal from Thewliss's cart wheels approaching the garden. Had her thoughts summoned the old man? Though he never spoke to her unless asked a direct question, he was a gentle, caring man and a good companion.

Maia rubbed her arms as she gazed at the trees and plants. The garden was beautiful and peaceful, yet the real world lay outside of it. She felt a little guilty about resting in this place of peace when her people were marching against their enemies. There were battles being fought throughout the realm. She thought about the Earl of Caspur and his valiant efforts to hedge the enemy's advance and protect those who were fleeing to Muirwood. She thought of Aldermaston Wyrich and his young maston warriors marching south to aid him. How many soldiers were wounded and bleeding? How many would only find sleep in their graves?

Please, if there is a way to prevent this bloodshed, she thought desperately, pouring out her heart to the unfathomable power of the Medium. *Would you have us be their slaves? Would that suffice? They promised they would butcher us, but would it save lives on both sides if we agreed to do their bidding? Is that what you will from me?*

She felt no answer from the Medium. Then a new thought nagged at her mind. Though she had visited every Leering around the grounds, she had not checked the Leerings that were actually hidden within the abbey. There were carvings inside that brought light, prevented plants from wilting, and served other purposes. She knew the story of how the residents of Muirwood had huddled within the abbey as the Queen Dowager began to burn it. Surely her entire kingdom could not fit inside, but was there another Leering that could be invoked to help them? Perhaps one capable of changing the heart of a man born to violence?

The thought niggled at her. Was such a thing possible? Her mind turned to the kishion, how his heart had softened and changed. What had happened to make it so? Her thoughts continued down this path as the door of the garden opened and Thewliss shuffled inside with his cart. Owen Page followed him inside.

"What is it?" Maia asked the breathless young man.

"My lady," he gasped. "The Aldermaston bade me to find you. A ship has been seen coming up the river!"

Her heart clenched with dread. "Whose ship?" she asked, the feeling of desolation welling inside her.

"Not a Naestor ship, ma'am. It is from Dahomey. The hunters sent word by pigeon. They said it is the *Argiver*. The Aldermaston wanted you to know right away. It will dock after nightfall."

Maia's eyes were wide with relief and a thrilling joy burst in her heart. She blinked away tears and started to tremble in relief and anticipation. "The *Argiver*! Tell the Aldermaston I will be there shortly. Tell him *he* is coming. The King of Dahomey is *coming* to help us!"

As Owen hurried away, Maia walked over to the bed of forget-me-nots. She plucked one of the tiny flowers and brought it to her nose. Then she pressed her lips against the tiny petals.

Come to me, my love. I have not forsaken you.

That young cub of Dahomey burned our ships in the harbor of Comoros. He has deceived my emissaries into thinking he was at war with Paeiz. Some truce has been secretly arranged between their kingdoms, and their combined fleets struck us by surprise. Even now, I see the fires glowing in the harbor. This vicious attack will not go unpunished. The cub will feel the teeth of the hound. After we have destroyed Comoros, we will turn the curse of Dahomey upon the rest of his shores and torch the vineyards of Paeiz. Vengeance will be swift. Even now his ships have departed. I have warned the fleet commanders to watch for them. This was a feint. I have no doubt he will strike next at the heart. And I will relish the news of his death.

—Corriveaux Tenir, Victus of Dahomey

CHAPTER THIRTY

Threat

Maia could hardly contain herself. Collier was sailing upriver to Muirwood on the *Argiver*. There was no doubt in her mind that he was coming to her as he had promised. Whatever Murer may have done, Maia would pardon and forgive. Everything would be right again so long as she could see him again, hold him again. Her emotions were in such tumult that she did not notice the shadow in the open doorway until the kishion revealed himself by stepping forward. Seeing him in *her* sanctuary brought a scowl to her face.

Thewliss had just set his cart by a stone bench and was fetching a hand spade. When he noticed the intruder, his white whiskers tightened into knots of concern, and he gave the kishion a black look.

"What is it now?" Maia asked, not wanting to spend this moment in his company. She had not seen him since their bleak conversation in her pavilion. She had hoped he would not intrude on the grounds of the abbey.

"I need to speak with you," he said. "There is something you must see. Come with me."

She felt a wrinkle of concern. "Tell me."

"I must show you," he insisted, extending his hand toward her.

Thewliss straightened from his crouch, the hand spade still in his grip. He started to edge closer to Maia, and she felt a stab of fear for the old man.

The kishion cast a fierce frown at Thewliss.

Feeling a tense pressure in the air, Maia said, "Very well. I will come with you."

"My lady," Thewliss said in a warning voice.

The kishion moved before Maia could react. In a moment, he had his arm around the old man's throat. Thewliss was nothing but bones and wrinkled skin, and he struggled in vain against the stronger man's iron grip.

"Let him go!" Maia said angrily. She rushed up and tried wrenching the kishion's arm free. "I said I would go with you!"

Thewliss's head lolled and his eyelids fluttered. His face was turning blue. The kishion dumped the body to the ground. Maia knelt by Thewliss, her heart pounding in her chest.

"Why did you do that!" Maia managed to choke out as she ruffled the gardener's white feathery hair.

"Because he saw me," the kishion answered. "And I do not want any witnesses." He unsheathed his dagger, and Maia went cold to her bones.

She shielded the old man's body with her own, her heartbeat thundering in her ears. She felt dizzy with fear and dread. "No . . . not this man. You will not kill him."

The kishion brandished the knife. "You think you can stop me, Maia?" He took a step toward her, looking determined and cruel.

"Do not *do* this!" she pleaded, feeling her arms and legs begin to shake. If she threw herself at him, he would only shove her aside. She had no weapon that could hurt him. She tried to focus her thoughts, to summon the Medium to defend her, but fear chased away her composure.

"If you come with me willingly, I will spare him," the kishion said in a whisper-like voice. "Walk alongside me. Do not speak to anyone, or they will die too. If you resist, I will murder this man and all his family. Do not think I will not. He is from the kitchen by the manor. There are two little girls who work there as well. I want to talk to you and I want to show you something. Are we agreed, Maia? I trust your word."

"Where are you taking me?" she demanded, her eyes tracing the sharp edge of the knife he held.

"Not far. Come."

She looked down at Thewliss and watched the slow rise and fall of his chest. He was breathing. There was a little scrape on his cheekbone, but it did not bleed. She touched his white hair softly again—a benediction.

"I will do as you say. Do not harm anyone. But you have betrayed my trust, kishion. I will not forget this."

He gave her a sardonic look. "I believe you."

He sheathed his dagger and then quickly unclasped his cloak and put it around her shoulders. He lifted the cowl to cover her hair and face. He gave her a pointed look. "You always did stand out too much," he said with a strange inflection in his voice. "Come."

Taking her arm gently, he escorted her from the garden and marched her across the grounds. There were people everywhere still, roaming the grounds in various directions. A few glanced at them, but the kishion said nothing and took no notice of anyone as he led her toward the Cider Orchard. The sight of the Aldermaston's manor was almost enough to make her break away and run for freedom. But she knew the kishion would keep his promise of violence. Yes, perhaps he would be captured himself. But he would kill many who were dear to her before he was brought down. Where was Jon Tayt?

She tried to tame her skittering thoughts, to find some answer to her dilemma. The ground was spongy against her shoes as they crossed the short distance to the grove of apple trees. They plunged into the sturdy rows and quickly left behind those wandering the grounds. The branches and leaves whipped at her cloak as they walked.

"Where are—"

"Shhh!" he snapped at her. His grip on her arm tightened as he began to maneuver through the woods. Occasionally he would glance behind, as if he expected to be followed. They reached a spot of ground that was exceptionally muddy and churned and plunged into it. Then the kishion surprised her by coming to an abrupt stop. He turned and hauled her off her feet, then swung her over his shoulder like a bundle.

She gasped at his rough handling and then again when she realized what he was doing—hiding their trail.

"Take me to the manor!" she ordered him.

"I will gag you if I must, Maia. Now be silent. This is to throw off your hunter a bit. Unless you *want* me to kill him like I did the dog. Not much farther now."

He stepped through the muddy spot and then stomped his boots on the other side to dislodge chunks of mud. A moment later he commenced walking again at a brisk pace, taking time to maneuver through the trees at odd angles and change direction several times. Maia felt his shoulder biting into her stomach and clenched her teeth, wanting to pummel his back with her fists. She saw the knife in his belt and was nearly overwhelmed by the desire to risk it all to snatch it.

When he reached the edge of the Cider Orchard, he set her down and then took her arm and led her away again. They were walking toward the walls of the abbey, the very spot where the sheriff of Mendenhall had taken her months before. It was where the kishion had killed the sheriff and his men. She ducked under a low-hanging branch that clawed at her, and continued to follow him, her stomach wrenching, her heart battering in her chest. A sick feeling wormed through her stomach. He changed his grip from her arm to her hand as he started up a short hill. The woods completely concealed them. She heard a horse nicker as they reached the edge of the wall, and the feeling of dread worsened.

"Why are you doing this?" she demanded. "Let me go!" She felt an impulse of panic, and in that instant she expected to see Corriveaux appear through the trees ahead, surrounded by Dochte Mandar. Could he be betraying her to the Victus?

The kishion snorted and did not reply. When he reached the opening in the wall, he held her back for a moment and glanced quickly around the edge to be sure it was safe. He looked back the way they had come and listened in the stillness. She could hear her own breathing from the pace of their hard walk. The only other sound was an animal snorting and pawing at the crackling brush.

The kishion then pulled her beyond the wall and led her past several thick trees to a large, sturdy horse—the kind a knight would ride into battle. One that would easily hold two. It had a mottled brown coat and specks of hay and straw throughout his mane. The beast snorted again as they approached.

"Do not try to run from me," he said, looking her in the eye. "Everyone will be heading for supper soon. I know the grounds and how they are run. It will be a little while before they find our trail, and by then we will be long gone."

Her stomach shriveled to the size of a peach pit. "Where?" she insisted.

"What I have to show you is in Bridgestow," he answered confidently. "It has been some time since you were there, has it not, Your Majesty? We will be there by dawn if we ride hard tonight."

"*Why* are you doing this?" she asked, struggling to control her emotions, her fear.

He gave her a knowing look. Then, without letting go of her hand, he brought her closer to the horse, stuck his foot in the stirrups and mounted. Pulling hard, he brought her up on the saddle behind him. "Hold tight."

As soon as she clenched his shirt, he kicked the animal's flanks, and the massive warhorse began to canter through the woods.

***

The road to Bridgestow was thick with traffic. Wagons and carts lumbered in either direction along the way—some heading to Muirwood laden with crates of food, some returning from Muirwood empty, to be filled again. Occasionally messenger riders would come from Bridgestow, riding fast and hard. The traffic on the left side of the road would veer away and let them pass. No one came from behind them, though. No one rode as fast as the war steed.

With the cloak fluttering behind her like a flag, Maia hugged the kishion to keep from tumbling down to the road. The horse was lathered and sweaty, but it was relentless in its mission. It had been bred for stamina and endurance, and the cart horses they passed look like ponies in comparison.

With the night, some of the carts had pulled off to the side of the road to rest and make camps, but many pressed on through the night regardless of the hour. The sun fell and Maia grew hungry, but they did not stop to eat or drink or rest. The kishion kept a punishing pace, which she knew was not helpful or healthy for the horse. But it was clear to her that the kishion did not care to spare the beast. He rode hard because he knew they were being pursued. How much of a lead did they have? In her mind, during the darkness of the night, she sent her thoughts toward Jon Tayt and Collier. *Bridgestow—he is taking me to Bridgestow. Hurry!*

She strained her ears for the sound of pursuit. But only the thudding of their hooves could be heard. The road was well traveled and it was built for the speed at which they journeyed. As the night stretched on, she had memories of riding in a carriage toward Bridgestow. Sometimes the memories were so vivid, she was afraid she had fallen asleep and the Myriad Ones had forced her to succumb.

But no, she did not sense the Myriad Ones. Even with the pale moon's arc in the sky, she did not feel herself to be in danger. There were thousands of glittering stars above, and she stared at them in wonder, amazed by their beauty. Occasionally, a shooting star would sizzle across the horizon, gone before she could blink.

She calmed her emotions and listened for whispers of insight, for the Medium's guidance. Jumping off the horse would be foolish. Not only would she likely break her leg, it would not be difficult for the kishion to halt and find her. She clung to him so tightly her fingers and arms hurt, but she endured the pain as she tried to sort through what was happening, why, and what she should do next.

Time seemed to race as fast as their steed, and soon the sky was brightening. They ascended a long hill, and the horse was struggling, weary and spent from the arduous ride that had lasted through the night. The animal would be in no condition to continue the race much farther. She began to hear birds calling to one another, greeting the day ahead, and small camps of travelers were stirring ashes and coaxing coals back to life for breakfast.

Pink turned to orange, and suddenly the dawn was there, radiant and dazzling. The Bearden Muir was far away now, and the lush woods and groves were glorious in the bright morning light. The beautiful sight gave Maia some small happiness—this land of hers was gorgeous—and she cherished it, despite—or perhaps because of—the danger she was in. Her cheek had been pressed against the kishion's muscled back, and she lifted up and turned back, holding tight to keep herself steady. The road behind them stretched down for miles, a clear and easy view.

It was then she caught sight of the lone horseman riding toward them at a full gallop. He was far in the distance, but she saw a small speck of dark hair, and could make out the man's approximate size and build. He rode as if on fire. The sound of the hooves had only just started to reach them, and the kishion quickly glanced back, his eyes narrowing with anger.

It was Collier. Maia was certain of it. Where was Jon Tayt? Where were her guardsmen? And she realized with a private smile that none of them had been able to keep up with Collier. Only he had managed to close a distance of hours. Her heart thrilled in excitement.

Just then, they crested the hill, and Maia saw Bridgestow appear before them, waving the banners of Comoros. Once more, she was the little girl whose father had sent her away at his chancellor's behest to begin her tutoring as the future queen. There was a garrison there. There were soldiers who would obey her commands. But how could she escape the kishion?

"Pray he does not catch us before we reach our destination," the kishion said in a threatening tone.

"Where are we going?"

"There is an inn on the outskirts of town. I have a room for us."

A feeling of revulsion and wariness seeped inside her at his words.

CHAPTER THIRTY-ONE

Queen of Dahomey

The inn was called the Battleaxes and was in the village of Wraxell, just south of Bridgestow. It was a large, stone building with a steep, multileveled roof. Part of the outer walls were made of brick and stone—the rest, timbers and plaster. There were easily five or six chimneys, and the inn was divided into several wings, reminding her of the Gables, the place where she and Collier had first danced.

Many wagons and carts were parked in the field near the inn, and there was a good deal of commotion as the teams prepared for the trek to Muirwood.

After the stableboy took their nearly collapsed horse to the paddock for tending, they were led to their room—a generous space with a tub, a broad bed, and several large chests that were stacked haphazardly through the chamber. The room had a door facing the back side of the structure, with easy access to the road and the yard.

The kishion stared out the window at the yard and then headed over to one of the chests and opened it. He drew out a servant's gown that Maia immediately recognized. She had just seen a similar gown on Maeg . . . it was the uniform given to the servants of Lady Shilton's household.

"What is this about?" she demanded, not bothering to conceal her anger.

"Change into this," he said, handing her the gown and motioning to the changing screen. "There is food on the table. We will eat before we go. Now change, quickly!"

Having ignored her question, he returned to his spot at the window, parting the curtain slightly to gaze outside. He went to the table, where the innkeeper had set out some repast for them, and grabbed a dark baked roll and nearly growled as he devoured it. When he noticed she had not moved yet, he turned back to the window.

"If you need help changing, I am glad to oblige you."

She clutched the gown to her bosom and hurried behind the changing screen. Her heart still thudded in her chest, but she quickly obeyed, hurrying to undo the lacings by herself. The room had a brazier, and it was not cold, but she found herself shivering as she pulled off the gown and dressed in the hated costume of Lady Shilton's household. She did up the lacings, determined not to ask him for anything ever again.

"Where are you taking me?" she asked over the screen.

"Where the Medium bids me," he answered mockingly.

She clenched her jaw in frustration. "Answer me truly. You dragged me from Muirwood to Bridgestow. Why?"

"Because this is where the ships are," he said flatly. He growled something under his breath. "Have you finished yet? I feel a pressing urgency to go."

"I am done," she said, coming around the screen. She clutched the other gown to her chest, not certain what to do with it. It felt oddly familiar to be wearing the servant's gown again. He looked away from the slit in the curtain to stare at her, his expression betraying just a hint of emotion. There was a longing in his gaze that made her experience a queer feeling of pity.

"Eat," he said, gesturing to the tray on the table—there was bread, Muirwood apples, and two cups. She was ravenous, having missed her dinner, and felt her stomach growl unbidden at the mere sight of the food. She tore into a hunk of bread and it tasted delightful and plain, a commoner's food. She quickly devoured it, then took a gulp from one of the glasses and tasted cider. It was sweet and slightly pungent and she put it down quickly, the flavor coursing over her tongue.

He nibbled on a fistful of roasted nuts from his pocket as he watched her eat, his glance returning to the window at regular intervals.

"The King of Dahomey is coming for me," Maia said. "I love him. Please . . . you must let me go."

"What will he think when he finds us in a room together?" the kishion asked, giving her another sardonic look.

Maia swallowed, now even more parched, but the sudden fear that he had tampered with her drink kept her from taking another sip. She wiped the sticky juice from her lips.

"Where are you taking me?" she asked.

He gave her a sidelong look. "I am doing this for your good, Maia. The Victus will murder you and destroy your kingdom. Every last man, woman, and child. If I believed there were any possible way that you could succeed, then I would gladly step back. But I know you too well. You are too compassionate. You are too forgiving. The Victus will destroy you, and I cannot abide that! I cannot bear to lose you. So we are going on a little journey, you and I. We are going *back* to the lost abbey."

She stared at him, thunderstruck. A stab of pain hit her abdomen, and she gripped the edge of a chair, feeling the needles begin to work.

The discomfort was . . . familiar.

"What have . . . you done?" she gasped as another wave of pain struck her bowels. She doubled over, feeling the waves of nausea and pain slash at her insides.

"You recognize the feeling?" he said with a smirk. "It is not the first time I have poisoned you with this particular drug."

Her knees became unsteady. She felt pressure in her ears as the twists of agony spread and deepened. Her stomach heaved and everything she had eaten spilled back onto the floor as she fell to her hands and knees. Through the pain, through the ringing of her ears, she *remembered* this feeling. She had last felt this way in Lady Shilton's attic, where she had been locked away for so long. Reliving the tortures of her past banishment made her tremble and shake, and her stomach clenched again, this time more violently.

Light from behind the curtains stabbed her eyes painfully as the kishion drew them open. The world was spinning in place.

"The poison will not kill you," the kishion said with amusement. "It only makes you *wish* you were dead. It will stop you from escaping while I fetch the men who will bring us to our destination. I will not be gone long. And I have another drug that will render you unconscious for the voyage. You will be easier to handle trundled up in a box."

He smirked at her as she lay on the floor near the puddle of vomit. Her body could not move and she convulsed uncontrollably. Twisting the handle of the back door, he opened it and stepped out into the yard beyond.

Find me, Collier, she begged in her mind.
Find me.

***

She did not know how long she convulsed and squirmed on the floor. Even though her stomach still clenched and roiled, she finally managed to drag herself up by gripping the chair's legs. Her movements were slow and painful and—even though her stomach was empty—she slumped back down to retch several more times. Then she started again, moving herself inch by careful inch, trying to reach the window. The bright morning light stung her eyes.

She got one hand on the bed, one on the chair, and began to laboriously lift herself. There was a sudden shadow at the window, but before she could see who it was, it was gone.

Before she could process what she had seen, the door burst open and Collier appeared, sword in hand. Sweat streaked his face. His disguise was dusty and sweat stained, but he had never looked more beautiful to her. His teeth clenched with rage and fury as he stared into the room, searching for his enemy. Maia tried to speak, but her tongue was swollen in her mouth. She had never felt so thirsty.

She reached out her hand, feeling her legs strengthen at the sight of him. A smile of relief spread across her face. They had to hurry. They had to flee back to Muirwood. But together they could do it.

A shape loomed behind Collier. Before she could even utter a word of warning, his face twisted with agony. He jerked his sword arm back, attempting to strike the kishion's jaw with his elbow, but instead he crumpled to the floor. The sight of the knife buried in his back, blood blooming on the fabric around it, made

Maia gape in horror. Without so much as glancing at her, the kishion shut the door and drew another dagger as he approached the fallen man.

Collier twitched with the spasms of pain. He tried to drag himself away on his arms, his sword having tumbled to the ground when he collapsed.

"No!" Maia shrieked, amazed at the strength of her voice. Even though she was dizzy and weak, she managed to hobble and claw her way to Collier's side. She knew all too well how damaging a knife to the back could be—she had heard of men who were crippled this way, who died from damage to their internal organs.

"You should have waited longer," the kishion sneered down at his fallen victim. "You rode ahead of your help. I thought you would do something foolish like that. I counted on it."

Maia's eyes filled with tears as she witnessed the suffering of the man she loved. Her heart groaned and she seemed to be drowning inside a black lake, sinking ever deeper. Panic and despair slashed all her hopes.

"No, no!" she begged. "Do not kill him! Please! I will do anything! I will go anywhere, but do not kill him! Do not touch him!"

The kishion shook his head. "Oh, but he *must* die, Maia. I won't have you *pining* over him. Your life here is over. You are not the queen anymore. You are banished from Comoros forever. And I am banished with you."

She stared into the kishion's face with a pleading look, her injured body filled with helpless rage and misery. Kneeling by Collier's side, she clasped his face in her hands. "I am yours! I have always been yours! I am faithful to you. Please! Please survive!" she sobbed, shaking her head, tortured by the sight of the mingled pain and love in his eyes.

Collier reached up and tugged at his tunic front. She saw a glimmer of silver, saw the pattern on the fringe. It was a chaen, the kind a knight-maston would wear.

Her eyes widened with surprise and misery. She stared, transfixed, as he lifted his hand and showed her the pink burn mark on his palm. He had . . . he had made his oaths? The realization only twisted the shards deeper into her heart.

"I am a maston," Collier whispered through his anguish. "Even now."

Maia crumpled with tears and hugged his face to her bosom, sobbing until her tears ran into his hair.

"Then you will die a maston," the kishion said coldly. Maia recognized the look of murder in his eyes, but she only held Collier closer.

"Maia," Collier whispered faintly. "I . . . love you."

She gazed down at his upturned face, his eyes strangely calm, as if he were no longer suffering. The bloodstain on the floor was spreading.

"You are the only man . . . I will ever love," she whispered through her tears. "Even in death, they cannot separate us. I would have married you by irrevocare sigil. Forever!" *Why? Oh, why!* She thought the pain in her heart would kill her.

Collier hooked his hand around the back of her neck and pushed himself up with one arm, pulling her down with the other. He kissed her tenderly, a farewell kiss, a kiss of love. She felt the mark on her shoulder flare, followed by the same tingle she had felt on her lips after Oderick's kiss.

She kissed Collier back, pouring all the ardor and love that devastated her heart into the caress. Then she cradled his face between her hands and smothered him with kisses—his lips, his nose, his eyes and cheeks. She wept as she kissed him, knowing he was already dying.

His strength gave out, and he slumped in her arms. She cradled his body, pressing her cheek against his, feeling the warmth of his skin. She mourned. Her heart had never felt so broken. Everything in her world was upside down. All was blackness and despair, a misery beyond enduring.

He blinked up at her, a small smile on his face as he lay listless. "My love," he whispered. "My queen. I named you my heir. You are Queen . . . of Dahomey now."

She tried to stifle her sobbing and could not. She kissed him again, but his lips did not respond this time.

The kishion shoved Collier onto his stomach with a boot and wrenched Maia to her feet. The knife still protruded from the back of her husband—her heart's husband. The kishion reached down and yanked the blade out, wiping the blood smears on Collier's tunic before resheathing it.

Maia covered her face with her hands. "Leave him!" she choked in fury.

"He is a dead man," the kishion said flatly. "If my blade did not finish him, your kiss surely will."

The Bearden Muir is a vicious swampland. They have demolished trees and made the road impassable. Archers plague us night and day. But my army is cutting a swath to the abbey. We have axes enough for the work. There have been several small battles on the flanks, but they are sending young men to do men's work. We will show them no pity.

—*Corriveaux Tenir, Victus of Dahomey*

CHAPTER THIRTY-TWO

The Cursed Shores

Maia awoke from a dreamless fog. Her eyelids were heavy and puffy from crying. Dizziness and nausea twisted her insides, but the sound of creaking timbers and the sway of the sea finally helped orient her and made her realize she was on board a ship. She tried to lift herself up, and found her wrists were lashed together with leather bonds. As she came more awake, the crushing weight of grief slammed against her once more.

The memory of Collier collapsing on the floor of the inn, his life blood seeping away, made it difficult to breathe.

She lifted herself up on the stuffed pallet, staring at nothing, just trying to get air into her lungs. The ship rocked and swayed, as if it were trying to comfort her, but she doubted she would ever be happy again. Her fingers tingled from the bonds at her wrists, and she lifted her heavy hands to try and smooth the clumps of hair from her face. She was weak from lack of food and drink. But that was nothing compared to the blot in her heart. A few trembling sighs and hiccups came. Had she run out of tears at last?

Her memories after they had left Collier behind were hazy and disjointed. The kishion had trussed her up, tied a foul-smelling rag over her mouth—which had made her fall unconscious, mercifully—and loaded her into a chest. She could only surmise the chest had been carried aboard some ship in the harbor of Bridgestow, for the next thing she knew, she was swathed in total darkness. At some point the kishion had released her from the chest and carried her to the bed. After telling her he would return with food later, he had disappeared from the cabin. She must have slumped back into unconsciousness.

Maia trembled and shook, realizing that every moment carried her farther away from Comoros, from her people and the dangers they faced.

The door of the cabin groaned, and she flinched as the kishion stepped inside and bolted it behind him. His face was half-hidden in shadows. He looked at her warily, his face devoid of guilt or concern. He held a small bag in his hand.

Maia smoothed the hair from her face again, staring at him with loathing and bitterness. "So we are going to the lost abbey," she said, her voice so small and delicate that it sounded strange to her own ears.

The kishion nodded. He approached the bed and opened the sack. He put down a heel of bread wet with honey. A piece of dried meat came out next. A small round cheese followed and then a Muirwood apple. The apple surprised her and stabbed her with pain, but she reached for it first, bringing it to her nose to breathe in the smell. A few tiny tears moistened her lashes, but it was not enough to fall. Not even the apple could comfort her. She set it down on her lap without taking a bite, then glanced up at him, frightened by the coldness she saw on his face. The detachment.

"You have robbed me, kishion," she said in a tremulous voice. "You killed my parents. You murdered the man I truly loved. Even Argus . . . faithful Argus . . . you are a monster."

His eyes narrowed, but she could see he had been expecting recrimination. "I am," he said with a chuckle. "Men like me exist to do that which is too difficult for the tenderhearted. Your mother's health was failing long before I arrived at Muirwood. I hastened her journey to her next life, where I am sure she will be rewarded for her patient suffering." He said this last part with a hint of derision. "Your father was a murderer himself, though he lacked the manhood to ever wield the blade for a killing blow. He was a coward. I will *never* regret killing him. I only regret not killing him sooner." His face twisted with anger. "The dog tried to attack me. I have never been fond of beasts. They make my work more difficult. And if you recall, Maia, your *husband* . . . your duplicitous *husband*, threatened to hang me when next we met. You recall the gallows in Dahomey he used to threaten me? But I was too cunning for him."

"I should have let him!" Maia said with barely concealed anguish. "Why did I plead for your life? Why did I not allow the Fear Liath to drag you away?" She groaned. "You have repaid my kindness and mercy with *blood*!"

Her words stung him and he flinched. She could see the pain in his eyes, but his resolve did not waver. He was hard as flint, as immovable as a Leering.

Without shifting his gaze from hers, he reached toward his belt and drew one of his daggers. Then he grabbed her arms—not pausing when she cringed—and slit the bonds at her wrists, freeing her. He knelt by the edge of the bed, eyes level with hers. His scars had never looked so grotesque, and utter revulsion almost made her shrink away. He gripped one of her hands and pressed the dagger handle into her palm.

"You want revenge?" he sneered softly. "Then cut out my heart and eat it." He dragged her wrist, blade first, toward his chest. Letting go, he quickly loosened his collar and exposed the skin and a thatch of hair. "Kill me, Maia. If you think it will make you feel *any* better."

The blade was heavy in her hand. It was sharp and well made. She stared at it in her hand and sat up on the bed, the apple ready to tumble from her lap.

The kishion stared at her defiantly, exposing himself to a mortal wound. But she could see in his eyes that he did not believe she would do it. He knew she could not kill a defenseless man. She stared at the blade, trying to hear the Medium's whisper through the haze of her grief and despair. She heard nothing.

Her hand grew heavy and her arm sank. The kishion snorted and took the blade, then slid it back into the sheath at his waist. He rose and scrubbed one hand through his untidy hair.

"That is why I am here. To do the things that you will not do."

She gazed up at him. "Compassion is not weakness."

"It is to the Naestors," he said gruffly. "You do not understand the enemy. There is a practice in Naess called the Blood Eagle. It is an execution that makes a headsman's axe seem tame. That is how they will destroy your leaders. Your chancellor, your Privy Council members. Your Aldermastons. They would have made you *watch* it, Maia." He shook his head, his face twisted with revulsion. "I wanted to spare you the memories. They will destroy everyone. But they are afraid of the cursed shores. They fear the magic down there. Even the Leerings are cursed. So that is where I will hide you. I know that only a woman can pass the

Leerings down in the lost abbey." The look he gave her was plaintive. "Even if they find me, you can hide. You will be safe."

She shook her head. "What is there is worse than death."

His looked hardened. "I do not expect you to forgive me, Maia. I do not ask that of you. I will do what I must to keep you alive." He gestured toward the food he had brought her. "You will need your strength to cross those lands. I have gathered supplies for the journey. It will not be long now." He gave her a crooked smile. "It will be like it was before. You will see." He left and shut the door behind him.

***

Maia's legs ached from the long march through the woods. It had been so long since she had wandered this place, and yet the memories haunted her. There were bite marks on her skin, and the gnats and insects were a maddening nuisance. Before, they had wandered the cursed shores with caution and dread, not knowing what they would find or how far it would be. This time, they knew the journey; they knew where to find the waymarkers that would lead them to the abbey. Memories lurked everywhere. As Maia trudged through the brambles and mud, she could almost hear Captain Rawlt and his men cursing the climate and the snake-infested woods.

Each morning they examined themselves for ticks, which were plentiful, and wolf spiders. Maia found that the creatures left her alone for the most part. There were never any bites beneath her chaen, so she did not need the kishion's help to remove them. There were also no whispers this time. No murmurings or premonitions of dread. Without the kystrel, the woods felt less haunted and foreboding. She wondered if the deadness in her heart did not leave the Myriad Ones enough emotions to feed on, or if something else was keeping them at bay.

The kishion's spirits rose the farther they went. He did not speak to her often, and she was mostly silent with him. He had warned her not to escape, but she did not feel that fleeing was the right thing to do. Strangely, as they walked, she began to feel the subtle guidance of the Medium compelling her to follow him. It was almost as if there were a trail of lampposts leading off into the woods, a trail that beckoned her onward much as the waymarkers did. More than once, she felt a smokeshape traveling with them—leading her. At first she worried it was a Myriad One, but it did not feel malign. In fact, it reminded her of . . . Argus.

She did not want to be there. It had not been her decision to come to Dahomey. But as she followed the trail into the woods, it started to feel . . . right. Of course, she still carried the weight of her horrible grief. It was so vast and so omnipresent she had even given it a name. She called it the Great Sadness, and it was as vast as a lake, constantly rippling at her side as she walked. If she thought on it too much, it would overwhelm her with bitterness and tears. She could not will the Great Sadness away, so instead she became acquainted with it. She thought on it, seeking to learn something of and from it. It taught her, silently, of the pain others had felt upon losing loved ones and spouses. Quotes from the tomes she had studied ran through her mind over and over again. One from Ovidius particularly resounded with her: *You can learn from anyone—even your enemy.*

The kishion had packed sufficient provisions and equipment, so this journey was slightly more comfortable than the last. Her heart was so broken and torn that she could not fill it with anything, not even hate or anger.

On a morning that had begun like any other since they started their voyage, she pushed a spiderweb away from her face and caught a little flicker of sunlight through the dense trees overhead. She was dirty and footsore, but the little stabs of light in her eyes felt good. It had been several days since their departure from Bridgestow. She worried about the invasion of her realm. What were her leaders doing in her absence? What did they think had become of her? She remembered Suzenne and Richard Syon with warmth and affection. She worried about her grandmother and wondered what was happening to her. She had a feeling that Sabine was also suffering. Perhaps her grandmother was merely on a different shore of the Great Sadness.

"I recognize this place," the kishion said, coming to a halt.

It was growing colder, and the winks of sunlight had disappeared overhead, replaced by a gray wall of mist that began to descend from the treetops.

A prickle of apprehension shot through Maia. She remembered this place too. The field of bones with a Leering in the heap. The kishion scowled and glanced through the woods.

"We should skirt around it," he said warily.

"No," Maia replied, sensing another Leering in the area, one she had not noticed before. "Come with me," she said, grabbing his arm and pulling him after her.

The mist grew thicker as they walked. The kishion looked around nervously, and she noticed he had unsheathed one of his knives. Maia felt no fear. Tendrils of wreathing fog swirled amidst the upper branches, descending lower, but there was no impulse to flinch away.

There.

Maia sensed the Leering at the perimeter of the enclosure. Then another one. Then a third. They were all summoning the mist. Through her Gift of Invocation, she realized that the Leerings were activated by the arrival of trespassers. In turn, the cover of the mist allowed the Fear Liath to emerge from its lair. Its only vulnerability was sunlight.

Maia silenced the Leerings with her mind, and their power immediately yielded to her request. The mist dispersed, and golden rays of sunlight showered down, streaming in slanting angles through the trees. The kishion stared in amazement.

"You did that?" he asked in confusion.

She nodded and then stared at the field of the dead. This was the final battleground of the Scourge. This was the place where thousands had been slaughtered. She stared at the moldering bones and armor, the rusted swords and spearheads. Sunlight glimmered on the pitted, rusty decay. The air had a metallic smell to it. She stared at the Leering in the center, the waymarker that had guided her to the lost abbey. But she already knew where it was. The trail was invisible, but it was clear in her mind, as if a blacksmith had forged a metal railing in the woods, leading the way.

The Fear Liath would not trouble them this time.

Maia offered a subtle thought, thanking the Medium for its assistance.

In reply, she felt a gentle murmur . . . so small and slight it was barely noticeable. The Medium was with her. She wanted to demand answers of it. She wanted to accuse and rage against it. She had been its loyal servant ever since her escape from Naess. It had rewarded her loyalty with the deaths of her parents, her true love. Feeling the Medium retreat from her, she crushed the negative thoughts with force of will.

No, she would have to continue to be patient. She would follow the trail through the woods. She would go to the lost abbey.

It struck her as a strange flash of insight.

Perhaps the kishion was doing the Medium's will after all.

CHAPTER
THIRTY-THREE

Ereshkigal's Daughter

When they had last journeyed the cursed shores, it had taken a week for them to reach the lost abbey buried deep within the uninhabited terrain. This time they had traveled more quickly, with more confidence. As the morning dawned and they began walking, Maia finally began to speak to the kishion again.

The thought from Ovidius had struck her again. *You can learn from anyone—even your enemy.*

"Tell me more about the Naestors," Maia said, huffing a little. The terrain was steeper. There was a haunting beauty about this land that reminded her vaguely of the Bearden Muir and Muirwood.

"What do you wish to know?" he responded, glancing at her with surprise. Their past several days had been spent in silence.

"Tell me about their customs, traditions," she said. "In Dahomey, they like eating melted cheese and skewered meats. Each kingdom has its own manners. Tell me about Naess."

The kishion looked at her with a wrinkle of confusion. He had not broached conversation with her, allowing her time to grieve and for her rage to cool. But he was not averse to talking. "They crave treasure," he said with a snort. "Treasure and fighting. They are fighters, raiders. They love mischief and plunder. There is a story that one of the chieftains went to conquer the shores of eastern Hautland. They were protected by keeps and walls and thought they could withstand a siege for some time. But the Naestors love cunning and trickery. They were not going to throw their lives away battering down walls. Instead, they sent a kishion over the wall to steal pigeons and doves from the dovecotes. When he got back, they tied burning strings to the birds' legs and released them. They flew right back to the dovecotes, and it set the thatch on fire. Soon the city was blazing and everyone came running out. It was an easy slaughter."

Maia looked at him. "That kishion . . . was you?"

He gave her a half smile and did not reply.

"So they love trickery and cunning. They prefer to steal their treasures than work for them. What of the dark pools? Tell me of them. Walraven shared some of that lore with me. What do you know?"

The kishion scratched the back of his neck. "That *is* lore of the Dochte Mandar. I am not sure I believe it."

"Why not?" Maia asked.

He shrugged. "Because I see how they manipulate the chieftains. When you went to Naess, did you see any of the revels?"

"No," Maia answered. She had only been there briefly, and all her time had been spent with Corriveaux and Walraven.

"They whip the fighters into a frenzy with the revels," the kishion went on. "They are plied with drink, pleasures, and violence. Any guilt is purged away with kystrels. The Dochte Mandar teach

347

that this is the second life. That each man . . . or woman . . . will be reborn again. Depending on how courageous and cunning you are, how fearless in battle and how cruel in strategy, you may become a chieftain in the next life. The Dochte Mandar say they speak to the dead in the dark pools and learn who should be the next chieftains. They tell us who has been reborn and what they were in their past life. To me, it is a bunch of nonsense. I think the Dochte Mandar say what they wish us to believe, to keep themselves in power."

Something nagged at the back of Maia's mind as she pondered his words. "I have heard about this teaching," she said. "Not about the chieftains or the rulers of the Naestors. But I know people give great credence to what the Dochte Mandar teach . . . and they believe we will all be reborn." She considered that for a moment. "It is an interesting thought. But it is not true."

He glanced at her, his eyebrows furrowing. "What does it matter whether or not it is true?" he said with disdain.

She gave him a pointed look. "It makes all the difference in the world. You know about the Myriad Ones?"

"They are spirit creatures," he said with a shrug. "The spirits of the dead."

"No, they are the spirits of the *Unborn*. They are spirits too wicked and cruel to pass on to the other realm. They tempt us, kishion. They feed on our fears and jealousies. They persuade us to murder and torture. To betray. To lie. And they feed on us, just like the ravens feed on a carcass. The Myriad Ones have dominion in this fallen world, but there is a better world we can reach if we put our trust in the Medium. What the Naestors do not understand is when they die, they will become *subject* to the Myriad Ones if they do evil. There is no rebirth. They will *feel* like they feel now in life, only without the ability to sate their cravings or purge their guilt. Imagine the *guilt* they will feel then, kishion, when there are no longer any kystrels to numb their pain. Think of yourself and what you have done. There is not another chance. There is no glory waiting, only misery. I may suffer *here*. But I long for a better world."

The kishion stared at her in suspicion. "And who is to say the mastons are right? The same logic turns against you, Maia. Perhaps nothing happens when we die. Like a fire that burns out, leaving naught behind but ash. We are simply no more. That is what *I* believe."

"You may be right of course," Maia said simply, not wanting to provoke him. "If you are right, then I have lost nothing in being good. I go to my ashes peacefully and am no more. But if we are right, where does it leave the Naestors?" She gave him a piercing look. "Where does it leave *you*? I know I am only reciting what the mastons have written in their tomes over the centuries. But I have felt the difference between the power of the Medium and how the Myriad Ones subvert it."

Danger.

She stopped short, feeling the whisper in her mind like a clarion call.

"What?" he asked her, stopping too, his body tense as he began searching the forest for trouble.

Maia stood silently and listened to the wind rustling through the mossy trees. Closing her eyes, she opened herself up to the Medium's will. She felt the breeze rustle her cloak, her skirts, her hair. She repeated the pledge she had made in Naess to serve the Medium, in an effort to cast aside all her pride, all her sorrow and grief. She shed these things like stained garments.

The breeze kicked up and she heard a marsh bird call.

Murer is here. Stop the hetaera from returning.

Maia opened her eyes. She had rarely heard the Medium's whispers so clearly, so cuttingly. In her mind, she could see the lost abbey, could see a small camp near the garden wall. There Murer was, dabbing ointment against the bite marks on her cheek, her expression angry as she felt the ugly welts. There were six Dochte Mandar as well. And a kishion.

"What do you hear?" the kishion asked her.

"We are not alone," Maia answered, opening her eyes.

***

The kishion scowled with anger as he regarded the small camp near the ruins of the lost abbey. He had anticipated finding refuge in this place, not enemies, but the Victus had ruined his plans.

"Do you see her over there?" Maia asked at his shoulder. Two Dochte Mandar were sitting before a small smoking fire, talking in low voices. The others were roaming the ruins, examining the Leerings and admiring the devastation of the place. Maia could feel the Leerings speak to her, like a chorus of dozens of small voices. These were the ruins of an actual abbey, and many of the Leerings still worked and had not been harvested by the Naestors.

One, in particular, struck her with the force of its power. It was coming from inside the abbey, and she could sense the power radiating from it. It was a Blight Leering. It was causing the land to become inhospitable. It seemed to recognize her, a maston in its presence, and she felt its will and power nudging against her mind.

"I see no sign of the girl," the kishion said, squinting. "Perhaps she went inside. A man cannot enter that lair."

"I must go after her," Maia said.

"Wait until dark," the kishion replied angrily. "It is barely noonday. We cannot approach without being seen. Why not wait until she comes out? Let me kill her."

Maia shook her head. "No, I must stop her now. The Medium bids me to go."

He grabbed her shoulder and pulled her back behind the boulder, his face angry. "There are six Dochte Mandar and a kishion down there!" he snarled.

Maia felt a burning confidence inside her as the Medium swelled within her breast. She felt the Leerings below them thrum in response. Some of their eyes began to glow. Shouts of warning rang out from the Dochte Mandar below.

"What are you doing?" the kishion demanded hotly, grabbing a fistful of her gown with his hand.

"Nothing," she answered, feeling a little helpless and giddy against the flood of power unloosing inside her. "It is the Medium. They cannot stop us. Believe in me."

Maia pushed him away. A mingled sense of confidence and determination filled her body. She took a deep breath and then started down the little hillock toward the encampment. The kishion swore under his breath and followed in her wake.

The voices down below were speaking in Dahomeyjan. These were Corriveaux's servants, Maia deduced. She strode quickly, as if a current of water were under her feet, carrying her forward. The sun was just overhead, a stab of light that pierced through the skeletal trees. Huge stone ruins and boulders crowded around, painted green and black with moss and lichen. She felt the Leerings of the area respond as she approached, and the sound of gushing water hit her ears.

"Who is that?" someone shouted. "From the woods!"

Maia heard the twang of a crossbow, and a bolt sliced through the air. As it approached her, the shaft veered wide and shattered against a boulder. She walked with confidence, unafraid of the Dochte Mandar foot soldiers—unafraid of anything. She felt a purpose, a firm purpose inside her. It was noonday. It was the moment of the Medium's greatest strength.

She felt its power flow through her. The two Dochte Mandar by the campfire had risen and dusted off their black robes. They came at her, their eyes glowing silver.

"Why are you here?" one of them demanded. He had a short beard and a look of rage on his face. The two joined their wills together and hammered at her with a wall of fear. It felt like a small trickle compared to the avalanche inside her. Maia looked at one of them, and suddenly a nearby Leering crackled with energy and a blast of white blinded everyone, followed by a huge clap of thunder.

The two men lay on the ground, their robes smoking. One of them groaned in pain, the other was listless.

Maia continued toward the ruins. Black robes fluttered between the columns of boulders and crumbled supports. She ignored them, focusing on reaching the entrance to the lost abbey. Followed by the kishion, she climbed up the wreckage, recognizing the hidden entrance to the abbey since they had found it once before. Maia scrabbled up the rocks, feeling the winds blow behind and around her. The sky rumbled, and lightning began to streak through the sudden clouds that converged on the hilltop of the lost abbey.

The sun was directly overhead, making Maia's shadow just a small patch on the ground. She sensed a Leering that could control the wind, and summoned its power, bringing another force to bear against those that the Dochte Mandar were harnessing. The Leerings of the abbey hummed with power. She felt the defenses begin to activate. Light began to shine around them.

She watched as one of the Dochte Mandar tugged the kystrel off his neck, tossed it away, and fled into the woods. As Maia and the kishion turned the corner, they saw the black gap descending into the depths of the hetaera's tunnel. There awaited the guardian, the defender—the other kishion.

"He is mine," said her companion, his knives held up.

The other man produced blades of his own, and the two saluted each other.

Her kishion vaulted himself at the other man, his face a rictus of fury. The two lunged and feinted at each other, grunting and stabbing at each other's bodies. Maia slipped around them to enter the blackness of the tunnel unobstructed. She did not have a kystrel this time, but the walls were still glowing, a mossy green light emanating from the spiderweb sigils carved into the stone. She moved cautiously down the tunnel—dreading the confrontation with Murer, but determined to follow the Medium's guidance. As she walked, she found a junction she remembered from her first journey to this place, one with an archway that went up instead of down. From that archway, a breeze carrying the scent of flowers and pine trees wafted against her face. She remembered it vividly. When she had last come there, whispers had warned her against taking that path. Those whispers, she now realized, had come from Ereshkigal. There was something important down there, but she felt the Medium tug her back down the other path toward the hetaera's lair.

She reached a set of stone steps carved into the rock and headed down them, descending deeper into the gloom. It ended at the stone doors carved with the shape of the kystrel. She paused, panting for breath, flooded with memories. This was where she had received the brand on her shoulder. This was where she had been deceived. Her thoughts prickled with apprehension.

The doors were shut.

As Maia approached, she felt a wall of blackness slam into her. Even with the massive power of the Medium surging inside her, the blow was almost forceful enough to knock her to her knees. She was surrounded by a miasma of doubt, despair, fear, and self-loathing. The mark on her shoulder began to burn.

You challenge me *in my* dominion? *You foolish, insolent child! I am the Queen of the Unborn. I am the Goddess of this world. Kneel before me!*

The compulsion was so powerful that Maia staggered. She felt the stones shuddering around her, trembling under the weight of the force being expelled.

You have no power here! the voice screamed at her.

But Maia felt something build within her, filling her with strength. She lifted herself and staggered forward. The doors were so close . . .

You cannot defeat a hetaera, said Ereshkigal vengefully. *She is mine! She is my pawn!*

Maia felt dizziness and sickness roar inside her. The sensation of her shoulder burning was painfully hot, but she forced herself to reach out and shove the doors with her hands.

The Leerings tried to resist her, but she forced them to obey with her will. The doors slid open smoothly, grating on the stone floor. Immediately a haze of steam and vapor rushed out.

She saw the hetaera Leering in the midst of the churning pool down below. Standing there, gown pulled low off her shoulder, was Murer, her eyes glowing silver. The serpent Leering glared red with heat, the light glowing off Murer's still-untouched skin. She stared at Maia with hate and loathing, her painted lips pulled back into a snarl.

"No, Murer!" Maia called out in warning.

They have huddled together like frightened children, believing themselves safe behind walls of stone. There are Pry-rian crows pecking at our flanks. Even with the army of Paeiz and Dahomey joining them, we outnumber their mass at least three to one. The odds are closer than I would have preferred, but I am near enough to see their detestable Muirwood Abbey. I will break it down. We have over four hundred and fifty Dochte Mandar gathered here and another four hundred novices with kystrels. The abbey will burn tonight.

—Corriveaux Tenir, Victus of Dahomey

CHAPTER THIRTY-FOUR

Murer's Truth

The expression of hate on Murer's face sent shards of blackness into Maia's soul. Her silver eyes were fierce and wild, like a lioness guarding its prey. The waters by the Leering churned, and the pool swirled as if circling a drain. The edges of Murer's skirts were damp.

"You came here to stop me?" Maia's stepsister challenged. "You were a fool to walk away from so much power. I will be the empress, Maia! I will rule them all."

Maia walked into the humid chamber, feeling sweat immediately gather along her brow. She passed the broken skeletons huddled near the door, victims who had doomed themselves in an effort to learn the hetaera's secrets, and started down the ledge along the perimeter, confident of her footing since she had crossed it before.

"You would rule over a graveyard," Maia said firmly. "You saw the Leering amidst the bones, did you not? That is the destiny that awaits you. Ereshkigal only destroys. She cannot create."

"You *dare* speak her name!" Murer shrieked. "She is the Queen of Storms. She is the Mother of Kings. This is *her* domain, maston. You have no authority here!"

"Murer, step away from the Leering," Maia pleaded, trying to close the distance between them quickly. She heard the stone doors slide shut above her, trapping her inside. She stared at the flaming brand of the entwined serpents in the livid rock, so near Murer's exposed skin.

"You would deny me another throne?" Murer said with venom in her voice. "You already stole mine from me."

"It was never yours by right. Please, Sister! I know what it is to bear that brand. It is a torture and an agony I would wish on no person. Even you."

"Was I ever your enemy, Maia? Was I as cruel to you as Mother? Did I afflict you as Lady Shilton did? I left you alone. And you repaid me by having your *husband* humiliate me in front of everyone!"

Maia had reached the lowest level of the chamber and lowered her gaze. "I did not," she answered, shaking her head. She approached the edge of the waters, which seemed to be boiling. The Myriad Ones surrounded her, drawn to the vortex of their mistress. "And yet you have *had* your revenge."

A flicker of mirth crossed the angry countenance. "Men are so easy to deceive. They *want* to believe they are loved . . . adored. They want to be strong, but they are weak. They want to be seduced. I have used *your* emotions to twist men's hearts. If only I had been a *true* hetaera then. Soon, mastons will fall before me." She nearly purred as she spoke, and Maia felt her blood grow hot with rage. "They will always fall to us. When I have the true power of this brand, even the *king* will be forced to worship me."

Maia felt a stab of hope at the words. "So you did not seduce my husband?"

Murer's face twisted with contempt. "It was his younger brother, his duplicate. He was not there. But rest assured, Maia. He will succumb once I have achieved my full powers."

Maia shook her head, feeling her love for Collier grow. "He is beyond your power now, Murer. He is dead. And he died a true maston." She glowered at Murer. "He is beyond your reach, Queen of the Grave." Maia lifted her hand in the maston sign. "I call you by your true name. You are Ereshkigal, the Unborn, and you will depart!"

With those words, the Medium surged inside her, a flaming torch against a windstorm.

Murer's lips pulled back as if the command burned. Then she pressed her shoulder against the burning Leering. There was a sizzle of smoke, and purple light spilled from the Leering. Something in the dark recesses of Maia's memory emerged. She had seen that light. She had experienced this moment—the fusing of Myriad One to host. The silver in the girl's eyes darkened to hard round rings. Hatred filled the air, hatred so fierce and feral it was like a rabid dog.

"I name you!" Maia shouted. "You are Ereshkigal, the Unborn, and you will depart!"

Murer pulled away from the stone, the dress still sagging. There it was, burned into her skin, the black mark of the entwined serpents. Maia watched as the other girl slid a dagger from a sheath fixed to her girdle and started across the water toward her, her feet gliding over the surface of the water as if it were paved.

"You would cast me out of this body?" Murer said with chilling fury. "In my own domain? In the heart of *my* temple? You cannot speak the words if you cannot breathe!"

Murer raised her hands, and a curtain of steaming water bucked from the pool, drenching Maia in scalding, salty water. The wave pummeled her and knocked her to the ground before crashing into the far wall of the chamber. There was water in Maia's ears, up her nose, and in her mouth as she gagged and spluttered, confused.

Turning on her back, choking, she saw the wave had parted and receded back into the pool. The dagger was poised in Murer's hand, and she lunged forward to stab her.

Twisting to roll away, Maia raised her arms to defend herself and pain slit down her forearm as the dagger shredded her gown. Murer jerked her hand back and came down again, slicing Maia's elbow next, each blow trying to find her heart.

On the ground, Maia felt the horror of a desperate situation growing steadily worse. She knocked Murer back with a kick to the stomach and scrambled to her feet, her gown sopping wet and heavy. Her arms were on fire, and blood dripped from her hands, mixing with the puddle on the floor.

Murer swung the dagger purposefully and jabbed it forward again, cutting at Maia's ribs. Grabbing the girl's wrists with both hands, Maia tried to use her weight to throw Murer off balance. Fingernails clawed at her.

Letting go with one hand, Maia grabbed at Murer's bodice and felt the hard edges of the kystrel—*her* kystrel. Walraven had given it to her, and she recognized the particular feel of its power. She gripped the edges of the medallion and then tore the chain free.

Murer kneed Maia in the back, making her arch with pain, and wrestled her arms free again. But Maia had the kystrel, and she held it tight in her fist as she backed away.

"I do not need *that* to destroy you!" Murer hissed. Her eyes still glowed silver, and the waves from the pool were bobbing again, threatening to smash into Maia once more. The Leerings in the walls gushed out more water, and the whorl-shaped pool was no longer draining. The chamber was filling with seawater.

Maia silenced the Leerings with her mind, commanding them to end the onslaught of water. They obeyed her.

Murer bared her teeth and rushed forward again, slashing down at Maia, who turned and caught the dagger's edge on her shoulder blade. Though blood dripped down her arm, she could not feel pain anymore. She felt power well up inside of her as she fought. The next time Murer rushed her, she caught the other girl's wrist and grappled with her for the dagger.

"I will kill you!" Murer screamed into her face, her teeth gnashing.

Maia held the other girl back and turned her around slowly, their muscles straining against each other. There was power in Maia's legs, from her long journeys across the lands. Her wrists and arms were stronger too, from hours of scrubbing clothes and polished brass. Murer had been raised in privilege, and had never done hard work before in her life. Maia saw the energy drain from the girl's eyes, saw her jaw quiver as her muscles began to tire.

"Stop," Maia ordered sharply, squeezing the girl's wrist hard. Murer's entire arm trembled with tension.

The waters bucked again, dousing both girls in a stinging flood, but Maia kept her feet, planting her legs wide to hold herself up. Still, she felt Murer slipping, and she knew that if the other girl fell, she would be dragged down on top of her as the waters receded back into the pool. The knife was twisted toward Maia's heart, so the blow would be a killing one.

She released Murer to keep from falling on top of her and retreated, ready to ward off another attack from the razor-sharp knife. Murer's legs were tangled in her drenched skirts, and she suddenly slipped, crashing to the stone floor.

She shrieked in pain.

Maia saw her stepsister's eyes go wide with surprise as she

pulled herself up onto her knees. The dagger protruded from her ribs. Her complexion drained of all color as a bloom of blood stained her bodice.

Rushing to Murer's side as she collapsed, Maia caught her and held her face above the swirling waters. The eyes blinked, stupefied at what had happened. She had managed, somehow, to stab herself. Her limbs began to seize with the pain, and she shuddered violently.

"Murer!" Maia groaned, pulling her stepsister onto her lap.

Murer's eyes, drained of silver now, gazed down at the hilt, looking at it as if she could not comprehend what it was. She took a breath and flinched with pain.

"Ah!" Murer gasped, wincing. Her face crumpled and tears leaked from her eyes. She gazed up at Maia, her expression beginning to soften from hatred to sorrow. "Maia," she whispered. Maia gripped her hand tightly as she stared down into her face.

"Sshhh!" Maia soothed.

"I still feel her . . . squirming inside me," Murer mumbled in confusion. "Leaving me . . . why is she . . . leaving me? I am broken."

Maia blinked with sorrow. "You are no longer any use to her," she whispered, reaching down and stroking the bridge of her nose. She was sorry to see Murer in such pain.

Murer's convulsions grew steadily worse, and a look of panic filled her eyes as she realized she was dying. "The kystrel . . . showed me how much . . . how much Gideon truly loved . . . you. He wore it . . . while they kept him in prison." She closed her eyes, squeezing tears from her lashes. "So jealous of you . . . how he felt . . . about you. So jealous . . . Maia. How I . . . *hated* you. He did not betray you. He was not . . . even there."

"I forgive you," Maia whispered, weeping softly.

"You are . . . wrong . . . though." Her voice was so tiny, Maia barely heard it. "I know . . . he is . . . not dead."

Maia stared at Murer, not certain she had heard the words correctly.

"Murer?" she pleaded, bending closer. "He . . . he lives?"

"I saw her thoughts. What *she* knew. His Family . . ." Murer paused, swallowing. "They . . . are immune . . . to the kiss. Cursed . . . to . . . survive. They cannot . . . be . . . slain in war."

Maia stared at Murer, the flickering of hope in her heart now starting to fan into vivid flames. She stared away, her mind conjuring the sight of Collier lying on the ground in a pool of blood.

"His father died," Maia said, her thoughts seething. "Dieyre is dead. He is . . ."

He is alive, the whisper in her heart told her.

The knowledge came open in layers, like flower petals bending to kiss the sunlight at dawn. Lia Demont had cursed the Earl of Dieyre before the Scourge. She had cursed him to live. That he would be the last man standing, a witness to the destruction she had prophesied would happen. He had not been killed at the last battle, the place where all the bones moldered near a Leering. He had lived through the wars that had decimated the kingdoms. He had survived the plague invoked by the hetaera's Leering. He would die of old age. But Collier could not be killed in a fight, which meant he had survived the death wound from the kishion.

Maia's kiss could not harm him.

She gazed down at Murer's face, which was now chalk white. There was just a little bit of light in her glassy eyes.

"Alive," Murer whispered. Her eyes looked haunted. "What have I done? What have I done? I feel them around me. They are dragging me away. Maia!"

Maia felt joy and hope shoot through her body as she bent to kiss Murer's forehead. "I name you. Ereshkigal, Queen of the Unborn. Depart from her . . . forevermore."

A small smile curled the corner of Murer's mouth. A sad smile. She sighed and breathed no more.

Maia gently set her down on the hard stone. She touched the cold hand, watching for a moment. Then, shakily, she stood and turned to face the hetaera Leering. The sigil burned and hissed angrily, glowering at her. Her injured arm burned now that the battle was done.

She silenced the Leering with her mind and closed the water Leerings that had summoned and drained the seawater. They obeyed her.

As she stood there in her drenched gown, staring at the cooling sigil of the entwined serpents—the one that had been unwittingly branded on her shoulder—she realized a deep truth. There was only one Family in all the seven kingdoms that was immune to the plague. Collier was a reckless swordsman because he could not be killed by a sword or a dagger. She doubted he even knew the truth. The kishion's wound had not been mortal. And she realized with sweet joy that she could kiss him, and she could kiss his Family, and she could one day even kiss her own children because they would share in his protection.

Closing her eyes, she sank to the stones on her trembling knees, overcome by an immense feeling of gratitude. The Medium had never deserted her. It had guided her path all along.

Thank you, she whispered in the silence of her mind. Her heart was overflowing. Collier was alive. And he was not as injured as she had supposed. *You did not have to bless me this much. I would have served your will regardless.*

Rising from her prayer, her arms stinging with pain, she walked up the ramp to the doors, determined to face the kishion and seal the hetaera's lair forever.

CHAPTER THIRTY-FIVE

Hunted

W
hen Maia emerged from the tunnel after revoking the door Leering's power, which would prevent others from entering the lair, the sun shone down on her in blinding rays, forcing her to raise her uninjured arm to shield her eyes. She strained for sounds to help her understand what had happened, but the story was laid out before her. There was a dead man guarding the porch. Her kishion had won the battle.

She stepped away from the corpse, sick of death, and wandered a short way from the entrance. The kishion approached her from a distance, his face hardened with determination and strength. In one hand he clutched the chains of several kystrels, the medallions swaying as he walked. She had fastened the one she had taken from Murer to her girdle, and it hung against her leg. His rucksack was slung over his shoulder. The kishion stared at her as he approached, his grave expression shifting to one of worry.

"You are bleeding," he said, rushing up to her worriedly. He looked over her shoulder at the dark tunnel, as if expecting another enemy to emerge.

"Murer is dead," Maia said.

The kishion stared at her in astonishment. "*You* killed her?"

Maia could read his thoughts in his expression. He could not believe she, of anyone, would harm another person. She gripped her cut arm tightly, wincing from the pain. "She fell on her own blade."

"After stabbing *you*, it seems," he said. Then, taking her by the arm, he led her away from the opening, back toward the little garden they had visited on their first journey. "The Dochte Mandar are all dead, even the one who ran away."

She was appalled by his brutal efficiency. They reached the small stone enclosure, and he quickly knelt in the soft turf and swung his rucksack loose. Inside, she saw a blue-stained leather bag of powdered woad, some needles and gut thread, and small strips of cloth for bandages.

"Sit here." He gestured next to him.

She obeyed, but she did not feel at ease. As she watched the sinking sun, a feeling of urgency thrummed inside of her. She had to return to Muirwood. Collier was still alive. Her people were in grave danger, and she felt the Medium warning her that it was time for her to leave the kishion.

He looked at the wound on her shoulder first, grunting at the size of it, and told her he would need to stitch it. He offered her a piece of root to dull the pain, but she shook her head no.

"If you will not chew it, then hold perfectly still," he warned her. "The needle will hurt as it goes through."

She nodded and shifted so that her back faced him. He undid some of the lacings of her gown and pulled the fabric down to expose the skin of her upper back. Then, with deft and experienced hands, he began to stitch the gut strings through her flesh. She flinched and hissed at first, but he worked quickly, and the pinch of pain became familiar. Once he was finished, he dabbed the area with woad to help stifle the bleeding and covered it with a bandage. He then covered her up with the dress.

"Let me see the arm. Those look painful."

Indeed they were. Maia untied the cuff string and pulled the sleeve up to reveal the angry red slashes on her arm and elbow. Taking out his water flask, the kishion undid the stopper and bathed away the dried blood. His eyes looked so determined as he bent over her wounds. How could a man with violent hands use them in such a tender way? Images swarmed in her mind of their many journeys together. She was no longer disgusted by his severed ear and his grim scars. There was a man behind the hard flesh. A man who had somehow, despite years of killing, managed to grow the semblance of a heart.

His gray-blue eyes glanced up at her once, but when he caught her gaze on him, he glanced away and scowled down at the gashes he tended. He scrubbed one of the cuts clean and began stitching it, his fingers handling the implements with skill and precision. How many of his own wounds had he treated the same way?

"You must let me go," Maia said softly, daring to speak the words that burned on her tongue.

His eyes flicked up again. He finished tending to one of the cuts and leaned back on his heels, eye level with her. He wiped his nose, his expression stony.

"There is plenty of food here," he said, sweeping his hand toward the gardens. "Strawberries. Peaches. The greens poking up over there are carrots, I think. The Leerings in this garden produce food. We have enough to survive here forever."

Maia looked into his eyes imploringly. "I *cannot* stay!"

His mouth turned angry and wrinkled into a frown. "It may take some time before you see I am right," he said flatly. "Perhaps it will not happen until the Medium has destroyed everyone else. You are safe here."

"I am *not* safe here," Maia argued, shaking her head. "The Medium brought me here to stop Murer. But now it bids me to go." She stared at the sun, watching as it slowly dipped across the trees, the light still blindingly brilliant. Suddenly, starkly, she knew something terrible would happen if the sun went down and she had not yet departed.

"Convenient," he said with a snort. "It always does what *you* wish it to do. I brought you here, Maia. If others come, then I will take care of them."

She felt the urgency grow more intense. "Please! You must let me go! The Medium is warning me to depart this instant."

He looked incredulous. "And where would you go? No ship is waiting for you. You want to cross the mountains again into Dahomey? I murdered their *king*."

She put her free hand on his wrist. "I know you believe you are doing right, but you must *trust* me," she said, then cast her eyes around the ruins, the moss-covered rocks and trees. There was a haunting beauty to the place, a feeling of ancient splendor ruined. In her mind's eye, she could see the ruins as Muirwood. No, she could not let that happen to her abbey. Not after all the sacrifices that had been made to rebuild it.

"You are a naïve young woman," the kishion snorted angrily, pulling his arm free of her grasp. He stood and began pacing in the garden, his expression turning angrier by the minute. "You want to forgive those who betray you. Pardon those who persecuted you." His scowl became menacing. "I watched you from the window, Maia. At Lady Shilton's manor. I saw how they treated you." His jaw began to quiver with suppressed rage. "Your father was so easily manipulated by Deorwynn. *She* is the one who summoned me. It was *her* connections with the Victus who arranged it. But she was too greedy; she wanted her own child to rule as empress. I poisoned you . . . but not to kill you. I could not . . . I did not *want* to hurt you." His face twitched with suffering. "I . . . *care* for you. I have never . . . cared for anyone."

She could almost see the thoughts swirling around his mind. Their journey together from Comoros to the lost abbey had changed him. She had gone from being another assignment to someone he cared for personally. She had never treated him as others did. The more experiences they had shared together, the more her kind ways had broken down his defenses. Maia could sense all of this—his confusion, his gratitude, his possessiveness. He wanted to re-create that perfect trust they had once shared. He had brought her back to this place for exactly that reason. But she realized that he would only find death here—if he did not release her, the Medium would destroy him.

Her heart grieved for him, panged for his loneliness and abandonment. He had saved her life multiple times. Even though he had killed those she loved, he had done it to help her, to push her on top of a throne he felt she deserved in a world hungry for power.

"But you *have* hurt me," Maia said, rising. She clenched a fist and tapped her heart. "After what you have done, I can never trust you again. You cannot *be* with me! This fancy you have is a dream from which you must wake!"

"You would rather see your friends tortured to death?" he scoffed.

"I would rather die *saving* my people," she answered. "Please . . . you must let me go. You must choose it, before it is too late."

He gave her a firm and angry scowl and shook his head. "You will feel differently later. I will not give you up so easily." He gestured to her wounded arm and said gruffly, "Let me treat those cuts. It will not take long."

She knelt again, her heart wringing with worry and compassion. She felt the Medium's disapproval. It brooded above her like a storm cloud. She knelt and watched the sun sink into the sky as he tended her. His head bent close to the wounds, his movements efficient and skilled. The wounds gave a dull ache and itched terribly. She let him heal her, for there was nothing else she could do. He would not willingly let her go. He never would.

As she stared at the crown of his head, bent over her, the idea whispered in her mind. She could kiss him. She had no weapons. She would not use her kystrel again. But her lips were a weapon. With one kiss, she could incapacitate him with sickness.

No, she pleaded in her heart, staring up at the sky. *Please do not make me!*

A kiss of betrayal. A kiss that would end his life.

As if he heard her thoughts, his head suddenly jerked up. His face was so near, his look wary and concerned. How easy it would be to dip forward and do it. It almost seemed as if he longed for it. As if he might kiss her himself—to rid his heart of misery.

Please! Not like this. I do not want to kill him.

Then she heard the noise. He heard it as well. It was the sound of a twig snapping, or a small branch crackling. Someone was coming toward them from down the hill. Maia turned to look at the woods as the kishion rose into a crouch, his healing hands wrapped around two knives.

"Someone is here," the kishion whispered. He gestured toward one of the fruit trees. "Hide."

Maia slipped away, keeping low, and quickly stole between the laden branches of an apple tree.

The kishion vaulted over the short wall and landed in a crouch behind a shaggy oak tree.

There was a whistle of metal, and a throwing axe embedded in the tree bark near the kishion's head. Maia had heard that sound before.

Jon Tayt lumbered into view. His face was sweating, his beard full of brambles, and he was dressed in his hunting leathers and bracers. The look in his eyes was frightening.

He pulled another throwing axe from his belt hook.

The two men stared at each other warily.

"I suppose we must get this over with," Jon Tayt growled.

The kishion said nothing. Maia stared at the hunter, her heart overflowing with joy and hope. In her mind, Maia thought, *Jon Tayt Evnissyen . . . I Gift you with speed. I Gift you with cunning. I Gift you with strength . . .*

Then, like a snake striking, the kishion leaped around the other side of the tree and hurled one of his daggers at Jon Tayt's head. The hunter dived to the side, the blade just missing his ear, rolled back to his feet like a boulder tumbling, and loosed another axe at the kishion.

Maia covered her mouth, staring at the two hunters who had become the hunted. Though it terrified her to see them in such danger, something told her this reckoning had been fated from the start.

The men rushed each other. Jon Tayt blocked the kishion's overhand thrust and kneed him in the stomach. Then the two men hammered into each other, and Maia felt true panic since the kishion was the faster of the two. Jon Tayt's head rocked back from a strike with the other man's elbow, but the canny hunter stomped on the kishion's foot and tackled him into a tree. Fragments of wood exploded from the impact, and both men clawed and grappled with each other. There was no room for weapons now—they fought with arms, fingers, heads, and hips. Jon Tayt slammed the kishion into the tree a second time, and Maia saw his grimace of pain from the blow.

The kishion flipped Jon Tayt over his back, making the hunter crash hard against the fallen branches and rocks. The man grunted in pain, but he managed to hook the kishion's boot with his own and yank him down as well. Scrabbling up quickly, both men tried tackling each other, grunting and hissing as they sought to shift leverage, gripping anything they could seize, and Jon Tayt managed to lift the kishion off his feet and slam him down on the rocks.

Maia winced with the pain of the landing, winding her way toward them. The kishion looked stunned and dazed, and Jon Tayt's hands were suddenly around his throat, choking him. The hold was broken by a quick jab to Jon's neck, and the two broke apart, panting and wheezing. Jon held his side and shuffled away as the kishion yanked the axe from the tree, giving the hunter a precious moment to draw another one from his belt.

The two men lunged at each other again, the axe blades glinting in the sunlight as they swung at each other. The clash of the blades was jarring, and then the kishion dropped low and hacked his blade into Jon Tayt's meaty leg, eliciting a howl of pain. Blood flowed from the deep wound, and the look of agony on the hunter's face made Maia shudder. She started toward the men at a run, determined to fling herself over Jon Tayt's body—she would not see another friend murdered.

Then Jon Tayt swept his axe down and lopped off the kishion's arm at the elbow while it still held the axe haft. The kishion roared with pain and staggered backward. He saw one of his daggers on the ground and jumped on it, fumbling with the blade to pick it up and throw it.

Jon Tayt's axe whistled twice, the blade burying itself in the kishion's chest.

He struggled to rise for a moment and then slumped to the ground, landing on his back. He lay still, eyes open and staring. His chest quivered with pain, but he could not breathe.

He was dying when Maia reached his side.

She gripped his dirty hand, tears stinging her eyes and falling hotly down her cheeks. The skin was still warm, but there was no strength in his grip. He had always offered that hand to her, to help her, to fight her enemies, to steer her through a crowd. Maia was not prepared for the devastation she felt when she realized she would never be able to see him again. She hung her head, the tears dripping from the tip of her nose onto his neck.

He blinked rapidly, unable to speak, and she watched as the life spark began to cool. She smoothed the hair from his forehead with one hand, gripping his remaining hand with her other, remembering how he had always stood at her side and tried to help her. She would never forget him. Her throat was so thick, she could not speak the words in her heart.

The tremors in his body stopped. He died gazing into her eyes, a small smile on his face.

We have the chancellor, Richard Syon. He left the abbey grounds to sue for peace, warning that the Medium would deliver them, and he surrendered himself to us. He is a short, fat man, completely contemptible in his false meekness and humility. I told the fool that there would be no truce. I told him that we fully expected the Medium to be summoned. It would be summoned by us. In consequence of his fool's bravery, I said we would tie him to a stake, flay his back open, break his ribs out, and burn his entrails as he died. This is called the Blood Eagle. I told him we would do this when the sun sets. And then at midnight, after he was dead, we would fulfill our oath and destroy the inhabitants in a Void. I reminded him that the tower on the Tor commemorated another Aldermaston who had watched his abbey burn.

—Corriveaux Tenir, Victus of Dahomey

CHAPTER THIRTY-SIX

Blight Leering

Jon Tayt yelled in pain as he torqued the two sticks, tightening the leather thongs wrapping his leg. The blood stopped flowing from the gaping wound on his leg, much to Maia's relief. He muttered terrible oaths in Pry-rian, his face a mask of suffering and fury, and tied off the sticks to keep pressure on the wound. He then collapsed back on the gorse, panting, his chest heaving.

Maia had fetched the woad and began to treat the cut on his brow and his smashed nose, using a handkerchief to mop the blood from his bearded cheek.

"Fine . . . kettle . . . of fish," he wheezed with hardly enough strength to utter it.

Maia felt tears swim in her eyes. "You came for me," she said in amazement.

"Was never . . . far . . . behind," he chuffed. He lifted his head a little and stared down at the leather thongs wrapped around his leg. "By Cheshu, a lucky stroke. Hit the bone," he added with a wince.

"But he suffered worse, I warrant. Never liked . . . that fellow much."
He gave her a hard look. "*Never* threaten a man's hound."

Maia stifled a sobbing laugh. "How did you reach me so quickly?"

He took some deep breaths to steady himself, lying still. "I will
be brief, for once, because I am not much in the mood . . . for talk.
I happened upon Collier at the Battleaxe. What a fine name for
an inn! He was near death, poor man, and swooned from the loss
of blood. I did what I could for him and then brought him to a
wagon bound for Muirwood. I was a bit . . . impatient with the
wagon master, grant me that, but I got him to the abbey straight
away. They all laid hands on him. Maston stuff. He roused enough
to tell us he had named you his heir in the event of his death, and
then charged me to go after you. I came on the *Argiver*."

"But how did you know where to go?" Maia asked, grabbing
his wrist and holding tight.

He smiled. "We were at *Muirwood*, lass. Do you know how
many Aldermastons are there right now? By Cheshu, one from
each kingdom, at the least!" He sighed and rested a bit, his green
eyes roaming the ruins around them. "Go to the lost abbey, they
said. And so I did. You left a trail easy to follow, I warrant you."
He sighed, his eyelids drooping.

Maia looked up and saw the sun fading quickly. As she stared
at it, feeling gratitude and concern for her friend, she noticed
someone approaching from the abbey ruins above. An older man
with a long, gnarled stick poked his way down the path at a breakneck pace. She recognized him instantly.

"Maderos," she whispered in surprise.

"What?" Jon Tayt muttered. He tried to lift his head and
failed. Maia cradled his head in her lap, watching as the crooked-
legged man made his way toward them.

Maderos was fat around the middle, his dark wiry hair silvered with gray. He paused to rest for a moment on the gnarled staff. His tunic was spattered with dirt and dust, and she could see the gleam of the chaen from his collar.

Jon Tayt's eyes closed, his head drooping.

"Jon!" Maia begged with concern, clutching his shirt to shake him.

"Let him rest, little sister," Maderos crooned with a wry smile. "He has not slept in many days, and he suffers a grievous wound."

Maia bit her lip as she watched the steady rise and fall of the hunter's chest. She stroked his chest and plucked a piece of bark from his tangled beard. In a moment, he started to snore, and the sound brought a wash of relief through her.

"Will he live?" Maia asked the wayfarer.

Maderos lifted his eyebrows. "I write the words *after* they happen, sister. Not before. Time heals. We shall see. But Muirwood needs you now. You must leave."

Maia stared at the bearded face, agonizing over the thought of leaving him so injured. But she felt the Medium's will clanging in her skull like a bell. She gently set Jon Tayt's head down on the heath. She stroked the copper curls off his damp forehead, feeling such deep tenderness for her friend. She had lost Argus. The thought of losing Jon Tayt too tortured her. It was painful leaving him.

"Come," Maderos offered, holding out his hand. "It is time."

She looked at the sinking sun again, watching as it descended toward the horizon. "Is there time, Maderos?" she asked. "Something terrible will happen at sunset. The Medium has been warning me of it."

"Yes, little sister. We must hurry. Hold my arm." He offered his elbow to her and led her back up the hill toward the ruins, his other hand wielding his staff. Instead of taking her toward the black gap of the hetaera's lair, he walked along to the left. They passed broken pillars and moldering stone. A few birds called down from the branches, the only witnesses of their presence in the woods. She glanced back one last time to the fallen bodies of the hunter and the kishion.

Maia had wandered the grounds on her first visit with the kishion, but she did not remember this area. A few toppled columns had fallen into each other. As she approached, she felt the presence of a Leering. She recognized it from earlier—it was the one that was causing the curse on the land. It was a Blight Leering. Maderos took her to it, crossing a broken archway that no longer supported anything.

The Blight Leering was a massive boulder surrounded by crumbling fragments of stone. The face on the Leering was so worn by time that she could not determine if it was a man or a woman. The boulder was smooth, almost polished. She felt power radiating from it, summoning the sickness and poisons that scarred the cursed shores. It brought the wolf spiders, the ticks, the venomous serpents. It created a haven that the Fear Liath was happy to call home. Power had been emanating from it for centuries, destroying the land bit by bit.

She felt the urge to touch it.

Maia reached forth her hand, but Maderos stopped her.

"You can silence it, child," he said respectfully, blocking her hand. "But do not touch it. The Blight is not what you must unleash upon the Naestors." He extended the staff and gestured to the ruins. "You must rebuild this abbey and safeguard these Leerings. End the Blight on this land. It will become an inheritance for those you trust. Those from Assinica and other lands who wish to stay here."

Maia nodded. In her mind, using her Gift of Invocation, she silenced the Blight Leering. The power thrumming through the boulder quieted. A breeze wafted into the ruins, and Maia heard the flutter of silk. Turning, she saw another archway by the toppled columns at the perimeter of the ruin, nearer to the rubble of the lost abbey. It was an Apse Veil.

Maderos smiled. "When you were in the tunnel, you sensed this place, sister," he told her. "Back when you *first* came here. The Medium whispered to you. It invited you to come to this place, but Ereshkigal clouded your mind. She made you fear what you did not know. Now that you have opened the Apse Veil again, you can pass back to Muirwood. You must save them, Maia."

Her heart dreaded the conflict, but she steeled herself. "I do not want to destroy the Naestors, Maderos."

He gave her another slightly crooked smile. "Of course, child. Why do you think the Medium has chosen *you*?" He patted her hand. "You will be remembered long after this second life has ended. Your memory will give others courage to live, to *be* what the Medium wishes them to become. Go now, sister. Return to your kingdom."

Maia started toward the billowing veil, but she hesitated before walking through it. "But what must I *do*, Maderos?"

He rested his arms on the mushroom-shaped top of the staff. "Is it really so difficult? Open your *mind*, child. Open your *heart*. The answer is there, if you will only believe it is possible. Do not doubt. Believe."

Maia looked into the aging man's eyes for a moment. Behind him, she saw the sun sinking low—a reminder that time was passing. It was going to be a glorious sunset, like the many she had enjoyed while walking the grounds of Muirwood.

The answer came to her in a thought, so small it almost passed without notice. She stared at the rays of sunlight, felt its warmth bathing her face.

It was so simple.

All she needed to do was stop the sun from setting.

***

Carved into the walls of every abbey there were Leerings with faces. The Leerings on the outer walls typically bore the faces of the sun, the moon, and the stars. These were light Leerings, enabling the abbey to glow at night and provide light to the grounds. But they could do so much more than that . . .

With her mind fixed on those Leerings, Maia stepped through the Apse Veil in the ruins of the lost abbey and emerged in Muirwood. She instantly felt the stains of her wounds and the filth and dirt she had carried with her, but she did not allow her thoughts to linger on them. There were mastons inside the temple—the entire place seemed full of people speaking in low voices, wearing maston robes. Many she did not recognize. Towering above those around him because of his height, she recognized Tomas, who had been Richard Syon's steward and now served Aldermaston Wyrich. When he saw her rush out from beyond the Rood Screen, his eyes widened with complete surprise and twin dimples appeared on his cheeks.

"Lady Maia!" he gasped, maneuvering through the crowd to reach her. "My lady! You came!" His look of cheer turned in an instant to worry and concern. "They have the Aldermaston . . . they have Richard Syon! He surrendered to them this morning so he could offer them a truce. He is to be put to death. Everyone has gathered outside, my lady. This way!"

His face pinched with concern as he took in her appearance. "You are wounded!"

"I am well enough, Tomas. Take me!"

She marched with him, passing dozens and hundreds of onlookers. A crowd began to follow behind her as she hurried to the abbey doors, which were opened for her before she reached them.

"Where is Aldermaston Wyrich?" Maia pressed.

"He returned with the warriors he led and has gathered the choir outside the abbey," Tomas answered. "They were going to start singing at sunset, to calm our people's fear."

The inner grounds of the abbey were packed with people of all ages and ranks. The choir from Assinica had gathered along a few rows of benches lining the abbey wall. Standing before them, she saw Aldermaston Wyrich. He was staring at the horizon, where the sun was just touching the border between land and sky. Long shadows were painted across the ground. The people were sitting together in a mass, waiting for the music to start.

"Aldermaston!" Tomas called, gesturing with his long arms.

Aldermaston Wyrich turned, his gray hair gleaming in the sunlight. He saw Maia, and his serious frown broke into a brilliant smile. He rushed forward to take her hands. "The Medium whispered that you were coming," he said smiling. "I had almost given up hope."

"Where is King Gideon?" Maia asked.

"Walking toward us now," the Aldermaston replied, gesturing.

Maia whirled and saw Collier striding through the dense crowd, his eyes wide with delight. He was walking! She had not dared to hope she would see him this improved.

"My lady, Richard Syon is with the Naestors," Wyrich said gravely. "They plan to execute him at sunset. I had hoped your coming would prevent it . . . but I do not see how."

"It will, Aldermaston. Cling to that hope," she told him.

She left the two men and rushed to Collier, who scooped her into his arms. She reveled in how strong and hale he looked—how *alive*. His eyes were bright as the blue sky, and in their reflection she could see the fading sunlight. She touched his face, her heart thrilling.

"Maia," he breathed, holding her close, hugging her fiercely.

She squeezed him as hard as she could, reveling in his continued life, ignoring for just a moment the vast crowds staring at them, then she pulled away and took his hands.

"The Naestors," he said. "They will attack tonight. We have tried to hold them back. To hold off killing them. But if they attack the abbey, we are certain they will be destroyed." He took her hands in his and clenched them hard. She could see the raw emotion in his eyes, the worry for so many lives that would be lost. "They do not know what they are doing!"

"And so we must teach them," Maia said. Still clinging to his hand, she turned and faced Muirwood Abbey. The light Leerings from the abbey were starting to glow, the eyes already brightening. She sensed the Leerings, felt their awareness of her, their eagerness to respond to her thoughts. The Medium swelled inside her breast and tingled down to her fingers, entwined with Collier's.

It felt as if a huge vault were opening inside her mind, metal grating against stone. The power of the Medium unfurled from her igniting every Leering within the abbey and outside. Her mind stretched, expanding until she could see every creature gathered on the grounds, then moved past the grounds, showing her the Naestors encamped in the valleys below. Her vision went farther still, spanning the country in an instant—she could feel the lives of every man, woman, and child as if in a single heartbeat.

Maia turned, feeling the weight of the Medium crush down on her shoulders, as if she were lifting the Tor itself. She stared at the sun, the dying embers of light slipping over the edge of the world.

Make it return, she commanded in her mind.

The Leerings in the abbey obeyed her. She felt the effigies of the sun, moon, and stars brighten, their power emanating into the nascent night. Their power was joined by that of the Leerings in distant abbeys in other realms, as if they were all anchors, weighing the sun in place and preventing it from being carried off.

The light in the sky seemed to wobble and then the sun started to rise again. Not from the east, but from the west. It rose in its majesty and splendor, bathing the walls with its light and warmth.

The looks of astonishment on the faces around her made her almost smile through the strain. If Collier had not been holding her, she would have collapsed.

It made sense to her. The Naestors were from the north, a land of darkness and cold. They were a superstitious people. Nothing would startle them or convince them of the power of the Medium more than seeing the very sun they worshipped obey the maston order. The shadows began to retreat.

Gasps of surprise came from everywhere around her. And then there was singing. The choir from Assinica was singing the same anthem they had sung at her coronation. Their voices were full of the Medium, inviting and invoking it, and their wordless chant spread a melodious wave of peace and serenity.

The sun continued to rise, pulled by the Leerings embedded in the abbey walls. The night was not beginning. It was day again.

"My love," Maia whispered to Collier, feeling her strength ebb. All she had endured came crashing down on her. Weakness broke her to pieces. She slumped against his chest, feeling the sunlight warm her cheeks as blackness carried her away.

CHAPTER
THIRTY-SEVEN

Covenant of Muirwood

M aia did not know how long she slept. She did not dream, which was in itself a blessing. As she gradually surfaced to consciousness, she sensed the soft mattress and blankets around her. The bedding smelled like the laundry soap the lavenders used at Muirwood and the scent of purple mint. She was aware of a dull, pulsing pain in her arm and shoulder as she slowly began to move. And then she felt lips press tenderly against her forehead and strong fingers entwine with her own.

"Are you awake?" Collier whispered faintly.

She blinked and saw her love hovering above her, sitting on the edge of her bed in the Aldermaston's manor. A Leering gave off a dim light, filling the room with supple shadows.

"Tell me this is not a dream," Maia answered, gazing up at him. She lifted her arm and saw she was wearing a nightgown. As the sleeve dropped down, she saw the ugly gashes Murer's dagger had given her.

Collier gazed at the wounds, his expression hardening. "Did he do that to you?"

Maia knew who he meant. The kishion. "No, it was Murer. I faced her at the hetaera Leering. She is dead now. So is *he.*"

He closed his eyes, as if uttering a silent prayer of thanks.

Then he opened them again. "We sent Jon Tayt after you," Collier said, rubbing his thumb across the top of her hand. "He found you?"

She tried to pull herself into a sitting position and winced with sudden pain. "He did, and I left him gravely wounded. Can you send someone? Can you send someone to save him?"

"Of course. Let me help you up," he offered. He arranged some pillows against the wooden headboard and helped her sit up, his strong arms shifting her easily.

"She is awake?" Suzenne said from across the room. She walked into Maia's line of vision, looking tired and worn, but relieved. "I have been holding back the flood of people who want to see you," she said with a warm smile. "I only let this one in after much persuasion." She nodded and gave Collier a genuine smile.

Because there were no windows, she did not know what time of day it was. "How long have I been sleeping?" Maia asked, wrinkling her nose.

Collier smirked and glanced at Suzenne. "It *should* be about midnight, by our best estimation." He looked at Maia with a wry smile. "It is a little difficult to tell, since the sun is directly overhead right now. Everyone is walking the grounds, gazing at the sky in wonderment." He gave her a pointed look. "The Aldermastons are all wondering when you intend to *release* the Leerings you invoked so that things can return to their normal state." He smiled and caressed her cheek.

Maia could hardly believe it. "I thought it would end the moment I collapsed—"

He shook his head. "Oh no, my love. You caught the sun in a net and captured it. People want to know what you intend to do with it next. The Naestors, as you can imagine, are terrified out of their wits. They have sued for peace and are imploring all the Aldermastons—there are *several* here right now, I should mention—to entreat you to release the sun before it scorches the earth. Richard Syon asked to be informed the moment you awakened." He tucked strands of her hair behind her ear. His fingers lingered against her skin a moment, making her shiver with pleasure.

"I suppose it would not be proper to greet anyone in my nightclothes," Maia said. She was aching and sore, but she felt rested and peaceful. She was afraid the tranquility was like a soap bubble and would burst in an instant, but she reveled in it nonetheless.

"Suzenne has a gown chosen for you," Collier said. "And it meets with my approval. I will go while you change." He started to rise from the bed, but she caught his hand and shook her head.

"No," she said. "There is a changing screen over there, and Suzenne is here to chaperone us." She gave him a longing look. "I cannot *bear* to be parted from you. Ever again." She squeezed his arm tightly, begging him to stay with her eyes.

Perhaps they were the words he most needed to hear. He looked humbled and a bit shaken, but he did not attempt to leave. He helped her rise gingerly from the bed, and as she walked slowly over to the changing screen, Suzenne holding her arm, she saw him wander to the dressing table and take up a comb. He turned and winked at her knowingly.

***

Maia would have savored soaking in a tub, but there was not time for that—nor would it have been appropriate, considering the

385

company. She asked Collier dozens of questions about what had happened to him and how he had managed to take the maston test in secret, but he would only promise to tell her all later, when they were alone in the garden.

Once Maia was dressed and Collier was busy combing the tangles out of her hair, Suzenne left to find Aldermaston Syon and his wife, Joanna. As soon as he entered, Maia painfully pulled herself to standing and went to him, hugging him hard, despite the way it made her injuries throb. She was too grateful to see him hale and uninjured after his brush with death. How horrible it would have been had she arrived too late to save him.

"Welcome home," Richard said soothingly, patting her arm and stepping back. "You could not have arrived through the Apse Veil at a more urgent moment."

"Indeed, a most desperate moment," Joanna agreed. She clutched Richard's hand as if she would never let it go. The look of relief on her face was palpable.

"Were you frightened, Richard?" she asked him, pulling away.

He frowned and shook his head. "If the Medium suffered me to die, I would have joined countless others who have lost their lives defending our beliefs. I was more concerned with how the Medium would punish the Naestors for my death. They have been humbled by what transpired this . . . day?" A smile quirked on his mouth. "I had not even considered halting the setting of the sun and reversing it, but it is mentioned . . . only once . . . in the tomes. A battle was being fought long ago, and the mastons knew they would be defeated if night fell. The Aldermaston leading the fight made the maston sign in full view of his army, and it halted the sun for three hours. That was centuries ago, and it is the only reference I am aware of to anyone invoking that power. The Medium obviously inspired you."

"Tell her about the Dochte Mandar," Joanna urged him.

"Let me get to the point quickly. The Naestors are convinced, utterly and completely, that the teachings of the Dochte Mandar are false. When the sun came back, many of their warriors fled in terror. The majority fell down and started worshipping me, thinking that *I* had done it. While the choir was still singing, they hurriedly escorted me back to the abbey as a peace offering, and that was when I learned that it was *you* who had summoned the Leerings. The chieftains rounded up all the Dochte Mandar and seized their kystrels, ripping the chains from those who did not cast the amulets away themselves in fear. They did not fight it. There were eight hundred and fifty to be precise. We have black-smiths destroying them even now. The Naestors are completely submissive, Maia, and fearful of the future. They rely wholly on the Dochte Mandar to invoke their Leerings in Naess and are afraid of living in the dark and by the light of torches."

Maia pursed her lips. "We must build an abbey in Naess for them," she said firmly. "We will send mastons—"

Richard smiled, pleased. "I already suspected you would feel that way. And so this is what I proposed after speaking to the Privy Council as well as the other Aldermastons and leaders who have gathered here at Muirwood. They all wish to know if you approve of their plan. If the Naestors enter into a covenant agree-ing that they will not attack the other kingdoms, they will be per-mitted to leave in peace without their weapons. We, in turn, will promise to continue trading relations with Naess and to teach them the crafts they do not know. Their people are mostly war-riors, Maia. Some are fishermen and a few are farmers. They have earned their bread mostly through stealing and raiding. They need to be taught, and we have knowledge to impart to them."

Maia liked the idea very much. "No retributions," she said,

nodding. "No punishments. But what if they refuse? And what of Corriveaux?"

Joanna looked at her intently and answered. "He and the other Dochte Mandar are under guard. Those who refuse to make the covenant will be banished from the kingdoms forever. The chieftains told us of an uninhabited island between here and Assinica where they can be exiled. The Naestors also promised to release all of their political prisoners, including Chancellor Walraven and your grandmother."

"Thank Idumea!" Maia sighed.

Richard nodded. "Indeed. Though many of the rulers of the other kingdoms still want vengeance and retribution. The Naestors have hoarded wealth, and there was talk at first about plundering their kingdom and leaving them in poverty. But I thought you would not approve, so it was not made a condition of the Covenant of Muirwood, as we are calling it."

Maia smiled, feeling her heart swell with love and admiration. "You know my heart, Richard." She turned and touched Collier's arm. "What do you advise, my lord?"

"We cannot change the past," he said softly. "We can only move forward. I say we forgive the Naestors. They have been cruelly duped by the Victus. They see now that they are guilty of the most grievous murders. They need time to heal, Maia. They need to know how the Medium feels when it is not forced. Some of the chieftains said they should be our slaves to repair the damage." He shook his head, chuckling. "We knew you would not accept those terms."

"You are right. I accept the terms of the covenant," Maia said. "If they will agree, then I will set the sun." She gave Richard a small smile, smoothing the fabric of her gown. "Make it thus so, Chancellor."

***

Maia and Collier walked hand in hand into the Queen's Garden as the sun slipped down past the wall. Though a new day should have been dawning, they were instead moments away from a second sunset.

She squeezed his hand. "Nightfall instead of dawn," she said. "The poor flowers are confused."

"Not as confused as the Naestors, I think," he said. Their pace was slow and languid. "And no Thewliss! He is well, rest assured. I should tell him never to grease the axles of his noisy cart, because I prefer to have a *little* warning that he is coming." He gave her an inviting look.

Maia smiled at him. "I want to hear your story," she said. "I am desperate to hear it."

"You have had a busy day, my love." He noticed her subtle limp. "You are tired. Here, sit by the flower beds." Taking her arm, he put his other hand on the small of her back and led her toward the bed with all the blue forget-me-nots. She suspected he did that deliberately and could not keep a tender smile from her lips.

"Thank you," she said, accepting his help to sit on the wide stone railing surrounding the elevated flower box. She smoothed her skirts and gazed up at him, drinking in the sight of him.

"What do you wish to know first?" he asked her. "I suppose you are wondering about Murer coming to get revenge on me?"

Maia shook her head. "I already know you are faithful to me. She told me herself. She was especially vengeful because of the way you had humiliated her here."

He winced at that. "Yes, I can see that. I believe there is a maston saying about a woman scorned. I should have remembered."

Maia smiled and rubbed her palms over the smooth stone of the bench.

"My goal was to fool the Dochte Mandar. I am rather cunning, my lady," he said with an impertinent look. "I warned you of that long ago. There is another maston saying—you can tell I have been reading my tome every day—about being as wise as a serpent yet as harmless as a dove. That describes the two of us perfectly, I think. I had a suspicion that my messages to Simon were being intercepted. So I deliberately sent him news that would misdirect our enemies, including any possible hetaera."

Maia stared at him in surprise.

"Devious, I know," he said with a smirk. "Sometimes I cannot help myself. For example, when I returned to Dahomey, I went straight to the Aldermaston of Lisyeux, confessed my many faults, and asked for his counsel on how to end the war with Paeiz in the shortest time possible, win them to our side, and pass the maston test . . . all in less than a fortnight." He grinned to himself at the memory. "I could only think of one way. And *that* would mean borrowing some of my then-wife's meekness and humility." He paced slowly in front of her, glancing at her periodically to see her reaction. She had the sense he rather enjoyed startling her. Though she admired his handsome looks, she tried not to make that admiration so plain on her face.

"Go on," she said.

"The Aldermaston suggested," he continued, "that instead of quarrelling with Paeiz over our shared borders, I should grant them the lands they contested in a secret agreement. That was my thought as well, so I believe the Medium had prompted us both. I sent my army marching to crush our invaders, but instead I rode ahead as Feint Collier and negotiated the treaty without the Dochte Mandar's involvement, persuading the king to pledge their support to Comoros. We had a merry time positioning our armies for battle and then moving them hither and yon, all while preparing our fleets to sail to your aid."

Maia could not help herself. She was impressed. "That was what happened, truly?" she asked. "You gave up a portion of your kingdom?"

He stopped pacing and gazed down at her upturned face. "I considered what I was *getting*—you—to be infinitely more important. And that land had been a source of contention between our nations for years, so I knew the agreement would benefit me in other ways as well. Having struck an understanding with Paeiz, I had time to focus on the maston test. I passed it several weeks ago and earned my chaen."

"Weeks ago?" Maia asked, perplexed. "Why did you not tell me?" She felt a small throb of resentment in her chest.

He held up his hands. "It was a secret! I absolutely *forbade* Simon to tell you. Even though I did pass the maston test, I still struggled to pass the Apse Veil on my own. Every time I tried, I would get sick and retch, but I worked at it, very hard. I told you in my letter that I wanted to come to *you*. I wanted to surprise you, which is why I refused when you offered to come to me." He shook his head guiltily. "Then that ship from Hautland came. Oh, by the Blood, how that tormented me! The Dochte Mandar annulled our marriage and began their invasion. Simon was murdered!" He threw up his hands. "I dared not reveal the truth then because my strategy required the armada to strike your coasts and move inland a bit. Only then did I move in on their fleet with my ships. The Naestors are *trapped* here, you understand. Their armada is no more. They require our leniency to return to their lands. While I attacked the armada, Paeiz challenged the army following Caspur. The Naestors were trapped between us, and we had the ships to move our forces around quickly. I do not think Corriveaux even understood how desperate their situation truly was. The only Void they were likely to create was their own."

Maia closed her eyes, trying to absorb the information flooding her. Collier had been a maston for weeks. Simon had known.

"It was only *later* that I learned you had kissed the Prince of Hautland," he said, drawing her from her reverie.

"That is not true!" Maia said defensively.

He smirked at her. "I know. Richard told me, and Aldermastons cannot lie." He then knelt down in front of her, resting one hand on the stone railing, one hand on her knee. Even with him kneeling and her sitting down, he was nearly at eye level with her. "Then," he said in a low voice, "I knew I had to tell you everything, so I came on the *Argiver* after I sacked the armada at Comoros. I knew that you would know it was me if I took that ship. You cannot know how it tortured me to learn that you had been abducted by that . . . man."

Maia touched his cheek with her palm, her heart fluttering with new emotions. She sensed he wanted to kiss her. "And you cannot know how it felt when I believed I had lost you," she whispered, her throat seizing up with tears. She moistened her lips, which suddenly felt dry as dust. The feeling in her stomach was like a whirlwind. "The dagger wound was fatal, I thought. But when you kissed me . . ." She shut her eyes and lowered her head, shuddering with the memory of those dark emotions.

She felt his fingers lift her chin.

"I was wounded, but not fatally as I supposed. Jon Tayt is quite able. When he brought me back to Muirwood, I could not stand up by myself. Within a day, I was walking. Within two, I could move freely. Richard told me that the prince's symptoms began immediately after he kissed you. They kept me apart from everyone else after I told them about our kiss. But there was no sickness. Nothing. And then the truth struck me."

Maia could hardly concentrate on his words. His face had gotten closer and closer as he spoke. She already knew the truth he was about to say. It sent tingles throughout her body.

"I realized your kiss would harm anyone else in the world . . . but me." He smiled. "Or my Family, but I do not feel inclined to share you very much." He gazed at her. "I have given you my kingdom, Maia. I have given you my heart." He snagged her fingers with his own. "Please tell me that you are mine. Forever. Always."

Maia stared into his vibrant blue eyes. "Forever," she whispered. And then she planted a kiss on his warm lips. She pulled back, barely noticing the little burn on her shoulder, her tingling lips. "For always," she whispered next and kissed him again.

Collier kissed her back and drew one arm around her waist. Then, parting from her for a moment, he gently lowered her onto the bed of tiny forget-me-nots. He joined her on the bench and proceeded to kiss her ardently, claiming her mouth with his own, claiming her heart and all that she was and wanted to be. And she kissed him back without timidity, digging her fingers through the thick locks of his hair until she was breathless.

The crushed blue flowers cushioned her hair, filling the air between them with the sweetest of fragrances. Her shoulder throbbed dully from her wound, but she could hardly feel pain through the blissful sensation of his mouth on hers. She surrendered to his kisses, feeling as if her heart would burst apart.

They both heard the creaking of the cart wheels as it approached the garden.

Collier lifted his head, cocking it to listen, sighed deeply and with exaggerated anguish, and they began to laugh.

Where there is darkness, there is courage. Where there is ambi-tion, there is power. Where there is will, there is dominion. I thank the Medium for an unconquerable soul.

—Corriveaux Tenir, King of the Kjavik Wastes

CHAPTER
THIRTY-EIGHT

Irrevocare Sigil

Never before in the history of the kingdoms had so many leaders assembled in one place at one time. Emissaries from all the kingdoms descended on Muirwood, either by ship or by Apse Veil, summoned to a Great Council by Maia, Queen of Comoros, and her betrothed, King Gideon of Dahomey. Some of the rulers were the age of her parents. Some were older. She and Collier were by far the youngest, but they were both treated with a deference and respect that surprised her.

A meeting had been called for that afternoon, during which all the leaders of the realms would be informed of what had caused the sun to linger in the sky. Every kingdom had experienced it. The people were frightened; they were struggling to understand what the Medium was saying. As she walked with Collier, greeting the various nobles, thanking those who had sent their support and assistance, Maia noted the conspicuous absence of one person she desired to see above all—her grandmother, the High Seer.

Collier touched her elbow and pulled her away from the chatter and noise. They were in the audience hall in the Aldermaston's manor, the same room where Collier had danced with her and declared that she was his wife.

"There is that look in your eye again," he told her softly. "And the fidgeting. I see how you keep glancing at the delegation from Pry-Ree."

She forced herself to stop wringing her hands and smoothing her dress. It still felt strange to her to wear a filigree coronet in her hair, but she had to admit that Collier's crown made him look even more handsome.

"You know me too well," she said. "I worry about my grandmother."

He took her hand, his fingers firm and steady. "You know that my fleet captains are assembling the provisions to strike for Naess tomorrow. If the Naestors will not surrender your grandmother, as they promised they would, then I will *make* them."

She saw his determination and did not doubt it. "Yes, but I *want* her here so desperately. I want *her* to be the one to marry us."

"It begins with a thought," Collier reminded her, brushing her chin with his knuckle.

"Thank you," she murmured, feeling her heart swell with gratitude for him.

"Tell me about the King of Paeiz," Maia asked, nodding toward the man Collier had persuaded to be his ally. "Tell me of his wife, his children."

Collier smirked. "I know the least about those things," he said with a chuckle. "He is a fencing master, though I think his training masters *let* him win. He was more than willing to seize part of my kingdom. Which I do not regret at all now that I know you revoked the Blight Leering." He looked at her with awe and adoration. "The cursed shores took up *half* of my kingdom. Think of what that means for us." He put his arm around her waist, pulling her closer to him. "I am not sure I have thanked you *properly* for that kindness yet."

"Consider it my wedding gift to you," she answered in a playful tone.

Maia noticed Tomas winding his way through the crowd toward them. He looked flustered, and his eyes were wide with excitement. She could see the dimples, so she knew it was good news, and her heart started to beat faster in anticipation.

As soon as he reached them, he said, "The Aldermaston . . . Richard—my apologies, I cannot help but call him that still—he wanted me to let you know that the *Holk* is docking at Muirwood as we speak. Would you both come with me? He thought you might appreciate a private reunion before the others know."

Collier took her hand, squeezing it so hard it almost hurt. "My mother arrived this morning as well," he said, whispering in her ear. "She came so that we could be married quickly when the High Seer arrives. If she is truly here, I do not want to wait any longer. Today, Maia? Can we marry today? If the sun actually sets, of course!"

Maia's heart thrilled at the thought. Pulling his hand, she led him out of the manor, following fast on Tomas's heels. Even Collier's long legs struggled to keep up with her as she hurried across the grounds. Several bystanders stood around gossiping, and Maia heard a few of their comments as she hurried toward the docks.

"The High Seer has come!"

"She is the queen's grandmother you know."

Maia ignored the words, her eyes searching ahead as they passed the fish pond and then rushed down the well-worn path leading to the docks. Finally she caught sight of the *Holk*, tethered to the bend of the river where there was more room to maneuver. A lone skiff manned by oarsmen clove the waters, slicing the way to where Richard and Joanna and Aldermaston Wyrich waited on the docks. Her heart began to pound as she recognized Sabine sitting in the skiff. Next to her was a wild-haired old man, a man she would have recognized at an even greater distance. It was Walraven, her longtime mentor and friend.

Maia surely would have tripped and fallen down the steps to the dock if Collier had not been gripping her hand so tightly. The skiff was already secured by mooring ropes by the time she reached the end of the pier.

Sabine looked tired as she disembarked, helped by Richard and Joanna, but her face brightened the instant she saw Maia and Collier, and she rushed over to them. Maia started to weep as her grandmother wrapped her arms around her neck and hugged her tightly, murmuring softly in her ear, "Well done . . . well done, dear heart!" Both women trembled with joy, clinging to each other for a long, sweet moment.

Then Sabine pulled away slightly and reached for Collier's hand. "I have news for you both. News I wanted to share immediately."

"What is it?" Maia asked, wiping her eyes. Her grandmother looked burdened, as if she had witnessed and experienced unspeakable things. But her fortitude and strength had carried her through. It was just like her to want to help someone else when she could easily have justified asking to sit and rest from a long journey.

Sabine pulled Collier closer and pitched her voice low, for their ears alone. "The Medium has taught me, through a vision, that you two were always intended for each other. While I was imprisoned in Hautland, before they sent me to Naess, I had a vision through my Gift of Seering of the Earl of Dieyre in Rostick. I saw him cavorting with hetaera after the mastons left. His *wife* was a hetaera! I saw her kiss him. So did others. But it did not harm him. The Medium taught me that his descendants are immune . . ."

But she must have noticed their flushed smiles and the knowing glance they exchanged, for she interrupted her own chain of thought.

"I think . . . you have already learned this truth yourself," Sabine said with a wry smile. "You cannot know how happy this makes me. Come, Maia, your friend wishes to see you again and to meet your intended. Walraven was tortured in the dungeons of Naess. He was broken and maimed when I found him there. The Medium bade me to heal him and adopt him into my Family. I would like to introduce you both to the future Aldermaston of Naess."

Looking over her grandmother's shoulder, Maia saw that her old friend was speaking with Richard, Joanna, and Wyrich. But upon Sabine's introduction, Walraven looked up and caught her eye. After speaking a few words to the others, he approached and bowed to Maia.

"To see you wearing the crown," he whispered huskily, tears gleaming in his eyes. "To see you at long last!"

She flung herself into his arms, sobbing as he hugged her. She was surrounded, completely surrounded, by those who loved and cherished her, those who had seen her through all her trials. When she finally pulled herself away from Walraven, she reached out and squeezed Richard's hand, then Joanna's. Her heart was so full.

As she turned back to Collier, she saw him looking at her with profound tenderness, tears trickling down his cheeks.

"She summoned you here," Collier told Sabine. "Her thoughts drove the wind. Will you please marry us? This very instant could not be soon enough!"

***

Although Maia had taken the maston test and crossed the Apse Veil, she had never climbed the winding steps to the high spire of the abbey. Each abbey contained a central tower or spike, and it was at the top of this tower where marriages were performed by irrevocare sigil. She wore the supplicant robes she had donned before taking the maston test. Collier walked with her up the steps, and they followed Tomas, who had informed them that the other witnesses of the ceremony awaited them in the spire.

The feeling of the Medium grew stronger as they climbed, and Maia felt her burdens lift the higher they went. Collier squeezed her hand, and she gave him a private smile, enjoying the look of anticipation she saw in his eyes.

When they reached the top of the tower, the room glowed with the light from the many Leerings that covered its walls. The stone buttresses were meticulously sculpted and inlaid with gold filigree patterns. There were stained-glass windows on each of the four walls, but the main source of light was the Leerings. There were no chairs in the chamber. Maia saw the other guests were all wearing maston robes, except for the Aldermastons present— Sabine, Wyrich, Richard, Joanna, as well as the Aldermaston of Lisyeux, a man whom she had met earlier that day. Suzenne and Dodd were also there with them, and both smiled at her with tenderness. Maia was so grateful to see him healthy. Collier's mother, the Queen Dowager of Dahomey, was also present. She was a stately woman with striking looks and silver streaks in her black hair. Maia was a little in awe of her, but she had enjoyed meeting her before the ceremony. The deep love she felt for her son was apparent, and that same affection had been readily shared with the girl who had tamed him.

As Maia and Collier approached the five Aldermastons, the row of people stepped aside, revealing a glistering Leering carved from an enormous white marble block. Unlike the normal Leerings Maia had seen in gardens and corridors, which had been carved from boulders, this Leering contained more than just faces. It reminded her most of the Leerings connected with the Apse Veil. She felt power emanating from it and understood that it was a marriage Leering, for an entire scene was depicted on it rather than a single face. Her Gift of Invocation told her the Leering's power was to invoke a Gifting on the married couple. The workmanship was exquisite and highly detailed.

Sabine motioned for them to approach and stand before the Leering, which they did.

"In every abbey, there is a special chamber," Sabine explained, "where marriages are performed. While this Leering is relatively new, it is modeled after the one that was originally in Muirwood, which I have seen in a vision." Sabine began to motion toward the scene. Now that she stood closer to it, Maia could see it showed a man and a woman standing next to each other, gripping each other by the hand. A woman stood between and behind them, one arm draped around either of their shoulders. Behind the man stood another man, as if looking over his shoulder and witnessing the marriage. All four figures were carved from the same block and formed an integrated image.

"It is so beautiful," Maia said, staring at it in awe. There were many details that caught her eye, making her wonder at the meaning. The man grasping the woman's hand had small scars on his face, claw marks like a beast had ravaged him. It made her think, momentarily, of the kishion, but she banished the thought, not wanting such a twisted memory to intrude upon such a sacred moment. The smiling woman behind the couple looked like an

Aldermaston. There was a scarf and veil wrapped around the head and shoulders of the bride in the statue. While her groom's free hand held a cylinder, hers clutched part of her robes, bunching them up and exposing her lower leg, where Maia saw an ankle bracelet fashioned like a serpent.

"Before you are married," Sabine said, noticing Maia's look, "I will explain the Leering. This sculpture represents the First Parents' marriage in the Garden of Leerings at the beginning of the world. They were immortal beings who chose to eat a certain fruit and take on a mortal state. This you know from maston lore. It is said the First Parents came from a different world, a world ruled by the Essaios. They were made stewards, caretakers of this realm."

Sabine motioned to the couple's linked hands. "The marriage ceremony is ancient, and we do not understand all of the symbolism behind it. But we do know much of it. The joined hands is called the *dextrarum coniunctio*, or the joining of the *right* hands. In his left hand, he holds what appears to be a capped scroll. It is called the *Tay Ard* scroll. The abbey contains one like it and your names will be written on it, joining you as husband and wife. The bride's free hand raises the hem of her robes. We do not know why, but it shows a bracelet around her ankle. The jewelry is called the *Idock*. Maia, you will wear one for the ceremony as well. You will notice the man has a belt and key. Gideon, you will wear that. It is called the *vacuata inanis,* or Voided Key. There must be at least one witness and, of course, the Aldermaston who performs the irrevocare sigil. Only an Aldermaston has the authority to perform this rite or the sigil. Now, come forward and emulate the Leering."

With assistance from the others, Maia was given a long white shawl to cover her head and wrap around her front and her shoulders. Collier was belted with the key. Both of their slippers were removed so that they stood barefoot, as if in the luscious garden of their ancestors. The ankle bracelet was wound around Maia's left ankle, and an ornate capped scroll was handed to Collier, which he held in his left hand.

Once they were both prepared for the ceremony, Maia stood by Collier, clasped his hand in hers, and stared into his piercing blue eyes. He was trembling slightly, his eyes fixed on hers. She felt the Medium so strongly it brought tears to her eyes.

Sabine stood behind them and wrapped her arms around each of their shoulders, her face peering between theirs. Richard Syon, the witness, stood by Collier's side where he could observe.

"I invoke this Leering," Sabine said in a soft voice, "to marry Queen Marciana of Comoros and King Gideon of Dahomey. Do you, Queen Maia, accept this man to be your lawful lord and husband, married and joined by the Medium in all holiness?"

Maia's heart burned inside her as she gazed at Collier and squeezed his hand. "Yes," she whispered, her throat tight.

"And do you, King Gideon, accept this woman to be your lawful lady and wife, married and joined by the Medium in all holiness?"

A tear trickled down Collier's cheek. "Yes," he said firmly, squeezing her hand in return.

Maia held her breath. She had been waiting for this moment her entire life. Her heart filled with gratitude, and she felt, unseen around them, silent witnesses to the union. Even as children, they had been meant for each other. All that had passed before, all the troubles and doubts and sadness, seemed to melt away.

"Then, as High Seer of the maston order, I join you two in marriage, bound by the *dextrarum coniunctio* to last beyond death itself. I invoke this Leering to grant you all the Gifts of the Medium. I Gift you both with blessings on your marriage. I Gift you with protection from the Myriad Ones. I Gift you with the perpetual sanctuary of this abbey, Muirwood. I bless you with the Gift of Firetaming that you may pass, when your mortal life is through, beyond the Apse Veil and into the world of Idumea. By the Medium, make it thus so."

"Make it thus so," Maia murmured, as did the voices of others.

Then, releasing her hold on their shoulders, Sabine used the palm of her hand and invoked the irrevocare sigil, drawing the eight-pointed star in the air between them.

"Forever and always," Maia said, releasing the hem of her robe and letting it fall down around her ankles.

"That is barely long enough," Collier answered with a smile, bringing her knuckles to his lips. Then, without waiting for permission, he dipped his head and kissed her again, this time as her husband.

***

They emerged from the abbey from the pewter doors they had entered a short time ago, holding hands as husband and wife. They were dressed in their beautiful wedding clothes, each wearing a coronet or crown. A sea of faces awaited them on the grounds of the abbey, and as soon as they emerged, this crowd of well-wishers raised their voices in a sustained enthusiastic cheer.

In the crowd, Maia saw many of the Ciphers with whom she had studied, several of them dabbing their eyes. Practically jumping up and down in the front of the mass were Davi and Aloia, and Thewliss and Collett were there too, trying to keep the girls' feet on the lawn and failing. The rulers of the other realms had gathered in a place of dignity near the front, along with the members of Maia's Privy Council who had not attended the ceremony. The lord mayor of Comoros, Justin, the Earl of Caspur, and Lord

Paget. They led the cheering. Small flower petals began to stream from somewhere above, coming down like little snowflakes.

Maia felt the Medium swell in her heart as she looked at her people with mingled love and gratitude.

Collier held up his hand for silence, and the murmuring praises quickly ceased. He turned to Sabine and gave her a knowing look and a wink, which alarmed Maia. The High Seer smiled, nodded to him, and stepped back slightly.

After releasing Maia's hand, Collier stepped off the porch of the abbey and turned to face her. She looked at him incredulously, her concern growing with each moment. His look said *just trust me*, but she was not certain what he was about.

Then, without a word, Collier knelt before her. He lifted his hands and removed his golden crown and set it before her feet. He bowed his head before her. Maia stared down at him and was trying to puzzle out his sudden gesture when the King of Paeiz left the crowd and spanned the short distance to her. He knelt next to Collier, removed his crown, and set it before her. Maia's heart hammered in her chest as the King of Avinion approached. Then they all came, removing their crowns and laying them at her feet. They were all kings and rulers in their own right, but they were paying homage and fealty to *her*.

Maia stared at the bowed heads, her eyes awash with tears. She felt Sabine's hand on her elbow.

"I know you do not want this," her grandmother whispered. "But they would all have you to be their queen and ruler." Addressing the crowd now, Sabine said, "Kneel."

The congregation obeyed, including Maia herself, and she felt tears gush from her eyes as Sabine lifted the coronet from her head and held it aloft.

As Maia shuddered from her shoulders down to her knees at

the responsibility that was about to be settled upon her, as she listened to her grandmother pronounce the words of authority, she saw Collier peeking at her, a smile on his face. A smile that said the Medium truly did give a person the fruit of their innermost thoughts and intentions. He had wanted to unite the realms under a single ruler. But only by giving up his crown had he achieved it.

And as difficult as the task seemed in that awful moment, she was grateful to have her husband with her to enjoy the long journey together.

EPILOGUE

Maia was a little weary from their ride from Briec to Roc-Adamour, but they had arrived at the city carved into the mountain before sunset. She and Collier had taken a secret path up to the manor at the top of the hill rather than using the normal roads. The grooms were stabling their horses, brushing them down and feeding them. So long ago it seemed when the king's collier had led her and her companions to this very manor and provided them with mounts and provisions.

Inside their bedchamber in the manor, she rubbed her sore arm and gazed out the window at the majestic view—the sunset over the ragged cliffs. Lights from the town below were already starting to dispel the encroaching darkness, and she imagined the pots of melted cheese and skewers of meat being served in the inns. There was a veranda outside the window decorated with ornate furniture and a sculpted garden full of Leerings. She did not want the light to ruin the view, so she kept them tamed for now.

Collier set aside his riding gloves and cloak, and she heard him approach behind her, then felt his stubble grazing the back of her neck, making her shiver.

"Does your arm still pain you?" he asked her, stroking her arms with his hands as he continued to nuzzle her.

"The wounds are mostly healed," she said, tilting her head to one side to expose more of her neck to him.

"Have you enjoyed your tour of the realm, my lady?" he asked her, nipping at her earlobe playfully. "There are many wonderful sights in Dahomey, of course, but this one has always been a favorite." He rested his chin in the nook of her shoulder and wrapped his arms around her waist, holding her. "You notice the difference when we are not at court. I prefer the anonymity. I think you actually prefer these simple gowns to the ornate confections at court. I have always fancied that about you."

"Have you?" she said. "Why spend so much on a costly gown that cannot be worn except for at state functions? I would rather give it to the poor."

"Yes. You have not despoiled all your treasures yet on the poor, though you try. It seems the faster you give it away, the faster new coins fill our coffers. Did you like staying at the Gables last night? The young folks who danced with us did not know who we were."

"Some may have recognized us from before," Maia said. She hugged his arms to her and swayed gently.

"I am going to fetch you a lute," he said. "I have two here, I believe. You and I will play music to each other before our meal arrives and then we will discuss where to go next. You want to rebuild an abbey in Mon, and I want to see the *lost* abbey. There are soldiers to protect and guard it, and I would like to make sure they understand its significance. Shall we play?"

"I would like that very much," Maia said. She turned, the window and view now behind her, and kissed his cheek and then took his hand, letting him lead her to the sumptuous couches nearby. The large four-post bed was crafted by master artisans and stained a dark umber color. She loved admiring the tapestries on the walls, the distinctly Dahomeyjan designs that she had always found appealing. She still could not get over the change in her life in the weeks since their marriage and her sudden coronation. Collier explored several chests on the other side of the bed until he found the hidden instruments. After picking one from the collection, he brought it over to her, and they tuned the strings together.

"Cruix or cursed?" he asked her, twisting the pegs.

"We are closer to the lands you wish to see," Maia said, testing the strings for the sound and adjusting them.

"I know," he said with a sly smile. "Why do you think I suggested Roc-Adamour? For the cheese and soup?"

"I forgot for a moment that you are extremely cunning, my lord husband," Maia said, striking a chord that resonated richly. It was perfect. She shifted the chord and made it sound strained. "But when you *boast* of it, it ruins the effect."

He smiled at the byplay and her choice of words. "Yes, I need your meekness to counteract my temperament. We are well suited for each other, truly." He strummed his instrument and nodded with satisfaction. "Speaking of which, I think I have a suitor for Jayn Sexton that you would approve of. I know you have worried about her."

"And who is that?" Maia asked, but they were interrupted by a knock on the door.

Collier frowned and stopped his little tune. "That was too quick for dinner. We only just arrived."

The door opened and the steward of the manor entered.

"What is it, Fouchon?" Collier asked pleasantly enough, though the expression on the steward's face showed he sensed his king's subtle annoyance.

"I am sorry, my lord," Fouchon said gravely, his voice perturbed. "I had no intention of interrupting you and my lady so soon, but there is a beggarly man just arrived who claims you owe him a great deal of money."

Collier looked confused and set down the lute. "Oh really? And did he say how much?"

"I think he may be jesting, but he said the sum was twenty-five thousand marks—or a sheriffdom—and . . . even with that limp . . . he said he would chop down the door if I did not let him in and tell you both he was here." He had an air of suffering. "Shall I have him thrown—?"

Maia shoved away the lute and sprang from the couch so she could rush to the door, hurrying to see *her* hunter once again.

AUTHOR'S NOTE

I was leery about writing a sequel to the Legends of Muirwood trilogy at first. But I like to challenge myself, and I loved the world and wanted to go back there again. I mentioned previously that the idea of this story came as a dream. But some of the details came as a result of being a history major in college.

As the main characters began walking around in my head and interacting, I wanted to ground them in a setting from our history, much like I did for Lia and the lost Welsh princess Gwenllian in the Legends of Muirwood trilogy. My first thought was to take the backstory of Elizabeth I of England as my inspiration. I once saw a great BBC miniseries *The Virgin Queen* and had studied her life during my college days. I liked the idea, but it did not work with the plot. As I snooped around Tudor history a bit more, I came across a figure with such a terrible reputation that they even named a drink after her . . . Bloody Mary.

Mary Tudor was the firstborn daughter of Henry VIII and Catherine of Aragon. As I researched her life, I was intrigued and fascinated, and she *became* Maia. Many of the scenes in the Covenant of Muirwood series came from Mary's life and inspired this work. Yes, she climbed out of a window in the manor house where she was locked away to wave to her father and try to bend him with compassion. Yes, she was poisoned in the garret, and they needed to call the court physician. Yes, an earl threatened to smash her head against the wall if she continued to refuse to sign away her station and status. Yes, she was promised to marry the heir of France when they were both little children, and she was sent to the borders of Wales to learn her role as a ruler. Yes, a prince from another realm vied for Mary's hand and impetuously kissed her. The coronation ceremony in this book came directly from the historical records. One place where I deviated from history is that Mary Tudor eventually capitulated to the threats and signed the act that disinherited her.

She regretted signing it all the rest of her life.

There are moments in history when it feels as if the Medium is controlling events. For example, after Mary became queen, there was a rebellion against her. The army marched on London, and there was no one to stop it. But when they reached the main gate of the city, the army seemed to lose its nerve, and it dissolved almost miraculously. For more on Mary's fascinating life during the Tudor period, I recommend the biographies by Linda Porter (*The Myth of "Bloody Mary"*) and Anna Whitelock (*Mary Tudor: Princess, Bastard, Queen*).

Not only was Maia's character influenced by the life of Mary Tudor, but I would also like to thank John Tomson, a reader, who pointed me toward the legend of Saint Aethelreda. She was the daughter of a king who wanted to live a celibate life, yet agreed to marry the king of another realm with the promise they would never consummate it. Part of the legend includes her fleeing to Ely Cathedral and a huge flood coming to surround the abbey to protect her. The story of Princess Aethelreda inspired the idea of having Maia and Collier marry early in the first book, then be kept apart throughout the series. I loved the tension that created in the story and how it led to many complications.

Sadly, the historical figure on whom Collier is based (Francis III, the Dauphin of France) was poisoned at age eighteen and never took the throne. I think the kishion was behind it. Francis was held hostage for many years as a young man and the imprisonment affected him deeply.

I will not get into all the other inspirations for this series. I will say that I started writing it shortly before being released as a bishop, and many of the experiences I had in that assignment added depth and feeling to the story. In many ways I felt like an Aldermaston trying to help people overcome the consequences of their mistakes or the devastating choices of others. And in so doing, I met some wonderful and memorable people who touched my heart and helped make the world of Muirwood even more real.

I hope this series helps people reconsider some of the "myths" they have grown up with and that public morality can impact society for generations. When I first began researching medieval history for *Wretched of Muirwood*, I learned that Glastonbury Abbey (the monastery on which Muirwood is based) was one of the abbeys that suffered from neglect after Henry VIII passed the Act of Supremacy in 1534. That is why only ruins of the abbey are left today.

Thankfully, Pasqua's kitchen is *still* standing.

ACKNOWLEDGMENTS

Many thanks to the wonderful people at 47North for bringing this series out so quickly. You should all send them a thank-you e-mail! Once again, I'd also like to express appreciation to my small cohort of readers for their continued feedback, input, and encouragement: Gina, Emily, Karen, Robin, Shannon, and Rachelle. And many thanks to the fabulous Angela Polidoro who proved her merit once again with this book!

ABOUT THE AUTHOR

Photo © Kim Bills

Jeff Wheeler took an early retirement from his career at Intel in 2014 to become a full-time author. He is, most importantly, a husband and father, and a devout member of his church. He is occasionally spotted roaming hills with oak trees and granite boulders in California or in any number of the state's majestic redwood groves.

Visit the author's website: www.jeff-wheeler.com

More ways to be enchanted by
Jeff Wheeler's
Muirwood

Legends of Muirwood

The Wretched of Muirwood
The Blight of Muirwood
The Scourge of Muirwood

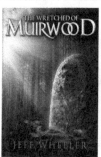

Covenant of Muirwood

The Banished of Muirwood
The Ciphers of Muirwood
The Void of Muirwood

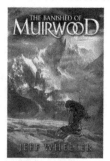

Muirwood: The Lost Abbey

Graphic Novel